# Love's Labor's Won

## *(Schooled in Magic VI)*

*Christopher G. Nuttall*

Twilight Times Books
Kingsport Tennessee

Love's Labor's Won

Copyright © 2015 Christopher G. Nuttall

Twilight Times Books
P O Box 3340
Kingsport TN 37664
http://twilighttimesbooks.com/

First Edition, August 2015

ISBN: 978-1-60619-308-2

Library of Congress Control Number: 2015947646

Cover art by Brad Fraunfelter

Published simultaneously in the United States and the United Kingdom.

To my son, Eric Jalil Nuttall,
who was born just after this book.

# Prologue

To someone without magic, Ashworth House looked fragile. It perched on a hillside, a mixture of a dozen different styles from all across the Allied Lands, as if each generation of the family had added a whole new wing to the house. And yet, Melissa Ashworth knew, as she walked through the wards, that the house was far from fragile. The nexus point pulsing below the giant building ensured that no conventional attack could hope to breach the defenses.

She felt the pull as soon as she passed through the last ward, an insistent tugging that compelled her to walk towards the center of the house. Gritting her teeth – she was eighteen, not a naughty little girl to be summoned – she resisted the pull as best as she could, dragging her feet as she walked into the house. A handful of servants bowed to her as she passed, then faded into the back of her awareness as the compulsion pulled harder. The Matriarch of House Ashworth was clearly impatient. By the time she reached the stone doors that barred the way into the central chambers, she was practically running – and steaming with humiliation.

The doors opened as she approached, revealing a single spotless room, empty save for a set of paintings on the wall, a wooden table and a pair of chairs. One of them was empty, Melissa noted as she stepped inside; the other was occupied by her great-grandmother, the Matriarch of House Ashworth. The compulsion snapped out of existence as the door closed behind her, but she knelt anyway. There was a long pause and then her great-grandmother slowly rose to her feet.

"You may rise," she said.

"Thank you, Lady Fulvia," Melissa said. No one dared address the Matriarch by any other title, not even *Grandmother.* "I thank you for summoning me."

"You may be seated," Lady Fulvia said. "I trust your exam results were satisfactory?"

Melissa felt her cheeks burn as she sat down and looked up at her great-grandmother. Lady Fulvia was tall and inhumanly thin, with a face so pinched with disapproval that she looked as though she were permanently sucking on a lemon. It was a testament to her power that she was still alive – and that no one dared to mock her, even in private. Melissa would sooner have dealt with her grandfather than the aging harridan. But no one would say no if Lady Fulvia chose to make Melissa's business hers.

"I believe I passed," she said, finally. "But we won't have the full results for another week."

"I suppose not," Lady Fulvia said. She sat down, her eyes never leaving Melissa's face. "It was my fault for sending you to that school, even though it was quite unsuitable for one of our bloodline."

"You told me I could not share the school with the Ashfall Heir," Melissa reminded her, daringly. "And so I went to Whitehall instead of Mountaintop."

"How true," Lady Fulvia agreed. "But we still expect you to do your very best." Her voice hardened. "And you have failed to make friends with Void's daughter."

Melissa winced at the cold scorn in Lady Fulvia's voice. No one had *known* Void had a daughter, right up until the moment she'd arrived at Whitehall. The Lone Power was so eccentric he hadn't even taught his daughter basic magic, although she *had* learned very quickly. But, by the time Melissa had received orders to befriend the girl, it had been too late.

"A girl who saved the school, *twice*," Lady Fulvia said. "A girl who crippled Mountaintop."

"Yes, my lady," Melissa said.

"And you have failed to befriend her," Lady Fulvia said. "That does not speak well of you."

Melissa cringed. Lady Fulvia never hit her grandchildren or great-grandchildren. She had other ways to discipline them. None of them were remotely pleasant.

"But, no matter," Lady Fulvia said. "There are other, more important issues to discuss. You are a young woman now, are you not? The measurement of blood-to-blood proves you are healthy and capable of bearing children?"

"Yes," Melissa said, embarrassed.

"Good," Lady Fulvia said. She gave Melissa a tight smile. "Because you're going to get married. The Matriarchy of House Ashworth will fall to you, one day, and it is important that you have both the right husband and the right father for your children. I have selected for you a suitable man."

Melissa felt as though she had been punched in the gut. She'd known her marriage would be arranged, but she'd always thought – her grandfather had promised her – that she would have the final say in who she married. To hear Lady Fulvia say, so casually, that her husband had already been selected...she stared, unable to conceal her horror. There was no point in trying to argue, or fight. She knew the Matriarch all too well. Lady Fulvia would simply override whatever she said and the wedding would go ahead anyway.

"My lady," she managed finally. "Who have you selected for me?"

"Gaius, of House Arlene," Lady Fulvia said. "He recently graduated from Mountaintop with impeccable marks and strong magic."

It took Melissa a moment to place the name. House Arlene wasn't a strong house, not by the standards of Ashworth or Ashfall. Their very lack of strength, however, made them ideal partners for Lady Fulvia. She could practically dictate the terms of the marriage contract, knowing they would have little choice but to accept. But... what little she had heard about Gaius hadn't been good. Women talked, after all, and stories were shared. Few girls had dated Gaius twice. She would have to write to them and find out why.

"You will be formally introduced to him at the Cockatrice Faire," Lady Fulvia continued, seemingly unaware of Melissa's innermost thoughts. "The wedding will be held on the final night of the Faire, once all the contracts have been signed. You and he can then enjoy the joys of married life."

Melissa colored, then frowned. "Lady Fulvia, I..."

"This is a great opportunity for you, and for your House," Lady Fulvia continued, smoothly. "I would take it greatly amiss if anything was to interfere with the planned wedding."

*Shit*, Melissa thought.

She hadn't wanted to get married until after her graduation – as a married woman, she might not even be allowed to return to school – but she knew there was no point in arguing. Lady Fulvia would have had the contracts drawn up already and also would have gone through the formalities of gaining the approval of the family's adults. The only person who might have been able to say no was Melissa's father – and he'd died years ago. And she was not of age. She couldn't refuse on her own.

"Go back to your rooms and prepare yourself," Lady Fulvia ordered. "We will leave for Cockatrice in four days."

Melissa winced, inwardly, as her mind caught up with what she was being told. Cockatrice. Of all the places they could hold the Faire, it had to be Cockatrice. It was not enough that she had to be pushed into a loveless marriage, was it? She had to endure her nuptials under the eyes of Lady Emily, Void's daughter and Baroness of Cockatrice. But again, there was no point in arguing. Lady Fulvia had made up her mind.

She rose, bowed again, and stalked out the door. There were letters to write, clothes to pack. And then...

*My life is going to change*, she thought, morbidly. *And who knows what will happen next?*

# Chapter One

"WE'RE DONE!"

Emily looked up from her book as Alassa and Imaiqah ran into the room, long hair streaming down their backs. They dumped their bags on the table and smiled at her. They'd loudly complained about Emily finishing her exams two days ago — they'd had to keep revising while Emily had been able to relax — but now it was over. Defensive Magic was the final exam of the year.

"Well done," Emily said, as Alassa sat on Frieda's bed. "How did it go?"

"Mistress Tirana hates me," Alassa said. She ran her hands through her long blonde hair as it fell out of her pins, framing her heart-shaped face. "I accidentally blew up one of her test dummies."

"Accident, my foot," Imaiqah said. She sat on the floor, crossing her legs. "You did it on purpose."

"The idea was to render any potential attacker harmless," Alassa countered. "I think I made the dummy *very* harmless."

"You can say that again," Imaiqah muttered.

"I think I made the dummy very harmless," Alassa repeated. She stuck out her tongue at Imaiqah. "And I did, didn't I?"

Emily snorted as she put her book down on the table. Alassa and Imaiqah were an odd pair by anyone's standards. One was tall, blonde and willowy, with a figure that wouldn't have been out of place on a Barbie doll; the other was shorter, with black hair and tanned skin. She couldn't help feeling a pang of jealously at how close the two had become, particularly in the days she'd been away from Whitehall. It was a natural reaction, she knew, but that didn't make it any easier to bear.

"So we leave in a couple of days," she said, softly. "Are you packed and ready to go?"

"Yes, *mother*," Alassa said, mischievously. "I have everything packed, save for my robes, dresses, underclothes, books..."

"Everything, in other words," Imaiqah cut in.

"Everything," Alassa agreed. "But don't worry about it. We can step through the portal at any time."

Emily nodded, ruefully. They could have left as soon as their exams were over — some of the students had already decamped back to their homes — but there was, as always, a leaving dance on the last night of term. *She* would have been happier skipping it altogether; her friends, on the other hand, had been looking forward to it since they'd started Third Year and there was no point in trying to argue with them. Imaiqah had persuaded Emily to try on various dresses for the last two months, while Alassa had threatened to ask her mother to send Emily even *more* dresses for her collection. It never seemed to matter that half of them were too revealing for Emily to wear in public, or that the other half were rarely used.

"You must be looking forward to the Faire," Imaiqah said, changing the subject. "Don't you think it will be wonderful?"

Emily winced. Last year, she'd been asked — in her persona as Baroness Cockatrice — to host the Faire on her lands. She'd agreed, and had then left the matter in the hands of her Castellan. There had just been too much going on in Third Year — first at Mountaintop, then at Whitehall — for her to pay close attention to her Barony. Now, she had the uneasy feeling that she was in for a surprise when she went back to the castle. The handful of reports she'd received had implied that the Faire would be larger than any before. *Everyone* wanted to get in on the game.

The door opened again, revealing the Gorgon and Jade. Emily waved cheerfully as the door closed, and winked at the Gorgon. In many ways, she was as much an outsider at Whitehall as Emily herself, all the more so because she looked utterly inhuman. Her body might be humanoid — if green, with scales in odd places — but instead of hair she had a writhing mass of snakes. She was one of the cleverest students Emily had met, yet also one of the most unfortunate. There might be no classical racism in the Allied Lands, but supernatural creatures — like Gorgons — were hated and feared.

Jade gave them all a bow. "A pleasure to be invited into this wondrous room," he said formally, with a smile of his own. "It could not be a greater honor."

"You're welcome," Emily said. Given that Jade had once, in all seriousness, asked her to marry him, it was astonishing how relaxed she'd become around him. "How did your last set of classes go?"

"Reasonably well," Jade said. He gave Imaiqah and Alassa a significant look. "But it all depends on the exam results now."

"I think we did well," the Gorgon said. "But *someone* blew up a dummy."

"There's plenty more," Jade said, unconcerned. "I blew up a dummy myself when I was a student."

"See," Alassa said. "Blowing up dummies is considered good practice."

"They made me pay for it," Jade said. "I don't think they thought I took it seriously."

Emily smiled at him. "Why?"

"Because I made a show of it," Jade said. He shrugged. "Sergeant Miles said it was a waste of time and energy."

The door opened again. Aloha stepped into the room, carrying a small wooden box under her arm. Her dark face twisted into a smile when she looked at Emily, then she closed the door behind her and walked over to the wooden table. Emily rose to her feet and walked over to join her as Aloha put the box down, then opened it. Inside, there were several sheets of charmed parchment. Magic crackled over them as Aloha picked them up and placed them gingerly on the tabletop.

"I had to spend several gold pieces to buy this lot," Aloha said, as the others gathered round her. "The price of parchment has skyrocketed in the past few months."

Emily winced, inwardly. That was her fault. Introducing paper had seemed a good idea at the time, but it was now so easy to produce that it was pushing parchment-makers out of business. Unsurprisingly, stocks of parchment itself had started to fall, even though it was used in a number of magic spells and rituals. Emily suspected that the problem would eventually sort itself out — there would still be a demand for parchment from magicians and their students — but for the moment it was harder to get decent parchment. It didn't make life any easier for struggling students.

"I can pay for it," Alassa offered.

"I managed to get a grant for materials," Aloha said, as she finished emptying the box. "But they may force me to repay some of it, once they've finished assessing my project."

She looked at Emily. "Or assessing the degree to which I...borrowed...one of your ideas."

"Don't worry about it," Emily said. "I don't intend to claim credit for anything."

The thought made her smile, inwardly. She knew she was no slouch when it came to practical magic, but Aloha was a genius. Emily suspected Aloha was the brightest — certainly the most capable — student in Whitehall. The idea behind the charmed parchment might have been *Emily's* — more accurately, it had been something copied from Earth — but it had been Aloha who had made it work.

"I don't feel good about using one of your ideas," Aloha admitted.

"You made it work," Emily reminded her. "I wasn't able to do that for myself."

"Yet," Aloha muttered. She cleared her throat. "I would remind you, all of you, that this ritual requires blood. If any of you have a problem with that, say so now or forever hold your peace."

Emily swallowed, uneasily. She knew — she had very good reason to know — just how dangerous it could be to let someone else have even a drop of her blood. Blood magic could be used to manipulate her mind, force her to do things she would normally never have considered, even control her body like a puppet. None of the others looked any happier at the prospect, even though they'd all known it was coming. To give up a drop of blood was to risk giving up control.

Jade stepped forward. "I'm ready," he said.

Aloha passed him a tiny silver knife. Like the others Emily had used in the past, it was charmed to prevent the cut from hurting. Jade held his hand over the parchment, then nicked his flesh with the knife. Blood dripped from his palm and down to the parchment, where it pooled on the sheets. Alassa shot Jade an unreadable look, then took the knife and made a cut in her own palm. Emily braced herself, when it was her turn, and then cut herself, very lightly. Cutting her skin wasn't easy, even with a charmed blade. It was hard to force herself to press the knife against her flesh.

"We begin," Aloha said, as she produced a silver wand and used it to mix the blood together. "Let the magic flow..."

Emily nearly took a step backwards as spells — complex spells — flared up around the parchment, shimmering into life. There was a moment when she thought everything had failed, but then the magic sank into the parchments and faded from her awareness. Aloha returned the wand to her belt — it was rare for any Whitehall student to use a wand, unless one needed to cast a series of complex spells — and then picked up the first sheet of parchment. It looked indistinguishable from the others.

"This would be yours, I think," she said to Jade. She passed it to him. "How does it feel?"

"Like magic," Jade said. "It's tingling."

Aloha nodded, passing Emily a second sheet. It felt like a normal piece of parchment to her, so Aloha took it back and gave her another. This one tingled with magic as soon as she touched it with her bare hands. The remaining pieces of parchment were rapidly exchanged until everyone had a piece that tingled for them, bound — literally — to their blood. Anyone else who happened to look at the parchment would see nothing but just another piece of blank parchment.

"Right," Aloha said. She reached into her robes and produced a pencil. "Let me see if this works."

She wrote a brief sentence on her parchment. There was a tingle of magic, then the sentence appeared on Emily's parchment. Emily scanned it, then produced a pencil of her own and wrote a response. Chuckles from the others told her that they'd all seen her words; they hurried to write comments of their own. Emily giggled as their words all appeared in front of her, shown in their handwriting. They all had neater handwriting than she did.

*But that isn't surprising,* she thought. *They were all taught to write precisely, because missing a line in one place could completely change the meaning of a sentence. I was taught to write in English.*

"We could do with a way to say who's writing," Alassa said, as she wrote another comment on her parchment. "And a way to send private remarks."

Imaiqah snickered. "You want to send a message to your boyfriend?"

Alassa flushed. "It would be a useful thing to do," she said.

Emily concealed her amusement. Alassa was the Crown Princess of Zangaria, Heir to the Throne, Duchess of Iron...as well as the holder of several dozen other titles, all of which were solemnly recited every time she stepped into her father's throne room. Whatever she might want, she couldn't have a boyfriend. Hell, it had only been two years ago when a number of princes had sought her hand in marriage. If the Iron Duchess — the *former* Iron Duchess — and her co-conspirators hadn't launched their coup attempt, it was possible she would *already* be married. The thought of her having a boyfriend was laughable.

"That's not possible," Aloha admitted. "These six sheets of parchment are bonded together. What is written on one of them, by the designated user, will appear on all of them. Anyone who isn't included in the original charm won't be able to see the words, no matter what revealing spells they cast."

"So don't go writing sweet nothings to your small army of boyfriends," Alassa said. Imaiqah flushed. "Can you add someone else to the list?"

"No, sadly," Aloha said. "If you wanted to include someone else, you'd have to have the entire spell redone."

"Which wouldn't be easy," the Gorgon said. As always, there was a very faint hiss underlying her words. "No one would want to leave their blood anywhere, no matter how secure, just so someone new could be added."

"Yeah," Aloha said. "That's the problem."

Emily shrugged. "But it's miles better than anything we had before," she said, reassuringly. "I think you will have passed with honors."

"It still wouldn't have been possible without you," Aloha muttered.

"But *you* made it work," Emily said, again.

Aloha was right, she had to admit. Emily had remembered the concept of Internet chat programs and tried to devise a way to make one work, magically. But it had been more — much more — than merely finding a way to link six sheets of parchment together. If she hadn't introduced English letters, it would have been hard for anyone to use the parchments without wasting a great deal of space. Old Script might be precise to the point of being thoroughly anal, but it was also far too complex for simple conversation.

"I have a question," Imaiqah said. "How do you wipe the sheet?"

"A simple erasing spell would suffice," Aloha said. "I did try to get the sheet to remember everything written, but it didn't last. If someone's parchment runs out of space, it will automatically start erasing the older messages."

*So no scrolling up or down,* Emily thought. *If someone writes something embarrassing, they can keep writing in the hopes of making it vanish.*

She shook her head as she placed her parchment on the table, then folded it up and placed it in her pocket. Everyone on Earth seemed to like the idea of instant gratification, but the Allied Lands knew better. The chat parchments were so much better than anything they'd had before, like the English letters, stirrups and several other minor ideas from Earth, that everyone would be delighted when they saw them. Aloha would probably become rich, just marketing the chat parchments to her fellow students. It probably wouldn't be long before they were unceremoniously banned from class.

*It may be years before someone comes up with something as functional as a computer,* she thought. *But I can wait.*

"Thank you," she said, sincerely.

"You're welcome," Aloha said. She ran her hand through her dark hair. "I had the idea of making the parchments tingle slightly when someone writes a message, so you can keep it in your pocket and look at it when someone writes you a message. You can alter the overlapping charms, if you wish, to make it sound a bell instead. But that would be rather noticeable."

*They'll be banned from class for sure,* Emily thought, amused. Her old teachers on Earth had always banned cell phones from their classes, which hadn't stopped a number of students from smuggling them in anyway and using them when the teacher wasn't looking. *But someone could always turn off the noise.*

Alassa frowned. "What would happen if someone burned the parchment?"

"You'd lose your link to the network," Aloha said. She'd learned that word from Emily, back when they'd been discussing the concept. "It might bring down the entire network, depending on precisely what happens. I've tried with a couple of linked parchments in the past, but never with six separate groups of interlinked charms. Try not to do it."

"We won't," Emily said. "How do you feel about *your* exams?"

"I should have the results in a week," Aloha said. Fourth Years were always marked first, Emily had been told; they were either leaving the school, with basic qualifications, or returning for Fifth Year. "And then...Fifth Year. I hear tell they're going to have someone special come to teach you and me."

"Martial Magic," Emily guessed.

"Yes," Aloha said. "We're outside the standard course now."

Emily shrugged. There was something to be said for repeating the standard course time and time again. She'd failed Second Year Martial Magic, after all, and even picking up on it again after returning from Mountaintop had still left her in limbo. She was expecting to have to repeat the entire year during Fourth Year. It would be a shame, in many ways, but she had to admit she needed the practice.

She looked up as the door opened and Frieda stepped into the room. Her former Shadow had blossomed in Whitehall, although Emily still felt a little responsible for her. It was almost like having a little sister.

"The Grandmaster wants to see you," Frieda said. "He didn't sound pleased when he spoke to me."

"Maybe that was because you were playing Freeze Tag again," Aloha said, not unkindly. "I thought you and the rest of the new bugs had already got in trouble for it."

"That was an accident," Frieda protested. "And they didn't say we shouldn't play!"

Emily smiled, and rose to her feet. "Do you mind the others staying here?"

"Don't worry about it," Jade said. "I have to go back to the sergeant, anyway. He probably wants me to do more hard work. Character-forming, he calls it."

"We will see you afterwards," Alassa said, with narrowed eyes. "You have to try on a dress or two."

Emily groaned, then smoothed down her robes. "If we must," she said, with a sigh. "But nothing *too* revealing."

Alassa grinned. "Just you wait," she said. "Wait and see."

# Chapter Two

ONCE, EMILY RECALLED, NAVIGATING THE HALLWAYS AND CORRIDORS OF WHITEHALL HAD been immensely difficult. They changed frequently, in unpredictable ways; a corridor that had once led to the library might, the following day, lead directly to the Great Hall. Now, finding her way was merely a matter of listening to the magic running through the school. She walked up three flights of stairs and down a long stone corridor, lined with portraits of famous people from the past, then stopped as she saw the new portrait hanging from the wall. It was yet another painting of her.

She groaned, inwardly, as she took in the sight. The artist had never laid eyes on her and it showed; she would have been surprised if he'd even had a first-hand description or a look at another, more accurate, painting of herself. He'd painted her with long brown hair, which was about the only detail that resembled Emily herself, but the portrait's hair hung down to the ground and pooled on the floor. The portrait, too, was stunningly beautiful. Indeed, if her name hadn't been written at the bottom, she would have doubted the evidence of her own senses.

*On the plus side,* she told herself, *anyone looking for me using this as their guide won't find me.*

She took one last look at her doppelgänger, then walked past the portrait and down towards the grandmaster's office. Here, the walls were lined with suits of armor, carrying everything from sharp spears to broadswords too heavy for Emily to lift. They were part of the school's defenses, she knew; they'd come to life, when Shadye had invaded Whitehall, and attacked his forces until they were battered into nothingness. Magic crackled around them as she looked into their blank helms, then walked onwards. The grandmaster's office lay open in front of her. She stepped into the room...

...And stopped, dead.

A tall girl, with hair as black as coal, was standing in front of the grandmaster's desk. The Grandmaster himself, seated behind his desk, looked coldly furious. His eyes, as always, were covered with a dirty cloth, but Emily had no trouble reading his mood. She hoped — prayed — he would never be *that* furious at her, ever. The girl, whoever she was, seemed to be in deep trouble.

The girl whirled around to face Emily. Her face was so pale that her lips, no redder than Emily's own, seemed to stand out against her skin. She was striking, rather than pretty, yet there was a grim determination in her face that mirrored Emily's own. The white dress she wore showed off her hair and drew attention to her face, rather than her body.

"Get out," she snarled.

"Ah, yes, Lady Emily," the Grandmaster said. He sounded annoyed, although not at Emily personally. "Wait outside. Shut the door behind you."

Emily hastily turned and walked outside, making sure to pull the door closed. She'd thought the door was open for her, not someone else! But she hadn't thought to knock...kicking herself for her mistake, she leaned against the wall and waited, trying to think of something — anything — else. There had been something in the girl's dark eyes that had scared her at a very primal level, yet she wasn't sure why. She'd seen so many unpleasant people since coming to the Nameless World that one more didn't seem much of a problem.

It was nearly half an hour, by her watch, when the door opened and the girl stomped out, closing the door sharply behind her. Her cheeks were still pale, but Emily could see two spots of color as the girl turned to face her. For a long moment, they stared at each other — Emily silently readied a spell to defend herself — and then the girl turned and strode off down the corridor. Her back was ramrod straight as she walked away, suggesting a desperate attempt to remain dignified. Emily watched her go, fighting down the childish impulse to fire a spell at the girl's retreating back, then turned and knocked on the door. The door opened and she stepped into the room.

"I'm sorry, sir," she said, as the Grandmaster looked up at her. "I didn't realize you had a guest."

"Knock in future," the Grandmaster advised, "even if the door is open. You don't really want to intrude on a magician's private space without his permission."

"Yes, sir," Emily said, feeling her cheeks heat. "Why...why was she here?"

The Grandmaster's eyebrows twitched behind the cloth. "I am not in the habit of discussing your discipline or the reasons for it with other students," he said. "Should I not grant them the same privacy?"

Emily looked down at the bare stone floor, embarrassed. "Yes, sir," she said. "Sorry, sir."

"Glad to hear it," the Grandmaster said, dryly. "Now, if you will give me a minute..."

He picked a piece of paper off his desk, and wrote a long series of Old Script letters. Emily looked away, her eyes skimming the office; for once, instead of bare stone walls, there were a handful of decorations. A large painting hung on one wall, while — below it — there was a small table, covered with artefacts and strange magical devices. There was something about the painting that caught and held her attention, reminding her of images she'd seen on Earth. The figure looked like Charles I, a tall aristocratic man with long dark hair, a goatee and expensive clothes. But there was something about the thin smile on the man's face that sent chills down her spine. He seemed to be permanently laughing at the universe.

"There's an interesting story about that painting," the Grandmaster said. Emily turned back to look at him. "There was a wealthy magician who had it commissioned, years ago. The artist was a powerful magician in his own right and infused a great deal of magic into the canvas. Once it was completed, it was hung in the magician's studio...and then, one night, when no one was watching, the figure crawled out of the painting and killed the original."

Emily frowned. "If there were no witnesses," she said, "how do they know?"

The Grandmaster snorted. "Stories have a habit of growing in the telling," he said. "But as you can see, the painting is surrounded by powerful magic."

Emily turned back...and started. The figure had changed. Instead of smiling, his face looked disapproving, as if he'd smelled something foul. The eyes were fixed on Emily's face...she took a step closer, wondering if she'd see the figure move again. But there was nothing until she looked away for a split second, then back at the portrait. This time, the figure seemed to be winking at her.

"It changes," she said. "Why are you keeping it here?"

"Certain parties would like to lay the legend to rest, once and for all," the Grandmaster said. She heard him rise to his feet, then walk around the desk to stand next to her. "Or have it confirmed, if it is real."

He pointed to the items on the desk below the painting. "These were pulled from the house of a magician who was killed in a duel," he explained. "Most of them are junk, without the owner, but a handful shouldn't have been in anyone's possession. Finding that" — he pointed to a gold heart-shaped artefact that looked scorched and pitted — "was worrying enough."

Emily knew better than to touch it, but she peered closely at the scarred metal. "What is it?"

"A corruptor," the Grandmaster said. "Certain kinds of magic, as you know, bring emotional resonances in their wake. These...devices...amplify the effects of casting such spells. A magician under their influence will rapidly become addicted to using dark magic, ensuring an eventual collapse into madness. Even the most stable of magicians, a very rare beast indeed, would be threatened by their magic."

"If one's mind was changing," Emily said slowly, "and all the tools one used to measure it were changing too, how would one *know* one's mind was changing?"

"Precisely," the Grandmaster said. He waved a hand at the space in front of his desk and a chair shimmered into existence. "Take a seat, Lady Emily. We have much to discuss."

Emily sat, resting her hands on her lap.

"Your exams were marked ahead of everyone else, including the Fourth Years," the Grandmaster said. "We needed to know if you were ready to move into Fourth Year yourself or if you needed to retake Third Year. Our general conclusion was that you were ready to move forward, as you did manage to close the gap quite nicely with the other students."

"Thank you, sir," Emily said. Mountaintop used the same basic exams as Whitehall, she'd discovered, but the educational pathway was different. She'd mastered some tricks that were only taught to Fourth Years, yet she'd lacked others that had left her ill-prepared for Third Year at Whitehall. "I worked hard."

"Indeed you did," the Grandmaster agreed. "No one would have blamed you for choosing to wait out the year, then redoing the Third Year from scratch. You can justly be proud of your achievements. However, they do tend to cause us problems too."

He took a breath. "The one thing you *don't* have is a proposal for a joint project," he continued. "Your classmates had already teamed up, so we had no one for you to work with on your joint project, particularly as there was no guarantee you would go directly into Fourth Year."

Emily had a feeling that there was no guarantee that *anyone* would make it into Fourth Year, but she held her tongue. Alassa and Imaiqah had been working together from the start, while she'd been at Mountaintop, yet they'd had great problems putting their project proposal together. She...hadn't had the time to do one for herself.

"This problem caused us some concern," the Grandmaster added. "The purpose of this project is to teach you how to work with another magician. Allowing you to submit a project of your own, without a partner, would defeat the object of the exercise. Several of my staff felt it would be better for you to repeat Third Year, which would allow you to work with another student. However, as you passed the exams, you could not be held back academically."

"I could submit a proposal in Fourth Year," Emily offered.

The Grandmaster smiled. "And would you then actually do the project itself in Fifth Year?"

Emily cursed under her breath. She saw his point; if she had to do both the proposal and the project itself, she would need a full two years. Hell, she couldn't pass Fourth Year without a completed project — or, at least, a determined attempt at one. The books Lady Barb had given her to read had made it clear that working together was the desired outcome, not a magical breakthrough. None of the tutors seemed to expect any of their students to come up with something *totally* new.

*Aloha did*, Emily thought. *But she had a concept from Earth.*

"Luckily, we have an alternative," the Grandmaster said. "Have you heard of a student called Caleb, of House Waterfall?"

Emily shook her head. She didn't pay much attention to students from outside her small circle of friends. House Waterfall was one of the smaller magical families, she recalled, from some of the books she'd been forced to study at Mountaintop, but she didn't know much else about them.

"He is — was — a Fourth Year student," the Grandmaster said. "His proposal involved working with complex spell-structures. Unfortunately, there was an explosion in the spellchamber during the early weeks of Fourth Year and he took the brunt of the blast, after shoving his partner out of the way. He had to spend the rest of the year recuperating at home."

"Ouch," Emily said. Magic could cure most physical injuries, she knew from experience, unless they were immediately fatal. It was odd to have someone recuperating for longer than a couple of weeks. "Why didn't he recuperate here?"

"His...experiment accidentally tainted his body with magic," the Grandmaster said. "It took longer for him to recover than it would have done if he'd merely broken a few bones."

He shrugged. "Be that as it may, Caleb has expressed an interest in resuming his project," he continued. "It holds great promise, I feel, so I have conditionally given my consent."

Emily looked down at her pale hands. "Conditionally?"

"He needs another partner, as the last one moved to assist another project team and barely scraped through the exams," the Grandmaster said. "I would like you to be his partner."

"I see," Emily said.

The Grandmaster held up a hand before she could say anything else. "You would have to meet him over the summer and go through his proposal with him," he warned. "If you rejected the proposal, your only real option would be to redo Third Year from the start, with a partner in the year below you. I have made it clear to him that the final decision will be yours."

Emily groaned, inwardly. She wasn't good at working with anyone, even her closest friends. Teamwork defeated her because it meant relying on somebody else — and her childhood had taught her, time and time again, that no one was truly reliable. But she knew the Grandmaster had gone out on a limb for both of them. The rules, stated at the start of Third Year, were being bent into a pretzel. Working with a stranger would be bad, but repeating Third Year would be worse.

*If only we could avoid doing some of the classes, the ones we already passed*, she thought, sourly. *But that isn't allowed.*

"I will be at Cockatrice," she said, slowly. "He will meet me there?"

"His family lives in Beneficence," the Grandmaster assured her. "He will have no trouble crossing the bridge into Zangaria and reaching your lands."

Emily braced herself. "I'll try," she said. "What happens if we fail? Or if we don't get along?"

"You get to redo Third Year," the Grandmaster said. He gave her a rather sardonic smile. "It wouldn't be the first time a project team managed to fall out, even when the project was working perfectly. Learning to work with someone else is part of the whole idea."

"You said," Emily muttered.

The Grandmaster reached into one of his drawers and produced a large sheaf of papers, which he passed to Emily. "This is the proposal he put before the tutors, last year," he said. "I advise you to take it with you and read it thoroughly once you are in Cockatrice, then get in touch with him to arrange meeting times. Lady Barb will assist with that, if you ask, although she is forbidden from offering any direct help with the proposal or the project itself."

"I will," Emily said.

"I would add," the Grandmaster said, "that these proposals are considered confidential. You could get in a great deal of trouble if you showed it to anyone without his permission."

Emily swallowed. "Yes, sir."

"And another issue," the Grandmaster added. "Do you still want to visit the Blighted Lands?"

"No," Emily said. The idea of returning to Shadye's fortress was terrifying. "But it has to be done."

"Then I will have you return to Whitehall a week before the remainder of the students are due to return," the Grandmaster said. He looked down at his desk. "You will be attending the dance, I take it?"

"Yes, sir," Emily said. She would have preferred to avoid it, but Alassa wouldn't let her hide in her room. "I have to try on dresses later."

"There won't be time for us to have another chat," the Grandmaster said. "I would have..._preferred_...to speak with you just prior to your departure, but circumstances have developed that have rendered that impossible. You will be the official host for the Faire, will you not?"

"Yes," Emily said, flatly.

"Be careful," the Grandmaster said. "There will be many powerful people visiting, some of whom will want to get a look at you personally. Be on your best behavior and don't hesitate to ask Lady Barb for advice. You could make enemies for life by doing the wrong thing at the wrong time."

"I already have too many enemies," Emily said.

"Quite," the Grandmaster agreed. "Good luck, Lady Emily."

Emily rose, curtseyed to him and turned to walk towards the door. The portrait had changed yet again; this time, the man was snarling at her as she walked past him. Emily wouldn't have cared to hang such a painting in her bedroom, even if it hadn't been shadowed by dark rumors. Outside, she couldn't resist looking at the painting of her, but it didn't seem to have changed since she'd last looked at it. Shaking her head in amusement, she walked down four flights of stairs and back into the dorms.

"Emily," Alassa said, as she stepped into the bedroom. "You're just in time."

"I can come back later," Emily said, as Alassa held up a long green dress. "I don't think that would suit me."

"That's for me," Alassa said. "I brought this for you."

She held up two strips of cloth. Emily stared at them, then realized that Alassa was pulling her leg. The Princess smirked, then picked up a long blue dress from the bed and held it out to Emily. It looked plain, save for the decoration embroidered over her chest. And, unlike some of the dresses Alassa had to wear, it could be donned by one person without help.

"Fine," she muttered.

She looked back as the door opened, revealing Imaiqah and the Gorgon. Imaiqah wore her dress robes, but the Gorgon wore a long brown snakeskin dress that set off her green skin nicely. Emily rubbed the bracelet at her wrist before pulling her robes over her head. There was no point in trying to stall when Alassa was determined to make sure they were all dressed for the dance.

"So," Alassa said. "Did anything interesting happen?"

"I think I have a project proposal, and a partner," Emily said. "But I will have to wait and see."

# Chapter Three

A LASSA WAS MERCILESS, AS ALWAYS; BY THE TIME EMILY FINALLY CONVINCED ALASSA TO allow her to stick with the blue dress, it was dinner time. They changed back into their regular robes, then walked down to the dining hall and joined the other students. Emily kept a watchful eye on Frieda as she ate and drank her fill — and took several potions in quick succession — then relaxed, slightly. Frieda seemed to have fitted into Whitehall far quicker than Emily herself, even though she had started late. But then, new students arrived for First Year all the time.

"I need to go to the library," she said, once dinner was done. "I'll see you all later?"

"We have to go play *Ken*," Alassa said. She was looking up at the High Table, where the teachers — and Jade — were chatting amongst themselves. "We'll see you when we see you?"

"Of course," Emily said.

She nodded to Frieda — the younger girl always seemed to be surrounded by friends — and then walked up to the library. The giant chamber seemed empty now that exams were over; there were only a handful of students sitting at the various tables, reading textbooks and making requests for copies they could take home. Emily smiled to herself — the printing press was one of her innovations — and walked over to the biographical section. If there was one thing the magical families had in common with aristocrats, both on Earth and the Nameless World, it was a tendency to brag about their accomplishments. She was sure there would be at least a dozen books devoted to House Waterfall. And they would definitely have an entry in *Magical Life*.

The first entry was shorter than she'd expected. House Waterfall had one main family and five cadet branches. Caleb was listed as belonging to a cadet branch; his mother, according to the entry, had married outside the magical families. She'd been a Mediator like Lady Barb, Emily noted, which was probably why no one had objected. Mediators were skilled fighters, using both magical and mundane methods. Caleb was the second child, of five, but there were few other details. The only really useful piece of information was that Caleb was twenty years old, two years older than Emily herself.

*He must not have done anything important,* she thought, although *that* wasn't really a surprise. Caleb was younger than Jade and *Jade* didn't even merit an entry. *They don't have room to give anything beyond the bare essentials.*

She glanced through a handful of other volumes, but found little beyond an assertion that Caleb's father had been a general, commanding a unified army in battle against the Necromancers. Emily wondered just what sort of son he would have produced, then put the matter out of her mind. There was no point in guessing, not now. She would meet him at Cockatrice and find out for herself. Carefully, she returned the volumes to the shelves and then strode back down to the bedroom. Inside, Frieda was sitting on her bed, reading a sheet of paper.

"They say I have to move to a different room next year," she said. "You can't talk them out of it?"

"They wouldn't let me room with my friends in Second Year," Emily said. Master Tor had been trying to help her, she knew now, but at the time she had regarded it as little more than unwanted meddling. "But you have so many friends you're *bound* to be with someone you like."

"Yeah," Frieda said. "But they're not *you*."

"True," Emily agreed. "On the other hand, you could wander around without me feeling as though I had to object. *And* you could host your friends in your room without worrying about me."

Frieda brightened. "There is that, I suppose," she said. One hand tugged at her pigtail, nervously. "Will they like me in Cockatrice?"

"They will," Emily assured her.

She felt her heart go out to the younger girl as she showered, then readied herself for bed. Frieda had nowhere to go, not really; her family had no interest in taking her back for the summer, even if she'd wanted to go home. Emily, still feeling responsible for Frieda, had invited her to stay at Cockatrice. It wasn't as if she didn't have the room for a single small girl.

"And there's the dance," Frieda said. "Will anyone want to dance with me?"

"I'm sure they will," Emily said. Mountaintop hadn't held dances, which — in hindsight — surprised her. "Just relax and try to enjoy yourself."

"I don't know how to dance," Frieda admitted.

"Just follow your partner," Emily said. "Most dances are simple, once you start moving. It's only the really complex ones you have to learn ahead of time."

She smiled at herself as she climbed into bed and lay down, pulling the sheets over her head. Once, she'd hated the thought of stepping onto the dance floor; she'd been nothing more than a wallflower, even at the best of times. Now...she found it easier to dance, if someone asked her to join him on the floor. But she didn't have the nerve to ask someone herself...

*I can ask Jade to partner Frieda first*, she thought, as she closed her eyes. *He can help break the ice.*

"Wake up," Frieda said, what felt like moments later. "It's time to get up."

Emily groaned, reaching for her watch. It was nearly ten bells. She was tempted to just roll over and go back to sleep, but she knew her friends wouldn't let her lie in bed for much longer. Reluctantly, she stood, walked into the shower and washed herself in cold water. It helped to push some of the tiredness out of her system.

"Just you wait until you're in Third Year," she muttered to Frieda. "You'll want more sleep too."

"I never had time to sleep since the day I was born," Frieda said. "There was always something to do."

"I suppose," Emily said. She pulled her robe on, then led the way down to breakfast. Half of the students seemed to be missing, she couldn't help noticing, but Alassa and Imaiqah were both sitting at their table. "Did you sleep well?"

"It could have been worse," Imaiqah said. "Did you have a good time at the library?"

"You should play with us instead," Alassa added, as Emily sat down. "Joliette is graduating and we're going to be a player down next year."

"I keep dropping the ball," Emily reminded her. "There's an entire school of people who would make better players than me."

"Yes, but they're not you," Alassa said. "And besides, you need the exercise."

Emily rolled her eyes as a servant placed a plate of bacon, eggs and bread in front of her. "I get enough exercise in Martial Magic," she said. "We do forced marches up and down the hills, then scramble up the rocks and down the mountainsides."

"It's not the same," Alassa said, dryly.

"Better for me," Emily said. She knew Alassa was trying to do her a favor, but she loathed team sports with a passion. "Besides, everyone knows I can't play *Ken* to save my life. It will stink like month-old potion for you to give me the slot."

"I suppose," Alassa said, reluctantly.

Emily eyed her breakfast, then dug in. It never seemed quite right to eat so much for breakfast, but magicians burned calories with frightening speed. The few times she had skipped breakfast, she'd regretted it by the first class. Beside her, Frieda ate with astonishing speed, then went back for seconds. It was a mystery how she remained so thin, despite both regular meals and potions. Emily had a private suspicion Frieda was practicing her magic far more than the average First Year.

*And who*, she asked herself, *could blame her for practicing?*

"The dance starts at four bells, in the afternoon," Alassa said. "That gives us *just* enough time to get ready."

Emily glanced at her watch. It was barely eleven bells in the morning. "We can start later, surely," she said. "I don't need five hours to get dressed."

"Count yourself lucky," Alassa said. "Do you know how long it will take me to get dressed when I marry?"

"Hours," Imaiqah said.

"If I'm lucky," Alassa agreed. "My mother was depressingly frank about *her* wedding day."

Emily groaned inwardly. "Why don't you just run off and get married at the nearest temple?"

"Because everyone who thinks they're someone would think they'd been slighted," Alassa said, after a moment. "They all have to be invited to the wedding."

"Then get dressed quickly today," Emily said. "It might be your last chance."

Alassa laughed. "But dresses are practically my armor," she said. "I need to be careful what I wear."

It was futile to argue, Emily discovered, as they finished their breakfast. Alassa practically dragged them upstairs, then started trying out more dresses herself while Imaiqah made mischievous remarks and Emily fought to stave off boredom. She knew, from bitter experience, that Alassa was right; the right dress, worn at the right time, would give precisely the right impression to any watching eyes. It wasn't enough for Alassa to *be* a princess, she had to *look* like a princess. But Emily, who had grown up buying her clothes at charity shops, had never had the chance to become a clotheshorse. Her trunk was full of dresses Queen Marlena had sent her, dresses Emily had never actually worn.

*I think I'm trapped in a time loop*, she thought, as Alassa tried on the same dress for the third time. *Or caught in a groundhog day. Or something.*

But Alassa was relentless. By the time four bells slowly rolled around, she'd not only donned the green dress for herself; she'd also outfitted Emily in the blue dress, Imaiqah in a white dress that clung to her figure and showed off her curves and, finally, Frieda in a dark dress that showed off her face and hair. Emily left her hair draping down her back — Alassa and the others did up their hair — and then followed them down to the Great Hall. As before, there were hundreds of students and tutors, some already dancing on the floor.

"You look lovely," Jade called, as he walked over to them. Like most of the male students, he wore his dress robes, rather than a proper outfit. "Would you care for the honor of this dance?"

"I would be flattered," Alassa said, primly.

She allowed Jade to take her hand, then lead her onto the dance floor. Emily watched them go, wondering if it had been arranged in advance. Alassa, whatever else could be said about her, was far from shy, but it was always awkward to wait for a man to ask one to dance. It was quite possible that she'd planned her first dance with Jade beforehand, just to break the ice.

Emily sighed inwardly before blinking in surprise as two boys she knew from Martial Magic came up to ask her and Imaiqah to dance. She turned to look at Frieda and smiled as she realized that Frieda had already been pulled onto the dance floor by another First Year student. Turning back to the boys, she allowed one of them to take her onto the dance floor too, while Imaiqah followed with the other. She switched partners as soon as the music changed, then again and again. But she couldn't help noticing that Alassa stayed with Jade for every dance.

*Maybe she arranged for them to share them all*, she thought, as she found herself dancing with an older student she knew from Martial Magic. *Or maybe she just wanted to stay with a reliable partner.*

She nodded to her partner as soon as the dance finished, then made her way off the dance floor and over to the buffet. A dozen students were standing there, chatting about nothing; Emily took a plate, then nodded to them as she piled her plate with food. She wasn't familiar with them and she had never found it easy or comfortable to talk to people she didn't know. Long moments passed before the next dance came to an end, allowing Imaiqah to join her. Frieda was still on the dance floor, seemingly enjoying the time of her life.

"You seem to have quite a few admirers," Imaiqah said, as she filled her own plate. "One of my partners even asked for an introduction."

Emily felt her cheeks heat. "And you said...?"

"I said he should ask you himself," Imaiqah said. She laughed. "You're not exactly a fire-breathing monster."

"No," Emily agreed, looking down at the bracelet on her wrist. "Some monsters are much smaller and harder to see."

She shook her head. Imaiqah had had so many boyfriends Emily had lost count, some of whom had lasted for only a few days before she dumped them. Sorceresses — even students — had a freedom denied to other women in the Nameless World, but Emily knew she couldn't share herself so openly. Magic could prevent any physical consequences from the act, yet it could do nothing about the emotional repercussions. She sighed at the thought, then shrugged and dismissed it. Maybe one day she'd find a boyfriend. But, until then, she could wait.

The afternoon wore on as more and more students joined the dancers. Emily danced several more dances, each time with a different partner, before she was finally able to escape to the wall once again. This time, Professor Thande was having a long discussion with Mistress Irene, complete with diagrams drawn out on the table and several heated disagreements. Emily listened for a moment, then realized she could make neither head nor tail of the discussion. Instead, she turned to watch the next dance began. Alassa was *still* dancing with Jade.

"Emily," Lady Barb said. Emily jumped, then turned to see the older woman standing next to her. "I trust you are ready for tomorrow?"

"Everything is packed, save for the items going into storage," Emily said. The last time she'd taken a full trunk to Zangaria, she'd almost lost everything. This time, they were going through a portal, but most of her possessions would be left at Whitehall. "All I have to do is shove a few things in my bag and we can go."

"We will probably be delayed," Lady Barb observed. Her voice hardened. "But do try and be ready at the appointed hour. It makes it easier to reprimand everyone else."

"Alassa," Emily said.

"Yes," Lady Barb said. She shrugged. "We have other matters to discuss, Emily, but we can do that later, once we have arrived in Zangaria. I trust you have been keeping up with political developments?"

"Barely," Emily admitted.

Lady Barb poked her chest with a finger, none too gently. "You cannot afford to leave matters in the hands of others indefinitely," she said, sternly. "They are acting in *your* name, Emily, and *you* will bear the brunt of any problems it causes."

"I know," Emily said, quietly.

"I know you find it boring," Lady Barb said, warningly. "But you don't really have a choice."

She looked past Emily, smiling as Sergeant Miles walked over to join them. It took Emily a moment to *recognize* him; he'd ditched his armor for a set of black robes, representing his rank as a combat sorcerer. Without his armor, he looked like just another sorcerer, she realized slowly. Alassa, she admitted again, definitely had a point about clothes making the wearer. And, in the sergeant's case, it was a definite form of camouflage.

"Lady Barb," Sergeant Miles said. "Will you grant me the honor of this dance?"

"Of course," Lady Barb said, in a flirtatious tone Emily had *never* heard her use before. "I would be honored."

Emily watched them step onto the dance floor, feeling an odd pang in her heart. She'd come to think of Lady Barb as a mother, of sorts, yet her *biological* mother had ruined her life when she had married again. Emily knew that Lady Barb wouldn't allow someone to ruin her life — and Sergeant Miles was a good and decent man — but it still bothered her. And it bothered her that it bothered her.

*I'm being selfish,* she thought, bitterly. *I should be happy for them, not sad.*

"Ladies and gentlemen," the Master of Ceremonies said. "If you will take your partners for the last dance..."

Emily blinked — she hadn't realized it was that late — then looked around urgently. Jade was *still* with Alassa, while both Imaiqah and Frieda had partners. The only person who was missing was the Gorgon, who seemed to have stepped out earlier. A handful of boys were standing on the edges of the crowd, looking around for partners of their own. Emily hesitated, fighting down the impulse to remain on the sidelines herself, and nodded to one of them when he looked at her hopefully. He stepped over to her, took her hand and tugged her gently onto the dance floor.

*Another year over,* she thought. On Earth, it would have been pointless to mark the passage of yet another year. She'd *known* her life was hopeless. But here...she would miss Whitehall, when she finally had to leave. She'd never realized it was even possible to miss a school. *And who knows what will happen next?*

After the dance, the students started to scatter. Imaiqah and her current boyfriend headed off somewhere; Alassa and Jade stayed in the hall, chatting together in low voices. Emily let go of her partner, then made her way up to her room. She was too tired to wash; she merely removed the dress, then lay down on the bed and closed her eyes. Another year of schooling was definitely over.

*And what,* she asked herself again, as sleep began to claim her, *will happen next?*

# Chapter Four

"I FEEL ROTTEN," FRIEDA COMPLAINED.

"It's that wine you were drinking," Emily said unsympathetically, as she pulled herself out of bed. She didn't feel much better, she had to admit, but at least she didn't have a hangover. "I thought you were used to drinking alcohol."

"That's *beer*," Frieda protested. "I didn't drink any beer at the dance..."

"Glad to hear it," Emily said. "Didn't anyone give you a lecture on not drinking more than a little alcohol in a magic school?"

Frieda shook her head. Somehow, Emily wasn't surprised. Mountaintop had allowed its students to buy alcohol, but the only ones who could afford to buy were the ones who already knew the dangers. Frieda probably wouldn't have tasted a drop of alcohol between her arrival at Mountaintop and the dance, last night. That would have given her two years, Emily calculated, to lose any tolerance she might have built up, once upon a time.

"Go see the healer," Emily ordered. "She can give you something for it. And a lecture too, probably."

"But..." Frieda rubbed her head. "She'll kill me."

"She will probably give you a telling off," Emily agreed. "But I don't think she will actually *kill* you." She shrugged. "But if you don't mind spending the day with a hangover, drink lots of water and then make sure you have everything packed. You do *not* want to have to explain to Lady Barb why we're late."

Frieda looked torn, then hurried out of the room. Emily smiled, removed her underclothes and jumped into the shower. It would be her last chance, she knew, to have a proper shower before she returned to Whitehall. Zangaria was a progressive kingdom by the standards of the Nameless World, but it didn't have any magical showers. The only way to wash was to have servants fill a tub of water, then use magic to warm it. Or have them heat the water, if one didn't have magic. It was perhaps unsurprising that even the nobility tended to smell faintly unpleasant, no matter how much perfume they drenched themselves in.

Emily grimaced at the memory, then washed herself thoroughly and stepped out of the shower. Lady Barb had told her they would be going through the portal rather than making the long journey from Whitehall to Zangaria by coach, so she donned a pair of loose trousers, a shirt and a jumper Imaiqah's mother had sent to her. It didn't look particularly aristocratic, but it was practical. Besides, she knew there would be a place to change into a dress at the far end, should it prove necessary. Half the social rules in the Allied Lands seemed to depend on people ignoring the breaches of conduct, as long as the formalities were observed.

The door opened, revealing Frieda. "She gave me something to drink and I feel better," she carolled. "But I have to write a long essay on the dangers of over-drinking and drunkenness in exchange."

"Serves you right," Emily said, dryly. "And don't forget to include the prospect of accidentally killing yourself with your own magic when you write the essay."

She waited for Frieda to dress, then went down to the dining hall. Alassa was already there, looking disgustingly fresh, while both Imaiqah and the Gorgon were missing. Emily sat down next to her, hastily ordering fruit juice and cereal rather than another huge breakfast platter. Beside her, Frieda ordered her usual and tapped her feet impatiently until it arrived.

"I've started to pack everything," Alassa assured her, before Emily could say a word. "But I wanted to leave a few boxes here in storage."

"Too many dresses and stuff," Emily said. She took her bowl of cereal gratefully and started to eat. "Or magic tools your father doesn't want you to bring home?"

"He wants me to do more ceremonial work over the summer," Alassa said. "I thought he'd let me have three more years of schooling, after my Confirmation, but he was hinting he might want me back earlier. It took hours of arguing to convince him to let me stay here for another couple of years."

Emily nodded in understanding. Alassa was the only heir King Randor had, the only person who could claim his throne without triggering a civil war. And she'd almost been killed — or replaced — by a Mimic, as well as the normal dangers of studying in a school of magic. Hell, *Emily* had almost killed her, back in First Year. She couldn't really blame Alassa's father for wanting his daughter back in Zangaria, under his protection.

But she knew she would miss Alassa when she was gone.

Imaiqah entered the hall, looking tired and worn. "You look tired," Alassa said, as Imaiqah sat down. "What were you *doing* last night?"

"It didn't involve sleeping," Imaiqah said. She yawned, loudly. "Can I sleep in the coach?"

"It won't be a very long drive," Alassa said. "But if you want to sleep, I dare say no one will dare stop you."

Emily colored, then finished her breakfast. "I'll take my stuff down to the Great Hall, then come back to meet you," she said, as she rose. "Frieda, did you finish packing?"

"I packed everything and it's in the trunk next to yours," Frieda assured her. "We can put the remaining boxes in storage now too, if you want."

"Good," Emily said.

She nodded to her friends, then walked back to the room, taking the time to say goodbye to the Gorgon on the way. The room always looked bare at the end of term, when the handful of decorations were taken down and either packed into storage or taken home for the holidays, but she knew they wouldn't be in the same room next year. She'd requested a chance to share a room with Alassa and Imaiqah, yet it was unlikely they'd get it. The other two had shared a room last year, after all, while Emily had already shared a room with Imaiqah. She might just have to get used to new roommates.

*Pity*, she thought, as she cast a levitation spell. The two trunks rose into the air, then followed her as she walked out of the room like obedient children. *We could have had more fun together if we shared a room.*

She wasn't the only student taking luggage down to the Great Hall, or to the Portals. Dozens of students moved up and down the stairs, some levitating their trunks, others showing off by carrying them physically. Emily moved past them and placed her trunks at the bottom of the stairs, where Lady Barb was standing. The older woman looked impatient, making a show of glancing at her watch from time to time. Emily looked up at her, then frowned. It might be quite some time before Alassa was ready to go.

"Tell her to hurry," Lady Barb said, when Emily said that out loud. "Her father will not be too pleased if she's late."

"I know," Emily said. "But I brought down everything of mine — and Frieda's."

"Good," Lady Barb said. "I wasn't worried about either of you."

Emily nodded and hurried back to Alassa's room. Alassa had finished breakfast and returned to pack, but clothes were strewn everywhere while she sat in the middle of the room, trying to pack them all into her trunk. Emily smiled inwardly — Alassa had never lived without servants before coming to Whitehall — then helped her friend push everything into the trunk and seal the lid. It was not only large enough to take everything she'd brought to Whitehall; the spells placed on the trunk by the enchanter who'd produced it would hold everything in stasis. The dresses could be unloaded later, once they were at Zangaria, and then the maids could sort them out.

"Thank you," Alassa said, as Imaiqah came into the room. "Did you put everything in storage?"

"Yes," Imaiqah said. "It will all be safe until we return."

Alassa nodded, then stood. "I'll take the trunk down, if you want to check on Frieda," she said, to Emily. "And I'll meet you both at the bottom of the stairs."

"See you there," Emily said. "And have fun explaining your delay to Lady Barb."

She smiled at Alassa's expression, then ducked out of the room and walked back to hers. Frieda was standing outside, levitating two large storage boxes in front of her. Emily took one, transporting it down the corridor and into the storage chambers. There were enough protective spells over the room, according to Madame Razz, to keep their property safe from everyone, save perhaps for the Grandmaster himself. Emily tried to imagine the Grandmaster breaking into their trunks over the holidays, then dismissed the thought. The Grandmaster had better things to do with his time.

"All done?" Frieda asked, hopefully. "Can we go now?"

Emily smiled at the excitement in her voice. "I suppose we can," she said. She took one final look at the secured boxes, then turned to lead the way to the stairs. "Did you leave anything in the room?"

"Nothing," Frieda assured her. "There's nothing left, but the sheets and blankets that came with the room."

"Good," Emily said. "Let's go."

Downstairs, Lady Barb was reproving Alassa, speaking in a soft tone that Emily knew, from experience, was worse than being yelled at.

"You cannot afford to be late, *Your Highness*," Lady Barb said. "There will be people who will see it as a sign of sloppiness, then weakness. Those people tend to have assassins on their payrolls. And, while I know you are skilled at defending yourself, those assassins will have more practical experience."

Alassa said nothing. Lady Barb gave her a long considering look, then looked past her towards Emily.

"Emily," she said. "Are you ready?"

"Yes," Emily said.

"I will have the coach brought up to the door," Lady Barb said, turning. "Be ready to load the trunks into the coach as soon as it arrives."

She walked out of the door. Emily looked at Alassa and frowned. Her friend looked angry, yet also — somehow — depressed. Very few people in her life had ever spoken so bluntly to her, Emily knew, and Alassa was realistic enough to know that Lady Barb was right. A display of weakness, or irresolution, would be used against her, even if it hadn't been her fault. And then...

Emily shuddered. Only a madman would risk starting a civil war, she was sure, but the Iron Duchess and some of the Barons of Zangaria had tried just that, two years ago. The aristocracy had been cowed, for the moment, but it wouldn't last. Alassa had even told her, only a few weeks ago, that they'd started scheming to undermine King Randor and his daughter once again. It seemed a handful of executions — including one Alassa had carried out personally — hadn't been enough to *keep* them cowed.

She rested a hand on Alassa's shoulder, just for a second. "You'll be fine," she said. "Just keep watching your back."

"My neck won't turn that far," Alassa said. She smiled, but there was no humor in her eyes. "I need a pair of eyes in the back of my head."

"There are spells that would give you eyes in the back of your head," Imaiqah said, in an effort to be helpful. "But you also need a good man."

Alassa merely nodded.

Emily gave her an odd look. Alassa had been accepting, at first, of the fact that her marriage would be arranged by her father. Later, after her Confirmation, she had insisted on having a greater say in any arrangements, when they were finally made. But now...there was something odd about her reactions, something *off*. Maybe she was just envious of Imaiqah, Emily wondered. It must be galling to watch her friend enjoy spending time with the boys, when Alassa could not compromise herself in such a manner.

*It's stupid,* Emily thought, as they picked up their trunks and headed to the door. *There are no shortage of potions to prevent conception. Alassa might not even need them because of the bloodline. She could have all the fun she wanted and no one would need to know.*

But she knew it wasn't that easy, not for a princess or a queen. The double standard was alive and well in Zangaria. If Alassa compromised herself, it would damage her ability to rule...when any male monarch could indulge himself as he saw fit. Indeed, if half the stories about Zangaria's male nobility were true, Emily had no idea how they managed to find the time to actually rule. Or do anything, beyond chasing pleasure.

Outside, a cold wind blew down out of the mountains, causing them to shiver as it rustled their robes. Emily cast a warming charm, then watched as the coach drove up to them and stopped right in front of the doors. Lady Barb jumped down and opened the storage space under the coach, allowing them to shove their trunks inside. Emily glanced back into Whitehall, feeling oddly as if she was leaving her home, then followed Alassa as she scrambled into the coach. It was easily roomy enough for all five of them, even with the light ball floating in the air, casting an eerie pale light over the scene. But the windows were covered by drawn curtains, preventing anyone from seeing in or out.

"You're late," she heard Lady Barb say. "I doubt your master would be pleased."

"He would be furious," Jade said. The coach shook as he placed his trunk underneath, then scrambled up to join them. "But he wouldn't have wanted me to go anyway."

Emily smiled as Jade sat down next to Alassa. "I hope you brought a book," she said. "There's not much else to do on the trip."

"It's only a short trip," Jade said. "I just need to meditate and prepare for the portal."

"True," Alassa agreed. "Emily, can you cope with it?"

"I don't think I have a choice," Emily said, as the coach lurched into life. Stepping through portals made her feel sick, unless she prepared herself beforehand. It was a sign of strong magic, Alassa had told her years ago, but it was one she could have done without. "Let me know when we're about to pass through the portal."

She gritted her teeth, then hastily erected mental defenses. Beside her, Frieda did the same, although she actually had more experience with portals than Emily. Mountaintop had used portals to keep its precise location a secret and Frieda had stepped through more than one. But then, Emily was morbidly certain that secrecy no longer mattered. Once the wards had fallen, the school's enemies would have no trouble locating it.

"We're about to pass through the portal," Lady Barb called, from where she was sitting with the driver. "Brace yourselves..."

Emily closed her eyes and focused her mind, then shuddered as magic crackled around her defenses. The entire coach seemed to heave, as if it was a ship caught in a particularly bad storm, then settled sharply. Emily swallowed hard, swearing to herself she would not be sick in front of her friends and forced herself to relax. It was a struggle to convince her eyes to open, somehow. They seemed to want to remain closed.

"Emily," Alassa said. Her voice sounded as though she were speaking from a very great distance. "Are you all right?"

"I think so," Emily gasped. None of the others, even Jade, the oldest, seemed to be affected quite so badly. Her head spun rapidly, then calmed. "What about you?"

"I've never felt it so badly," Alassa said. Her voice was curiously flat. "I should have asked Lady Barb to teleport you here, Emily. I'm sorry."

Emily ran her hand through her hair, which suddenly felt uncomfortably sweaty. "It wasn't your fault," she said. "I could have asked her myself."

Alassa eyed her for a long moment, then turned her attention to peering through cracks in the curtains. "We're in Alexis," she said. "The last time I was here, the streets were lined with people cheering."

"You're here incognito now," Jade pointed out, dryly. "And no one knows who's in the carriage."

Emily would have been surprised if that was actually true. No matter how incognito Alassa wanted to be, there were armed guards outside and the coach was heading right for the castle at the heart of the city. But, like so much else, if Alassa wanted to pretend to be someone faceless, the citizens would gladly go along with her. It was one of the many little understandings that allowed rigid protocol to be tempered with compassion and understanding.

*Like we are allowed to change before greeting the king, even though we are not meant to enter the castle without greeting the king,* she thought. Like so much else, it exasperated her, but it had to be endured. *Alassa needs our support.*

The coach came to a halt. Outside, she could hear men shouting backwards and forwards, then the coach lurched and drove forward again. It stopped a moment later. Emily heard Lady Barb jumping down from the driver's seat and scrabbling with the handle. The door opened a moment later, allowing cold air to waft into the coach. Emily peered out and saw, once again, the cold grey stone of Castle Alexis, home of the royal family. A handful of guards peered back at her curiously, then hastily lowered their gazes as they remembered she was a baroness. The only person in the coach who didn't have a noble title was Frieda; Jade, being a combat sorcerer, was effectively considered minor aristocracy.

*Because if someone didn't treat him well,* she thought, *he could turn them into a toad — or worse.*

She jumped out of the coach and helped Frieda scramble down to the ground. The younger girl looked around in awe, her face glowing with astonishment. Behind her, Alassa looked amused, while Jade looked understanding. Frieda would never have seen anything like the castle before, apart — perhaps — from Whitehall itself.

"You can freshen up before being presented to the king," Lady Barb said, as a maid hurried over to them and curtseyed quickly. The maid muttered hastily in her ear. "There are dresses and other clothes waiting for you upstairs."

Emily sighed, but knew — once again — that there was no real choice. Besides, she wanted a quick wash after passing through the portal. Her skin felt sweaty and unclean.

Gritting her teeth in anticipation of the coming ordeal, she followed the maid through a tiny doorway set in the grey stone and into the guesthouse.

# Chapter Five

FRIEDA CLUNG TO EMILY AS THEY ENTERED THE WASHROOM, WHERE A SMALL ARMY OF maids was waiting for them. Emily hastily fended them off as they started trying to remove her clothes, their faces expressing a disapproval they would never express out loud, and glared daggers at a pair of young girls carrying sponges and towels. Baroness or not, she could still wash herself — and besides, she had never been comfortable allowing someone else to undress her and wash her, as if she were nothing more than a doll. She took a sponge and towel, then found a private corner next to where the dresses were waiting.

"Why…" Frieda coughed and started again. "Why do we have to come here?"

"Tradition," Alassa said. Two of the maids were already undressing her, while a third was wiping her face with a warm cloth. "We cannot enter the castle until my father has greeted us, but we cannot be presented to the king while wearing undignified clothes. So we come here, to the guesthouse, and wash and dress in proper clothes, all the while claiming that we have not actually entered the castle. By such sleights of hand the formalities are maintained."

Emily rolled her eyes. "You'll find that everyone is obsessed with formalities," she added, dryly. "If you wear the wrong dress at the wrong time you will never hear the end of it."

"I only have two dresses," Frieda said, slowly. She looked down at the floor, nervously. "What else can I wear?"

"Don't worry about it," Alassa said. "My mother will find something for you to wear, never you fear."

*Of course she will*, Emily thought. She'd offered to buy Frieda a pair of additional dresses, but the girl had turned her down. *It won't make Frieda's life any easier.*

She sighed, inwardly. Frieda had grown up in the Cairngorms, where she had worn homemade clothes, certainly nothing particularly fine. Mountaintop had given her a pair of school uniforms, but nothing more elaborate. Now, the poor girl was faced with the prospect of either having to buy dresses herself or accepting charity from the queen. And the dresses were so expensive, by her standards, that she didn't have a hope of buying one. Alassa, on the other hand, saw nothing wrong with buying a dress for a single occasion, then putting it away for the rest of her life.

"There was a big tiff last year, while you were gone," Alassa said, looking up at Emily. The maids were washing her feet, paying careful attention to the dirt between her toes. "Two noblewomen, having bought their dresses from the same exclusive designer, discovered to their horror that they were wearing the *same* dress. They wound up fighting in the middle of the Great Hall."

*The more things change, the more they stay the same*, Emily thought.

She took the dress that was meant for her, and pulled it over her head. Two seamstresses closed in and made a handful of minor alterations, pointing her towards a mirror. Emily scowled at her reflection, then looked down at her chest. The gown

covered everything, but it was tighter around her breasts than she would have preferred. She hesitated, unwilling to make a fuss in front of everyone, then cast a charm
over the dress. It would be hard for anyone to see her chest clearly.

Frieda caught her arm. "Another blue dress?"

"It seems to be my color," Emily said. Imaiqah had started it, followed by Alassa
and Queen Marlena. They'd all sworn blind that blue was the best color for Emily.
"And yourself?"

"Blue too," Frieda said. "Do you think she wanted us to match?"

Emily shrugged, watching the maids finish dressing Alassa. She had a long white
outfit that reminded Emily of a wedding dress, complete with flowers in her golden
hair and a pair of golden slippers. As soon as she was ready, Alassa stepped forward
and motioned for them to follow her down the stairs, towards the throne room. Jade
was waiting at the bottom, having changed into a dark set of clothes that marked him
as a combat sorcerer. Emily had to admit they looked good on him, showing off his
muscles as well as his magical prowess.

Jade struck a dramatic pose, whirling his cloak around him. "How do I look?"

"Powerful," Alassa said. "But you really need something gold to catch the eye."

"My hair," Jade said, deadpan.

Emily looked from one to the other, surprised, then followed Alassa up to the
grand wooden doors leading into the throne room. A pair of armed guards eyed them
curiously, but looked away as a herald, wearing a uniform that made him look alarmingly like a walking trifle, stepped forward and bowed so deeply Emily thought he
would brush his nose against the stone floor.

"Your highness," he said, as if Alassa were alone. "I welcome you to your father's
grace."

"You may announce us," Alassa said, grandly.

The herald threw open the doors and stepped forward. "My Lords, Ladies and
Gentlemen," he said, in a voice that carried right across the throne room. "I present to
you Crown Princess and Duchess of Iron Alassa, Baroness Emily of Cockatrice, Lady
Viscount of Steam Imaiqah, the Sorcerer Jade and Frieda Wandbreaker, Daughter of
Huckeba."

Emily felt Frieda tense beside her. It wasn't just that she lacked a title, although
Emily understood precisely why someone would find the throne room intimidating;
it was the simple reminder of her father, a man who had sold her to Mountaintop as
soon as the recruiters came calling. Emily gave her a reassuring glance, then followed
Alassa into the throne room, looking neither to the left nor the right as they walked
up the carpeted path towards the throne. The back of her neck prickled as she
walked, reminding her that everyone would be staring at them, looking for signs of
weakness or malleability. Zangaria's politics were very much a dog-eat-dog universe,
she knew; it hadn't been *that* long since some of the barons had tried to kill the king.
The urge to run grew stronger as she stopped at the base of the dais and looked up at
the king. Alassa's father, if anything, seemed to have grown harder in the two years
since they'd last met.

He was a powerful, barrel-chested man. Long blonde hair, a shade darker than Alassa's, hung down from the golden crown perched on his head, while a neat goatee poked down from his chin. His face was stern, projecting the image of a patriarch who had neither fear nor favor, but his eyes were colder than ever before. Emily recalled Aurelius's warning and shivered, inwardly. King Randor might *like* her, even *respect* her, but he wouldn't hesitate to *use* her. And he had already been more than willing to use his own daughter.

"We welcome you back to Our Kingdom, my daughter," Randor said, as Alassa dropped to one knee. "Your throne awaits you."

Alassa rose, then walked forward and climbed onto the dais. A simple golden throne, almost a chair, was positioned next to the king's throne. She turned in one smooth motion, sat down and smiled at the crowd. They cheered so loudly the entire room seemed to shake.

"Baroness Emily, We welcome you back to Our Kingdom," Randor said. His gaze moved over Emily's face as she knelt, then to Frieda. "And who is this you have brought with you?"

"This is my friend," Emily said, flatly. It had taken a week of messages exchanged between Alassa and her father to come up with a formula for introducing Frieda to the court. She couldn't be Emily's sister or daughter because she was no blood relation, but she couldn't be introduced as a commoner because she was a magician. "I bid you welcome her to your court."

King Randor rose slowly to his feet, taking a step forward. Emily reminded herself that she'd faced two necromancers and remained where she was, forcing down the urge to rise to her feet or to run. She hated being on her knees in front of anyone, particularly someone used to getting whatever he wanted. King Randor peered down at her for a long moment, then moved his gaze to Frieda. Emily sensed, more than saw, Frieda freeze like a mouse caught in a spotlight.

"We welcome you to Our Court," Randor said, finally. He stepped backwards and sat back on the throne. "You may rise."

Emily rose, gratefully. "I thank you, your majesty," she said.

"There will be a meeting of the barons tomorrow morning," King Randor added, smoothly. "You will attend, of course."

"Yes, your majesty," Emily said. She groaned, inwardly. If she'd known just how many obligations had come with the barony, she would have turned it down in front of the whole court. "I will attend."

Randor greeted Imaiqah, who took the whole process in stride, then motioned for Emily and the rest of the girls to stand to one side. Jade stepped forward and bowed, but remained on his feet. Emily felt a hot flash of envy — the social protocols for qualified sorcerers made them the equals of anyone else — and then watched, curiously, as the king met Jade's eyes and held them. She couldn't help wondering if they would have started to arm-wrestle if they had been alone.

"My daughter informs me you wish to become a Court Wizard," Randor said. "Do you feel qualified to serve as my sorcerer?"

Emily blinked in surprise. She'd known that Jade would be accompanying them to Zangaria, but she hadn't known he intended to become the Court Wizard. God knew King Randor needed someone trustworthy to serve as his wizard...and yet, why Jade? Why a newly-qualified combat sorcerer, just out of his apprenticeship, when there were more experienced magicians out there? Someone like Lady Barb? Or, even though she hated to admit it, someone like Master Grey?

"I do, your majesty," Jade said.

There was a long pregnant pause. "Then we will see, young man," King Randor said. His tone was light, but his eyes never left Jade's face. "Please, join us at the high table for dinner. I would see what you are made of."

Imaiqah poked Emily in the side. "Can you see the queen?"

Emily frowned, then looked around. Queen Marlena should have been sitting beside her husband, if on a lower throne, but there was no sign of her. None of her letters had mentioned an illness, or something else that would have kept her from greeting her daughter; everything she'd written had suggested she was looking forward to seeing Alassa and her friends again. Emily glanced back at the king, who was dismissing his court, then at Alassa. Her face was tightly controlled, but Emily could tell she was worried.

*We have to keep acting like noblewomen here*, she thought, as the crowd started moving into the Great Hall. *There will be a chance to talk about it later.*

"It's dinnertime?" Frieda asked. "We only just had *breakfast?*"

"Time difference," Emily said. She groaned inwardly. They would probably have something akin to jet lag the following morning. "It's late afternoon here."

The Great Hall seemed larger than she remembered, she noted as they were shown to their seats. As before, there were ten huge wooden tables, one set higher than the others, but they all seemed to be larger, with more places laid for the guests. Emily rolled her eyes as she and Frieda were escorted to seats three and five and sat down, remembering how the whole event was organized. The closer to the king, who had seat one, the greater the prestige. She would have gladly traded her position with someone else, perhaps one of the barons who looked unhappy at having to suffer the humiliation of sitting in the ninth chair, but she knew that wouldn't be allowed. The seating plan would have been worked out after months of careful negotiation.

Frieda took her seat and peered at the chair between her and Emily. "Who's sitting here?"

Emily shrugged. Imaiqah or Jade? No, Imaiqah was seated next to her father, the newly-ennobled Viscount Steam, while Jade was seated on the king's other side. She wondered, briefly, if King Randor intended to give him a job interview right there and then, then realized it was yet another test. The Court Wizard had to endure much more than merely working spells on the king's behalf. There would be dinners and ceremonies and hundreds of other boring arrangements that couldn't be ignored, merely endured.

She looked up as someone pulled the chair away from the table. "Lady Emily," a very soft voice said. "I believe I am sitting here."

"Welcome," Emily said, although she wished she were sitting next to Frieda. "Please, join us."

The newcomer looked...odd. She had white-blonde hair, skin so pale it was almost translucent and large blue eyes. Her pale blue dress was cut low, revealing the tops of her breasts, and clung neatly to her hips. Emily couldn't help being reminded of Alassa, save for the fact that while Alassa looked stunningly human, there was something oddly *inhuman* about the newcomer. There was nothing she could put her finger on it, yet it was there.

"I am Alicia, Heiress to the Barony of Gold," the newcomer said. There was almost no emotion in her voice at all. "I admire you greatly, Lady Emily."

"Thank you," Emily said, feeling her face heat. Heiress to the Barony? Baron Gold, the third most powerful nobleman in the kingdom, had been beheaded in the wake of the coup attempt, two years ago. Alicia had to be his daughter. "You're not the baroness in your own right?"

"No, my lady," Alicia said. "His Majesty has not yet seen fit to confirm me as baroness."

Emily studied her for a long moment. King Randor had never liked the idea of a female heir — he'd spent *years* trying to have a son before giving up and accepting that Alassa would be his heir — and he might have denied Alicia the title for the same reason. Or he might have viewed her in the same light as her father, as a potential traitor. Keeping her powerless might be nothing more than self-defense.

But Alicia didn't look very threatening.

*You should know better than to judge by appearances*, she reminded herself, savagely. *Lin didn't look very threatening either.*

Alassa elbowed Emily, catching her attention. "Mother is apparently unwilling to attend the feast," she said. "We will be talking to her later."

Emily blinked. "Unwilling?"

"Apparently," Alassa said. "Father says we will discuss it later."

*That* was odd, Emily knew. It was rare, very rare, for aristocrats to show any signs of weakness. Lady Barb had been right; the slightest sign of weakness or carelessness would have people licking their lips and hiring assassins, or coming up with cunning plans to take advantage of the weakness. Queen Marlena would have attended a function on her deathbed, if she had to bring her deathbed with her. And now she was absent...

She cast a privacy ward hastily, then leaned forward. "Do you think they've had a row?"

"My parents wouldn't have allowed a fight to get in the way of showing a united front," Alassa said, scornfully. "That's what worries me."

Emily nodded, then dispelled the ward as the servants arrived, each one carrying a colossal plate of food. She felt her stomach clench at the plates of meat, roast potatoes and vegetables, strangely bland compared to the food at Whitehall. Behind them, other servants carried trays of condiments and jugs of gravy, each one strong and thick. She recalled one experiment with mustard she had no intention of repeating and wished, just for a moment, that she was close enough to Frieda to whisper a warning. But she'd never met anything her younger friend couldn't eat.

She waited, with the others, until everyone was served, then started to eat. As she'd expected, the meat was bland, but the gravy was surprisingly tasty. Emily ate enough to satisfy the hunger pains, then looked around, studying the guests. Alicia ate with a daintiness that surprised Emily, picking at her food as little as possible. Perhaps she just wanted to keep her figure, Emily thought tartly, although she hadn't seen many fat teenagers in the Nameless World. Beside her, Frieda seemed intent on cramming as much as she could into her mouth before the servants could take it away.

*Her table manners need work*, Emily thought, remembering how Alassa had taught her how to handle herself in a royal court. *But she didn't grow up learning the ropes from her parents.*

Jade was chatting to the king, his words hidden behind a privacy ward. Emily wondered just what they were saying to one another, then looked for Lady Barb in the crowd. The combat sorceress was missing, she realized, after sweeping the tables twice. Maybe she'd gone to visit the queen.

"We will dance, after this," Alassa said. "And then we will drink potions and sleep."

Emily nodded. "Do you know what the meeting tomorrow is about?"

"I don't, but it was put off so you could attend," Alassa told her. "I suspect it's probably important."

"Yeah," Emily agreed. If it was something that Bryon couldn't handle, it had to be important. But it was also odd. Randor could have summoned her at any moment, at least after she'd left Mountaintop. Lady Barb could easily have teleported her to Zangaria. "Will you be attending?"

"I don't think so," Alassa said. "Tell me about it afterwards, okay?"

Emily blinked. "What sort of meeting is so secret even *you're* out of the loop?"

"I don't know," Alassa said. "Father...has been sharing a lot with me, now I've been Confirmed. But I don't know what this is about."

"I'll tell you," Emily promised. "You can look after Frieda while I'm gone."

"Mother will want to meet her," Alassa agreed. "I'll take Frieda to her room."

"Thanks," Emily said. "Would it be terribly wrong of me to skip the dancing and go straight to bed?"

"Probably," Alassa said. "They all want to know you're healthy."

# Chapter Six

EMILY HAD KNOWN, FROM HER FIRST VISIT TO CASTLE ALEXIS, THAT KING RANDOR HAD A private set of rooms that were locked and warded away from most of the castle's residents. He'd even *shown* her a set of such rooms, when she'd first visited the castle. But she'd never known there was a meeting chamber below the throne room, or that it could be entered by stepping through a seemingly solid wall. If one of the king's private servants hadn't shown her to the chamber, she knew she would never have seen it at all.

*Subtle magic*, she thought, as the rune carved into her chest burned uncomfortably. *Not enough to be dangerous, but enough to keep this room hidden unless someone is shown how to reach it.*

It was surprisingly bland, compared to the throne room. A large portrait of Alexis I, the founder of the kingdom, hung on the far wall, while the other two held maps of Alexis City and Zangaria itself, respectively. A wooden table was placed in the center of the room, surrounded by hard wooden chairs. King Randor, she assumed, had the only chair that had a comfortable seat, probably intended to help remind the noblemen of their place. Besides, it would also ensure that meetings didn't last very long. She'd sat on enough hard wooden chairs at school to know it was never pleasant.

She kept her face impassive as the other barons eyed her, their faces under equally tight control. There were only four barons in the kingdom now, including Emily herself; Alicia, it seemed, had not been invited to the meeting. None of them liked Emily or trusted her, she knew, even though they feared her power. To them, she was the person who had defeated the coup and killed some of their friends and allies, even though it hadn't been *Emily* who'd executed them after the coup had failed. They thought of her, she suspected, as someone between a tattletale and an agent of chaos.

A door at the far corner opened, revealing King Randor. The barons — and Emily — hastily went down on one knee; the king eyed them for a long moment, before motioning for them to rise. He looked surprisingly pleased with himself, Emily noted, as he took his seat at the head of the table. It struck her, suddenly, that he had been looking forward to the meeting.

"Please, be seated," King Randor said. He waited for them to sit, then continued with an air of mischievous amusement. "It has been years since we have been gathered together, has it not? Then, there were six of you and my poor charmed brother. And now there are only four."

He smiled, rather coldly. The former Duke of Iron had been packed off to an isolated castle; a prison, in all but name. Even if he escaped, he was powerless. Alassa had claimed his title, Emily knew, after executing the duke's treacherous wife. No one would risk their position to back his weak claim to the throne, particularly now that Alassa had been Confirmed.

*And the barons are powerless too*, Emily thought. Their private armies had been scattered, their sorcerers packed off to other countries...they were weaker than they'd been for nearly a hundred years. *They have to hate it.*

"We shall begin by discussing my will," Randor continued. He produced a sheaf of paper from his pocket and dropped it on the table. "My kingdom will, of course, go to my daughter. She is, as yet, unmarried, but she is Confirmed. And, I might add, a powerful magician in her own right. Who would be fool enough to dispute the title with her?"

There was a long pause. No one answered.

"There are a handful of other bequests," King Randor added, "but they are comparatively minor. You will be expected to uphold the terms, should I die before my appointed time."

He passed the sheaf of papers to Baron Silver, who read it quickly and then passed the will to the next baron. Emily winced inwardly when the papers came to her — the will was written in Old Script, rather than English — and then started to read it. She wasn't anything like an expert, but as far as she could tell there were only a handful of bequests. Queen Marlena would receive enough money to keep her in luxury for the rest of her days, a handful of loyal servants would be rewarded for their service and...a number of payments were marked out to various women of the court. Emily's eyes narrowed at the final section. What the hell did that mean?

"I do not intend to divide the kingdom," Randor said. "It is my intention for my daughter to inherit a unified land."

"Your majesty," Baron Gaunt said. "When is your daughter to marry?"

Emily winced, inwardly. Alassa had to produce an heir at some point, someone who shared the Royal Bloodline as well as a strong claim to the throne. And whoever married Alassa would have a chance to make himself king, in fact as well as name. She had a feeling that the three barons, all easily old enough to be Alassa's father, would have happily put their wives and children aside for a chance to marry the princess.

"When she has found a suitable husband," King Randor said. "One will be found, I have no doubt, and then she will marry. She has time."

"She should have been married sooner," Baron Silver said.

"But she was not," King Randor said, sharply. "And this leads us to the second part of the discussion."

He placed his hands on the table and smiled at them. There was something cool and deliberate about his movements, as if he had planned the meeting beforehand. Emily felt a cold shiver running down her spine as she realized that, whatever the King had to say, the barons were not going to like it.

"A number of noble families have lost their heads," he said. "Their children, alas, have been cast out in the world with no one to protect or discipline them, let alone guide them through the rocks and shoals of the path towards adulthood. The estates, held in trust for them, will languish without a firm hand to keep their clients in line. Their peasants are already fleeing the fields for the opportunities of the cities."

Emily felt her cheeks heat as two of the barons tossed her sharp glances. It was *her* fault, more than anyone else, that so many opportunities had opened up in the cities. Now, peasants who were legally bound to the land were fleeing to the cities, seeking a chance to make new lives for themselves. The barons were furious; clearly, it had never occurred to them that no one liked working hard, then only being allowed to keep a tiny portion of their crops. Taxes were so high in some parts of Zangaria that they were literally impossible to pay. And then the barons wondered why so many peasants became bandits.

"This is, of course, a grave concern to the kingdom," King Randor continued. "I will therefore be assuming guardianship of all the minor aristocratic children, effective immediately."

Emily didn't understand what he meant, but it was clear the other barons *did*. They looked, very much, as if they wanted to protest, to object to what the king had said. If they'd had weapons...she shook her head, inwardly. She rather doubted King Randor would have been defenseless, if they'd gone at him with swords or daggers. The wards surrounding the room were light, compared to Whitehall's, but they would be effective against men without magic.

"The children will come to the castle to live with my family," Randor said. "Once they reach their majority, they will assume their titles and serve as aristocrats in their lands."

He paused. Emily realized, suddenly, that he was effectively gloating, rubbing their helplessness in their faces. But why? What did the guardianship of minor children *matter*? But there was no way she could ask, not now. She would have to discuss it with Alassa later, and perhaps Lady Barb. And then...she wondered, briefly, if there was anything she should or could do. But she couldn't say without knowing what was going on.

"Your majesty," Baron Silver said. "You have yet to confirm *Baroness* Alicia in her lands and title, even though she is of age."

"She is a girl," King Randor said, dismissively.

"So is Baroness Cockatrice," Baron Silver said, indicating Emily. His voice dripped honey...and sarcasm. "And *she* saved your throne, for which we are all truly grateful."

"Baroness Emily was rewarded for her services to the crown," King Randor said. "What has Alicia done to merit being confirmed in her lands and title?"

The barons sucked in their breath. Even *Emily* was astonished. King Randor had targeted, intentionally or otherwise, the cornerstone of the aristocratic system. Noble titles and power were passed down from father to son — or daughter, if there was no suitable male heir. For him to deny Alicia her rank and titles...she shook her head, promising herself that she would go over it with Alassa at the earliest possible moment. There was too much here she simply didn't understand.

*Maybe I should just give up the title,* she thought, ruefully. *There is probably no shortage of others who want it.*

"She is the only surviving heir of Baron Gold," Baron Gaunt said. "And she was not involved in his treachery."

Emily frowned inwardly as something clicked into place. The three most powerful barons were called Gold, Silver and Bronze. Collectively, they controlled enough
lands and power to bring the king to heel. Or they had, before Baron Gold had
been beheaded and King Randor had deployed a new and powerful army. Was King
Randor delaying because he didn't want a new Baroness Gold? Alicia might be very
far from harmless with such wealth and power in her hands. She would be only
human if she didn't want some revenge for her executed father.

"We will see," the King said. He held up a hand as the barons started to object.
"The third matter is considerably more alarming."

He waved a hand in the air. Moments later, a pair of dark-clad servants entered,
carrying a box of documents between them. Emily's eyes narrowed as she spotted
the jewels implanted in their foreheads, anchoring the enslavement spells in place.
The servants — no, the *slaves* — would do whatever they were told by their master,
without the slightest hope of resistance. It wasn't something she would wish on her
worst enemy.

"These...pamphlets have been spreading through the kingdom," King Randor said.
"You will, I suspect, find them quite disturbing."

Emily took one of the pamphlets and read it, quickly. It was written using English
letters, but, as always, the local spelling left something to be desired. Words were
spelled out phonically, ensuring there were several different, but technically correct spellings for many different words. Hell, the writer couldn't be bothered being
consistent; he'd used the same word several times, spelling it four different ways.
But it didn't matter, she knew. As long as the words could be sounded out, they were
readable.

Her eyes went wide when she finally parsed out the first section. Years ago, she'd
read Karl Marx. She hadn't been impressed, either with the arguments or the ver-
biage; it had seemed to her that Marx had been trying to hide the weakness in his
thinking behind a mountain of long and complicated words. But the writer who'd
written the pamphlet seemed to be channeling the ideal of Marx...

"Baroness Emily," King Randor said. "Why don't you read to us?"

Emily looked down at the pamphlet. "Our society is shaped like a triangle," she
read. "The king and his aristocracy are on the top, peasants and slaves are at the bottom. This is the one truth we are taught right from birth, when we become aware of
both society and our place in it. The higher up the triangle, the more power a person
possesses over his inferiors. But the question we are taught never to ask is why? Why
is our society so fixed?

"We are told that peasants deserve to be peasants and slaves deserve to be slaves.
We are told that peasants are slow, stupid, incapable of being anything more than
grunt animals in the fields. And yet, when given the opportunity, peasants who
escape the fields can make their own lives, earning wealth for themselves, rather
than their owners. Is it true, therefore, that there is something *inherently* slavish
about the peasants?

"And if this is not true, and common sense tells us it isn't, is there something *inherently* noble about the nobility? Why should they have power when they have done nothing to earn it, save being born lucky?"

King Randor held up a hand. "These have been found everywhere," he said. "Some argue that the nobility should be elected, or that real power should be placed in the hands of the Assembly. Others call for the total destruction of the aristocracy and a grand sharing out of the wealth and power we have built up over centuries. They are, of course, hideously subversive."

*You would think that*, Emily thought acidly. She couldn't blame the king for wanting to protect his position, but she'd never liked the idea of an aristocracy. Why, indeed, should some people have the right to rule others, merely through having been born to the right families?

"I have issued orders to ban these documents and discover the producers," Randor continued. "I expect each and every one of you" — his gaze rested on Emily for a long moment — "to concentrate on finding the writer of these...these pieces of toilet paper and arresting him."

That wouldn't be enough, Emily knew. The printing press ensured that thousands of copies could be produced very quickly, while English letters made sure just about anyone could *read* the subversive papers. It would be impossible to suppress them completely, not without completely destroying the printing presses and killing anyone who knew how to read English letters. And *that* would cripple the newborn economy beyond repair.

And she wasn't sure she *wanted* to catch the person or persons responsible. She'd seen too much of the nobility, mundane or magical, to have any faith in aristocracy as a basis for long-term government. Alassa had been a brat when they'd first met, a brat armed with magic, while half of her would-be suitors had been lecherous fools. And Melissa was a member of the magical aristocracy...

"Change is coming to Our Kingdom," Randor said, softly. "We cannot avoid it. But we can, we will, manage it so that all that is noble and good about our lands is not destroyed."

"Of course, your majesty," Baron Gaunt said.

"But there are other issues to be discussed," Baron Silver said. "The broadsheets, for example. They should be controlled."

King Randor looked at Emily. "Can they be controlled? Should they be controlled?"

Emily swallowed. It was hard, in all honesty, to actually answer the question. On one hand, she knew from Earth that freedom of the press was the cornerstone of a healthy democracy. But, on the other hand, Zangaria wasn't exactly a democracy. King Randor was practically all-powerful, with an army powerful enough to threaten both the Noble Estates and the Assembly. And even if it *had* been a democracy, too much press freedom had proved as corrosive as too little...

"They shouldn't," she said, finally.

"I see," King Randor said. "And would you like to explain that statement?"

Emily forced herself to think. "Most of the broadsheets will not survive," she said, after a moment. "There were hundreds established just after the printing press became freely available, but the economy simply cannot support them all. However, those that do survive will often point to very real problems that need to be fixed, if you allow them the freedom to do so. And, because you have allowed them freedom, you will be believed when you use them to spread your own words and statements."

"But they will also make people question their betters," Baron Silver observed, darkly.

"People always question their betters," Emily said. She rather doubted anyone in Zangaria believed a word of the official statements, even the ones read out by heralds in the center of town. "But this way, you start making connections with the people..."

She hesitated, unsure if she wanted to say anything else, then plunged on. "The events of two years ago upset the kingdom," she said. "You cannot afford to proceed as if nothing has changed."

"Well said," King Randor said. He sounded amused, although Emily wasn't sure if he was laughing at her or the discomforted barons. "We will continue to review the situation."

"That is not enough," Baron Silver said. "Indeed, only two weeks ago it was stated, in a broadsheet smuggled into my lands, that my son and daughter were engaged in an incestuous relationship."

"But it will serve, for the moment," King Randor said.

He rose. "You will all, of course, be required to sign copies of the will," he added. "If you have any comments on the proposed bequests, you can make them up until the day my daughter returns to school. The documents will be signed on that day. Until then...return to your lands and consider, carefully, just how you wish to proceed."

*Proceed with what?* Emily thought, as they were dismissed. *And why is he raising these issues now?*

She mulled it over as she walked back up the stairs and out into the corridor, marveling at the sheer precision of the magic used to hide the hidden chamber. Some of the maids would have seen her appear from nowhere, yet their minds wouldn't acknowledge the fact, not even to themselves. They would think she had always been standing there...

Shaking her head, she walked up to Alassa's suite and allowed the herald to open the door and announce her. It was high time she sat down and talked through the politics with her friend.

# Chapter Seven

"MY FATHER IS A VERY CUNNING MAN," ALASSA SAID, WHEN EMILY HAD FINISHED. "HE
played them like...like pieces on a Kingmaker board."

Emily shrugged and looked around the giant room. It was staggeringly luxurious
by the standards of the Nameless World — a single piece of silk alone cost more
than Frieda's family could hope to make in a decade — but oddly uncomfortable by
Earth's. Without magic to heat the room, it was cold and windy, while the windows
weren't even covered by glass. Outside, she knew from the last time she'd been in the
castle, one could look down on the courtyard and the city beyond.

"I don't understand," she confessed. "What has he done?"

Alassa had been sitting on the carpeted floor when Emily had entered, reading a
document written in Old Script. Now, she stood up and led the way into her office, a
smaller room lined with bookcases and maps of the surrounding countryside. Emily
stiffened as she felt the privacy wards surrounding them, then relaxed slightly as
Alassa closed the door and cast a pair of her own.

"We should have been in here from the start," she muttered. She waved a hand
towards a comfortable chair, then sat down in another armchair. "Please, sit. You
really need to understand all this."

She waited for Emily to sit, then went on. "You understand, of course, that a person isn't really confirmed until they have been Confirmed?"

Emily nodded.

"I was my father's heir from the moment I was born," Alassa continued, "but
I wasn't actually going to inherit the throne, in my own right, until after I was
Confirmed. Before then, my uncle would have become my guardian, if my father had
died, and ruled in my name until I was old enough to take the throne for myself."

"Which would have given him and his wife plenty of time to organize matters to
suit themselves," Emily said. "Perhaps even to deny you the throne altogether."

"Perhaps," Alassa agreed. "Point is, I couldn't have done anything on my own. I
would not have been considered an adult. My uncle would have assumed all my
father's powers over me and I would not have been able to complain about it."

"That would have been bad," Emily said.

"Yes," Alassa said. "But the same thing has happened with the minor children who
were left without parents, following the attempted coup. They need guardians or
nothing can be done on their lands. And, by claiming their guardianships for himself,
my father has secured control of their estates at a stroke. He can keep them here, in
the heart of his power, as hostages, ensuring their former subordinates don't dare to
try anything stupid."

"But Alicia is old enough to rule," Emily said, slowly.

"My father is the one who will determine when she's old enough to be granted her
title and power," Alassa said. "He will also determine who gets her hand in marriage,

among other things. She can be treated as a minor child until she's old enough to be a grandmother and there's nothing anyone can do about it."

Emily felt a stab of sympathy. "Is there nothing you can do?"

"My father wants to break the power of the barons, once and for all," Alassa said. "And if he gave her the power without, as you say, arranging things to suit himself, she could turn against him. This way...her ability to do harm is minimized."

She shrugged. "And besides, I agree my father is probably right," she added. "The barons cannot be allowed a chance to launch another coup."

Emily shook her head, tiredly. Every so often, when talking to her friends, she ran into a cultural gulf far wider than anything she had seen on Earth. To Alassa, there was nothing particularly wrong with her father taking Alicia's guardianship, still less organizing her life and marriage to ensure she remained harmless. Alicia had been on the wrong side, her position determined by an accident of birth; she was a danger, simply by being born. The same fates that had made her a baron's heir had also ensured that her life would never be her own.

But Emily couldn't agree. There was something wrong with organizing another person's life, with controlling their every move from birth till death. Alicia might get lucky and receive a decent husband, but it was far more likely that she'd be given away to one of Randor's loyal supporters, the ones who depended on the king for everything from power to place. And, until then, she would be trapped in the castle, a bird in a gilded cage.

*Poor girl*, she thought.

Was there anything she could do? She thought, but nothing came to mind. Randor wouldn't listen to her, she suspected, and even if she talked Alassa into trying it was unlikely the king would listen to his daughter. He would probably argue that he was neutralizing Alicia as a boon to Alassa, who would have to deal with the younger girl when she assumed the throne.

*I could help her leave the castle*, Emily thought, *but where could she go then?*

"I know that look," Alassa said. "You're planning something, aren't you?"

"I don't know," Emily admitted.

Alassa's blue eyes met Emily's. "I can speak with my father, if you wish," she said. "But I don't think he will change his mind easily."

"Yeah," Emily said. She sighed. "How's your mother?"

"Feeling down, apparently," Alassa said. "She's been in her bed for the last week, just reading and feeling sorry for herself. I don't understand it. Maybe she thinks I should be married by now."

"The barons discussed your wedding," Emily said. Alassa's blue eyes opened, wide. "They wanted to know when it would be."

Alassa looked down at the floor. "When I have a suitable man," she muttered. "But my father is still looking for someone who can actually bolster the position of the throne."

"Good thing Alicia isn't a boy," Emily said.

"Don't even joke about it," Alassa said. She shuddered, dramatically. "I can't decide if it's worse to be courted by a man old enough to be my father or pushed towards a boy young enough to be my son."

Emily shuddered, too. The Allied Lands had a long tradition of betrothals between children, betrothals between children too young to understand what they were doing, let alone that they might have to get married one day. Few of them lasted more than a year or two, but as long as they did they were...convenient, underpinning agreements between various aristocratic factions. But the whole concept still seemed disgusting to her.

"That won't last, surely?" She asked. "You're old enough to actually *marry*."

"I know," Alassa said. "So my father is being very, very careful."

She shrugged. "I can't say I like the thought of people using the written word to spread propaganda either," she added. "My father may have to do something unpleasant."

"I don't think he can do much," Emily warned. "The printing press is out of control now."

"And that will be blamed on you," Alassa said. "As will everything else."

Emily shook her head. *She* hadn't introduced the rudiments of communism or socialism into the Allied Lands, let alone democracy. But it only took one person to look at the world and start asking *why* for the ideas to spread. Why *shouldn't* people elect their leaders? Why *should* the aristocrats have the power when some of them had tried to overthrow their king and make his daughter a mindless slave? They would look at the history of Zangaria and demand answers. Alexis and Alexis II had been strong monarchs, but Bryon had been a weak fool and his son a ruthless, but charismatic bastard. And he'd screwed the middle classes, such as they were, in favor of his own power.

"I think more and more people hear the news now," she said, instead. "And then they start wondering why things are the way they are. And then you and yours cannot give them any good answers."

"Uneasy lies the head that wears the crown," Alassa muttered.

"Quite," Emily said.

There was a knock at the door. Alassa waved a hand, unlocking the spell that held the door closed. Imaiqah entered, followed by a tired-looking Frieda. The younger girl was wearing a dress of white silk, which seemed to shimmer around her as she walked. Emily had never thought of Frieda as conventionally pretty, but she had to admit her charge looked striking, particularly with her hair hanging down in a single long ponytail. Queen Marlena hadn't lost any of her gifts for dressing people, she decided. And at least it had kept Frieda out of mischief.

"I feel strange," Frieda said, as the door closed behind her. She looked at Alassa. "Why does your mother keep dressing people up?"

"She likes it," Alassa said. "I think she was dressing me in royal clothes from the moment I was born. There are paintings of me in the gallery that show me as a young girl, wearing a hundred different outfits. Mother must have spent hours making half of them..."

*Or maybe*, Emily thought in a flash of insight, *she wanted some control over something in her life.*

"But I can't keep this," Frieda said. "It's...it's expensive."

"It's a gift from someone who will never notice the expense," Alassa reminded her, firmly. "And you do look good in it."

Frieda turned a pleading gaze on Emily, who shrugged. She understood Frieda's concerns — there was no way she could repay the queen for the dresses — but she also knew that there was no formal price tag attached. Queen Marlena was just trying to ensure that her guests looked as though they belonged in a castle. She had showered Emily in dresses until Imaiqah's father had been ennobled and welcomed into the court.

"We're leaving tomorrow morning," she said, instead. "You can endure the dresses until then."

She looked at Alassa, then Imaiqah. "You're not going to come with us?"

"Not at once," Alassa said. She waved a hand towards her desk, which was covered with paperwork. "The downside of being Confirmed is that I now have to actually do my duties as a crown princess. Each and every one of those papers has to be read, stamped with my seal and then sent down to my father's chambers. And I have to hear court cases tomorrow too."

"At least you take it seriously," Emily said. The old Alassa, the one she'd first met, wouldn't have bothered to do her duty at all. Being judged by her would have been a nightmare. "Just remember you're going to rule one day."

"Yes," Alassa said. "And then my son or daughter will have the powers of justice in my place."

"I have to stay with my father," Imaiqah said, after a moment. "But I think we'll be up in a few days, though. He's sending a hundred devices to the Faire for people to see...I think he wants to show off the cutting edge of *technology*."

Emily had to smile. *Technology* was a word she'd introduced to the Nameless World, along with the concepts for everything from steam engines to typewriters. The first steam engines might be slow and prone to breaking down, but she knew they would be improved rapidly, now the basic idea was loose. Typewriters, too, would be along soon, once someone managed to put together a purely mechanical device. Magical typewriters required too much power to work for more than a few hours.

"I look forward to it," she said.

She rose to her feet. "I have to find Lady Barb," she said. "Can I leave Frieda here with you?"

"Of course," Alassa said. She tossed the younger girl a droll look. "She might be very bored though."

"I can read," Frieda protested.

Emily smiled, and walked out of the chamber. Jade was standing outside, talking to one of the guards in a low voice. Emily blinked in surprise, then waved for him to join her. Jade nodded to the guard, then strode over and stood next to her. He was still wearing the black sorcerer outfit, carrying a staff in one hand. Emily wasn't sure if he expected trouble or he was showing off, just a little.

"I didn't know you were planning to apply for a position here," she said. "Why didn't you tell me?"

Jade looked down at the stone floor. "King Randor would accept me, if you told him to," he said. "I wanted to succeed or fail on my own."

"I don't think King Randor would let me push him into anything," Emily said. "Unless he actually wanted it for himself and was prepared to let me *think* I'd pushed him into it."

But she understood. Jade wanted to prove himself — and yet, at the same time, he was in a world where connections could mean much more than competence. It had to be galling to know that someone could — and someone would — put a word in on his behalf. Or, worse, put a word in on someone else's behalf.

"Take care of Alassa, if you do get the job," she said. "Do you know where Lady Barb is?"

"She was in the barracks, last I heard," Jade said. "Something about an old grudge with an officer."

Emily frowned, then hurried down the corridor towards the stairs, hitching up her dress so she could move faster. One thing the designers never seemed to take into consideration was that women might have to run...unless, of course, they didn't actually *want* women running away from an unpleasant fate. She moved down the stairs as fast as she could, stepped past a couple of guards and into the barracks. Lady Barb was crossing swords with an older man, the blades flashing in the light, while some of the soldiers placed bets. She looked, from the smile on her face, to be having the time of her life.

*No magic*, Emily saw, as the two fighters thrust and parried at one another. *Just skill.*

She shivered as Lady Barb jumped backwards, narrowly avoiding a thrust that would have skewered her. The sergeants had taught Emily the rudiments of sword-fighting, but it wasn't something she'd taken as seriously as her magic studies. Somehow, the prospect of injury or death seemed much more *real* when swords were involved. She looked down at the smooth floor, then up at Lady Barb, just in time to see her knock her opponent's blade out of his hand. It clattered to the floor and lay there.

Her opponent held up his hands. "I yield," he said.

"Honor is satisfied," Lady Barb said. She returned the blade to its scabbard, then shook her opponent's hand firmly. "You fought well."

She turned to face Emily before her opponent could say a word. "Emily," she said. "What are you doing here?"

"Looking for you," Emily said, feeling her cheeks flush as the soldiers sniggered. "Can we talk somewhere?"

"Of course," Lady Barb said. She strode past Emily and out of the room, motioning impatiently for Emily to follow her. "What can I do for you?"

"We're leaving tomorrow," Emily said. "What time?"

"Seeing it's just you, Frieda and I," Lady Barb said, "we will try to leave around nine bells. I suggest you don't spend the entire night dancing, not tonight. Make sure you don't let anyone put a mark in your dance card."

Emily nodded, quickly.

"I'll just stay for the meal," she said. There was always an opportunity to slip away after the dinner, if one didn't want to dance. Alassa would have to stay, of course, but she would understand Emily leaving early. "And I'll tell Frieda to do the same."

"That would be wise," Lady Barb said. She paused, her eyes sweeping Emily's face. "And what else do you want to talk about?"

"I don't know," Emily said. She wanted to ask about Alicia, but she wasn't even sure how to frame the question. "Do you...do you know about the king's plans for the minor orphaned children?"

"I believe I can guess," Lady Barb said. She'd lived in Zangaria for several years before meeting Emily — and, perhaps more importantly, she knew Randor personally. "And this bothers you...why?"

"It just feels wrong," Emily confessed.

"I imagine it does," Lady Barb said, briskly. "Now, tell me. If you were in King Randor's shoes, what would you do?"

*Make friends with them*, Emily thought. But that might not be an option. Alicia was hardly a child...and the others, too, might be nearing their age of majority. They might already be as dangerous as Alassa had been, when she'd first come to Whitehall. *Or find them somewhere to go, out of the country.*

"I don't know," she mumbled, reluctantly.

"King Randor will organize matters to suit himself," Lady Barb said, "but I do not believe he will be openly abusive. You can watch and wait and protest, if necessary, should that change. Or, if you like, you can offer the children the chance to give up their ranks and titles and go elsewhere. There are places for them to go, if they wish."

"But then they would lose their lands," Emily said. "They would lose everything."

"Yes, they would," Lady Barb agreed. She reached out and gave Emily a tight hug. "Emily, young lady, you can't fix everything."

She cleared her throat. "Enjoy the rest of the day with your friends, then report to the gates in time to leave tomorrow," she added. "You will have no shortage of work at Cockatrice, I promise you. The Faire alone will consume most of your working day."

Emily swallowed. "I will," she said. "Can we go through the papers on the way?"

"We can try," Lady Barb said. "Make sure you get plenty of rest. You'll need it."

# Chapter Eight

Emily was mildly surprised that King Randor wasn't present as she and Frieda prepared to take their leave, but he might have just been trying to give Alassa more time with her friends. His daughter looked tired — Emily had learned to recognize the signs, even though her face was as beautiful as ever — as she hugged Emily goodbye, then gave Frieda a hug too. Frieda, who had gratefully changed back into her working clothes, hugged her back and scrambled into the coach.

"Take care of yourself," Alassa said. "And remember to at least *try* to relax along the way."

"I can try," Emily said. "You take care of yourself too."

Alassa gave her a quick hug, then waved goodbye as Emily climbed into the coach. Lady Barb was already inside, a leather folder of papers resting on her lap. The door was closed, then the coach rocked once as the driver cracked the whip, encouraging the horses to move. Moments later, the spells designed to compensate for every jerky motion started to work, ensuring a smooth trip. If they hadn't been there, Emily knew from bitter experience, it would be impossible to do anything while the coach was driven over potholes and cracks in the road.

*Springs*, she thought, sourly. The idea was on the list of concepts to develop. *We'd make a fortune.*

"A word before you start," Lady Barb said, as she held out the folder. "I cannot give you advice on the proposal or how best to make it work. Furthermore, I am required to inform your supervisors of any attempt to wheedle information out of me. It will be counted against you when they consider your work."

Emily swallowed. "I understand," she said. "We could be marked down for it?"

"Yes," Lady Barb said. "If the supervisors are in a particularly vile mood, they could insist you redo Third Year from the beginning, even after having worked your way through Fourth Year."

"Ouch," Emily muttered. Redoing Third Year wouldn't have been too bad, but redoing Third Year *after* Fourth Year would leave her two years older than everyone else in the class, alternately bored and humiliated. And they would have made her redo all the practical work, including the lessons she had mastered on her first run through the year. "What *am* I allowed to ask?"

"How to contact your partner," Lady Barb said. "There's nothing else that you can ask me without compromising yourself."

Emily tugged at her hair, nervously, and looked over at Frieda. The younger girl had pulled a book out of her bag and started to read, her lips moving soundlessly as she parsed out the English letters. Emily was amused to note that it was one of the newly-published novels, although *she* privately suspected it would be forgotten within the year. The Nameless World had yet to produce any great writers, as far as she knew. Most stories had been handed down from person to person before the printing press had been introduced.

She smiled, and started to read through the project proposal. It was comprehensively detailed in so much minute detail that she started to wonder if Caleb was as obsessed about magic as Aloha. Every section was explained in tedious detail. Caleb seemingly had never seen fit to use a word when a sentence could do, nor a sentence when a paragraph could explain everything. And yet, she had to admit, it left little room for misunderstanding. Everything was detailed, defined and carefully placed in context.

*Clever,* she thought, as the idea slowly took shape in her mind. *Did he learn something from the magical computer?*

It was a tempting thought. She'd tried, back in First Year, to explain a computer to Aloha, who had produced something akin to a typewriter. Unfortunately, it had required constant replenishment of magic to make it work for longer than an hour or two, while it hadn't been able to master even the simplest functions of a computer. But Caleb seemed to have put his finger on the key to eventually producing a *real* computer...and even if it couldn't stretch that far, it would revolutionize some aspects of magic.

*They must have thought it was workable,* she told herself, as she came to the final sheet of paper. *The Grandmaster wouldn't have approved the proposal if he'd thought it couldn't be made to work.*

She bit her lip as she read through the final sheet. Unlike the other parts of the proposal, it was short and to the point. Caleb and his partner had been producing a variant of *Manaskol* they could use for their experimental devices. Somehow, the modifications they had made to the recipe had caused an explosion, which had crippled Caleb and sent him home for the year. They hadn't quite known what they were doing, Emily realized; Mountaintop taught Third Year students how to produce *Manaskol*, but Whitehall waited until Fourth Year, believing the students needed more grounding first. Caleb would have had to learn very quickly, once he'd realized it was necessary...and he might not have considered just how temperamental the liquid could be.

"It could have been worse," she muttered to herself. "They could have killed themselves."

"They could have," Lady Barb agreed. Emily looked up to see the older woman eying her with a sardonic eye. "I don't believe anyone told them that producing *Manaskol* was *safe.*"

Emily nodded. It had taken months for her to master the recipe...and she still lost one wok in three, whenever she brewed it for Professor Thande. She was mildly surprised that they'd let her keep producing it, but in hindsight she suspected the Grandmaster had intended to pair her with Caleb all along. He must have seen real potential in Caleb's proposal for spell mosaics. Looking at the papers, Emily could see it too.

"I would like to try to work with him," she said, nervously. Working with others wasn't one of her strengths, particularly when the other was a boy she didn't know. "Would you send him a message?"

"I'll have a letter sent on from Cockatrice," Lady Barb said. "He should be here in a week or so, just in time for the Faire. Do try and find some time to actually work together, all right?"

"I will," Emily promised. She had plans for the summer and they didn't *just* include the proposal. It was high time she put everything she'd learned at Mountaintop to work and actually started on the first magical battery. "Do you know him?"

Lady Barb shrugged. "He wasn't in my classes at Whitehall," she said. "I know his mother, if that's any help. She is — *was* — a strong-minded woman."

"Like you," Emily said.

"You have to be strong-minded if you want to be a Mediator," Lady Barb said, bluntly. "The people you have to work with won't respect you if you seem weak, or inclined to compromise. I was surprised she married a general. We're normally inclined to bicker with senior officers instead of marrying them."

"Maybe it was love," Frieda said, abandoning her book. "They might have been deeply in love and chose to spend the rest of their lives together."

"I think you should spend more time on your schoolwork and less on soppy romantic novels," Lady Barb said, crossly. She hadn't been in a good mood since the coach had left the castle, although Emily had no idea why. "The real world is rarely driven by people who fall in love at first sight."

Emily rolled her eyes as Frieda blushed. She'd read a couple of what passed for romantic novels in the Allied Lands and she hadn't been impressed. One of them had been incredibly soppy, to the point where she'd found herself wondering how anyone could stand the heroine, while the other had been a tale of a strong macho man who beat down a shrewish woman and convinced her to marry him. It hadn't seemed to occur to the writer that there was something *wrong* with the hero's actions...or, for that matter, that the heroine might have good reasons for being something of a bitch. And the less said about the sex scenes, the better. She'd read bad fan fiction that had included more realistic sex scenes.

She placed the papers back in her bag and looked at Lady Barb. "When I went to see the Grandmaster," she said, "there was someone already there. Who was she?"

"I heard about that," Lady Barb said. She thinned her lips. "Let us just say that Cabiria did something she shouldn't have done, something no sensible magician would have done. And I hope you will never be stupid enough to do the same."

Emily sighed, inwardly. She knew Lady Barb wouldn't be drawn if she didn't want to be drawn.

"If she doesn't know what Cabiria did," Frieda piped up, "how would she know to avoid it?"

"Common sense," Lady Barb said, crossly. She looked back at Emily. "And you shouldn't try to pry, young lady. People will be prying about you."

"I get that anyway," Emily said.

"Then don't do it to someone else, if you don't like it," Lady Barb said. "What happened was enough to get Cabiria suspended for a whole year, so I suggest you leave it at that."

They stopped, briefly, at an inn to find dinner and answer the call of nature, then resumed their journey up towards the mountains. Emily read a book she'd borrowed from Whitehall's library, while Frieda, tired of her book, closed her eyes and went to sleep. Boredom didn't sit well with her, Emily knew; she'd always been kept busy at home, then at Mountaintop. It had been all Emily could do to stop Frieda from acting as her servant.

*And if we were allowed servants,* she thought, *Alassa would have had a small army crammed into her room.*

She smiled at the thought, and returned to her book. It was complex and engrossing, so enthralling that she barely noticed when the coach came to a halt and Lady Barb peered outside. A moment later, she leaned back and tapped Emily on the knee, making her look up.

"I think you'll want to see this," Lady Barb said, as she opened the door. "Come and look."

Emily put the book to one side — Lady Aliya would do something unspeakable to her if the book got damaged — and clambered out of the coach. The cold air struck her at once, making her hastily cast a warming charm as she peered into the distance. Cockatrice Castle rose in front of her, near Cockatrice City...surrounded by tents. Hundreds of tents. Emily recalled the last Faire, near Lady Barb's house; surely, she asked herself, it hadn't been as big as this.

"It's huge," she said, in disbelief. "How big is it?"

"At least three times the size of the last one," Lady Barb said. "I'd say you should be expecting hundreds of thousands of visitors. They're probably planning to set up a few portals in the city, or perhaps closer to the Faire itself."

"I didn't realize it was going to be so large," Emily stammered. "It...it just grew."

Lady Barb gave her a reproving look. "That's what happens when you leave the matter in someone else's hands," she said. "I just hope Bryon had the sense to organize a roving patrol of Mediators. Holding the Faire this close to a proper city means there will be no keeping the magicians apart from the mundanes."

Emily shivered. Lady Barb had told her more than a few horror stories about previous gatherings, back when she'd been a full-time Mediator. They always ended with drunk — and sometimes not so drunk — magicians playing tricks on helpless mundanes. Sorting out the mess was never easy.

She looked at Lady Barb, who was watching her with a gimlet eye. "Can I count on you?"

"I should charge you a salary," Lady Barb said, sardonically. She motioned Emily back into the carriage with one hand. "But I dare say I could stick around for a while, unless something pops up."

Emily sat down in the carriage, again, as the driver cracked the whip. This time, she pulled back the curtain and watched as the Faire came closer. It wasn't due to open for another week, she knew, but there were already thousands of people there, preparing their stalls for the grand opening. Last time, there had been potions, books and rare magical artefacts; this time, there would be all of that and more. Her eyes narrowed as she saw a set of iron rails, carefully embedded in the ground. A railway line?

*Imaiqah said her father intended to show off a few things,* she recalled, as she felt a sinking sensation in her stomach. *What have I let myself in for?*

The coach drove around the city and up towards the castle. It was a squat brooding monstrosity, dominating the landscape around it by its sheer presence. The previous baron, a thoroughly unpleasant man, had bragged that his castle could never be taken by storm, but he hadn't counted on being caught red-handed trying to overthrow the king. His execution had been pretty much a foregone conclusion. And now it was hers. Emily braced herself as the gates opened, feeling the thin edge of the wards pass over her as they acknowledged their mistress. Inside, only Bryon was waiting for her.

"I was expecting a crowd," Lady Barb said, tartly.

"I asked him not to organize a greeting party," Emily said. She packed her books in her bag, and placed it on the seat. "I always hated being greeted by everyone."

She opened the door as soon as the coach came to a halt and jumped down to the stone courtyard. Bryon went down on one knee as soon as he saw her, lowering his head until he was looking at the ground. Emily sighed inwardly, and took a long moment to study him. He seemed to have grown up a little since they'd last met, but he was still terrifyingly thin, with short brown hair. Perhaps that was a good thing, Emily decided. He'd certainly had ample opportunity to eat himself sick while he'd been working for her.

"You may rise," she said.

"My lady," Bryon said. "I welcome you back to Cockatrice."

Emily nodded. The castle — and all the surrounding lands — were hers, but she didn't feel as if she owned them. It was strange and terrifying to realize that she effectively owned hundreds of thousands of people, people who would have no recourse if she went mad and started to abuse them. The previous baron had written so many laws that no one could live without breaking a few, giving him a ready-made excuse for killing or jailing anyone he didn't like. Emily had repudiated most of the laws when she'd been granted the barony, but she knew there were still problems. How could there *not* be?

"I thank you," Emily said. She turned and beckoned Frieda out of the coach. "This is Frieda, my friend. I trust you have prepared a room for her?"

"I have," Bryon said. He bowed to Frieda, then straightened up. "Would you like to be shown to them now?"

"Yes, please," Emily said. "We will need to sit down tomorrow and have a long talk."

Bryon looked relieved. "Thank you, my lady," he said. He nodded briefly to Lady Barb as she climbed out of the coach. "The servants will bring in your bags."

"I'll go down to the Faire and see who's there," Lady Barb muttered to Emily. "I'll catch up with you later."

Emily nodded, and allowed Bryon to lead her through the wooden doors and into the castle. It was not just her home, but the administrative center for the entire barony. Even so, it still surprised her to see so many people in the building, ranging from a handful of ceremonial guards to dozens of servants, maids and bureaucrats. The Scribes' Guild might have had problems adapting to the brave new world, but many of the scribes had managed to master English letters and find themselves work. After all, just because someone *could* do their own records didn't mean they *wanted* to do them.

The wards grew stronger as they walked up two flights of stone stairs into the level set aside for Emily and her personal guests. Emily made a mental note to work on them once she'd had a chat with Bryon, but stopped as Bryon opened a wooden door. Inside, there was a roaring fire, a bed easily large enough for four people and a large window, peering out over the growing Faire.

"Your room, Lady Frieda," Bryon announced.

Frieda stared into the room, then at Emily. "This is for *me?*"

"As long as you want it," Emily promised. As far as the castle was concerned, Frieda would always be an inhabitant. "Welcome home..."

She broke off as Frieda wrapped her arms around her and squeezed, tightly. Emily gasped for air before hugging the younger girl back. She understood, better than she cared to admit, what it was like to have a place of your own, somewhere where you *belonged*. Frieda might never have seen such luxury in her life, but it was hers now.

"My apartment is just down the corridor," Emily said. She yawned, suddenly. The coach ride hadn't been *bad*, but she wanted a long soak in a bath. "We'll eat dinner later, once Lady Barb returns."

She looked at Frieda. "Just be careful when you heat the bathwater," she said. "You don't want to scald yourself."

"There's only cold water on tap," Bryon confirmed.

Emily hid her amusement. It had been hard enough explaining why she wanted running water in the first place, not when the castle kept a dozen servants gainfully employed ferrying water up to the higher levels. But, in the end, she'd got what she wanted.

"We'll talk in the morning," she said. "Until then, thank you."

Bryon recognized it as a dismissal. He bowed, then retired, leaving them alone.

"Thank you," Frieda said, again. "I...no one has ever done this for me."

"It's nothing," Emily said. "I'll key you into the wards properly tomorrow, but until then..."

She gave Frieda a gentler hug, then glanced at her watch. There would be an hour until dinner, then they could go to bed and rise early, with the sun. And then...she would have to have a long chat with Bryon. She needed to know what had been done in her name.

# Chapter Nine

SOMEONE WAS IN HER ROOM.

Emily stirred, woken by a sense she'd had beaten into her by Sergeant Miles. She'd rarely slept deeply, not since her mother had remarried; she'd always been nervous about someone coming into her room when she was asleep. It had been hard to share a room with two people — and then a dorm, at Mountaintop — and she'd welcomed the chance to sleep alone. But now, someone was in her room.

She braced herself, listening carefully. The newcomer was trying very hard to remain quiet, which set off alarm bells in her head. Two years ago, a maid had tried to assassinate Alassa — or Emily — in Alluvia, before the attempted coup. Gritting her teeth, she slipped her fingers out of the bedding and cast a spell. There was a flash of light; the sound of someone moving stopped abruptly.

Emily sat upright, conjuring a light globe into existence. A maid stood by the fire, frozen in place. Emily winced inwardly as she realized dawn was breaking over the mountaintops and the maid had been attempting to build up the fire. Feeling like a fool, she hastily cast the counter-spell. The maid jerked violently, dropped several pieces of wood to the floor, and spun around. Her eyes were wide with fear.

"My lady," she said. "I..."

"I'm sorry," Emily said. The maid was so young that Emily couldn't help feeling like a bully, picking on a child who looked at least five years younger than her. It wasn't uncommon for girls to go into service as soon as they entered their teens, she knew from bitter experience, but she'd never had a personal maid. "I didn't know who you were."

The maid hastily prostrated herself on the floor. "I am Janice, Daughter of Lanark," she said. "I only meant to light the fire..."

"Get up," Emily ordered, embarrassed. She didn't *like* people bowing and scraping to her, let alone falling on the floor whenever she passed. "I didn't mean to scare you."

"I didn't mean to wake you," Janice said, as she rose. She kept her eyes downcast at all times. "I..."

"Don't worry about it," Emily said, firmly. She couldn't help noticing that the maid wore a uniform that showed off her assets, a legacy from the previous baron. She'd have to have them changed, she resolved. He'd probably insisted his maids prostrate themselves too. "I need to rise soon, anyway."

Emily watched as Janice hastily laid the fire with shaky hands, and felt another wave of bitter guilt. Janice had probably known her mistress was a magician, but there was a difference between knowing something and actually *believing* it. Now she would probably be scared of Emily, no matter what Emily said or did. She'd seen that reaction before, once or twice, during the walk through the Cairngorms. And if Hodge had had that reaction, it might have been a very different trip.

"Thank you, my lady," Janice said, when she had lit the fire. "I'm sorry I woke you."

"I know," Emily said, patiently. She didn't blame Janice for being scared. A word from Emily could have her sent back to her family — or worse. In hindsight, she told herself again, she should have rejected the barony. "What is it like to work here?"

"I really couldn't say, my lady," Janice said.

Emily sighed, inwardly. She wouldn't get a straight answer out of any of the staff, with the possible exception of Bryon. They knew better than to complain, even if their superiors were making their lives intolerable. It was no wonder, Emily knew, that so many of the former staff had decamped when Emily had taken over. They'd only been kept at the castle through threats and blackmail.

She watched the girl curtsey, then back out of the door, careful never to turn her back to Emily. Emily had to bite down the impulse to tell the maid that it hardly mattered if she did walk out the door properly, knowing it wouldn't matter. The maid was probably old enough to have worked for Baron Holyoake, who would have taken sadistic delight in punishing each and every mistake. It would be a long time before they became comfortable with Emily instead...

*And even if they did, they might recall a few royal brats and decide it would be better not to call attention to themselves*, Emily thought, as the door closed. *What would I do, if I was in such a place?*

Pushing the thought aside, she stood and walked into the bathroom, where an enormous bathtub waited for her. It wasn't quite large enough to qualify as a small swimming pool, but it was certainly larger than anything she'd seen on Earth. She twisted the tap and watched as cold water cascaded into the tub, then carefully cast a warming spell. The water started to bubble furiously, but cooled as more water fell from the tap. Emily removed her nightgown, climbed into the tub and washed herself, hastily. It was tempting, very tempting, to just cast a spell to allow her to breathe underwater and just relax into the warm water. But she knew she couldn't allow herself to relax.

She used a spell to wash her hair, climbed out of the tub and cast another spell to dry herself. A new dress waited her in the wardrobe; she pulled her underclothes on, then the dress itself. Red didn't suit her as well as blue, she decided as she looked at herself in the mirror, but she couldn't wear blue all the time. Alassa would have had a fit. Shaking her head, she cast a handful of spells to protect the room and walked out the door. She would need to have a word with Bryon about keeping the maids out of her room, even to light the fire. Some of the items she had brought from Whitehall were dangerous.

*Or just seal the room with magic*, she reminded herself. *But I was too tired to think of it.*

"Emily," Frieda called, as she stepped into the *small* dining room. It was larger than anywhere she'd eaten on Earth, even a fast food restaurant. There was a single table in the center of the room, with three places laid. "Did you sleep well?"

"As well as I ever do," Emily said. She would definitely need to do something to make it up to Janice. "And yourself?"

"It felt strange to sleep alone," Frieda confessed. "But I made it, eventually."

Emily had to smile. She liked her privacy, but Frieda had grown up in a tiny hovel and then moved to the dorms of Mountaintop. Frieda had never known true privacy from the day she'd been born until the day Emily had taken her to Whitehall. Even then, she'd shared a room with Emily rather than one of her own.

"I'm sure you did," she said, softly. A maid — not Janice — appeared with a menu, which she placed in front of Emily. It was written using English letters, but half of the dishes still made no sense to her. "I'll just have scrambled eggs, please."

The maid looked astonished, either at the simplicity or the politeness, but merely curtseyed and departed, leaving the menus behind. Emily sighed inwardly, then looked at Frieda's plate. It was crammed with bacon, eggs and pieces of unidentifiable vegetables. After a moment, she decided she didn't want to know.

Frieda leaned forward. "What are we going to be doing today?"

"I'm going to have a long chat with Bryon," Emily said. She cursed under her breath. It hadn't occurred to her that she should have organized something for Frieda. "I think Lady Barb might be willing to show you around the city."

Frieda looked doubtful. "I don't think she likes me that much."

Emily snorted. "I think that was because you and your friends managed to catch her and two other tutors in the crossfire," she said. "Why were you playing Freeze Tag near the tutor's lounge when there's no shortage of empty floors in Whitehall?"

"It's more exciting down there," Frieda said.

"I bet it was," Emily said, dryly. It was hard to blame the tutors for being annoyed, even though they hadn't banned the students from playing. "But it wasn't a very clever place to play."

"I suppose not," Frieda said unrepentantly. "We had detentions for months afterwards."

Emily opened her mouth to point out that she obviously hadn't suffered that much, but closed it when her breakfast arrived. There was more on her plate than she could have eaten, even after a day of casting spells at school. She sighed, made a mental note to ask for a smaller portion later, and started to dig into the eggs. It wasn't easy to estimate just how many eggs had been broken to make her breakfast, but she would have bet it was somewhere around six or seven.

Lady Barb entered the room, looking disgustingly fresh and cheerful. "There's a couple of people I know down there," she said, nodding in the vague direction of the Faire. "I'd like to see them after breakfast, if you don't mind."

"Can you take Frieda with you?" Emily asked. "She really needs an escort."

Lady Barb gave her a knowing look. "*You* need an escort," she said. "But you can't hide behind me here, not during the Faire. You're their host."

"I know," Emily said.

She finished her breakfast, shaking her head at the waste, then rose. "I have to see Bryon," she said. "But I'll catch up with you later."

Lady Barb smiled. "Don't let him get away with anything," she said. "You have to watch people carefully when you give them power."

Emily swallowed the comment that came to mind — she'd been granted power, which suggested King Randor would keep an eye on her — and then walked out of the door, down towards the office that had been set aside for her. It was a chilly room, despite the roaring fire; Emily had a private suspicion, from the number of stuffed heads mounted on the wall, that Baron Holyoake had used it for something other than actual work. The desk, made out of stone, looked laughable to her. If she ever came back permanently, she promised herself, she would have the whole room turned into a proper workroom.

"My lady," Bryon said, as he entered the room. "You wished to see me?"

"Yes," Emily said. Several questions rose to the top of her mind as they sat down, but she focused on the most important one. "How large is the Faire going to be?"

"It grew," Bryon admitted. "We had the first request, the one you signed, last year. And then we had more requests from several magical families. And then Viscount Steam made his own request, followed by several others. Right now, we are looking at hundreds of stalls, thousands of exhibits and hundreds of thousands of guests."

Emily fought down the urge to put her head in her hands. "And you have this under control?"

"I believe so," Bryon said. "Only a handful of the guests, the most important ones, will be granted rooms in the castle. The remainder will be staying in the city or traveling through the portal network. They've been organizing rooms for the last two months, my lady, and prices have been rising constantly."

"I bet they have," Emily said. Cockatrice City might be large, by local standards, but it wasn't *that* big a city. These people would be astonished if they'd ever set eyes on Washington, New York or London. "And have there been problems?"

"Not many, my lady," Bryon assured her. "They have all been handled."

"I'm glad to hear it," Emily said. Lady Barb's horror stories echoed through her head. "And security...?"

"They would not dare to cause trouble," Bryon said. "Not in *your* lands."

Emily shook her head. She knew magicians too well to assume her reputation, both as the Necromancer's Bane and Void's supposed daughter, would provide any protection. Some magicians would go out of their way to show they weren't scared of her, while others would take one look and instantly dismiss her reputation as nothing more than a tissue of lies. Only people like the Grandmaster, or Void, seemed to command the sort of respect that led to instant obedience.

"Put Lady Barb in charge of security," Emily ordered, flatly. "Pay her if she wants to be paid. She can muster support, if she thinks we need it."

"Yes, my lady," Bryon said. "Do you expect trouble?"

Emily shrugged. There hadn't been any trouble at the last Faire, as far as she knew, but there had been a dozen Mediators there, along with a number of other senior magicians. Here, there would be her and no one else...she cursed herself under her breath. In hindsight, she should have thought harder before agreeing to host the Faire. It might have been a mistake.

*No*, she told herself. *It was a mistake.*

"Lady Barb can handle security," she repeated. The older woman wouldn't be happy, but she would do it, even if she did extract a price afterwards. "Putting that aside for a moment, are there any other issues I should know about?"

Bryon smiled at her before he started to speak. "Local taxes have been sharply reduced, as you ordered," he said. "However, there have been enough new taxpayers in your lands to more than compensate for our loss in revenue. Furthermore, scrapping the tax collection policy has actually saved us a considerable sum of money. Currently, we have a surplus of gold and several hundred requests for low-level microloans."

Emily nodded. Microloans had been an idea she'd heard about on Earth and introduced to the Nameless World. They had to be paid back, of course, but they made it easier for any would-be entrepreneurs to start their own businesses. In the long run, she knew, some of the businesses would fail, yet she was sure enough would succeed to keep her in the black.

"However, we have complaints from some of our neighbors," Bryon continued. "Beneficence hasn't bothered to register any complaints, but Earl Wycliffe and Baron Gaunt have both filed formal complaints about peasants, slaves and even traders moving from their lands into yours. In addition, my lady, the Temple Master of Solis has filed a complaint of his own."

"I see," Emily said. "Why?"

"The Word of Solis, the dictates of the god, were meant to remain verbal," Bryon said. "One of their senior initiates took the word and actually wrote it down, then produced hundreds of copies. The entire country can now look into the heart of their religion."

Emily shrugged. "Is that our fault?"

"They want someone to blame," Bryon said. "And we do have the largest printing press industry in the world."

"True," Emily said. King Randor had wanted her to watch for subversive printings...and she would have bet good money that most of them came from Cockatrice. She'd never bothered to supervise what was being printed, let alone try to censor it. "Can they actually cause problems for us?"

"I don't know," Bryon admitted. "But it should be watched."

He smiled, thinly. "On the other hand, the Temple of Justice has been having its holy texts printed and distributed to the faithful," he added. "They *love* the printing press."

"It will sort itself out in time," Emily said. "What else?"

"Some minor issues," Bryon said, uncomfortably. "There are a handful of court cases that require you to make a final judgement. I've been keeping them frozen in the hopes they would go away, but I can't delay them any longer now you're here."

"I'll hear them later today, if they're urgent," Emily said. "How serious are they?"

"Mostly, they concern land distribution," Bryon said. "I'm afraid that one of them is...sensitive."

Emily groaned. "How sensitive?"

"Sensitive enough to upset a great many apple carts," Bryon said. "A couple of smallholder freemen made a contract that one's son would marry the other's daughter, thus combining their lands. The contract was due to come into effect last year..."

He paused, allowing his voice to trail off.

Emily met his eyes. "But?"

"But your laws say that no one can marry until they're sixteen," Bryon said. "The contract specifically states that they have to marry as soon as they are of marriageable age. And, at the time the contract was signed, that was twelve. The girl is twelve, the boy is thirteen and their parents want them to get married."

Emily felt sick. "No," she said, flatly. "The contract didn't take the change in the law into account, did it?"

Byron shook his head. "How could it?"

"Then they can get married, if they want to get married, at sixteen," Emily said. How could she explain, even to Bryon, just how fundamentally *wrong* it was to push such a young couple into marriage? Even if the girl was capable of bearing children — and the boy old enough to sire them — they were both too young to make responsible decisions for themselves. "And if they don't want to get married, they will not be forced into wedlock."

"Most similar contracts are based around marriage ties," Bryon said, quietly. "If you choose to bar this contract from going into effect, it will certainly cause problems for others."

*Of course,* Emily thought, savagely. *Who gives a damn about the young couple when land and money is involved? They can just make the best of it!*

But it was wrong. And she was damned if she was going to condone it.

"I don't care," she said, shortly. "If the contracts were signed before I changed the law, they can be altered to fit the current circumstances. Or they can be scrapped; they *should* be scrapped."

Bryon slowly bowed his head. "As you command, my lady," he said. "But the problems..."

"We will deal with them," Emily said, firmly. Maybe it had happened, in the past, on Earth. But that didn't mean she had to tolerate it here. "And if they complain, tell them they're getting away lightly. There are worse things that can happen than having to tear up a contract!"

# Chapter Ten

E MILY STILL FELT COLDLY FURIOUS THREE HOURS LATER, EVEN AFTER A LIGHT LUNCH AND A long session in the wardchamber, slowly and carefully reprogramming the hearthstone. It should have helped calm her down, but even the most complicated part of the task hadn't done more than sharpen her anger. She knew, all too well, that her rage might prove a danger to anyone she encountered.

She sighed as she tried to concentrate. The castle had never had anything beyond basic wards, not when its former owner hadn't been a magician in his own right, and it was something she knew she needed to fix before the guests began to arrive for the Faire. She concentrated, keying both Frieda and Lady Barb into the wards before she devised a series of new ones, one after the other. Finally, she scanned the castle for unexpected magic and blinked in surprise when she discovered that two of the maids used potions regularly.

*I'll have to see what they're doing,* she thought, as she disconnected her mind from the wards. *Something to keep themselves pretty...or something more sinister.*

"My lady," Bryon said, startling her. He bowed as she turned to face him. "The first case is ready to be heard."

Emily nodded. He'd tried to convince her, several times, to *hear* the case of the invalid contract, but Emily had flatly refused to even consider it. Instead, he had organized a handful of other cases she needed to hear, all of which had considerable implications for the future of her lands. She checked the wards one final time before allowing him to lead her back up the stairs into the Great Hall. No matter how often she stepped into the chamber, she couldn't help feeling faintly absurd. It was, in intent if not in name, a throne room.

*King Randor would have pulled it down, if he had known,* she thought, as she sat on the large chair. It, too, was a throne in all but name. *It was clear that the baron had regal pretensions.*

Bryon stood next to her. "My lady?"

Emily gritted her teeth. Judgement, Lady Barb had shown her, was part of a roving magician's job, but this was different. She would have to live with the consequences of her decisions, which might be taken on the spur of the moment. In hindsight, she understood precisely why headmen and even kings were so relieved to have visiting magicians handle their cases. The magicians wouldn't stay in the village, allowing them to take the blame if the population didn't like the decision.

"Bring in the claimants," she ordered.

The doors opened, revealing five men. Two wore farmer's clothing; two more wore city outfits, while the fifth wore a simple grey outfit that marked him as a scribe and recorder. He was here, Emily knew, to record everything that happened, good or bad. King Randor had been quick to see the advantage of keeping careful records, even before English letters had spread through his kingdom. It was astonishing just how much could be drawn from records, she had learned from experience, if some-one read them with a gimlet eye.

"My lady," Bryon said. "The dispute is between Farmer Giles and Farmer Wolsey, both sons of Hamish. Both lay claim to the farm Hamish left behind when he died."

Emily frowned as all five men knelt before her. Unlike almost everything else, land laws in Cockatrice had been simple even before Baron Holyoake had been beheaded. The land went from the father to the oldest son, while the younger sons were either expected to remain and work for their brother, or go elsewhere to find their fortune. Daughters, on the other hand, were married off as advantageously as possible. They were rarely considered as productive as men.

*That might change,* she thought. *As farms start to consolidate, daughters will have their own roles to play.*

She pushed the thought out of her head and pasted a calm expression on her face. "You may rise," she said. She wasn't going to pay any attention to the lawyers. "The claimant may speak first."

Farmer Giles looked up at her, then down at the stone floor. He was a strong man, wearing clothes that had been patched so many times they might have very little of the original garment left. His hair was dark, his eyes darker still; beside him, his brother looked almost identical, except for longer hair. It was difficult to be sure, but Emily suspected that Giles was the older brother.

"My lady," he said, in a rough tone. "I am the firstborn son of my father. I seek nothing more than clear title to my lands, which were passed down from my father."

And that, Emily knew, was his argument in a nutshell. He was the firstborn, thus he was his father's natural heir. Nothing else needed to be said.

"Thank you," Emily said. "Farmer Wolsey?"

"My lady," Farmer Wolsey said. His voice was lighter, but still bore traces of some-one who had lived his entire life in one location. "My brother is correct; he is indeed the firstborn son of our father. But he chose to leave the farm, ten years ago, and seek his fortune in the wide world. He only returned a week before our father died, leav-ing the farm to me."

He paused. "I was the one who stayed with our father," he continued. "Our father saw fit to leave the land to me, the son who remained. It was I who, in our father's declining years, took control of the farm, planted the crops, organized marriages for my sisters and trained my children in the skills they would need to be farmers. Giles, for all of his adventures, has done none of those things. He hasn't even married or fathered the next generation of farmers!"

Emily concealed her amusement with an effort. Everyone seemed to be obsessed with having children, but then it *was* the only way to ensure immortality. For nobles and commoners alike, it was the only way to keep their lands and possessions in the family. Giles might have had adventures — there was something oddly familiar about the story — but he hadn't attended to his duties.

*The prodigal son,* she recalled. She'd read the story once, before she'd largely dis-missed religion as anything other than the pre-TV opiate of the masses. The moral of the story, according to the book, had been that one should always welcome one's children and siblings home. But she'd always been convinced that the youngest son had had a point. Why bother to work for one's rewards when rewards went to everyone alike?

She sighed, inwardly, as the full scope of the problem became clear. Giles *should* have succeeded his father, but he hadn't worked for the reward. And yet his brother, legally, had no claim to the farm, even if his father *had* willed it to him. Upholding the law or turning it upside down would cause problems, no matter what she decided.

*Damn*, she thought, crossly. No *wonder* Bryon had stalled until she returned to Cockatrice.

She looked at Giles. "You have no wife or children?"

"No, my lady," Giles said.

*None that you know about*, Emily translated, mentally. A bastard child could inherit, in certain circumstances, and having such a child could only have strengthened Giles's claim to the farm. There had to be a next generation, after all. *But what the hell do I do with you?*

She closed her eyes for a long moment. "Did you disavow your claim to the farm?"

"No, my lady," Giles said.

"You *left*," Wolsey snapped. "You certainly did nothing to *keep* the farm!"

Emily tapped her lips, urging them both to the quiet, then ran through a set of possible options. Cut the baby — the farm — in half? But that would leave Wolsey trying to maintain his family on half the land, while Giles would be unable to farm his own lands alone. And who would have all the items the family had built up over the years? Separating the farm into two equal shares might prove tricky. It would certainly take a great deal of time.

"Do you really want to be a farmer," she asked, silently casting a mild truth spell into the air, "or do you merely want land?"

"I want land, my lady," Giles said. He blinked, no doubt wondering why he'd told the truth so openly. "I'm growing older and I have little to show for it."

Emily sighed and made up her mind. "Wolsey remained on the land and worked it, while you left to have adventures." She wondered, absently, what Giles had done with his life. Served in the Baron's illicit army? Or something worse? "He has a family who will take the farm themselves in time, while you have no family and chose to leave the land as soon as you could. Your father, I suspect, understood that you had no true claim to the farm."

"My lady," Giles began. "I..."

Emily held up a hand, cutting him off. "Wolsey's children will inherit unless you have children of your own," she added. "I can understand you wanting to find your own niche in the world, but not trying to take a farm you don't want. Therefore, I have no choice but to deny your claim.

"However, there are other options, other places you can work. Why not see what you can find here?"

She watched as Bryon dismissed the group, then shook her head. Maybe Giles would find somewhere he could work, or maybe he would do something stupid. Maybe something from his father could be sold to give him a small stake, upholding family feeling if nothing else. But, in the end, she'd told the truth. She couldn't throw a hardworking man off the farm — or subject him to his older brother — just because he'd been unlucky enough to be born second.

"You handled that well, my lady," Bryon said. "But what will Giles do with his life?"

"There's no shortage of opportunities," Emily said. "Perhaps we could find him a place here, if nowhere else."

The next case was relatively simple. A traveling trader, completely without any magic Emily could discern, had sold his own medicines to villagers, medicines that didn't actually work. Emily listened to his lies of having studied under several famous alchemists, including Professor Thande, then ordered him handed back to the villagers for punishment. The trader was lucky he hadn't actually managed to kill someone with his brews. He probably would have, Emily suspected, if he'd fed one of them to a child.

But the one afterwards took on a darker tone. "They took me in to work for them," a dark-haired girl said, pointing to the defendants. "I worked for them for years, enduring everything, until they said I was a thief. They took me to the headman and cut off my hand! And then their oldest son said *he'd* taken the food."

Emily blanched. The girl was thinner than Frieda had been when Emily had first met her at Mountaintop, and her skin was marred by nasty bruises. Her right hand was missing, her lower arm ending in a stump. Someone had cut it off and wrapped a cloth around it before kicking her out of the village. She'd been incredibly lucky it hadn't become infected.

"Yin was always rude andungrateful," the woman said. Her voice was high enough to be unpleasant, grating at Emily's ears. "How were we to know she wasn't the thief?"

"You could have waited for a magician," Emily said. She shuddered in horror, unable to hide her reaction. "If you had, your son would have been able to clear her name before she lost her hand."

She looked at the girl and shuddered, again. It was a miracle Yin had survived long enough to reach the castle, let alone press charges against her former master and mistress. Emily didn't want to *think* about what she might have been doing to survive, or what prospects she might have had if she'd been kicked right out of the castle. The Nameless World could be very cruel to a cripple, even one born into the aristocracy.

Magic crackled over her fingertips as she fought to keep a hold on her temper. She could kill them both, easily, and no one would say her nay. Or she could crush their souls, turn them into toads, cripple them so completely that they would be turned out of their home by their family...there were so many options it was hard to decide. The old baron wouldn't have cared, she knew. But *Emily* cared. How could someone just cripple a helpless servant on suspicion? It wouldn't have been *that* hard to obtain a truth potion.

"First, a healer will tend to your victim," Emily said. Her voice sounded strange in her ears, as if someone colder and harder was speaking through her. "She will have her hand rebuilt and her body cleansed of damage. You will pay for her treatment, without argument, no matter how expensive it becomes."

Yin gasped. "They can do that?"

"Yes," Emily said.

Yin fainted. The woman opened her mouth to object, but her husband caught her arm and silenced her.

"Second, after the medical bills have been paid, you will surrender half of your remaining property to Yin, to compensate her for your mistreatment." Emily wondered, absently, just how involved the husband had been. No matter; he'd either supported his wife or lacked the moral courage to stop her. He could go to the devil. "Third, you will no longer be considered freemen. You will be placed in the hands of your oldest son as serfs. And I hope, for your sake, that you taught him better than it seems."

The woman started to scream abuse. Emily ignored her — she'd heard worse from her stepfather — and watched, dispassionately, as they were hustled out of the chamber. It wasn't quite what she'd wanted to do to them, she admitted privately, but it would utterly destroy their lives. Serfs had no legal rights; they couldn't own property, sign contracts or go where they pleased. Indeed, they would be the only two serfs in Cockatrice.

"There will be talk," Bryon observed, once the maids had helped the stunned girl out of the chamber and down to the castle's small clinic. "And people will wonder."

"Let them," Emily said, tiredly. It *was* a terrible punishment...but they'd deserved worse, much worse. She could have taken their hands, if she'd wanted. "Maybe it will stop people from abusing their servants in the future."

She rose from her seat and stepped down to the stone floor. "Are there any others?"

"Not at the moment," Bryon said. "There will be several more by the end of the month."

"We can put time aside for it," Emily said. Two weeks...the Faire would be well underway by then. And Caleb would probably have arrived. She was tempted to drop it all in Bryon's hands, but knew she couldn't. "Have them hosted in the city, if there's space, then brought up when we have a free moment."

"Yes, my lady," Bryon said.

"You handled that well," Lady Barb said. Emily jumped. Beside her, Bryon looked as though he would very much like to have jumped too. "But your wards need work."

"I know," Emily said, embarrassed. "When did you get back?"

"Twenty minutes ago," Lady Barb said. "But I trust you are not trying to make *more* work for me? That girl needs a proper healer."

"I appointed you as the security chief," Emily said, before Bryon could say a word. "But if you would help the girl, I would be very grateful."

Lady Barb gave her a long, considering look. "There are several healers in the city," she said. "The girl can be taken to one of them, but you'll owe me something."

Her voice was very cool. "I'm your advisor, Emily, not your servant. It isn't a good idea to take me for granted."

"I know," Emily said. She looked at Bryon. "I'll see you later."

Bryon bowed, hastily backing out of the chamber, leaving the two magicians alone. Emily didn't blame him. *She* wouldn't have wanted to get between two magicians, particularly if she'd lacked magic of her own.

"This was my mistake," she said, before Lady Barb could say a word. "I didn't realize how large the Faire would become. And I didn't know who else I could ask."

"That's what you get for making decisions in haste," Lady Barb said, tartly. "I will serve as your security chief, if you want, but you'll owe me a very large favor."

"I understand," Emily said. *She* would have been annoyed if someone had signed her up for something without consulting her first. Lady Barb had every right to be annoyed. "What would you like in return?"

"I'll tell you when I think of it," Lady Barb said. "You should know, by now, not to make open-ended bargains with *anyone*." Her voice lightened. "You might find yourself doing something embarrassing or humiliating to pay off the debt."

Emily blushed, embarrassed.

She shrugged, turning to lead Emily towards the door. "I would start by modifying your wards," she added, darkly. "I crept up on you and you never even had a hint I was there."

"You were keyed into the wards," Emily countered.

"You should still have known I was there," Lady Barb reminded her. "Emily..."

She took a breath. "Emily, you are treating this" — she waved a hand at the chamber — "as something you can pick up and put down again, whenever it suits you. But you can't; you can either be their baroness, which comes with its own obligations, or you can pass the lands to someone else. Alassa and Imaiqah, even Alicia, are not considered powerful in their own right, not yet. You, on the other hand, are a full baroness."

"I know," Emily said.

"Then I suggest you live up to it," Lady Barb said. "Or walk away, now, before you change too much to allow anyone to consider themselves on solid ground."

She opened the door, then paused. "I sent the letter to Beneficence today," she added. "I suspect Caleb will be here within the week. You will need to find time to work with him, too."

Emily swallowed, nervously.

"And I advise you to spend the evening with Frieda," Lady Barb said. "*I* will be sending notes and calling in favors. You'll need some additional Mediators at the Faire and they won't be pleased at being summoned so quickly."

"I could ask Void," Emily said.

Lady Barb snorted. "Not unless you really hate your guests," she said. "And what have they done to deserve your hatred? *You* invited them here."

And that, Emily knew, was all too true.

# Chapter Eleven

"I CONTACTED A NUMBER OF OLD FRIENDS," LADY BARB SAID TO EMILY, AS SHE JOINED THEM for breakfast the following morning. "A number have agreed to assist with the Faire, in exchange for money or future considerations."

Emily stared at her. "Did you use my name?"

"I used *mine*," Lady Barb said. "Like I said, you owe me."

"I know," Emily said. Magicians hoarded favors like dragons and kings hoarded gold. Lady Barb had done a great deal to help her. "And I'm very grateful."

"We will be meeting them after breakfast," Lady Barb said. "You and I will walk down to the Faire, together."

"Thank you," Emily said. "I...I didn't handle this very well, did I?"

Lady Barb shrugged, then waited impatiently for Emily and Frieda to eat their breakfasts. Emily wolfed down her food, donned a long cloak that should protect her from being recognized at a distance, and then waited for Frieda.

"I would advise you to leave Frieda here," Lady Barb said. "There's a great deal you have to see."

"I promised I'd show her the Faire," Emily said. "She won't get in our way."

Lady Barb seemed unconvinced, as they made their way down to the gate, but showed no inclination to continue the discussion. Frieda looked from Emily to Lady Barb and then back again, then quietened, like a child suddenly caught up in adult conversations. Emily smiled at the back of her head, making a mental note to ensure that she spent more time with Frieda after the Faire. There wasn't so much for her to do at the castle.

"We will work on expanding your protections later," Lady Barb said, as they passed through the outer edge of the wards. "Consider it an additional lesson in protecting your property."

Emily looked back at the castle and sighed. Whitehall had a nexus point to power its wards — and she knew, all too well, just how far Mountaintop had gone to protect itself. *She* lacked both options...and the castle was too big for her to protect with more specialized wards. It would be simple enough to add an alert to inform her if anyone used magic within the walls — she'd already done that, to some extent — but actually stopping someone from using magic would be a great deal harder. She really needed more magicians to help her maintain the wards or a smaller castle. And she doubted she would get either of them.

"I don't know how to make the protections any stronger," she confessed. "This building wasn't designed by magicians."

"No, it wasn't," Lady Barb agreed. "You might consider building a new castle."

"I thought I wasn't allowed to build any new fortifications," Emily said. King Randor had made that clear to her, after he'd granted her the title. *No one* was allowed to build any fortified structures without the king's specific permission. "Or do you think the king would let me build something if I asked?"

"You don't lose anything by asking," Lady Barb said. "I dare say he trusts you more than any of his other barons."

*Maybe about as far as he can throw me*, Emily thought, dryly. *Which would be quite some distance, if he used magic.*

She sighed, inwardly. She'd never had the impression that Randor was a trusting person...and he was a monarch, a monarch who couldn't *afford* to trust anyone. Even Alassa was locked out of some secrets, and she was his *heir*. Emily knew Randor had needed to reward her, after the thwarted coup, but she also knew he intended to use her to benefit himself as much as possible. And the only real question was just how long she intended to put up with it?

A cold wind blew across the field as they reached the edge of the Faire. Emily couldn't help thinking it looked rather depressing, with the stalls battened down and the wagons drawn up in tight circles. Some of the wagons carried families who spent most of their lives going from faire to faire, either mundane or magical, showing off for a few measly copper coins; others belonged to magicians who wanted to show off while bringing their own accommodations with them. Beyond them, she saw a handful of cages, each one holding a rare animal from elsewhere in the Allied Lands. She fought down a smile as she saw the lion in one cage, watching the nearby humans with beady eyes.

Frieda gasped. "What is *that?*"

"A lion," Emily said. She wasn't particularly impressed. Compared to a dragon, or a Mimic, a lion was surprisingly commonplace. But Frieda would never have seen anything like it before. "They eat people, sometimes."

The lion growled deep in its throat. Emily did her best to ignore it as they walked past the cages, then down towards a set of empty stalls. The stallkeepers were arguing, in quiet voices, over just which of them should have the stall closest to the walkways. Lady Barb snorted, rudely, then led Emily past without stopping. She didn't seem inclined to intervene.

"That's the problem with not organizing everything properly," she warned, as soon as they were out of earshot. "There's no one here to say where someone can and cannot go."

She led them towards a large tent before Emily could muster a response and pushed the flap aside. A gust of warm air struck Emily in the face as she entered. She looked around, seeing a handful of tables and plain wooden chairs. A dozen workers sat there, drinking beer and chatting happily amongst themselves. Behind the tables, there were a handful of mugs, and barrels, ready to be tapped. And, Emily noticed, a grim-faced man wearing a long black robe and hood.

*You could have warned me*, she thought at Lady Barb, as Master Grey stood to greet them. *You could have told me he was here.*

"Master Grey," Lady Barb said. "Thank you for coming."

Master Grey bowed to her, then nodded politely to Emily. Jade's former master hadn't changed from the last time they'd met, just after she'd escaped Mountaintop. He was a tall muscular man, his head shaved bald, carrying a staff in one hand. Emily was sure he disliked her, although she wasn't sure why. The sense of abiding disap-proval had followed her ever since they'd first met, a year ago. He'd even objected to Jade keeping in touch with her.

"I was planning to visit anyway," Master Grey said. His voice was deep, but tinged with cold amusement. "Being asked to assist you is always a pleasure."

*And he will make Lady Barb pay for asking him,* Emily thought, sourly. *But what will he want?*

"Glad to hear it," Lady Barb said, as they sat down and cast privacy wards in the air. "What do you think, so far?"

Master Grey gave Emily a long, cold smile. "You do realize you've done something very brave or very stupid?"

Emily fought down the urge to bow her head. She'd met many strong men, both muscular and magical, since she'd entered the Nameless World, but Master Grey intimidated her in ways she hated. It would have been easier to bear, she thought, if she'd known *why* he'd hated her, yet none of her theories seemed to make sense. Maybe he, like Master Tor, disliked her for something that was out of her control. Or maybe Master Grey just hated the thought of anyone distracting his former appren-tice from his duties.

"Yes," she said, curtly. She was damned if she was calling this man *master.* "I under-stand my mistake."

"Do you?" Master Grey said. "I would be surprised if you did. Your father does not seem to have prepared you for magical life."

Emily shrugged, although she couldn't help feeling a flicker of concern. Now what?

"No one would trust Void to raise a child properly," Lady Barb said. "If you have a point to make, make it."

"You've invited *everyone,*" Master Grey said, as if that in and of itself should be enough.

Emily waited, but didn't understand.

After a long moment, his bushy eyebrows twitched, sardonically. "Everyone who happens to think or believe they're important. And among those who have accepted your invitation, whose names are blazing across the guest list, are the Ashworth and Ashfall Families."

Emily blinked. "As in Melissa and Markus?"

"As in the magical families who have been fighting and feuding for the last hun-dred years," Master Grey said. His voice darkened. "They've been trying to *kill* each other, young lady, and when they haven't been trying to kill each other they've been trying to tear each other down. I don't think they're going to agree to get along just because you've invited them both to the Faire. Most people try very hard to avoid inviting both of them to the same event."

He smiled, coldly. "There was a *reason* Melissa was sent to Whitehall," he added. "Or don't you know that?"

Emily frowned. Melissa had never been a friend. She'd taken a dislike to Alassa from the start, before the princess had grown up a little, and extended it to Emily and

Imaiqah when they'd both befriended Alassa. In their first two years at Whitehall, Melissa had done everything she could to make them miserable...and, Emily had to admit, they'd not been on their best behavior either. The only reason they hadn't continued their private war in Third Year was that they'd all been kept desperately busy, trying to keep up with the course load.

And Melissa had only attended Whitehall, Emily had been told, because Markus Ashfall, her family's rival, had been at Mountaintop.

"I know," she said.

The timing didn't quite make sense, she thought. Markus had been Head Boy... hell, given the politics, it was possible that everyone had *known* he would be Head Boy, even three years before he'd entered his final year. The temptation to use that power against Melissa would have been overpowering...but Emily had always had the sense he was a decent person. He'd even offered Emily some good advice.

*But perhaps it would have been different,* her thoughts whispered, *if you'd belonged to his family's rivals.*

"Then you really shouldn't have invited them both," Master Grey said. "Putting them together is like adding Basilisk Blood to powdered Dragon Scales."

Emily swore, inwardly. Professor Thande had warned them, more than once, that certain materials could *never* be allowed to blend. Adding Basilisk Blood to powdered Dragon Scales would always result in an explosion.

*Lady Barb must have known,* she thought, darkly. *Why didn't she tell me?*

She took a breath. "But...if someone invites one family and not the other," she said, "how do they keep the other family from being insulted?"

"They roll dice, normally," Master Grey said. He smirked at her discomfort. "Everyone would have understood, young lady, if you had only asked *one* family to attend."

"But there are people who would be offended if they weren't asked," Emily said. Alassa had once had to manage a ball in Zangaria, in what King Randor had called a lesson in practical politics. Everyone had to be invited, but seating had to be sorted out based on who was fighting with whom, or who wasn't speaking to whom. And not inviting someone could be seen as an insult...or a threat. "And..."

*And you didn't even think to supervise the invitations,* a voice at the back of her head pointed out. *You just assumed Bryon, a mundane, could handle it.*

"This isn't the mundane world," Master Grey said. "Everyone would have understood you inviting one of the families, but not both."

"Master Grey," Frieda asked, suddenly, "why *are* they fighting?"

Master Grey smirked, again. "It depends who you ask," he said. "I was told that the head of the Ashworth Family had a brother...and they both fell madly in love with the same girl. A few years of increasingly bitter fighting later, the younger brother was expelled from the family and, in his rage, swore to bring down the Ashworths. They've been fighting and feuding ever since."

"No one knows who actually got the girl," Lady Barb said. "I was told that the woman in question was sent to break the family up and succeeded, magnificently.

The brother who left swore to liberate his family from her cursed spawn."

"Or that the younger brother leveled the charge against an innocent women," Master Grey added. "Thus ensuring, after such insults had been exchanged, that it was war to the knife."

Emily held up a hand. "Does anyone actually *know*?"

"It's been over a hundred and fifty years," Lady Barb said. "There are so many conflicting versions of the story that it is impossible to know which one is the truth. They might all have some grains of the truth in them...or they might all be lies, tall tales spread to hide the *real* issue. We may never know why the younger Ashworth split from his family and declared war. Or, for that matter, why so many saw fit to follow him."

She sighed. "But Master Grey is right," she admitted. "Inviting them both is asking for trouble."

"Quite," Master Grey agreed.

"I see only one option," Lady Barb continued, ignoring him. "Cancel the Faire. Tell them all to go home."

"That *would* be an insult," Master Grey warned.

"Better an insult than a war," Lady Barb said. "The last time there was a fight at the Faire, between two small groups of magicians, it took years to sort out the mess. This time, two entire families will be involved."

"It wouldn't just be the two families," Master Grey said. He looked at Emily, his grey eyes boring into her face. "Hundreds of carnies have already made their way here — and more are on the way. Countless sellers have paid the nominal fee to establish a stall where they can sell their wares to the visitors. Thousands of magicians have planned trips here. Many of those trips will have been planned months in advance."

His eyes never left Emily's face. "If you cancel the Faire now, young lady, you will put a great many noses out of joint. At the very least, you will have to pay out a great deal of gold in compensation. It will certainly damage your reputation for a very long time to come. At worst..."

"You don't need to scare her," Lady Barb snapped.

"I'm just pointing out the problems she would face if she wanted to cancel the Faire," Master Grey said. There was a hint of mocking amusement in his tone. "And it *will* cause her a great many problems."

Emily cursed him under her breath, then thought hard. She trusted Lady Barb — and if Lady Barb said she should cancel the Faire, it was certainly something to consider. But Master Grey was right. Hundreds of thousands of people, many of them powerful magicians, had already hired their stalls, booked their tickets and planned their trips to Cockatrice. None of them would be pleased at having to cancel at short notice, particularly the ones who had turned down opportunities to go elsewhere. And people like Jasmine's family — she remembered the young singer with a touch of fondness — would be put out of pocket by the sudden change.

"This is my territory," she said. "Wouldn't they respect it and not start fights?"

"I imagine the grown-ups would understand the dangers of picking a fight with someone who has killed two necromancers," Lady Barb said, her lips so thin they were practically invisible. "But the hot-headed younger generation might be so dunderheaded as to start picking fights anyway, regardless of the wisdom or lack thereof."

Emily groaned inwardly. She had two ways to kill necromancers, neither of which could be used in Cockatrice. One required a nexus and the closest one she knew about was several days journey, the other would cause far too much damage to the surrounding countryside, if she unleashed it. And it would start magicians wondering precisely what she'd done...it had been sheer luck, in hindsight, that most people believed Mother Holly had lost control of her magic and died when it broke free. The prospect of hundreds of magicians experimenting with ways to split atoms was horrific.

"Damn it," she said, softly. "Damned if I do, damned if I don't. Right?"

"I'm afraid so," Master Grey said. He didn't seem too upset at her dilemma. "I can have a few words with the senior leadership, if you like, but..."

"You're tied to Ashworth, aren't you?" Lady Barb said.

"A cadet branch of the family," Master Grey said. He shrugged, expressively. "I would be surprised if they consider me one of them, these days. But I can have a word with both families."

"It's your choice, Emily," Lady Barb said. Her voice was flat, but Emily could tell she was displeased. "But you should be prepared for the consequences."

*I should walk away from Cockatrice*, Emily thought, angrily. She hadn't known what she was getting into...or what was going to be done in her name, merely because she hadn't been paying attention. *Leave the lands to someone else and just go.*

But that wasn't an option, not now.

"If we hold the Faire as planned, we risk them starting a fight," she said. "But, if we cancel the Faire, we definitely upset hundreds of people."

"Thousands of people," Master Grey corrected. "Your reputation would not recover."

"Not to mention causing problems for everyone who bought a ticket in good faith," Emily continued. "It would not be easy to compensate them all."

"No," Master Grey agreed. "You wouldn't even be able to calculate what you owed."

Emily nodded. It would be simple enough to reimburse everyone who had bought a ticket, but what about everything else? How many profits might be lost because someone had thought they would be going to Cockatrice? Master Grey, as much as she hated to admit it, was right. The legal wrangling over who owed what could take years to resolve. And it would be far too expensive. She was a wealthy woman, by the standards of the Allied Lands, but was she wealthy enough to cover everything?

"We hold the Faire," she said. "And you sit on anyone who feels like causing trouble."

"That might be hard if most of the families show up," Lady Barb said. "I hope this is the right decision, Emily."

"Yeah," Emily said. She had a feeling she would have regretted it no matter what choice she made. "I hope so, too."

# Chapter Twelve

T HE NEXT FEW DAYS PASSED QUIETLY, QUIETLY ENOUGH FOR EMILY TO START BECOMING nervous. She worked with Lady Barb on the wards, watched as the older woman hired a dozen experienced magicians to assist with security and tried to study the barony's record books. The latter were both extensively detailed and incredibly confusing, leaving her feeling as if she couldn't make head or tail of them. Bryon, it seemed, had kept good records, but the system didn't make sense to her.

"Everything has to be logged," he said, as they sat together in the records room. "You can track everything by going through the records."

Emily groaned. "Wouldn't it make more sense to merely log the essentials?"

"If the king asks for information," Bryon countered earnestly, "you have to give him everything, or he will think you're hiding something."

There was a tap on the door. Lady Barb stood there, looking amused.

"I hate to interrupt," she said, "but you have a visitor."

Emily blinked, then remembered. "He's here?"

"He's here," Lady Barb confirmed. "Would you like me to show him into the hall?"

"No," Emily said, suddenly flustered. It was hard enough using the Great Hall to pass judgement, when she was clearly in charge. She didn't want to meet Caleb somewhere where they wouldn't meet as equals. "Um...can you show him into my study? I'll be there in a moment."

She stood, brushed dust off her dress, then hurried back to her rooms. The maids had agreed after the first day not to enter without Emily's permission, even early in the morning. There were spells, after all, to ensure the room remained warm and comfortable, rendering a fire unnecessary. Besides, it was easier to find things when the maids hadn't tried to help by tidying up the room. She hastily dug out the proposal paperwork, pulled her hair back into a long ponytail, and headed down to her study. There was barely any time to sit down before there was a tap on the door. Emily rose to her feet as it opened, revealing Lady Barb and a young man.

"Lady Emily," Lady Barb said, with tight formality. "Please allow me to introduce Caleb, of House Waterfall."

"I thank you," Caleb said. His voice held the same accent as King Randor's, but lighter, as if he'd grown up in a place where several accents blurred together. "Lady Emily, it is a pleasure to make your acquaintance. I've heard a great deal about you."

"Thank you," Emily said. She held out a hand. "I've heard a great deal about you too."

Caleb took her hand and shook it, gently. Emily found herself studying him as he released her hand, his brown eyes looking back at her. He was tall and gangly, with short brown hair, a lightly-scarred face and damaged hands. The black shirt and trousers he wore were unmarked, but she couldn't help being reminded of a military uniform. There was something about the way he wore it that reminded her of Sergeant Harkin, who had dominated a field of magicians through sheer personality.

And yet, she was sure that he wasn't a military man.

"Please, sit," she said, waving to one of the chairs. "I can have food and drinks brought in, if you like."

"Thank you," Caleb said. He sat, resting his hands on his lap. "It was good of you to agree to work with me."

"I think I should be thanking you," Emily said. "You had every right to restart your project and search for someone new, from the year below."

"Too much like hard work," Caleb said. He gave her a smile that reminded her, suddenly, of Rory Williams. "Besides, I still qualify for Fourth Year. I didn't want to repeat Third Year if it could be avoided."

"I know the feeling," Emily said.

"I will have food and drinks sent to you," Lady Barb said. "Until then, behave."

Emily found herself flushing as Lady Barb bowed and retreated from the room. She glanced up at Caleb and saw that he was flushing too, his cheeks a dull red. She gaped, then started to giggle, despite herself. Caleb laughed a moment later, breaking the ice. By the time Janice entered with a tray of food and drink, they were laughing together like loons.

"Thank you," Emily said, as Janice placed the tray in front of them and retreated. "Please, feel free to eat what you want."

"I've never had cakes like these before," Caleb said, picking up a honey cake and eyeing it thoughtfully. "Do you eat them all the time?"

"Not if I can avoid it," Emily said. She liked sweets, but she'd never had very many of them on Earth. "Tell me about yourself?"

Caleb shrugged. "There isn't much to tell," he said. "I was at Stronghold for the first two years of my education, then transferred to Whitehall for Third Year. My father was less than pleased when the Mimic started killing people; I think he thought I should have killed it personally. Father always was a demanding person."

Emily winced. "It wasn't easy to kill the creature," she said. Very few people knew about the Mimic's true nature and she hoped it would stay that way. "You would just have been killed."

"That's my father for you," Caleb said. "Charge! Death before dishonor! Take no prisoners! Last one in is a rotten egg!"

"I know the type," Emily said.

"And you?" Caleb said. "What was your family like?"

"There isn't much to tell either," Emily said. She knew he was asking about Void. "I didn't know I had magic until I was sixteen, whereupon I was sent to Whitehall."

Caleb frowned, but seemed to sense she didn't want to talk about it and didn't ask any further questions. Emily was relieved; they'd worked out a cover story shortly after she'd arrived at Whitehall, but somehow she didn't want to lie to him. Let him believe, if he wished, that Void had been an absentee father, or one who had been ashamed of his daughter failing to develop magic early. She could always tell him the truth later.

She took a bite of her cake, then a sip of Kava. "Your project is fascinating," she said, as she put her mug back on the table. "But can you make it work?"

"I hope so," Caleb said.

He took a breath. "The problem with casting spells is that one has to account for all the variables," he said. "Most magicians eventually develop the habit of casting spells without thinking through every detail, which allows them to cast the spells quickly, but not to alter the variables. And some magicians never learn how to do more than trigger spells already embedded in wands and staffs."

Emily nodded. "I understand," she said. She had a hundred spells memorized that she could use to turn a person into an animal, or an object, but changing any of the variables would require her to take the spells apart, then rebuild them. "And you plan to change this?"

"Spell mosaics," Caleb said. He reached into his pocket and produced a sheet of paper, which he placed on the desk in front of her. "Every magician knows that channeling magic is like channeling water, merely a case of allowing it to flow though the spellwork and produce the defined end result. This...allows the spell to be built up piece by piece, the variables to be changed at will, and then cast with minimum effort."

Emily studied the diagram for a long moment. "Each piece of the mosaic represents a different variable," she said, slowly. "You could change one and the entire spell alters itself."

"Yes," Caleb said.

He dug into his pocket and produced a small wooden object. Emily took it, when he passed it to her, and turned it over and over in her hand. She couldn't help being reminded of a bourbon cream; there was a layer of light wood, sandwiched between two layers of darker wood. And, judging by the smell, the glue holding the wood together was *Manaskol*. Magic would embed itself in wood, given half a chance, but the *Manaskol* would ensure it fled onwards to its final destination.

"Clever," she said. It looked sloppy, but neatness was very much the last problem. "Does it actually work?"

"The basic concept is sound," Caleb assured her. "We embed complete spells in wands, after all. But the trick is learning to separate out the components so they can be placed together in the correct order."

Emily looked down at the diagram, feeling her thoughts churning. She had a concept for a magical battery — she intended to make the first test version over the summer, if she had time to actually do anything for herself — and, merged with the spell mosaics, it might actually prove more workable than she had thought. It would be risky — Caleb had already managed to injure himself once — but it was doable. And then...

She looked at Caleb, wishing she dared trust him enough to talk about the batteries. *They* would make one hell of a project proposal, but they would be literally earthshaking. She didn't dare discuss them with anyone, save for Lady Barb. And *she* had taken an oath of secrecy.

"I would understand if you didn't want to work with me," Caleb said, after a moment. "June worked with me and she...she came very close to being hurt."

"I know," Emily said. She looked at Caleb's twitching hands and shuddered. "How long did it take you to recover?"

"Six months, more or less," Caleb said. "Father was most unimpressed. He kept pointing out that I should have stayed at Stronghold, where they would beat the clumsiness out of me."

Emily frowned. Caleb moved with an eerie precision, as if he was carefully considering each and every movement before he made it. Or, perhaps, as if he didn't dare to relax and move naturally. Had he been genuinely clumsy as a child? Or was something else wrong?

"I don't think it would have helped," she said. "*Manaskol* has a tendency to blow up if you look at it the wrong way."

"Tell me about it," Caleb said. "I had to convince Professor Thande to teach me how to make it a year ahead of schedule, just so I could produce it for the project. Father was not amused when he saw the bill."

"I bet he wasn't," Emily said. *Manaskol* was expensive, largely because the ingredients were expensive...and because most magicians would prefer to purchase it from someone else, rather than make it for themselves. "You didn't actually try to buy it for yourself?"

"I need to modify the recipe in the final moments," Caleb said. "It's detailed in the proposal."

Emily could have kicked herself. She'd seen it, but she had not remembered.

"I can make it," she said, instead. "But I don't know if I would be any more reliable than you."

"I think you'd be doing most of the brewing," Caleb admitted. He held up his bandaged hands. "My hands twitch like...a recruit facing his sergeant for the first time."

Emily nodded. "We can certainly try and make it work," she said. They would be graded on how well they worked together, rather than what — if anything — they managed to produce. "Do you mind working with a Third Year?"

"You're not just *any* Third Year," Caleb pointed out. "And besides...we'll both be in Fourth Year. I barely got through a couple of weeks before I managed to put myself in a bed for the next few months."

"It won't be easy," Emily warned.

It was a galling thought. She paid little attention to anyone outside her circle of friends, but she had heard that students who were held back a year rarely had an easy time of it. They were older than their new classmates, yet regarded as suspect because they'd already failed once. It didn't make sense to her, but magicians regarded incompetence with more than a little fear. Not that they would ever admit to it, of course.

"It's that or go back to Stronghold," Caleb said. "And I don't think they would want me back."

Emily frowned. "What's it like?"

"Horrible," Caleb said. "You'd hate it."

"Worse than Mountaintop?"

"I've never been to Mountaintop," Caleb said. "You walk into the school and you're instantly assigned to a regiment. That regiment will be your family for the next six years. If you do well, that regiment will be composed of your best friends; if you do badly, the regiment will turn on you. The life of a social outcast at Stronghold isn't worth living. Oh, and if you make a mistake, everyone in your regiment gets punished."

Emily shuddered. "Were you a social outcast?"

"I might have been, if I hadn't had an important father and pompous older brother," Caleb said. "As it was, I got a little leeway...which is what saved me from nearly being expelled, once upon a time. But they wouldn't take me back now, even if my father pulled strings."

"Oh," Emily said. "What did you do?"

Caleb looked embarrassed. "I turned one of my regiment into a snail," he said. "The bastard deserved it, but...they would have expelled me, if my father hadn't had a few words with them."

"That's it?" Emily asked. She'd lost count of how many times she'd been turned into something small and embarrassing...or done it to someone else, for that matter. "They wanted to expel you for *that*?"

"Stronghold isn't just for magical students," Caleb explained. "Two-thirds of the regiment were mundanes, without magic. Using magic on one's fellows is considered a grave offense, no matter how much they deserve it."

"I see," Emily said. She'd always had the impression that magical students were gathered together, at Whitehall and Mountaintop, to keep them from being a threat to the mundanes around them. A little spell, nothing more than a prank, could be devastating if used against a defenseless mundane. "But if you were defending yourself...?"

"You are expected to defend yourself using your fists," Caleb said. "Not magic."

Emily looked down at her pale hands. She couldn't help understanding, through bitter experience, what it was like to go through school as an unpopular child. It would be worse, she suspected, if everyone's marks depended on hers. The staff didn't need to expend effort in keeping the students in line, not when the regiment would do it for them. And children who were pushed out of the regiment entirely would fall by the wayside, lost forever.

"I'm sorry," she muttered.

"Don't be," Caleb said. "It wasn't your fault."

He sighed. "I understand we will be spending the summer rewriting the proposal," he said. "Or we could simply sign your name to the bottom, then send it back to Whitehall."

"I think I need to read it first, then understand," Emily said. She'd signed quite enough papers without reading them. "I've had a room prepared for you here, if you want to stay in the castle. I don't know how much time I will have, though."

"We have a couple of months before we're due back at Whitehall," Caleb said. "I dare say we will have enough time, if you want to go through it line by line."

He reached into his pocket and produced a small bag. It must have been charmed to be larger on the inside, Emily realized, as he produced more spell mosaics from the bag than should have been reasonably possible. Piece by piece, he put them together on the desk, pressing his fingertip against the head piece. There was a flare of magic, and a tiny light globe appeared at the far end.

"It works," Emily said.

"This is something so basic that anyone could do it, with a ward," Caleb said. "It's the more complex spells I need to make work, but they don't hold together so well."

"Maybe you need to bind them together," Emily mused.

"I tried," Caleb said, with a hint of irritation. "But anything I use to hold them together would interfere with the magic."

"Then use something mundane," Emily said. She reached for a sheet of paper and drew out a very basic jigsaw pattern. "Something like this, perhaps."

Caleb looked at it, then frowned. "It might work," he said. "But I'd need something very precise to make sure they fit together."

Emily smiled, remembering one of her old teachers from Earth. He'd tried to teach his students how to produce chessboards, something so complex that few of the students had managed to master it. But she still recalled the basic idea...

"You made these small," she said, picking up one of the spell pieces. "Why not make one big sandwich" — she demonstrated with a piece of paper — "and then carve them out piece by piece. Pile two or three layers on top of one another, and you might have something that would work."

"That might work," Caleb agreed. He gave her a look of unmitigated respect. "They said you were a genius."

Emily blushed. "I'm not that smart," she said. "And I don't know if it *will* work..."

"It's better than my idea," Caleb said. "But we'd still need to..."

He broke off. "We could make it work," he said. "I *know* we could make it work."

There was a tap on the door, which opened a moment later to reveal Frieda.

"Emily, there's a party at the door," she said. She gave Caleb a long glance before she looked again at Emily. "Lady Barb says you'll want to meet the Duchess of Iron personally."

Caleb blinked. "The Duchess of Iron?"

"A legal fiction," Emily said. Alassa wouldn't be fooling anyone...but traveling as the duchess would save her from tedious formalities. "Please ask Lady Barb to show the duchess and her party into...into my living room. I'll be along in a moment."

She rose. "I'll see you for dinner?"

"Of course," Caleb said. "By then, I might have rewritten the proposal."

# Chapter Thirteen

"I DON'T KNOW WHO YOU THINK YOU'RE FOOLING," EMILY SAID, AS SHE STEPPED INTO HER living room. It was one of the few rooms she'd managed to have redecorated since she'd inherited the castle, lining the walls with bookcases and stuffing ugly, but comfortable furniture into the room. "Everyone knows who the current Duchess of Iron is."

"Yes, but everyone also knows the Duchess of Iron doesn't have to be greeted by everyone in the castle," Alassa countered. She sat on an overstuffed sofa, next to Jade. Imaiqah sat opposite her, wearing a long dark dress. She'd accompanied Alassa from the city. "Or would you rather have everyone line up so they can bow in unison?"

"Not really," Emily said. She touched the parchment in her pocket. "You could have warned me you were coming."

Alassa looked embarrassed, although someone who didn't know her would probably have missed the faint flush of her cheeks. "I forgot," she confessed. "Besides, I didn't know I would be coming until yesterday, when father finally agreed to let me go."

Emily sighed and sat down next to Imaiqah. "How are things in Alexis?"

"Good enough," Alassa said. "Father wanted me to hear a couple of complex court cases, but the lawyers have been very inventive in coming up with reasons why I shouldn't."

"They remembered you from before Whitehall," Emily commented, dryly.

"Probably," Alassa agreed, ruefully. "How much time did I waste when I was a child?"

She elbowed Jade. "The good news is that this...*person* is now my personal bodyguard," she added. "Father wouldn't let me come here without someone watching my back."

"You mean you convinced him to let you go with a combat sorcerer, instead of a small army," Imaiqah offered. "I thought he was going to ban you from leaving the castle before he finally changed his mind."

Emily lifted her eyebrows. "Why did he change his mind?"

"I'm Confirmed," Alassa said. "I imagine he thought I should be treated as more of an adult now."

"Oh," Emily said. She doubted that was the truth — or *all* of the truth. King Randor should never have let his only heir risk her life, not when there was no one else who could succeed him without triggering a civil war. She glanced at Jade. "He must have been very impressed by you."

"All that arm-wrestling," Alassa said, before Jade could say a word. "It was a dreadful male-bonding experience."

Jade colored. "He *actually* asked me hundreds of questions about my training," he said. He gave Emily a sharp look. "And about you."

Emily frowned. "What did he ask about me?"

"Your life, basically," Jade said. "I had to tell him that I'd only shared one class with you before I went to apprentice under Master Grey."

"He's here," Emily said. "Did you know that?"

Jade shook his head. "Because of me?"

"I think Lady Barb called him," Emily said. She quickly outlined the problems with the Faire. "I'm glad to see you here too."

"Call Sergeant Miles," Jade advised. "There aren't many young combat sorcerers who weren't taught by him, once upon a time. He'd command respect with ease."

"I'll suggest it to Lady Barb," Emily said. But surely Lady Barb would have thought of asking her lover, if she'd thought he'd come. "Do you think I've made a mistake?"

"Yes," Alassa said, flatly. "You are the baroness. You need to live up to the title."

"Lady Barb said the same thing," Emily said.

"She was right," Alassa said.

Emily shook her head slowly. "Is it wrong of me to want to give up the title?"

"Alicia would give her...her maidenhead to get her title confirmed," Alassa said, sarcastically. "And you just want to abandon it?"

"I'm not suited to this life," Emily said.

"My father said the same thing," Imaiqah said. "But he's doing better, now that he's organized himself."

"Your father knew how to run a small business," Emily countered. "I don't know how to run my own life, let alone the lives of thousands of others."

"Yes." Alassa raised her eyebrows in emulation of Lady Barb. "I heard about your judgements. The broadsheets were full of them."

"Some people agreed with you," Imaiqah added. "But others thought you acted badly."

"The marvels of a free press," Emily muttered. Somehow, she doubted the other barons would be anything but amused at the outcome. "How did I act badly?"

"You chose to alter the terms of a contract, after the contract was signed," Alassa said. "It didn't exactly *break* the contract, but it did upset the signers. Then you chose to turn a law intended to prevent farmers from dividing their lands on its head, by choosing the person you wanted to inherit, rather than the person who should legally have inherited."

"But he abandoned his claim," Emily said. "Even his own father told him he'd abandoned the farm and everyone on it. All he wanted was land. How was I wrong?"

"I don't think you were," Imaiqah commented. "But messing with the inheritance principle could be dangerous."

Emily scowled. "I did the right thing."

"You still have to live with the consequences," Alassa pointed out.

"You've had years to study the history of this country, the laws and judgements, the precedents and exemptions," Emily snapped. "I haven't had time."

"Then *make* the time," Alassa said. "Or allow my father to send someone to act in your name."

Emily considered it, seriously. It was tempting...but who would King Randor send to govern her Barony? Would it be someone smart enough to keep up with the reforms she'd championed, or would it be someone bent on rolling them back? She wasn't blind to some of the long-term implications of the changes she'd made...and, after the printing press had blossomed into life, nor were most of the aristocracy.

"I'll think about it," she said, slowly.

"I suggest you do," Alassa said. "But if you gave up power, the title would be largely worthless."

Emily nodded. There was no shortage of exaggerated titles in the Nameless World, now the emperor and his family were gone. A person could call himself Lord High Admiral and Noble Ruler of the Seven Seas, if he wished, and no one could deny him. But if the title came with no power, it would be effectively meaningless. She might be baroness in name, if she gave up the power, but she wouldn't have any power to change the world. Or even to defend herself.

*But King Randor is cutting back on our ability to raise independent forces of our own,* she thought. It was hard to blame the king, but she'd heard rumors that some of the barons had returned to their plotting. *And what will that do to the kingdom, in the future?*

She pushed the thought aside and leaned forward. "Are you going to stay for the entire Faire?"

"Unless there is real trouble," Jade said, firmly. He gave Alassa a sidelong look when she seemed inclined to protest. "I gave your father my oath that I would protect you, and I meant it."

"She has a habit of leading us into danger," Emily said. "Or at least into pointless duels with Melissa." She shook her head. "Melissa is going to be coming, by the way. Please don't pick a fight with her."

"I won't," Alassa said. She gave Jade a wink. "I think he's just waiting for a chance to lock me in a room, under the guise of protecting me."

"It would keep you safe," Jade said, deadpan.

"It would also be boring," Alassa said.

Emily winced, inwardly. She knew that some noble families considered it better to have their women neither seen nor heard. The girls were kept in their castles and rarely even presented at court, at least until their marriages were already arranged. Would Alassa have been trapped in her room, if her father had managed to sire a son? Or would she have merely gone to Whitehall and never looked back?

"You should order her to stay in her room," Jade said, to Emily. He winked, mischievously. "This is your castle."

"I value my sanity," Emily said.

"Quite right," Alassa agreed. "And besides, I know a dozen good blasting spells. The walls wouldn't survive more than one or two."

"Please don't wreck my castle," Emily said. Inwardly, she recalled Mother Holly smashing through a castle's walls as though they were made of paper. Cockatrice Castle looked strong, but she had no illusions about how long it would survive if a necromancer decided he wanted to destroy it. "I'm sure we can keep you safe here."

"I'm not," Jade said. "There are two families who happen to hate each other on their way. Most of them are powerful and well-trained magicians. Then there are quite a few other magicians who might want to settle grudges against their fellows here, once they see how few security people you have on staff. And then there's the normal run of thieves, conmen and duelists who want to duke it out in public to see who has the bigger pair. It's a recipe for disaster."

Alassa gave him a brilliant, teasing smile. "What happened to the Jade who went into the Forest of Shadows to recover a missing girl?"

"He didn't have to worry about the safety of a princess," Jade pointed out. "I was on my own, free of all obligations to protect anyone else."

Emily blinked. "What did you do?"

"We — Master Grey and I — walked around the edge of the forest," Jade said. "There was a small town in mourning, because the headman's daughter had been lured into the forest."

"It's a place infused with wild magic," Alassa explained. "Someone who goes into the Forest of Shadows might not come out again."

"I couldn't leave her in the forest," Jade said. "So I went, found her and brought her back home."

"Why do I have the feeling," Emily asked, "that there's a great deal of the story you're not telling me?"

"Because there are things in there I don't want to remember," Jade said. For a moment, his eyes looked haunted. "I found the girl, brought her back and left the forest behind. And yet, it still left a mark on my soul."

Emily nodded in understanding, one hand playing with the snake-bracelet. She still had nightmares about the Cairngorms, although they tended to focus on what humans did to their fellow humans, rather than magical creatures and waves of wild magic. Human cruelty was so much worse, somehow, than anything else she'd seen.

"But enough of that," Alassa said. "I understand that Caleb has arrived?"

Emily blinked. "How did you know?"

"Lady Barb told us," Imaiqah said. "I don't think I ever saw him in Dragon's Den. What's he like?"

Emily hesitated. "Studious," she said, finally. "And smart. Very smart."

"As smart as you?" Imaiqah asked. "Should we start planning the wedding now?"

"*No*," Emily said. She felt her cheeks heat as her friends giggled. "We only met today!"

"At least you met him," Alassa commented. "Some people get married without ever meeting their partner, at least until the day of their wedding. And some people get married without meeting their partner at all."

Emily rubbed her flaming cheeks. "We're going to do a project together," she protested. "A project! And you have us practically married off!"

"You could always go on a double-date with me and..."

"And who?" Alassa asked sweetly. "What's his name? What's his name, Mark II? You know who? You know who else? You possibly don't know who...?"

Imaiqah blushed prettily. "There's nothing wrong with exploring the possibilities..."

Emily shook her head. Imaiqah had grown and blossomed at Whitehall, becoming friendly and outgoing...words that no one would ever apply to Emily herself. She'd had so many boyfriends that Emily had lost count, yet she didn't seem to have fallen in love with any of them. Emily, on the other hand, couldn't bear the thought of dating someone she didn't know, personally, beforehand.

She carefully didn't look at Jade. He'd kissed her once, and she'd let him. And he'd asked her to marry him. But she knew now it would have been a disaster. She was flattered that he'd asked, yet she knew she couldn't have married him. It would definitely have been awkward.

*And that*, she told herself, *is one hell of an understatement.*

"Just be careful," Alassa advised. "My mother was *very* frank about the dangers."

Imaiqah nodded. "I use potions," she said. "And other precautions."

She looked at Emily. "This is the first time I think you've worked with a young man of about the same age," she said. "Be open, but be careful."

"We're working on a project," Emily repeated. She'd liked what she'd seen of Caleb, but she had no idea if he was always like that. Her stepfather had been charming too, until he'd convinced Emily's mother to marry him. And then he'd turned into a monster. "I don't know if we will have any other relationship."

"Take it as it comes," Imaiqah advised. She glanced at Alassa. "Or will your father try to have a say?"

"I don't think he could," Alassa said. "Emily isn't his daughter or one of his wards. And her...*father* might not be inclined to let *my* father try to marry her off."

Emily frowned. "Do the other barons need the king's approval to marry?"

"Depends who they want to marry," Alassa said. "If they wanted to marry me or the wards...or my aunt, before I killed her...they'd need his permission. I think any marriages that might bind two estates together would also need the king's permission. Emily would probably need his permission if she wanted to marry Baron Silver."

"That is not a pleasant thought," Emily said. Baron Silver was old enough to be her father, if he'd started early, and only escaped execution through proving he knew nothing of his father's plot. Unfortunately, as a Confirmed heir, he couldn't be kept from claiming the rank and title. "He's far too old."

"But you have huge tracts of land," Alassa said, blandly. "And so does he."

Emily cringed, mentally.

There was a tap at the door. "Begging your pardon, my ladies, my lord, but dinner is about to be served," Janice said. "Please would you make your way to the small dining room?"

"Thank you," Emily said. She rose, wondering briefly where Frieda had gone. Lady Barb might have found something for her to do, or she might just have found a book and started to read. "We'll be down in a few minutes."

Alassa caught Emily's eye as Janice retreated. "You're really not comfortable here, are you?"

Emily swore, inwardly. Alassa was more perceptive than most people realized. Even before Emily had told her the truth about Earth, she'd still realized that Emily knew very little of the Nameless World. Alassa had grown up with servants tending to her at all times, helping her to undress and wash herself before dressing again, but Emily...Emily was used to doing things by herself.

"No," she admitted, finally. "I will never be used to having servants."

Dinner was a surprisingly cheerful affair. Alassa and Imaiqah chatted happily to Frieda and made plans to spend tomorrow having fun, while Jade chatted to Caleb and Lady Barb watched them all, her blue eyes revealing nothing of her innermost thoughts. Emily forced herself to relax and eat as much as she could. The first guests were due to arrive tomorrow, and she would need to be ready to greet them. It wasn't going to be easy.

"The last time we had a transfer student," Alassa said, "she turned out to be a spy. What about you?"

It took Emily a moment to realize she was talking to Caleb, who took it in good part.

"I have better things to do with my time than spy on Whitehall," he said. "Besides, I don't think anyone at Stronghold really cares enough to send a spy."

"That could be just what they want you to think," Alassa countered. "Or they could have sent another student to spy on us — and you."

Emily sighed inwardly. Alassa knew the meaning of the word *tact*, but she rarely used it.

"As far as I know, I'm the only transfer student from Stronghold," Caleb said. "And I don't think they would have let me go if they'd valued my mind."

"I heard that Sergeant Harkin graduated from Stronghold," Jade said, entering the conversation. "Is that actually true?"

Caleb smiled. "Would you know the name of every halfway famous student who left Whitehall?"

"Maybe not," Emily said. She knew of some who could be considered famous — or infamous, in Shadye's case — but she had to admit she didn't know everyone who had graduated. The only reason she knew a handful of Jade's contemporaries was through Martial Magic. "But Sergeant Harkin was special."

"I don't know if Stronghold considered him special," Caleb said, softly. "We are only told to honor those who served in our regiments. I don't recall any *Harkin* being mentioned on the rolls, during Memorial Day."

*Their loss*, Emily thought. She still mourned Sergeant Harkin, who'd given his life to save hers. *They should remember him.*

The conversation lasted long into the night, only ending when Lady Barb dryly reminded everyone that they would have to be up the following morning. Emily rose, called the maids to show the others to their bedrooms, and walked slowly back to her own rooms. It was funny, but the castle felt livelier now that her friends had arrived.

She stopped at her door and touched the cold stone. It was an honor, she knew, to be a baroness...but it was also a prison. If she chose to remain at a distance, she would have to run the risk of Bryon making mistakes...and if she chose to stay in Cockatrice, she would never be able to leave. And she really *wasn't* suited for this life.

"I can't stay here," she muttered. "But where can I go?"

There were options. Whitehall felt like home...and there were other places she could live, if she wished. But what did she want to do with her life?

*Magic*, she thought. *But I need to do more than just magic.*

Shaking her head, she opened the door and walked inside. Her room felt warm and welcoming, yet it didn't quite feel like *hers*. Emily sat down on the bed, undressed quickly, then climbed under the covers. Lady Barb had been right, she knew. She would need her rest.

Tomorrow, everything was going to become more than a little hectic.

# Chapter Fourteen

"THE ROOMS ARE ALL READY," BRYON ASSURED HER AFTER BREAKFAST. "THEY'VE BEEN cleaned as you ordered, and the maids have been given their orders."

"Good," Emily said. The castle could hold nearly a hundred guests, which was fortunate; Bryon had assigned every last one of the guestrooms. He'd even hired extra maids and manservants to assist with the guests. She couldn't help thinking that he would make a much better ruler of the barony than her. "Remind them of the rules when dealing with magical visitors."

"It has been done," Bryon told her. "All is in readiness."

Emily nodded, tiredly. She hadn't slept well.

"Emily," Lady Barb said, walking up to them. "We need to discuss the other arrangements for the guests."

"I know," Emily said. "I'm coming."

She'd hoped to spend an hour or two with Caleb, or even work on her own projects, but it was not to be. Lady Barb talked her through everything from basic security to what to do if there was an emergency, then Bryon wanted her to approve the dinner menu and authorize additional expenses for some of the guests. Emily couldn't help wondering if the barony was going to be in debt after the Faire was over, even if they didn't spend any more money than they'd spent already. It seemed unlikely that the money they made through hosting the Faire could meet their expenditures.

But when she asked, Bryon disagreed. "It shouldn't be a problem," he assured her. "We get a small commission on everything sold at the Faire, as well as the flat fee for allowing the merchants to set up their stalls in our territory."

Emily sighed. "I hope so," she said, as she sensed the wards flicker. The first set of guests had started to arrive, on schedule. "We're out of time."

She allowed Bryon to lead her back to the Great Hall, where she sat on her throne-like chair and watched as the first set of guests were ushered into the hall. It was custom, Lady Barb had told her, for the host to greet the most important sets of guests personally, which very definitely included both the Ashworth and Ashfall Families. Thankfully, she'd gone on to say, most of the remaining guests would understand why Emily had granted the two families precedence; they wouldn't expect her to greet them, although they *would* expect her to say a few words to them during social gatherings.

"If I ever even think of hosting anything like this, again," she muttered to Lady Barb, "tell me to my face I'm being an idiot."

"My Lady Emily, Necromancer's Bane, Baroness of Cockatrice," the herald thundered, "I present to you Fulvia, Matriarch of House Ashworth; Balbus, Patriarch of House Ashworth, Caelian of House Ashworth, Melissa of House Ashworth and Iulius of House Ashworth."

Emily straightened up in her chair as the Ashworth grandees came into view. She knew Melissa already from Whitehall, but the others were new to her. Fulvia was the oldest woman Emily had ever seen, perhaps even older than Void, yet her back was straight and her eyes were bright with cold calculation. Emily shivered. Fulvia looked *formidable*, the sort of person who would always get their way, whatever the cost.

Beside Fulvia, her son — Balbus — looked more like a professor than a patriarch. Indeed, if Emily hadn't taken the time to look the family up in the record books, she would have mistaken the white-haired gentleman for Fulvia's *husband* rather than son. There was something kindly about his face, but also something else that disturbed her, even though she couldn't put her finger on it. He leaned on a staff and smiled at her, vaguely.

Caelian, Melissa's mother, didn't look happy. Emily met her eyes for a brief second, wondering if it was her fault somehow, but it didn't seem to be the case. Caelian looked no older than Lady Barb, with long red hair that fell to her knees, yet there was something about her gaze that suggested the fire had long since gone out of her. Melissa half-hid behind her mother, her expression sulky. Emily couldn't help feeling a flicker of amusement. For Melissa to have to pay court to someone she saw as a rival, if not an enemy, had to be a humiliation in and of itself. And her younger brother, standing beside his mother, seemed almost bored.

"I welcome you to Cockatrice," she said, politely.

"We thank you," Fulvia said. Her voice was cool, collected...and surprisingly young. "We pledge to hold our hands in your house."

Emily nodded. The ritual words still sounded odd to her, but she knew their underlying meaning. Her guests wouldn't start fights with her other guests — or her. If, of course, they could be trusted. The rivalry between the houses made the Capulets and Montagues sound like amateurs. She glanced briefly at Melissa and frowned, inwardly, as she realized that something was bothering her rival. Something more, she suspected, than merely having to bow to Emily. But there was no time to figure out what it was.

"Then I will have my people show you to your rooms," she said. Bryon had given each member of the family a private room, although Emily had a feeling that Fulvia would demand access to all of them. There was something about the woman that suggested she would be incredibly controlling. "And I will see you all formally at the dinner and dance tonight."

"We thank you," Fulvia repeated. "Others will be arriving later. Have them sent to our rooms."

Emily felt a flicker of irritation at the blunt command. Did Fulvia think *Emily* was a servant — or one of her family? Or was she making a power play, right in front of the rest of her family and Emily's friends?

"If that is what they wish," Emily said finally, "that is what we shall do."

Fulvia eyed her for a long moment, and nodded once, curtly. She turned and strode majestically out of the room, to where the maids were waiting. Her family turned in unison and followed her, apart from Melissa, who shot Emily an unreadable glance before turning herself. Emily felt a shiver run down her spine as the Ashworth Family left the Great Hall.

"That could have gone worse," Lady Barb commented, from the sidelines. "You need to watch those people, though. They're used to claiming every advantage they can."

"I noticed," Emily said. She was surprised to discover she was sweating. "Are they going to cause trouble?"

"I doubt they will try to cause trouble for you personally," Lady Barb said. "But they may succeed in causing trouble anyway."

Emily nodded, sat back on the hard chair, and thought hard. Their names had sounded *Roman*, save for Melissa; indeed, there was a considerable amount of Greco-Roman influence in parts of the Nameless World. Coincidence? Her memory playing tricks on her? Or was it something else? She had long since concluded that humanity couldn't be native to the Nameless World, not when evolution had produced creatures like dragons and other monsters right out of fantasy novels. And she, of all people, knew it was possible to move from one dimension to another.

*And Melissa might actually be derived from a Roman name*, she thought, as the wards shimmered again. *It must have been long enough for languages to change quite a bit, before the Empire froze everything in place.*

"My Lady Emily, Necromancer's Bane, Baroness of Cockatrice," the herald thundered once again. "I present to you Marcellus, Patriarch of House Ashfall; Lady Nova of No Name; Markus of House Ashfall, Maximus of House Ashfall and Maxima of House Ashfall."

Emily smiled as the Ashfall Family stepped into her hall. Marcellus looked younger than his rival, a tall thin man with a long brown beard and thin, almost feminine hands. Beside him, his wife looked slight, her dark hair shading to grey. She couldn't help smiling in welcome at Markus, then glancing at his younger brother and sister. The two children, too young to have developed magic of their own, looked almost like twins. If Maximus hadn't been a head taller than Maxima, she would have believed them to be the same age.

"My Lady Emily," Marcellus said. He had a gravelly voice that reminded Emily of Professor Lombardi, although it was clear he was trying to be friendly. "My son speaks highly of you."

Emily felt her cheeks heat as she looked at Markus, who winked. The last time they'd met, it had been just before Mountaintop had been exposed to the world... and *that* had been Emily's fault. Markus had never struck her as a bad person and he'd given her a great deal of useful advice, but she knew he might resent her turning Mountaintop upside down. And yet, there was no trace of any of that on his face. Indeed, he seemed almost pleased to meet her again.

"I thank him," Emily said, flustered. "I welcome you to Cockatrice."

"We thank you," Marcellus said. He paused, significantly. "Am I to understand that we will be sharing quarters with the Ashworth Family?"

"You will be sharing the same castle," Emily said, carefully. "But you will not have to share the same rooms."

Markus snickered. His father glowered at him before looking back at Emily.

"That is fortunate," he said, dryly. "I would not care to share a bedroom with *dear* Fulvia."

"You won't have to," Emily said. She tried to imagine the ancient woman's reaction to having to share a room with her dread rival, but decided it would probably bring the castle tumbling down on top of her. "You each have your own apartments within the castle."

"We *definitely* thank you," Marcellus said. "And we pledge to hold our hands in your house."

Markus nodded. "I hope I will have the chance to speak with you later, Lady Emily," he said. "I have messages for you."

"We will talk after dinner," Emily promised.

"We have other guests coming," Marcellus said. "Please, will you have them shown to our rooms?"

Emily's lips twitched. At least he was politer than Fulvia.

"I will have them sent to you, once they've had a chance to freshen up," she said, simply.

"I thank you," Marcellus said. He shook his head. "Inviting both us and the Ashworths. I could think of few braver things to do. You are truly Void's daughter."

Emily blushed. *That's probably the nicest way to put it*, she thought.

"We will attend your dinner and perhaps, if these old bones are up to it, dance," Marcellus continued. "Until then, it was our pleasure to meet you."

He bowed, turned, and walked out of the room. His wife and younger children followed him at once, but Markus hesitated before following them. Melissa had done the same, Emily recalled. It was an odd coincidence. If, indeed, it *was* a coincidence. Melissa, like Markus, might have preferred talking to Emily to staying with her family. She certainly hadn't *looked* very happy.

Lady Barb cast a privacy ward as soon as Markus was out of sight, then stepped forward so she was facing Emily. "Question time," she announced. "What was actually happening there?"

Emily took a moment to think about it. "He was trying to befriend me," she said. "Or at least trying to get on my good side."

"Correct," Lady Barb said. "Marcellus is a manipulator, Emily; there isn't a single person at that level who *isn't* a manipulator. He will want you to like him because it will make it easier for him to influence your thoughts and feelings. Do *not* make the mistake of thinking he's a decent person because he acts like a decent person."

Emily swallowed. Her mouth was suddenly dry. "Why...?"

"Do I feel that way?" Lady Barb finished. "Do you recall, last year, that I told you that Alassa would not be welcome at the Faire?"

"You did," Emily recalled. "Something about her inheriting her power?"

"Correct," Lady Barb said. "Alassa never had to struggle to rise to power within her family, Emily. Marcellus — and Fulvia — unquestionably *did* have to struggle for power, first to grasp it and then to keep it. There are cadet branches of the family who would happily seize the chance to put forward a rival Patriarch or Matriarch, if they thought the ones in charge were losing their grip. The strong survive, while the weak...are pushed aside."

"You're stronger than me," Emily said. "But would you be stronger than my entire year, put together?"

Lady Barb snorted. "The day I can't handle a schoolroom of whining brats is the day I cut off my hair and sell myself into slavery," she said, darkly. "But you have touched upon the crux of the matter. Fulvia and Marcellus will be skilled at getting others to support them – that, too, is a form of strength — as well as being strong themselves."

She took a breath. "Tell me something," she added. "Why is there so much bitterness and hatred between the families?"

"Master Grey said..."

"No, not the story," Lady Barb interrupted. "The underlying truth."

Emily shook her head. She didn't know.

"There is an agreement among most magical families that...there are limits to how much infighting is tolerated," Lady Barb pointed out. "You weren't born to one, so you won't know, but most of our internal struggles were verbal arguments, rather than magical duels for supremacy. Once I was an adult, I was invited to take my place in the family council and add my voice to the debates."

She shrugged. "You know how my father was treated. I wasn't really interested in steering the family, not when I could move away from it.

"But for one family to split into two, for dozens of people to simply walk away from the original family...that is largely unprecedented. The agreements binding the family together should not have allowed it. Whatever the council decided, the entire family should have accepted. Whatever happened, whatever the root cause of the split, it sent shockwaves through the entire community. It should not have been possible."

"But it happened," Emily said, quietly. "Why?"

"If we knew that," Lady Barb said, "we might know just what went on in the first place."

Emily considered the problem. "Can someone leave the family? I mean...without suffering any ill-effects?"

"Someone can leave simply by renouncing his ties to the family," Lady Barb said, flatly. "But he wouldn't be able to call on the family in the future. He would be an outcast, to all intents and purposes, a wandering magician on his own. It happens, and more often than you might think, but never on such a large scale."

Emily stood and started to pace. "What do I do now?"

"You serve as host, you talk nicely to both of them, and you pray some young idiot doesn't start a fight," Lady Barb said. She paused as the wards tingled around them.

"And some of your other guests have arrived. You'll probably need to say hello to them, too."

She was right, Emily discovered, as the herald showed a line of men and women, all magicians, into the Great Hall. Some of them had links to the Ashworth or Ashfall Families — Emily was amused and horrified to meet Steven of House Lansdale for the second time in her life — while others were independents, or came from other families. Steven explained, with a glint in his eye, that he'd come to support Markus, but he too would like to have a chat with Emily at some point. Emily sighed inwardly, but agreed. There was no point in trying to put it off.

Later, she allowed Lady Barb to lead her on a roving patrol through the castle. It was almost as chaotic as Whitehall on the day the students came back to school; maids and menservants were everywhere, carrying trunks through the building and placing them in different rooms, while the guests watched and chattered, catching up on affairs. Emily wasn't surprised; she'd learned, from the last Faire she'd attended, that magicians loved to chat and spread rumors. She would have been happier about it if she hadn't known that most of them were chatting about *her*.

The wards tingled in alarm. Lady Barb sensed it, too; she glanced sharply at Emily before plunging down the corridor towards one of the smaller guest rooms. Emily followed, cursing under her breath. Someone had just used magic on someone else. Lady Barb stepped into the room, then stopped. A tall man with a thin, cruel face was peering down at the floor, where a trembling frog sat.

"Using magic on the maids is not permitted," Lady Barb snapped.

"She dropped my trunk," the man said. His voice was very calm, but there was an undertone of entitlement that made Emily wince. "I have the right to punish her."

"No, you don't," Emily said, stepping past Lady Barb. Using magic on magicians was one thing, but using it on helpless maids was quite another. "If you have a problem with one of my servants, you bring it to me."

"I am Gaius, of House Arlene," the man said. He hadn't been important enough to be shown into the Great Hall, before he'd been escorted to his rooms. "And who might you be?"

Emily silently cursed the rumors — and the paintings — under her breath. She knew she didn't look impressive, but surely the artists could have made the paintings reasonably accurate. No one would recognize her if they weren't introduced to her...

"I am Emily, Necromancer's Bane and Baroness of Cockatrice," she said. She held the older man's eye, unwilling to back down. "I will not have my servants abused."

Gaius eyed her for a long moment, then bowed and snapped his fingers. The frog shimmered, then popped up into a terrified-looking maid. Emily winced in sympathy — she'd been scared too, when she'd been transfigured for the first time — and shot her a reassuring look. The maid had to have thought that no one would ever recognize her.

"As you wish, my lady," Gaius said.

Emily scowled at him. She had a feeling he was going to be trouble.

# Chapter Fifteen

"FOR THE DAUGHTER OF THE MOST POWERFUL SORCERER KNOWN TO EXIST," FULVIA SAID, AS the servants started serving dinner, "you seem remarkably shy. I don't believe that anyone knew you existed before your arrival at Whitehall."

Emily groaned, inwardly. She had hoped that seating Marcellus on her left and Fulvia on her right would help defuse tensions, during dinnertime, but she hadn't realized that both of them would take the opportunity to pump her for information.

"I didn't develop magic until I was sixteen," she said, which was true enough. "And my father sent me straight to Whitehall."

"He never told anyone he had a daughter," Fulvia said. Her brown eyes probed Emily's face, watching for signs she wasn't being completely honest. "I would have expected him to shout your birth — and survival — to the entire world."

"My father is a very private man," Emily said. It was true, too; her *real* father had abandoned his family so long ago she barely remembered him. "He wouldn't want to share anything of himself with the world."

"But a daughter...Void could have taught you himself," Fulvia pressed.

"He isn't a very good teacher," Emily said. Void had admitted it himself, back when they'd first met. Lady Barb had confirmed it, later. Void was one of the strongest known magicians, a Lone Power, but a poor teacher. "I think he thought I should have a proper grounding in the magical arts."

"That was wise," Fulvia said. "But it is also irresponsible of him to let you walk out on your own. *My* children and grandchildren know better than to act without consulting me."

Emily felt a brief flicker of sympathy for Melissa. Emily's mother might have largely ignored her daughter, but it was clear Melissa had suffered from too much supervision in her life. Perhaps she hadn't known any real freedom, any real chance to make up her own mind, until she'd gone to Whitehall. The price of having a real family had been a complete lack of real independence, or even freedom of choice. It wasn't a pleasant thought.

"I believe my father figures I am old enough to handle myself," Emily said, instead.

"How careless," Marcellus offered. "You kill a necromancer, thwart a coup, become a baroness, kill a Mimic, kill another necromancer, leave a school in ruins...I'm starting to think you shouldn't have been allowed out of his tower, let alone left to *handle yourself.*"

He had a point, Emily knew. Void might never have claimed to be Emily's father, but everyone believed it, knowing that power didn't come from nowhere. She had a feeling the Grandmaster had encouraged the rumors, in the hopes they would give Emily additional protection. But, in truth, Emily was not his daughter. He had shown concern for her, in the past, but how far did that go?

*He never seemed to care that people were branding me his daughter,* she thought. *But I only made his reputation more fearsome.*

"My father believes in the school of hard knocks," she said. "I have to learn through doing."

"But you will make mistakes, of course," Fulvia said. "He should offer you firm, but considerate, guidance."

Emily shrugged before looking around the dining hall. It was still decorated in the manner the previous baron had preferred; the stone walls were covered in animal heads, tastefully preserved to show off the baron's hunting skills. Emily had never seen the attraction of chasing deer through the woods, let alone wild boar and a handful of magical creatures; her one experience with hunting for fun had been quite bad enough. Dozens of servants brought in plates of food and drink, while the guests ate, drank and chatted away. She couldn't help noticing that cliques had already started to form, with the Ashworths leading one group and the Ashfalls leading the other. That promised trouble in the not-so-distant future.

She caught sight of Melissa and frowned, inwardly. Melissa was sitting next to her younger brother, barely touching her food. It wasn't as if she couldn't eat, Emily was sure; she'd taken pains to ensure that a wide range of food and drink was served, instead of the standard roast meat, potatoes and vegetables that seemed to dominate local tables. Indeed, after some explanation, she'd even managed to convince the cooks to produce pizza! But Melissa still wasn't eating.

"My great-granddaughter is to marry," Fulvia said, following Emily's gaze. "She will meet her husband tonight."

Emily blinked. "You're choosing her husband for her?"

"The family picked a suitable man," Fulvia said. "I was surprised your father did not respond to my letters, requesting he considered bequeathing your hand in marriage to one of my great-nephews."

"My father thought I should choose my own husband," Emily snapped, feeling a hot flash of anger. Void had told her he'd received such letters, years ago, and she'd asked him to burn them. "I think he incinerated the letters."

"You could not possibly make a decent choice for yourself," Fulvia said. She showed no reaction to Emily's anger. "Marriage is for life, not for some...*passion*...that will burn itself out, given time. It is far more important to choose a husband who will give you good children, like my sons and grandsons."

"And yet, one must offer the illusion of free choice," Marcellus put in. "Children become far more temperamental when they think they're being dictated to."

"Nonsense," Fulvia said, evenly. "Illusions are eventually dispelled by the cold hard light of reality. Better to start without any illusions and work from there."

Emily felt another flicker of pity, for Markus as well as Melissa. Both of them would have their elders deciding their marriage partners, perhaps — in Markus's case — with the illusion of free choice. She couldn't help wondering just what would happen when — or if — the illusion fell apart. Would there be an almighty fight, followed by a separation, or would the married couple merely have affairs on the side?

The dinner wore on until, finally, the dessert was served. Emily took a small portion of Summer Pudding for herself, casting another glance at Melissa. The girl wasn't eating anything, not even the sweet treats Emily knew Melissa loved. Both Fulvia and Marcellus had taken considerable portions for themselves, reflecting just how much magic they needed to use on a daily basis. The power had to come from somewhere.

"If you will excuse me," Fulvia said, once the dinner was finished. "I need to speak to Melissa."

Emily watched her go, and turned her attention to the servants as they hastily pushed the tables against the wall or carried them out of the hall. A band took up their position in the far corner, casting a handful of spells to ensure that everyone could hear their music before they actually started to play. Emily rose to her feet and nodded at Alassa, who had been chatting to Imaiqah and Jade. Beside them, Caleb looked thoroughly out of place.

"You haven't done badly," Alassa assured her, as the band started to play. Couples formed up on the dance floor, spinning to the music. "All you have to do is keep them from killing each other for the next two weeks."

Emily groaned as she looked at the dancers. It was clear there was *some* tension in the air; junior Ashworths were glaring at junior Ashfalls, while their seniors were trying hard to put a damper on problems. A handful of minor arguments broke out as the first dance came to an end, then faded away as the second tune began. Alassa gave Emily a quick hug, waved to Jade, and led him onto the dance floor. Emily was almost tempted to invite Caleb to dance with her...

She frowned as she caught sight of Fulvia, Melissa...and, to her surprise, Gaius. The three were talking together, their voices obscured by a privacy ward. Emily narrowed her eyes, frowning as two middle-aged members of the rival families started snapping at one another, followed by pushing and shoving. Lady Barb descended on them like an angel of vengeance and separated them by force. No one seemed inclined to take the matter any further.

"Lady Emily," Markus said, as he separated himself from the crowd and walked up to her. "Do you have a moment to talk?"

"I dare say," Emily said. At Lady Barb's advice, she'd put a number of rooms near the Great Hall aside for private wheeling and dealing. "Will Steven wish to accompany us?"

"I don't think so," Markus said. "He will want to talk to you later."

*Politics*, Emily thought, sourly. Steven was the Head of Crystal Quarrel — or had been, given that he'd been a Sixth Year student at Mountaintop while Emily had been there — and he probably wanted to see where Emily stood, now she was back at Whitehall. In hindsight, Master Grey's advice had been very good indeed.

"Come with me," she said, and led the way through a doorway. Two of the rooms were already occupied, sealed tight with magic; a third lay open and unclaimed. Emily closed the door, cast a handful of privacy spells, and then took a seat. "It's been a few months."

"Yes, yes it has," Markus said. He gave her a beaming smile. "I bring you greetings, felicitations, and curses from the MageMaster of Mountaintop."

"Zed," Emily recalled. It had been *her* fault he'd become MageMaster. "He sent me curses?"

"I think that while he likes some of the perks of the job, he resents the time it takes from his own studies," Markus said. "But he has been something of an improvement over Aurelius's stewardship."

Emily wasn't too surprised. Aurelius had been ambitious; he'd intended to become MageMaster as part of a plan to eventually reshape the Allied Lands. Zed, on the other hand, had no interests beyond pure magical research. And, despite having good reason to dislike Emily, he'd actually been an effective teacher. She might just have finally begun the process of mastering alchemy, thanks to his patient tutelage.

"I'm glad to hear that," she said. She wondered, briefly, just how much else Markus might know. The dread secret of Mountaintop was known to a scant few. "What else did he tell you to say?"

"Apparently, he's begun negotiations with Red Rose," Markus said. "He was quite clear I was to mention that to you, but he didn't give me any other details."

*The nexus point*, Emily thought.

"I see," she said, out loud. "And Nanette?"

"Missing, presumed rogue," Markus said. "She must have made her escape once the wards fell, as we never found her body. Aurelius was found dead in his chamber, near his daughter. Did you kill him?"

Emily shook her head. "He was unconscious the last time I saw him," she said. "How did he die?"

"Magical burns were found all over his body," Markus said. "Someone wanted to make very certain he was dead."

"It wasn't me," Emily said.

She ran through a short list of suspects, but came up with nothing. Anyone who learned the truth would want to kill him, starting with the friends and relatives of the students he'd fed to the school's wards. Maybe it had been Master Grey, who'd graduated from Mountaintop years ago. He'd been shocked to learn the truth...

*Or Void*, she thought. *He did say he had business to complete at Mountaintop.*

"I'm glad to hear it," Markus said. "You'll be interested to know that Aurelius changed his will, two weeks before he died. He left you his private library. However, as many of those texts are either rare or unique — and most of them are very dark — the MageMaster is reluctant to let them out of his sight."

Emily stared at him. "He left them to me?"

"He did," Markus confirmed. "Didn't he mention it to you?"

"No," Emily said. She frowned, puzzled. Aurelius had granted her access to his library, a gift beyond price, but he'd never suggested that he would leave her anything in his will. And yet...maybe it had been a planned attempt to make trouble for his successor, if his plan went off the rails. "I never thought I had a claim."

"Well, you do," Markus said. He sighed, then spoke with the air of one reciting a memorized message. "The MageMaster thinks it would be unwise for a nineteen-year-old girl, who has yet to complete her formal training, to have possession of the books. However, he has no grounds to stop you from taking them. He would like to propose a compromise."

Emily frowned. She practically *collected* books, now she had the money to fund her habit. It wasn't in her to just surrender an entire library, even if she hadn't known she owned it until now. Zed had to be trying to take a subtle revenge...or, perhaps, he was genuinely concerned. She *had* promoted him, after all.

"A compromise," she repeated. "What sort of compromise does he have in mind?"

"He would like to keep them at Mountaintop, where they will be secure," Markus said. "You will have the freedom of the school, able to come and go as you please, allowing you to consult them whenever you wish. In addition, you would have access to the school's library at all levels."

"I will have to consider it," Emily said.

She drew in her breath. It was a tempting offer, on the face of it, but simply *getting* to Mountaintop presented a whole series of problems. She didn't have the power to teleport, which meant she would need assistance in teleporting to the school, and using portals presented their own problems. On the other hand, there *were* volumes at Mountaintop that weren't duplicated at Whitehall. Having the ability to read them, and other books that were normally considered above her level, was very tempting indeed.

"Please inform the MageMaster that he will have his answer at the end of the Faire," she said. "Does he plan to attend personally?"

"I don't believe so," Markus said. "He dislikes politics, I think."

Emily nodded. "Is that everything you wanted to talk about?"

"For the moment," Markus said. He struck a preening pose. "You'll be pleased to hear, despite your...disruption, that I passed my exams with flying colors. You are now looking at a certified sorcerer."

"Very good," Emily said. The magical families had a great deal of influence over Mountaintop, but even they couldn't fiddle with the grading system. Even if they had, fixing a student's grades would have been disastrous in the long run and they were smart enough to know it. "What are you going to do with your life?"

Markus shook his head slowly. "My father expects me to take up his position as Patriarch when he dies, or chooses to lay it down," he said. "It isn't really what I want in life."

"I suppose not," Emily said. "You'd be responsible for maintaining the feud."

"Oh, the stupid feud," Markus snapped, annoyed. "Do you realize how much energy is wasted fighting the Ashworths?"

"Too much," Emily said, quietly. "But why do you fight?"

Markus shrugged. "I was always told that the founder of House Ashfall was unfairly evicted from the family by his brother for daring to question his choices," he said. "The family council was split on the matter and half of the cadet branches decided to declare him the true head of House Ashworth, which was later changed to Ashfall after the original family attempted to break truce and slaughter the rebels."

"And how much of that," Emily asked, "is true?"

"I have no idea," Markus said. He grinned at her. "I was also told that House Ashworth drowns Ashfall babies, then eats them for lunch. Do you think *that's* true?"

"I rather doubt it," Emily said, primly. "What do you think they say about you?"

"Probably the same, just with the names reversed," Markus said. "You'd think we'd notice if we kept losing children." He sighed. "I'd better get back to the dance. Maximus was talking about doing something stupid, and father told me to box his ears if he actually did."

"You were Head Boy," Emily reminded him. "I'm sure you can control an eleven-year-old."

"Maximus knows I'm not allowed to kill him," Markus said, as Emily started to take down the wards. "It makes it harder to intimidate the little brat."

Emily smiled. She'd never had siblings, but Imaiqah had told her that she'd found herself competing with her siblings for very limited attention. It wasn't something she regretted.

She opened the door, looked out, and stopped in surprise. Melissa was leaning against the stone wall, looking tired...and upset. She looked up and scowled when she saw Emily, then looked past her at Markus. And then she struggled to straighten up.

"Emily," she said, tiredly. There was a bitterness in her voice that made Emily shiver. "And who is your friend?"

"Markus, of House Ashfall," Emily said. There was no point in trying to hide Markus's house from her; indeed, she was surprised that Melissa hadn't recognized him. But then, maybe Markus's portraits were as inaccurate as hers. "Markus, this is Melissa, of House Ashworth."

"Pleased to meet you," Markus said. "Do you actually eat babies for breakfast?"

Melissa snickered. "Do you? I was told you prefer them with chilli and raisins."

Emily opened her mouth, but stopped as she felt the wards shimmer again. "I have to go," she said. It crossed her mind that it might not be a good idea to leave them alone together, but she couldn't drag them both with her. "Please don't kill each other."

"I don't think that will be a problem," Melissa said.

"We won't," Markus said. He'd rubbished the whole idea of the feud, minutes ago. "I promise."

Emily nodded, then turned to hurry back to the Great Hall.

# Chapter Sixteen

"A HANDFUL OF MINOR HEXINGS, TWO CURSES, AND SEVERAL LOUD ARGUMENTS," LADY Barb said the following morning, as they walked down towards the Faire. "I expected more trouble, to be honest."

Emily nodded, thankfully. The remainder of the dance had been surprisingly peaceful, largely because Fulvia and Marcellus had glared anyone who felt like picking a fight into uneasy silence. She'd been unable to leave until the end of the dance, whereupon she'd gone straight to bed without bothering to undress, let alone wash. Fortunately, nothing had been planned for breakfast.

She peered down towards the Faire and frowned, inwardly. It had seemed big when they'd arrived, but now it was even bigger, with hundreds of stalls and thousands of people, magical and mundane. A stream of people was moving down from the castle, while another was heading in from the nearby city. Emily hoped, silently, that unfortunate incidents were being kept to a minimum. There was a reason, after all, why such gatherings were normally held far from any mundane settlement.

Frieda caught her arm. "You don't have to do anything today, do you?"

"You do have to host the dance tonight," Lady Barb said, quickly. "But you don't have to make any speeches until then."

"Thank God," Emily said. She knew the morning would be spent at the Faire, but she had plans for the afternoon. Perhaps, if she were lucky, she could make a start on the battery. Or maybe work on Caleb's project. "We can just relax and wander around until lunch."

"If you wish," Lady Barb said. "But I do have to wander through the Faire, keeping an eye on people."

She nodded politely to Emily before hurrying off ahead of them. Emily sighed inwardly, and looked back at her little group. Alassa and Jade looked disgustingly fresh, as always; Emily honestly couldn't remember a time when Alassa had looked anything but beautiful, never a hair out of place. Imaiqah and Caleb, at least, looked as if they hadn't had enough sleep, although Imaiqah hid it well. Emily couldn't help wondering if she'd chosen to break the taboo on using makeup, or if she'd just used a well-constructed glamor. The latter would be quite understandable.

They reached the edge of the Faire and passed through the VIP entrance, guarded by Master Grey. He exchanged a few words with Jade as Emily looked around, drinking in the sights of the Faire. It was definitely larger than the previous one, with hundreds of interesting stalls; in hindsight, perhaps she should have insisted on a private viewing of the bookstalls, before they opened formally. Shaking her head — she knew she would never get used to being an aristocrat — she turned, just in time to see Alassa and Jade heading off on their own.

"They thought it would be less exciting if they went off on their own," Imaiqah said. "She does tend to attract attention."

Emily rolled her eyes. *That* was an understatement. Alassa was stunning...and there were portraits of her scattered all over Zangaria, now she was Confirmed. There wasn't a single person who wouldn't know who the "Duchess of Iron" was, but it would be a very bold or stupid person who tried to kidnap her from the Faire. Jade was a skilled combat sorcerer, Alassa had powerful magic herself, and besides, there was plenty of help within easy shouting distance.

"Come on," she said. She looked up at Caleb, who seemed even more out of place. "Are you going to come with us?"

Caleb hesitated, noticeably. Emily understood. It was easier for an introvert, such as herself, to stay on his own. If she hadn't been so completely unique on the Nameless World, if she hadn't been forced to share a room with her fellow students, she might have remained friendless too, by choice. And Caleb had come late to Whitehall, after friendships and rivalries had already been formed. In many ways, he was even more of an outsider than she was.

"I will," he said, finally.

"Great," Frieda said. "Let's go!"

Emily smiled and allowed Frieda to tug her towards the bookstalls, where hundreds of people had already gathered. Copies of various newly-printed novels, some with lurid covers that made her blush, were selling like hot cakes, while reprints of older books were being scooped up by magicians who would never have been able to afford originals. Frieda headed towards the first stall with grim determination, but stopped dead. Emily realized it was because Frieda didn't have any money.

"Here," Emily said, passing her a handful of gold coins. "Don't spend them all at once."

Frieda frowned, clearly torn between desire for the books and reluctance to accept any form of charity. "You don't have to," she mumbled. "Really."

"Yes, I do," Emily said. She gave the younger girl a gentle push towards the stall. "Just don't spend them all at once."

"That cover is inaccurate," Imaiqah said. She pointed to a thin book with a cover so detailed that Emily couldn't bear to look at it. "No one could do that without warping their own bodies..."

"I don't want to know," Emily said quickly. She shared a look with Caleb and realized he was just as embarrassed. "I *really* don't want to know."

Imaiqah picked up the book and glanced at a handful of pages. "I don't think anyone could do this either, unless they wanted to kill themselves," she said. "And *this* was clearly written by a man pretending to be a woman."

Emily sighed, hastily moving to a stall selling magical textbooks. Most were fairly common, she noted to her disappointment, but a couple were new. The prices, though, were staggeringly high. She made a mental note to look up both of the volumes, just to see if they really were rare or unique, then glanced at a couple of reprints. They were on demand in the library, she knew, and she could use a copy or two of her own.

"I'd like to buy some of these," Caleb said. "Do you want to share?"

Emily blinked, then realized they would be sharing Fourth Year, even if the proposal fell though. They would both need copies. It wouldn't be quite as convenient as having one of her girlfriends own half of the book — she dreaded to think what Madame Beauregard would say if she keyed Caleb into the wards protecting her room, to say nothing of her roommates — but it would be useful. Besides, they were going to be spending a lot of time together.

"Yes, please," she said. She scooped up a handful of volumes and checked her money pouch. "Four gold each?"

"Looks that way," Caleb said. "But try to haggle first."

He stepped forward as the seller wrapped up the books, then started haggling. Emily watched in some amusement; the bookseller demanded ten gold, while Caleb offered one. Eventually, after much bickering, they finally settled on three, then went through another round of arguments over which coins should be accepted. The bookseller weighed the coins, bit them and finally tapped them with a wand, before grudgingly accepting them.

"Definite keeper," Imaiqah muttered in her ear. Emily flinched. She hadn't sensed her friend slipping up behind her. "You would have been overcharged by five gold if he'd just let you have your way."

"I know," Emily said. Bargaining wasn't something she'd learned to do on Earth. But then, the value of coins was always what it said too, rather than going by both weight and the amount of pure gold in the metal. One thing she definitely intended to do, once she was established, was set up a proper bank and begin coining money. "Good thing he was here."

"Quite," Imaiqah said.

Caleb dropped the books into his bag, and followed them as they walked past the next set of stalls, all selling various different kinds of potions or enchanted artefacts. Emily couldn't help noticing that one was manned by Yodel, who'd sold her the first two trunks she'd owned. But she'd also managed to get him into trouble...she knew she should go talk to him, but she didn't want to face him again. She promised herself she'd visit him after the Faire, and walked onwards.

"I think some of those are colored water," Imaiqah commented, pointing at a stall selling love potions. "Anything really strong would be illegal."

Emily nodded. Love potions were almost always forbidden; even brewing the mildest version could get a student in real trouble. They were no better than date rape drugs, she considered...and, for once, the locals agreed. If they weren't used, sometimes, for legitimate purposes, they would be banned outright. The Faire wouldn't tolerate anyone selling *really* strong brews in the open.

"It's a common trick," Caleb said, suddenly. "But they also help people overcome their nerves."

"If they don't know the trick," Emily said. She shook her head. "Placebos only work if someone doesn't know they're useless."

"That smells lovely," Frieda said. She caught Emily's hand and pulled her towards a food stall. "What is that?"

Emily smiled. "Burgers," she said. She had tried to explain the concept to Bryon, last time she'd been in Cockatrice, but she hadn't realized it would spread out of the castle. "Real burgers."

She joined the line of people waiting for a burger, smiling at just how much the cooks had duplicated from Earth. They hadn't produced fast food-sized burgers; they were offering burgers the size of dinner plates, with everything from makeshift relish to mustard and mayonnaise. Large bowls of lettuce, tomato and everything else one could want were piled next to the barbeque, where the burgers were being prepared. She took her burger — the cook's eyes went wide when he finally looked up and saw her; he shoved it at her and refused to take any money — and then loaded it with relish, mustard and lettuce. It tasted heavenly.

"It looks like a giant sandwich," Caleb said. He'd gone to a nearby stall selling fried chicken and, Emily was amused to notice, French Fries. "What does it taste like?"

"Wonderful," Frieda said, between bites.

"You have to make your own," Emily said. It wasn't something she had ever been able to do on Earth. Cheap burgers weren't particularly healthy — or meaty. "Take a burger, pour everything you want into the bun, then eat."

"These are good, too," Caleb said. He held out the paper wrapper of fries. "Try one."

Emily took one of the fries and nibbled it, thoughtfully. It didn't taste anything like she'd expected; it tasted far better. Perhaps it was the open air, she decided, or perhaps it was the natural ingredients. Caleb finished his chicken, then went to get a burger for himself.

"What do you think he would say," Imaiqah asked, "if he knew you'd suggested these foods?"

Emily shrugged. The Allied Lands might have been unified under the Empire, but no one had ever tried to make everyone eat the same foods. Indeed, while the kingdoms tended to stick to their native foods, the city-states were remarkably multicultural. Burgers, pizzas, kebabs and anything else she introduced from Earth would just blur into the mainstream — or vanish, if they didn't find niches of their own. It would be quite some time before anyone could set up a proper fast food restaurant.

*But that isn't a bad thing*, she thought. *Is it?*

Once they had eaten, Imaiqah dragged them towards the edge of the Faire, where her father had his stall. A small steam engine sat on the rails, blowing smoke into the air, while dozens of children were eagerly lining up for a ride in the small carriages. Frieda laughed and ran forward, jumping into the rear carriage as the train started to move. Emily smiled before she took a good look at the adults. The mundanes seemed to be terrified, even though the train was moving so slowly anyone could have outpaced it, while the magicians seemed to be thoughtful. They had to know there was no magic in the steam train.

Caleb put their puzzlement into words. "How does it work?"

"Steam technology," Emily said, uncomfortably aware that *technology* might as well be magic, as far as the Nameless World was concerned. "It..."

She shook her head. "I'll explain later," she added. "It will need diagrams."

Caleb nodded. "I look forward to it."

Emily smiled at him before turning to watch as the steam train slowly made its way around the Faire, puffing up smoke. It was a basic version; it would be years before more complex versions started to link the cities and towns together. But it would change the world in many ways, just like the railways had done on Earth.

"It's an iron dragon," Caleb said, as the steam train returned to the station. "Isn't it?"

"No," Emily said. *Iron Dragon* sounded magical, too magical. "It's a steam train. There's no magic inside at all."

"That was fun," Frieda called, as she scrambled off the train and ran back to them. "Can I go on it again tomorrow?"

"You'll get bored with it soon enough," Emily said, smiling indulgently. "You can go on it every day if you like."

"Unless it breaks down," Imaiqah said. "Or someone steals the rails. We've had problems with people taking up the pins and pinching the rails when we started laying the first mainline tracks."

Caleb gave her a surprised look. "Why?"

"Because metal is expensive," Imaiqah said. "And we can't afford to police every last piece of the line."

"You could use subtle magic to keep people away from the line," Caleb offered. "Once you carve out the rails, have the runes stamped directly into the metal."

"It might work," Emily said, slowly. She fought down the urge to rub her chest, where the rune was still there. "But the magic might keep everyone away."

"You would have to tune it properly," Caleb said. He turned to look at the train. "If the magic was tuned perfectly, you could keep the people on the train safe from its influence, while anyone who tried to steal the rails themselves would be unable to escape."

"I'll suggest it to father," Imaiqah said. "But he's quite keen to keep magic away from the steam engines. We even had a boiler explode because he didn't want to put a binding spell on the metal."

"It might not have saved the boiler," Emily said. "The blast would have needed somewhere to go."

"That's what he said," Imaiqah said. "He was quite annoyed with me when I pointed it out."

"He was probably concerned about relying on magicians," Emily said. "But once the runes were described, he could just produce them for himself."

"He could," Imaiqah agreed. "I'll speak to him later today."

Caleb frowned. "Your father invented these things?"

"*Emily* designed the first engines," Imaiqah said. "We've improved quite a bit on the original designs."

"They have," Emily confirmed. She jabbed a finger at the steam engine as it started its trek around the Faire, once again. "I didn't design that."

"You still started it," Caleb said.

Emily shrugged. She wasn't comfortable with the look of admiration in his eyes, not when she knew all she'd *really* done was draw out a very basic steam engine from Earth. It had been the designers in Alexis who had really made it work, then started improving the design until they had something they could scale up into a full-sized steam train. And they'd done the same with other ideas too. Gunpowder, in particular, would reshape the world...

*And Nanette might well have stolen those notes*, Emily thought. There had been no hope of recovering her original notes, certainly not in time to prevent them being copied and redistributed. God alone knew who else now had the basic formula for gunpowder. *And where the hell is she?*

"I'm going to speak to my father," Imaiqah said. "If you'll excuse me..."

"Can I speak to him too?" Caleb asked. "I'd like a chance to talk about these... steam engines?"

"Just talk to him as an equal, and you will be fine," Imaiqah said. "Emily?"

"I'm going to head back to the castle," Emily said. She had a feeling she wouldn't see either of them for the rest of the day. Imaiqah's father was a great believer in putting his children to work, while he'd probably bond with Caleb over a discussion about steam theory and practice. "Frieda?"

"I'd like to stay," Frieda said. She looked around at the nearest stalls, then back at Emily. "Do you mind?"

"Just stay close to Lady Barb," Emily said, firmly. She looked around for Alassa, but saw no sign of her. "And stay out of trouble."

"We'll take care of her, if you can't find Lady Barb," Imaiqah said. "It might help keep my father from keeping me too long."

Emily concealed her amusement with an effort. "Stay with them, then," she said. "I'll see you all later, at the dance."

"Don't forget the fireworks," Imaiqah said. "They will surprise your guests."

Emily smiled. There was no shortage of magical fireworks, including some that looked like they had been taken from *The Fellowship of the Ring*, but the fireworks she intended to display were completely mundane, without even a hint of magic. She wondered what the two families, much less all the other guests, would make of them. She shrugged; they'd find out soon enough.

"And don't forget to bring Frieda back before the dinner," she warned. "I need company for the night."

"You'll probably have to sit in the middle again," Imaiqah said, unsympathetically. "Try not to let them fight, or you'll get hexed from both sides."

"I know," Emily said. "I almost wish I was sitting between Markus and Melissa instead."

"That would be worse," Imaiqah said. "Melissa hates you."

"Maybe," Emily said. She had a feeling that Melissa had other problems now. "But she wasn't very aggressive last year."

She nodded, turned, and started her stately walk back to the castle.

# Chapter Seventeen

"IS THIS ROOM SUITABLE, YOUR LADYSHIP?"

Emily stepped into the workroom and looked around. It was larger than she'd expected, with a cheap wooden table, a pair of wooden chairs, and a rickety — and empty — bookcase perched against the far wall. Compared to the spellchambers she'd used at Whitehall, it was pathetic, but it was *hers*. She could organize it to suit herself.

"More than suitable, Janice," she said. "You have warned the other maids that the rules about my rooms extend here, too?"

"Yes, your ladyship," Janice said. "This room will remain sealed, without any attempt to clean it, unless you give your specific permission."

"Good," Emily said. She levitated her trunk into the room, and nodded. "You may go."

Janice curtseyed hastily and retreated out the door. Emily didn't blame her. She remembered touching quite a few things she shouldn't have in Whitehall, during her first year, and that had been in a school of magic, where help had been available for anyone who ran into trouble. As soon as the door closed, she raised her hand in concentration and cast the first set of wards. Piece by piece, they fell into place, providing both privacy and security. Thankfully, the room was small enough for her to put up a comprehensive set of wards, rather than the relatively weak set covering the castle as a whole.

*I need to isolate this section completely*, she thought, as she carefully linked one set of wards to the other. *I don't need to set off my own alarms when I do experiments.*

Once the final set of wards was in place, she opened the trunk and dug out her equipment, placing it on the table. Some of the equipment was fairly common — by now, she was used to using both wand and staff — while other pieces had been designed by Professor Thande or Lady Barb. They both believed that a magician should have all the tools he or she could possibly require; Emily had purchased everything she thought she'd need, as well as a few other devices that had caught her eye. She rather liked the idea of tinkering on her own, even if she didn't want to seek total isolation. Magicians who did that tended to be a little strange.

"Well," she said, although there was no one to hear her. "Here we are."

She rooted through her equipment until she found an iron ring and placed it in the middle of the table, carefully moving the remainder of the equipment to the bookshelves. There had been nothing particularly special about the iron ring when she'd purchased it, but she'd used magic to carve a handful of runes into the metal, gathering magic that would help shape and contain her own magic. Lady Barb had helped her with the theory — she'd forced Emily to produce a new pocket dimension every weekend — but she'd done the runes herself. It simply felt like the way it should be done.

Emily braced herself before picking up the ring. It felt oddly heavy in her palm, even though it wasn't any bigger than the snake-bracelet and shouldn't have been much heavier. She eyed it carefully, fixing its dimensions in her mind, then closed her eyes in concentration, running through the first set of spells to form a pocket dimension. For a long moment, nothing seemed to happen...

And then the space inside the ring expanded, like a child blowing up a balloon.

She'd had problems, at first, grasping how it actually worked — Earth science refused to admit the possibility of something being larger on the inside than on the outside — but two years of work had helped her overcome that issue. Besides, it was hard to deny it was possible when living at Whitehall.

*It still seems like a TARDIS*, she thought with droll amusement. *What will happen if they ever lose control of the interior dimensions?*

She pushed the thought aside, concentrating on the pocket dimension. It fluctuated, like air alternatively being pumped in and allowed to escape from a balloon, but remained intact. The magic she was allowing to flow into the ring was holding it firmly in place, even though nature resisted its presence. Emily silently thanked Lady Barb for her endless lessons — not to mention the blunt insistence that Emily practice, time and time again — then carefully picked up the wand with her right hand. The spells twitched at her touch — she checked them, just to make sure they hadn't decayed — and shimmered as she held the wand close to the ring. For a moment, she thought the magic would interact badly, before the two seemed to blur together. Bracing herself, she pushed the wand through the ring, into the pocket dimension, and triggered the spells. The pocket dimension expanded rapidly, but froze as the spells fitted themselves solidly into place. It could no longer collapse in on itself, even after Emily stopped feeding magic into the ring.

*The spells hold it up*, she thought, as she watched the spells interlock together. She couldn't help thinking of building blocks, from kindergarten. If they were interlinked together, they were much stronger than if they were merely piled on top of one another. *And the dimension is secure.*

Emily ran a hand though her sweaty hair, placed the ring on the table and stepped backwards, monitoring it from a distance. The magic holding the spells in place, which in turn held the pocket dimension in existence, shouldn't have anywhere to go. It was, in a sense, a perpetual motion machine. But even the tiniest leak could be disastrous, in the long run; the dimension would either deflate slowly, like a balloon, or explode like a bubble pricked by a pin. She wasn't quite sure what would happen if the dimension exploded — there wasn't anything in the dimension apart from her spellwork, which would shatter before the dimension burst — but she doubted it would be pleasant. But, as she watched and waited, it became clear that the dimension was firmly fixed in place.

*Wait*, she told herself, firmly. *You need to know it remains solid.*

She reached into her trunk and found her copy of Caleb's notes, reading through them once again. The proposal didn't need many changes, she was sure, but she did need to leave her fingerprints on it somewhere. They were already going to be marked down, Lady Barb had warned, because she'd come to the project late. Emily wasn't sure if she should be annoyed on Caleb's behalf, because he hadn't expected his partner to desert him, or irked because she'd been denied a chance to claim full marks.

*And you should stop feeling sorry for yourself,* her own thoughts mocked her. *Would you rather redo Third Year from the start?*

It would be humiliating, she thought. And yet the idea had a certain charm. She could delay any long-term decisions about Cockatrice until she graduated, but then she would have to make a final decision. Should she stay and remain baroness — as well as Alassa's closest advisor — or should she abandon the barony? The question haunted her; she disliked the idea of giving anything up, yet she knew she was ill-suited to the role. And there were limits to how much Bryon could do in her name.

She pushed the thought aside, and started to make notes on the proposal paper. Caleb could review what she'd done — she wondered, suddenly, what he would make of her project — and then they could decide how best to present the revised paper once they returned to Whitehall. She'd be going back early...maybe Caleb would like to go back, too. Or maybe he'd want to go be with his family for the last week of holidays. Just because his father was strict and wanted a soldier, instead of a...well, a nerd...didn't mean they didn't love each other.

An hour later, she put the papers to one side and picked up the ring. It felt warm to the touch, but not warm enough to burn her skin. Carefully, she tested the dimension, probing the spellware with her mind, and relaxed when she realized it was solidly in place. The magic hadn't faded at all.

*Thank you, Lady Barb,* she thought, as she put the ring back down. The project might have been Emily's idea, but it had been the older woman who'd made it work. *And now for the final test.*

She stood and walked to the bookshelves, picked up a leather bag, and opened it. A handful of knives sat inside, each one made from a different material. She picked up the silver knife, checked the charms placed on the blade carefully, and carried it back to the table. Once she was seated, she picked the ring up again, and used the knife to make a thin cut on her palm. Blood — and magic — welled up in front of her.

It felt weird, almost uncomfortable. Lady Barb had taught her how to focus and channel her magic for rituals, but she'd never had to do it alone. Indeed, rituals were almost never performed by fewer than three magicians, allowing them to balance their power. Her head swam for a long second before she managed to gather herself long enough to direct a stream of raw magic into the ring. The spellwork inside shimmered, then seemed to collect itself, steering the magic — *her* magic — into the heart of the pocket dimension. Emily shivered violently, suddenly feeling very cold, and carefully sealed the dimension before she could collapse. It was all she could do to put the ring and knife back on the table before her legs buckled. If she hadn't been sitting, she would have fallen to the floor.

*It might be better to do this on a rug*, she thought, as she leaned on the table and tried to pull herself back together. It felt thoroughly weird, as if she was both happy and sad at the same time. She rubbed her eyes as she felt tears starting to form, but forced herself to stand up and pace the room. The motion made her feel better, although she still felt drained. But then, she *had* pumped a considerable amount of magic into the ring...

Opening her trunk, she removed a ration bar and nibbled it carefully. Lady Barb had also told her to have something sweet on hand, ready to eat, as soon as she had completed the experiment. The ration bar tasted almost *too* sweet, but it made her feel better. She kept pacing, trying to drive away the last vestiges of the strange feelings. What she'd done had made her feel vulnerable, and she didn't like it.

*Well*, she thought, as she finally turned back to the ring. *Did it work?*

She touched the ring...and felt, instantly, her own magic welling up to meet her. It reminded her of some of the exercises Mistress Irene had taught her, when she'd first entered Whitehall, but different, although she couldn't put her finger on why. She was sensing her own magic, yet it felt separate from her...but she was sure, if she wished, she could absorb it back into her own body. She'd just have to be very careful not to overwhelm her mind, she reminded herself sharply. Necromancers went insane because no mortal mind could handle the sudden influx of magic without going mad.

*Dear God*, she thought. *I've done it.*

The Nuke-Spell had been bad enough, she knew. If the theory leaked out, every magician with a grudge against his neighbor would be setting off atomic blasts, utterly destroying civilization. But at least the Nameless World didn't know about atoms, let alone what happened if someone started splitting them. Pocket dimensions and rituals...? Far too many magicians knew about *them*. It was something of a mystery why enchanters like Yodel hadn't invented their own batteries long before Shadye had kidnapped her from Earth.

*Unless they did, and decided no one would want to use them*, she thought. Pouring so much magic into the ring had left her exhausted, easy prey for anyone with bad intentions. *But if the magic has nowhere to go, it can stay where it is indefinitely.*

She looked at the ring, picked it up, and placed it in her pocket. It wasn't something she wanted to leave lying around, not when there were so many trained and experienced magicians wandering the castle. They might have been *told* not to go past the first two levels, but she rather doubted they would heed the warning. Magic-users might be protected by the Sorcerer's Rule, which prevented magicians from being forced to share their secrets, but it didn't prevent other magicians from engaging in industrial espionage. And she knew, all too well, that she was a target.

*This will change the world*, she thought. Lady Barb had warned her that it might even make necromancy practical, which would be disastrous. *And what do I do with it?*

She dug the charmed parchment out of her pocket and glanced down at it. Aloha and the Gorgon were chatting about charms, including a handful of twinned charms that would be covered in Fourth Year. They'd seemed to become friends, of a sort, Emily noted. She was surprised — it was rare for students to socialize with students from other years — but she had to admit that Aloha and the Gorgon had a great deal in common. They were both brilliant and, to some extent, determined to prove themselves. And the Gorgon had actually been held back a year.

*HI*, she wrote. *THE FAIRE IS HUGE.*

*HI, EMILY*, Aloha wrote back. *ARE THERE ANY RARE BOOKS?*

*A COUPLE*, Emily wrote. *BUT NOTHING SPECIAL.*

*WHY AM I NOT SURPRISED?* The Gorgon wrote. *NO ONE WOULD SELL A UNIQUE BOOK.*

Emily smiled, then swore as she felt the wards tingle. Someone — somewhere — had used magic, *hostile* magic, in her castle. And yet, most of the guests were at the Faire...she glanced at her watch, but it didn't seem likely that any of them would be coming back so early. Dinner was at seven bells, after all.

*MUST DASH*, she wrote. *CRISIS TIME.*

# Chapter Eighteen

S HE HEARD THE SOUND OF SOMEONE SHOUTING AS SHE TURNED THE CORNER AND STRODE towards the guest quarters. A woman was shouting at a man, who didn't seem interested in shouting back; Emily flinched, remembering some of the arguments her mother had had with her stepfather, but forced herself to go on.

"I told her to clean the room," the woman said. "Father, you should have left the charms *off* the bed!"

Emily peered into the room. A maid stood in front of the bed, frozen in place, while a middle-aged woman shouted at a man who looked as old as Fulvia. He waved a wand with one hand, while the other held a tankard of something that smelled suspiciously like mead. Emily gritted her teeth and stepped into the room, crossing a protective ward. The old man glared at her, but the woman caught his wand arm before he could point it at Emily.

"I let no one make my bed!" The old man thundered. He pulled away from his daughter, but she managed to pull the wand out of his hand before he could start casting spells. "I refuse to allow anyone..."

"Shut up, father," the woman snapped. "Lady Emily, I apologize for my father."

"Good," Emily said. "Please explain what happened."

The woman sighed. Just for a moment, Emily saw a look of resignation cross her face, the look of a woman who found herself trapped, taking care of her elderly father.

"I asked the maid to clean our rooms," the woman admitted. "I explained all of this to my father, but...but he's deaf..."

"I am not deaf," the old man bellowed.

*You mean he hears what it suits him to hear*, Emily translated, silently. She felt a flicker of sympathy for the woman. Having to take care of an elderly man would be bad enough if the man hadn't had magic.

"And he froze the maid when she started to change his sheets," the woman continued, desperately. "Please forgive him, Lady Emily. He's not what he once was."

"I'm as fit as I ever was," the old man thundered. He leered at the maid, an expression that was strikingly repulsive. "Give me back my wand!"

"Not until you've had your nap," the woman countered. She waved the wand at the maid, who unfroze and staggered. Emily caught her before she could collapse to the floor. "I am sorry, Lady Emily."

"I'm not the person you should be apologising to," Emily said, tartly. She had told Bryon to warn the maids to leave the magicians alone, but she hadn't anticipated one magician inviting the maid in, then another freezing her. How many other problems had escaped her notice? "I wasn't the person you trapped."

The woman looked as if she'd had to taste something vile, but she reached into her pocket and produced a handful of silver coins. "I thank you for your service," she said to the maid, as she passed her the coins. "You can clean the room later when my father is at dinner."

"I won't have anyone touching my bed!" The old man thundered. "Young women cannot be trusted with my bed!"

"There isn't a single woman who wants to get into your bed," the woman muttered. "And I can't imagine why you would feel differently."

Emily looked at the maid and jerked her head towards the door. The maid scurried away, gratefully. Emily turned her attention back to the arguing couple and watched as the man stumbled to his feet, muttering under his breath all the while. The woman sagged the moment the man entered the bathroom, looking exhausted.

"I'm all he has," she said. "And..."

"I understand," Emily said. "But I can't have him abusing my people."

"I'll speak to him," the woman promised. "But he's never listened to anything I've told him before, Lady Emily."

"Just do your best," Emily said. "If he acts up again, I reserve the right to take more...extreme steps."

The woman looked downcast, but nodded. Emily left the room, closing the door behind her. The maid stood just outside, looking at the floor. Emily felt another stab of pity, mingled with guilt; she'd frozen Janice, too, when Janice had surprised her. The maids hadn't signed up to work in a magical household, nor had they realized the dangers when Bryon had hired them. It was something that was going to have to change.

*Bryon should have told them,* Emily thought. *But how could he tell them to ignore a guest's wishes?*

"My lady," the maid said. "I..."

"Don't worry about it," Emily said, sharply. An idea was starting to take shape in her mind. "Go find Bryon and tell him I want to see the staff, all of them, in the Great Hall."

The maid curtsied and hurried off. Emily took a moment to steady herself before she walked down to the Great Hall. A pair of workmen cleaned the floor, which needed it after the previous night's dance, while a set of maids were putting the tables back together. Bryon walked in moments later, followed by a confused array of cooks, maids and manservants. Emily had known there were over three hundred servants in the castle, but she'd never really grasped it until she'd seen them all together. And they all worked for her...

"I asked the guards to remain on duty," Bryon said. "The gates have to be watched at all times. But everyone else is here."

*Let's hope the food doesn't burn,* Emily thought. It could take hours to prepare the food for even a small gathering, when "small" could mean hundreds of guests. She honestly didn't understand how Alassa tolerated it. How could she hope to have a private dinner, perhaps for a handful of friends, when everyone who hadn't been invited would resent it?

"Thank you," she said. "I need to speak to you afterwards."

*The more I do for myself, the more it belongs to me,* she thought. It was something she doubted she would ever fully understand. Magic behaved oddly, compared to science; if she performed magic on herself or her tools, it worked better than magic performed by someone else. She rubbed the rune on her chest absently, then walked back to the trunk. Carefully removing a wand and one of her journals, she placed both on the table next to the ring. *And it's time to finally see if I know what I'm doing.*

She sat down on one of the chairs, which rocked alarmingly, and picked up the journal. Lady Barb had ordered her to protect her writings carefully, using several different security spells, and untangling them all took time. It wasn't convenient, she had learned from experience, but she'd already had one set of notes stolen. This set would be worse, if it fell into the wrong hands; she'd drawn lessons from Mountaintop's library as well as the books she had access to in Whitehall. Someone could use them to build a case against her – she knew that all too well.

*And there are already idiots who believe I'm a necromancer,* she thought. It didn't seem fair, somehow — Shadye and Mother Holly had both been completely insane — but logic and reason rarely had any influence with people who already disliked her. *They'd start thinking I was a Dark Wizard, too.*

She shook her head before opening the journal to the correct page to run through her notes one final time. Lady Barb had offered to assist her with the experiment, when she ran through every step for the first time, but Emily had declined. If there were risks performing the experiment, even here, she didn't want anyone else to face them. The notes seemed as clear as ever, now that she understood the theory...but she knew there was a considerable gulf between theory and practice.

*Here we go,* she thought, and picked up the wand. *Please, let this work.*

The wand was nothing more than a piece of wood, she knew. Frieda had told her there were students in Mountaintop who bragged of the modifications they'd made to their wands, but Emily knew from experience that such modifications were pointless. All one could do with a wand was lodge spells within the wood for later activation. In many ways, she reflected, it seemed the ultimate end result of Caleb's spell mosaics, save for the simple fact that a spell couldn't be modified, once lodged. It could only be triggered.

She gritted her teeth — she distrusted wands on principle — before assembling the first set of spells in her mind. They glimmered in her awareness, slid through her fingertips and out into the wand. She felt the wood grow hot as the last spell slipped into place — she hastily raised a ward to protect herself, just in case — and then cooled, rapidly. They wouldn't last, she knew; the spells were too complex to remain in the wand for more than an hour, if she was lucky. But they would last long enough for her to complete the rest of the experiment.

*Good,* she thought. Her heart was suddenly racing. Two years of research, two years of practice, all boiled down to the ring and wand in front of her. The first time she'd tried anything like it, Master Tor had been horrified, with reason. Now...now, there was no one at risk, but herself. *Let's see if this works.*

She cleared her throat as she stepped up to the dais and looked around. Alassa had taught her how to address servants, but she'd privately resolved never to speak to *anyone* in such a manner. Servants were stripped of their dignity by a language that was cool and utterly impersonal, as if the servants were nothing more than automatons. It explained a lot, Emily felt, that servants were dehumanized. Perhaps their masters and mistresses mistreated them because they didn't think of them as *human*.

*And if people spoke to the help like that on Earth,* she thought, *they'd be hit with lawsuits that would put them permanently in the red.*

"Thank you for coming," she said. Alassa would probably say she was showing weakness, but she wasn't going to be rude to the servants. God knew they had enough problems without her adding to them. "I won't keep you long."

She paused, marshaling her thoughts. "There was an incident, just now, when one of the maids was invited to clean a room by one magician, then frozen by another, who happened to be sharing the same room," she said. "This was the second incident I have seen, personally, involving magic. Have there been others?"

There was no response, but she saw several maids looking uncomfortable. Emily sighed inwardly, feeling cold rage bubbling in her heart. Abusing servants was strictly forbidden at Whitehall, with draconic punishments for any offender, but that was very much the exception rather than the rule. The previous baron had been a nightmare, Emily recalled, even before he'd tried to overthrow the king. She'd heard enough horror stories to last her the rest of her life.

*And subtle magic could make things worse,* she thought. *They will need to sew runes to protect themselves.*

"There are rules," she said. They should know already, but they bore repeating. "Do not enter a room belonging to a magician without permission, not even to light the fires. If they do ask you to enter and clean the room, check what you can and cannot touch. They will probably *not* want you to touch their trunks, their books or any other magical possessions."

She paused, long enough for her words to sink in. "Do not enter a room when the magician isn't there," she added. "If they don't respond when you knock, assume they're absent or they don't want to see you and leave them alone. Most magicians have a habit of leaving traps around to catch unwary intruders and those traps won't care if you're cleaning the room or trying to steal from them. You could wind up trapped — or worse.

"Finally, be polite," she concluded. "If they ask for something reasonable, give it to them, but I will not tolerate them abusing my employees. If there is a problem, come and tell me about it. I can't do anything unless I *know* there's a problem."

There was another uneasy rustle, but no one spoke. "I will be in my office until dinner time," Emily told them. "If you want to speak to me, you are welcome."

"There are always incidents," Bryon said, once the remainder of the staff had left the Great Hall. "Do you really want them all reported to you?"

"Yes," Emily said. "How many have been reported to you?"

"None," Bryon said, "but I have eyes and ears. A couple of maids were paid to spend last night in the arms of a magician. It happens."

"And as long as it is consensual, I don't mind," Emily said. "But if it isn't, I will need to do something about it."

"Few of them would dare accuse a magician," Bryon said. "They'd fear being taken for liars."

Emily sighed, inwardly. She'd seen enough of what passed for justice in Zangaria to know she wouldn't want to be on the wrong side of it. A high-ranking man was automatically believed over his juniors, if he happened to speak in court. It didn't matter who or what he was, or how much proof there happened to be; his rank protected him from the consequences of his actions. She couldn't help wondering why so few aristocrats didn't end up murdered by their staff. It wasn't as if they didn't have an excellent set of motives.

"Then tell them I won't consider them liars," she assured him. "There are spells to find out if someone is telling the truth, after all."

Bryon met her eyes. It was so forward that Emily sat up, surprised.

"And what," he asked, "will you do about it if you learn the truth?"

"Whatever I need to do," Emily said.

"It is my duty to offer you advice," Bryon said, after a moment. "If you...if you evict a magician, no matter how unpleasant, from the castle, you will risk your relations with the rest of the magical community. The same can be said of anyone from the aristocracy. They will close ranks around him...and against you."

*Yet another reason to walk away*, Emily thought, coldly. *Leave...and don't look back.*

"I understand what you're saying," she said, instead. Bryon *was* giving her good advice, from his point of view. "But I will not stand by and let my people be abused."

She walked back to her office and sat down, then started to go through a huge pile of paperwork that required her signature. It was nearly an hour before the first visitor arrived, a junior maid who refused to look Emily in the eye as she told her how one of the guests had groped her breast when she'd cleaned his room. Emily cast a covert truth spell and winced, inwardly, as she realized the maid was telling the truth. Two more followed in quick succession, both telling similar stories. A fourth told of entering a room upon invitation, only to be ordered out seconds later. Emily puzzled over that, then put it aside. The magician might have realized, after inviting the maid to enter, that he'd left something exposed and wanted to cover it up. By the time Lady Barb returned from the Faire, Emily was tired, cranky and feeling murderous.

"Some minor incidents, but nothing worth mentioning," Lady Barb said, as she entered. "The Faire is winding down now for the day."

"Good," Emily said, absently. She'd wanted to tell Lady Barb about the battery, which still felt warm in her pocket. But instead she needed to talk about other problems. "There were some...incidents with the maids."

Lady Barb listened, carefully, as Emily ran through what she'd heard. "I think the old man must have been Douglas, of House Douglas," she said. "He was a very strong magician in his day, before he started to go senile. There was a problem with the rejuvenation spells, or so I heard. Too many wives in his life."

Emily blinked. "Too many wives?"

"He had seven, if I recall correctly," Lady Barb said. "And at least twenty children." She shrugged. "But that isn't the issue at hand, is it?"

"No," Emily said. "I need to deal with these...these molesters."

"Well," Lady Barb said. "Do you know who they are?"

"No," Emily admitted. She shuddered, remembering Hodge's hands on her...and the moment she'd knocked him down, then hit him with a spell. "I could get them identified, couldn't I?"

"Not easily," Lady Barb said. She frowned. "And most of their families wouldn't give a damn."

"I care," Emily said. She thought, frantically. "If the maid was asked to clean a room, logically the groper was someone *staying* in the room..."

"Logically," Lady Barb agreed. "But you would still have to convince their families that what they did was *wrong.*"

"Because they don't see servants as human," Emily agreed, bitterly.

"No," Lady Barb said.

Emily looked down at her hands, feeling helpless. "So...what do I do about it?"

Lady Barb reached out and rested a hand on her shoulder. "Are you asking me for advice?"

"Yes," Emily said.

"Speak to them all this evening," Lady Barb said. "Tell them that you won't tolerate your servants getting hurt, molested or treated badly. Or bespelled. Do not show any signs of weakness as you speak. Make sure they know it isn't a request, but a demand, and don't give them any wiggle room at all."

Emily winced. Lady Barb could quirk her eyebrows and people would fall into line. *Emily* didn't have the same presence, and doubted she ever would.

"I don't know how to do it," she admitted.

"Talk bluntly and firmly," Lady Barb said. "Don't show your power, because they won't be impressed; show them that you will not be pushed on this issue. You do not want to leave any room for doubt."

"I'll do my best," Emily said. She shook her head. "But..."

Lady Barb cast a privacy ward into the air. "Was this a problem where you came from?"

"Sometimes," Emily said. There was no magic on Earth, but there was still power... and people willing to abuse it. "But most people would agree it was wrong."

"Changing something like that will take a lifetime," Lady Barb said, softly. "Don't expect results immediately."

Emily rested her head in her hands. "I did, didn't I?"

"Yes," Lady Barb said, flatly.

"Damn," Emily said.

She cleared her throat. "I'll speak to them," she said. "And now, can we talk about something different?"

Lady Barb's lips quirked. "If you wish," she said, "we can talk about anything."

Emily drew the ring out of her pocket. "One battery," she said. "It works."

"Good," Lady Barb said. She touched the ring lightly, then frowned. "I could draw on this, too."

"I think so," Emily said. "If rituals allow us to combine magic, surely a battery could allow one magician to draw on the power of several."

"You'd still run the risks of channeling it through your mind," Lady Barb said. "Or do you have a solution in mind?"

"I have half of one," Emily said. "But I don't know how well it will work."

Lady Barb smiled. "You can discuss it with Caleb, if you like," she said. "I think you and he were getting on."

Emily blushed. "Why is it that...that everyone seems to think we'll start dating?"

"Probably because they're your friends, and they like teasing you," Lady Barb said. "And probably because they want you to be happy."

"Oh," Emily said. She cringed. "But I barely know him!"

Lady Barb made a rude noise. "You don't have to jump into bed with him," she said, sharply. "And, no matter what anyone else may happen to say, you don't *have* to do anything with him. I would actually advise you to finish the project first, then consider going out with him, if you wish. The last thing you want is to fall out with him before the project is completed."

"Because repeating Third Year would be horrible," Emily said.

"It will be worse if you're two years older than everyone else in the year," Lady Barb pointed out, dryly. "You will be a mature student, considered old enough to be treated as an adult, yet you will still be subject to childish penalties and punishments. The humiliation will be unbearable."

She shrugged, turning the ring over and over in her hand. "But he's a decent man and you're...better than you were, certainly. Just be careful."

"I will," Emily promised.

"And if you happen to need advice on protection and suchlike, go to the healers," Lady Barb added. "They will not be happy if I start dispensing advice."

"You *are* a healer," Emily said. She hated the idea of asking anyone for help with protective charms, even her closest friends. "Can't you teach me?"

"Not unless I want to get into trouble," Lady Barb said. "Healers can be quite sharp about tutors dispensing advice. They prefer to make sure students get it directly from them."

She glanced at her watch. "It isn't long until dinner," she said. "You might as well start planning your speech. And try not to make it a long one."

Emily nodded. She hated long speeches, too.

# Chapter Nineteen

EMILY WAITED UNTIL EVERYONE WAS IN THE GREAT HALL AND SEATED BEFORE SHE ROSE TO her feet and used a very minor spell to catch their attention. Aurelius had taught it to her, claiming that strong magicians always used magic to make speeches. He'd used it himself when he'd welcomed the students back to Mountaintop, although she hadn't pushed so much power into the spell. There was no point in encouraging them to fight back.

"Before we eat," she said, "there is a matter I must address."

She allowed her gaze to sweep the hall. Markus and Melissa, sitting with their respective siblings, both looked bored. Alassa and Jade were sitting together, watching her attentively, while Frieda and Imaiqah were both frowning. There was no sign of Caleb at all. He'd probably decided to skip the dinner and eat in private, or down at the Faire.

"It has come to my attention that magic has been used, twice, against my servants," she said, bluntly. "My servants, in *my* house. Furthermore, some of my servants have been abused by my guests. I consider this to be an offense against my person."

There was a long pause. Lady Barb had advised her to frame the incidents as offences against her personally, rather than against individual maids. It was something they'd understand, she'd explained; they'd respect Emily's right to be angry, even if they didn't quite grasp *why* she was angry. Emily's home was, quite literally, her castle.

"I do not have time to come running to attend to each and every incident," she continued, "so I will say this now. If anyone, and I mean *anyone*, abuses my servants, they will be evicted from the castle and banned from the Faire. You may ask them to clean rooms, or to provide food, or to assist you in carrying your supplies, but nothing else. I will not tolerate such activities in my home."

After giving them one final glance, she sat down. They'd have to be mad to start a fight, Lady Barb had commented, but some magicians were more than a little unstable. Or proud; they would go out of their way, Emily knew, to show they weren't scared by the Necromancer's Bane. And yet...the others would have to stop them, or risk seeing the sacred laws of hospitality torn asunder. Emily just hoped it would be enough to keep them from doing anything stupid.

*And to make you decide*, a voice whispered at the back of her head, *if you're bluffing or not.*

"A pretty speech," Fulvia said, as the servants started to bring in giant tureens of soup. "But I'm sure my family will behave themselves."

"I'm sure," Emily said, dryly. Gaius had been invited as part of the Ashworth party, she knew, and *he* had turned a maid into a frog. "But it needed to be said."

"It comes of young magicians having no respect for their elders," Fulvia said. She peered past Emily, at Marcellus. "I believe you helped your father die before his time."

"My father died through one of his experiments," Marcellus said, pleasantly. "But tell me, Lady Fulvia, just how your grandson died."

"He drank an overdose of painkilling potion and poisoned himself," Fulvia said, tightly. "It was most unfortunate."

"Particularly as it left a malleable toddler as your heir," Marcellus observed. It took Emily a moment to work out that he meant Melissa. "How...coincidental."

Fulvia eyed him coolly. "Are you accusing me of murdering my grandson?"

"It does seem off," Marcellus said, "that you should jump to *that* conclusion."

He smirked, then went on. "Painkilling potion tastes horrible, by design," he said. "I fancy few people could swallow more than a teaspoon, certainly not willingly. They wouldn't need to, either. One teaspoon would be more than enough to make their bodies go numb. Why would anyone set out to drink a whole *bottle* of the stuff?"

"My grandson was always emotional," Fulvia said. "It seems to run in the family."

"I had noticed," Marcellus said. He looked at Emily. "How is her great-granddaughter at school?"

Emily paused to consider her answer. She didn't *like* Melissa, full stop. Melissa had had a feud with Alassa, which had widened to include Emily and Imaiqah after they'd become Alassa's friends. She still cringed at the memory of some of the humiliations Melissa had heaped upon her. But, at the same time, she couldn't deny that Melissa was a powerful and skilled magician. She'd always been in the top ten each year.

"Talented," Emily said, finally.

"A very diplomatic answer," Marcellus said. "But is it true?"

"Of course it is," Fulvia said. "Talent runs through the bloodline. Indeed, I fancy Melissa's children will be powerful indeed."

Emily frowned. "Her children?"

"She is to marry Gaius," Fulvia said. "It will bring his bloodline into the fold."

Emily had suspected as much, but the confirmation left her feeling sorry for Melissa. If Gaius was so cruel as to turn a helpless maid into a frog, who knew what he would do to his wife? But, on the other hand, Melissa was hardly defenseless. The marriage might end with her murdering her husband, perhaps on their wedding night. It would be hard to blame her for blasting Gaius into thousands of pieces.

*Not that that would stop Fulvia from trying*, Emily thought.

The soup arrived, thankfully cutting off conversation. Emily took her bowl with relief and tucked in as soon as everyone was served. Fulvia and Marcellus seemed to welcome the pause too, given how badly they'd been sniping at each other. Emily couldn't help wondering if they were going to start trying to kill each other, if they kept picking fights throughout the Faire. It was going to be a long two weeks.

She glanced at Melissa and frowned, inwardly. Melissa seemed torn between hope and a grim despair that flickered over her face, then faded away when she clamped down on her emotions. Emily wondered, vaguely, if there was anything she could do, but there was nothing. And even if there was, Melissa had been thoroughly unpleasant to her. A part of Emily's mind thought she deserved a little humiliation...

*Shut up*, she told herself, sharply. Her eyes found Gaius, who was chatting to a pair of magicians of roughly the same age. *No one deserves that kind of man as a husband.*

"Your cooks have done a wonderful job," Fulvia said, as the soup bowls were taken away and the next set of dishes were brought out. "I must ask them for the recipe."

"I doubt you cook for yourself," Marcellus sniped, unkindly.

"There is something to be said for cooking for one's family," Fulvia said. "There are ancient protective charms that can only be worked by the mother when she's cooking for her children."

She gave Emily a sidelong glance. "There are tricks passed down through the bloodlines that are rarely shared with outsiders. Talk about the prospect of learning them with your father, if you wish, then see who might offer you the most knowledge."

Emily's eyes narrowed. Melissa might have realized that Emily prized knowledge above all else...but it had been Nanette who had been the first to *really* grasp it. Mountaintop wouldn't have been able to try to use the offer of knowledge to seduce her if they hadn't realized it was a possible ploy. And Fulvia had gone to Mountaintop. Had someone passed the word to her?

*Or are you just over-thinking it?* She asked herself. *Fulvia might have been making a sincere offer, of sorts.*

"I'm not familiar with such magics," she said, truthfully. "How do they work?"

"Through the blood," Fulvia said. "The family is bound by blood and honor."

"Except when it isn't," Marcellus said. He smiled at Emily. "Blood and honor is one thing, but only true power can bind a family together."

Fulvia snorted, rudely, and turned her attention to her food.

Emily sighed, and took the opportunity to glance at her friends. They seemed to be having fun, as they were totally without the problem of being caught between two powerful and dangerous magicians who happened to hate each other. She ate quickly, despite her lack of appetite, and rose to her feet again once the plates had been taken away.

"There will now be a short intermission," she said. "If you would care to accompany me to the battlements, you will be able to watch the fireworks as they light up the sky."

"I would be honored," Fulvia said. "But an aging lady like myself needs to be helped up the stairs."

"You'll outlive us all," Marcellus said, bluntly. "How old are you, really?"

"A lady never says," Fulvia said. She held out her arm to Emily. "If you will, my dear?"

Emily scowled, but took Fulvia's arm. She had wondered if Fulvia was actually *younger* than she seemed, or was draining someone else's youth to keep herself young, but Fulvia moved like an old woman. There was nothing keeping her going but sheer power and bloody-minded determination. Emily didn't like Fulvia, any more than she liked Fulvia's great-granddaughter, yet she had to admire her determination. She was older than Douglas, and yet her mind was still working perfectly.

The battlements were shrouded in darkness when they reached the top of the castle. High overhead, the stars were starting to come out, twinkling in the night sky. Emily caught her breath — perhaps it was her imagination, but the stars always seemed brighter in the Nameless World than they had on Earth — and glanced at her watch. There were only a few minutes to wait until the fireworks began.

"Cold enough to keep a body awake," Fulvia said. She hadn't let go of Emily's arm. "But warm enough to keep one from going back inside."

Emily shrugged. Moments later, the first set of fireworks began to shoot into the sky and explode. The children whooped as bangs and cracks echoed through the night sky. Brilliant flashes of multicolored light burst through the air, some twisting madly while others just flared once and vanished back into the darkness. They'd been experimenting, Emily realized, as more and more fireworks were launched from the Faire. She hadn't known they could produce so many colors, the last time she'd checked.

"Impressive," Marcellus said. "But where is the magic?"

"There is none," Emily said. She couldn't help wondering how he'd react, when he realized the truth. "Just chemistry."

"No magic," Marcellus said. He didn't sound if he believed her. "How is that even possible?"

"Chemistry," Emily said, simply.

She would have said more, but her attention was drawn away by a sudden exchange of blows between two young men, followed by a handful of hexes. Emily cursed and let go of Fulvia, just as the hexes started to reflect in all directions. One spell flashed towards Alassa's back, only for Jade to knock her down a moment before it slammed into her. Emily met Jade's eyes, just for a moment, as he lay on top of Alassa, covering her with his body. But there was no time to think about what his expression meant...

"Stop this," Fulvia bellowed, as several others raised their hands, ready to launch hexes of their own. Somehow, she no longer looked like a weak and feeble elderly woman. "Garth, Holston; put your hands down at once."

"And you do the same," Marcellus bellowed at his family members. "Honestly, Roland; I thought Markus could keep you in line!"

Emily looked around. There was no sign of Markus. Or Melissa.

Fulvia caught Garth by the ear and dragged him back to where Emily was standing. "I offer my apologies, Lady Emily, for the disturbance of your peace," she said. Her voice was coldly furious, each word making Garth jump. "You may punish him as you see fit."

Emily thought, fast. No one had been hurt, fortunately, although it had been a very near thing. If Alassa had been struck in the back, it might have burned through her protections and spelled doom for Zangaria. Civil war would have been inevitable.

"Roland will also submit himself to your judgement," Marcellus said, as he walked back to Emily. Roland trailed him, looking like a child who didn't quite understand what he'd done wrong. In other places, Emily suspected, fighting with the Ashworths would have been considered commendable behavior. "We offer our apologies, too."

"They can spend the rest of today and tomorrow in their rooms," Emily said. It was a light punishment, but she had no idea just how far she could press them. Besides, she had a feeling that both Fulvia and Marcellus would be meting out punishments of their own. The battlements were not a good place for a battle. "And they can apologize to Alassa and everyone else they nearly hit."

"Matriarch," Garth said. "I must..."

He yelped loudly, his protest cut off, as Fulvia twisted his ear. Emily winced in sympathy; she'd lost count of how many times she'd been injured in the Nameless World, but having one's ear twisted had to hurt badly. And there was the humiliation of being treated like a child in front of everyone, friend and foe alike.

"Go to your room," Fulvia ordered. "I will discuss the matter with you later."

Garth glared at Emily, then stalked off with as much dignity as he could muster. Emily watched him go, resolving not to turn her back on him while he was in her castle. People could do stupid things out of injured pride, she knew all too well, even if they had been in the wrong. Garth might just try something to avenge himself...

"I'll see you tonight, lad," Marcellus said, to Roland. "And I suggest you prepare yourself for a long explanation."

He turned to face Emily. "I apologize, once again," he said. "Those two hotheads have no common sense."

Fulvia, for once, didn't seem inclined to snipe further. Instead, she turned and watched as the remaining fireworks exploded in the night sky. Emily checked her watch — the firework display was due to last twenty minutes — but decided they must have burned through their stockpiles quicker than they'd expected. A final firework rose up to the heavens, then exploded...sending a wave of multicolored light cascading in all directions. The air tingled with magic, just for a second, and faded away to nothingness.

"Let us go down to the dance," Emily said.

The servants had been busy while the guests had been admiring the fireworks. They'd pushed tables against the walls and placed desserts there for anyone to eat. A line, mainly composed of young children, was already forming beside the bowls; Emily watched in some amusement as the children squabbled over who should eat first.

"My Lady Emily," a voice said, behind her. "I was wondering if you could tell me where Melissa has gone."

Emily turned...and looked up at Gaius. He didn't seem any pleasanter now, she noted, than when she'd seen him for the first time. She didn't really feel like helping him — and even if she had, she lacked the ward network necessary to track and monitor each and every one of her guests.

"I'm afraid I couldn't tell you," she said. She made a show of looking around. "But she isn't here."

"But we are to be married," Gaius protested. "I have a right to know where she is."

*I think Melissa has a right to do horrible things to you,* Emily thought, coldly.

"I can't tell you where she is," she said, instead. "If you want to find her, I suggest you go looking for her."

"We are to be married," Gaius repeated, "and yet she doesn't want to spend time with me."

Emily shrugged, battling down her temper. Gaius...seemed odd, a mixture of entitled brat and passive-aggressive victim. There were some men, Sergeant Harkin had told his class, who saw the world divided into two sets of people: masters and slaves. The trick to controlling them, he'd said, was to keep them convinced that you were the master. Emily couldn't help wondering if Gaius was torn between the two extremes. Maybe Fulvia had considered him biddable...

*But he turned a maid into a frog,* Emily reminded herself. *He doesn't deserve sympathy.*

"Emily," Steven said, coming up behind them. "A word, if you don't mind."

Emily nodded to Gaius and turned to Steven. Gaius snorted and stalked off, muttering rudely under his breath.

"We need to talk," Steven said, bluntly. "Can I request an appointment tomorrow morning?"

"Tomorrow afternoon, before dinner," Emily said. It wasn't a discussion she wanted to have, but she knew there was no choice. "I'll see you in my office, if that's acceptable."

"It will do," Steven said. He looked around. "Have you seen Markus?"

"No," Emily said. She sighed, inwardly. "I have no idea where either Markus or Melissa happens to be."

The band struck up a merry tune, inviting the dancers onto the floor. Steven bowed to her, before heading towards a pretty girl from one of the cadet branches of the Ashfall Family. Emily sighed, and started to make her way towards the dessert table. Alassa waved to her as she passed, then beckoned her into a corner.

"Emily," she said. "Do we have time to talk?"

"I'd be glad of the distraction," Emily said. She looked at the dancers and felt a flicker of envy. She had never had the confidence to just glide onto the dance floor and make up her own steps. "Would you like to run the rest of the Faire for me? I'm sure your father would consider it good practice."

Alassa shrugged, although it was clear her mind was elsewhere.

"No," she said. There was something in her voice that caught Emily's attention, something...wrong. She was nervous. But Alassa was never nervous, not really. She could be happy or angry or even depressed, yet she never lost her poise. "But we do need to talk."

# Chapter Twenty

Emily frowned as Alassa led her into one of the private rooms, locked the door and started to erect a set of complex privacy wards. Some of them she knew from Martial Magic; others were unique, as far as she knew. Alassa might have had a few private lessons during her Third Year...or she might have some specialized spells that had been devised for her family. Either way, no one would be able to spy on them without breaking through the wards and setting off a multitude of alarms.

"That's a very complete set of wards," Emily said. She felt she should say something, if only to break the tension. Alassa was practically nibbling on her fingernails. "Where did you learn those?"

"I don't like the idea of people spying on me," Alassa said. She gave Emily a sidelong glance before sitting down in one of the comfortable chairs. "My aunt...who knows how long she was watching me, before she made her move?"

"Years, perhaps," Emily said. It might have been her fault. The barons would probably have been quite happy to have a spoiled brat on the throne. They wouldn't have been able to marry her — and who would have wanted to marry her? — but at least she wouldn't have been interfering with them. "I think she was an obsessive woman."

Alassa smiled, thinly. "I think she was," she agreed. "Please, sit down."

Emily sat, feeling a chill running down her spine. Alassa was always direct, always certain the straightest path to the target was right *through* any barriers in her way. For her to be so hesitant was strange, utterly out of character. Alassa had never been shy about saying what she needed to say. Emily smoothed her dress, reminding herself of the value of patience. There was no need to rush things.

*Unless there's another problem*, she thought, morbidly. *Or a disagreement that turns to outright violence.*

Alassa looked down at the floor, her hands twisting and turning in her lap. "I need you to tell me something," she said, finally. "Something important."

Emily stared at her friend, who refused to meet her eyes. What did Alassa want? Had her father asked her to make a particular request of Emily? Something she knew Emily would refuse? Or was it something else, something more personal? It wasn't like Alassa to be shy about anything. She'd happily built her own sports team in Year Two and set out to knock the older students off their comfortable perches.

"You can talk to me about anything," Emily said, slowly. Lady Barb would have known what to say, she was sure. "I promise."

Alassa took a deep breath. "Emily," she said. "How do you feel about Jade?"

Emily blinked in surprise. Her imagination had provided a multitude of possibilities, from Randor having figured out the nuke-spell to trying to arrange Emily's marriage, but she hadn't even considered the possibility that Jade would be involved. She thought fast, trying to sort out her own feelings...and parse out the motives behind the request. But she could come up with nothing.

"He's a friend," she said, finally. She found the whole embarrassing interlude difficult to talk about, even to her best friends. Jade had asked her to marry him, perhaps out of sympathy, and changed his mind shortly afterwards. "He...you know...we're better off as friends."

Alassa looked up. "You really think so?"

"Yes," Emily said. She'd found his proposal a little flattering, but also worrying. "I don't think we would make good partners."

She frowned. "Although I seem to recall *you* talking about the advantages of such a match," she added. "You thought it was a good idea."

"That was before I knew where you came from," Alassa said. She looked back down at the floor. "And before you became a baroness, for that matter."

*So I'm too grand for Jade now*, Emily thought, sourly.

"Alassa," she said slowly, "why are you talking to me about this?"

"I wanted to know your feelings," Alassa said.

Emily shook her head in bemusement. "You could have asked without" — she waved her hand to indicate the wards — "all this trouble."

"I needed to ask you in private," Alassa said. She sucked in a breath, as if what she had to say pained her. "Emily...over the last year, while you were at Mountaintop, Jade and I became very close."

She rushed on before Emily could say a word. "I want to marry him."

Emily stared at her in absolute shock. Alassa wanted to marry Jade? Jade wanted to marry Alassa? But...

She closed her eyes as memories surfaced in her mind. Jade had served as a teaching assistant, taking Defensive Magic. Jade had clearly spent extra time working with Alassa, who needed the skills before she left Whitehall. Jade and Alassa had chatted and danced together...he'd traveled with them to Zangaria, to seek a post that would tie him down to one kingdom, even limit his employment elsewhere. And he'd managed to get himself assigned as Alassa's personal bodyguard...

In hindsight, it was all too clear.

*I missed it*, Emily told herself, savagely. *Why?*

"Does he...?" She coughed and started again. "Does he want to marry you?"

"Yes," Alassa said.

Emily felt as if she'd been punched in the chest. Jade had wanted to marry her, *her*. Now he'd moved on to her best friend. To a princess. To...someone who was far more his match. She hadn't wanted him, she knew she hadn't wanted him, but it hurt.

Why did it hurt?

"There are advantages to the match," Alassa said, as if she were relieved she could finally talk about it. "Jade is a commoner, but he's a sorcerer, so he would be a social equal to anyone below a baron. He's powerful enough to protect me and father strong children, but doesn't have a kingdom or family ties of his own to urge him to take power for himself. He could serve as a regent without selling out the throne to either the barons or another kingdom..."

Emily glared at her. Alassa had always been cold-blooded about relationships — she'd once casually outlined all the advantages to *Emily* marrying Jade without sparing a moment's thought for either of their feelings — but this was too much. The pain seemed to grow stronger, outrage that Alassa could pursue Jade mixing with astonishment that they'd never told her. Had they assumed it was obvious? Perhaps it would have been, to anyone else. But Emily knew she was hardly the most observant person where emotions were concerned.

"We would like your blessing," Alassa finished. "And perhaps your support..."

"Why?" Emily demanded, feeling tears prickling at the corner of her eyes. Why was she almost crying? Why did it hurt so much? "Why didn't you tell me?"

Alassa looked uncomfortable, just for a second. "We didn't want to upset you," she said, finally. "I..."

"You didn't want to upset me," Emily snapped. She had to fight down the urge to throw a spell, or perhaps a slap. "You didn't want to *upset* me?"

"No," Alassa said. "I didn't want to see you hurt."

Emily gritted her teeth. "You didn't want to see me hurt?"

Alassa's face darkened. "Do you want to marry him yourself?"

"No," Emily snapped. "I..."

"Then why do you have a problem with *me* marrying him?" Alassa demanded. "If you don't want him yourself, why do you object to me marrying him? Or is there something wrong with him that I should know about?"

Emily shook her head, but said nothing. Jade...was decent. He'd helped Emily, back when she'd been dumped into a class intended for students three or four years her elder, and had been her first real male friend. They'd walked the hills together, enjoying the sunlight and the chance to explore places touched by wild magic. In hindsight, it had been obvious that he'd been courting her, but at the time she'd just learned to relax and enjoy herself. Jade...had made her feel safe.

And now Alassa was taking him away.... And Jade was taking *Alassa* away. Emily's feelings were such a tangled mess that she didn't know how to handle them. Logically, she *knew* she should be happy for her friends, but what did logic know about emotion? She wanted to lash out, to hurt someone, and yet she felt helpless to do anything.

What could she do?

"I don't know," she muttered. "I just don't know."

"Then what is the problem?" Alassa demanded. She rose to her feet, towering over Emily and glowering down at her. "Do you think he's a little too...*common*...to be my husband?"

"No," Emily said. She rose, too, meeting Alassa's eyes. "I don't know how I feel."

"Then figure it out," Alassa snapped. "If you don't want him, why do you object to him marrying me?"

She glared at Emily, magic sparking from her fingertips as she placed her hands on her hips. "Or are you just being selfish?"

"I'm not being selfish!" Emily shouted.

"Yes, you are!" Alassa shouted back. "You want everything to suit you! You want this barony, and yet you also want to stay at Whitehall and study magic! You don't want Jade, but you don't want anyone else to have him either! You want everyone to be your friend when it suits you, and leave you alone when it doesn't!"

Emily forced herself to step back, despite the overwhelming anger. There was a great deal of truth in Alassa's words, she had to admit; she was torn between keeping the barony, even though it might mean having to leave Whitehall and settle permanently in Cockatrice, or simply handing it back to the king. And she knew she wasn't the most sociable of people, even when she wasn't busy. There were times when she just wanted to be alone.

"I don't want him," she said, although the words tore at her soul. Why did it hurt? What was she missing? It wasn't as if she'd imagined having Jade even after he'd made his interest clear. He was fun, she had to admit, but not as a long-term partner. They were simply too different. "I don't..."

"Then why," Alassa demanded again, "do you have a problem with me marrying him?"

"I don't know," Emily confessed. She wanted to find Lady Barb, to ask her for her advice, but she had no idea where the older woman was. But for all Emily knew, Lady Barb might just agree with Alassa and point out that Emily was being selfish. Somehow, the thought of the older woman's disapproval hurt, too. "I just don't know..."

Alassa thinned her lips and sat down, clearly furious. Flickers of magic were sparking over her hands. "We need you to help present our case to my father," she said. "He would need to approve the match."

"You want me to help convince your father to let you marry him?" Emily demanded. "You..."

"You saved his kingdom," Alassa said. She rose again, her eyes meeting Emily's. "He would listen to you!"

Emily almost slapped her. It hurt too much for her to think clearly. She hadn't wanted Jade, but he'd wanted her, but now he'd moved on...and it hurt! It should not have hurt, she told herself, and yet it did. She sagged back into her chair, feeling suddenly tired and worn.

"You didn't tell me," she mumbled. She recalled, suddenly, the moment she'd met Jade's eyes, just after he'd knocked Alassa to the ground and saved her life. He'd thought she'd realized at that moment, she saw suddenly. Perhaps Alassa had planned to tell her later, when the Faire was over. "You didn't tell me, and yet you want me to help?"

"We didn't want to upset you," Alassa said. "You were trying to catch up with us and help Frieda adjust to her new world..."

"You didn't want to upset me?" Emily yelled. "How will it upset your father if he finds out you're marrying a man who wanted to marry someone else, first?"

Alassa took a step forward, then but stopped herself. "Do you really think that's uncommon? Half of the imbeciles we brought to Zangaria two years ago were already engaged, probably several times in a row. Royal children are currency on the marriage market..."

"Jade isn't," Emily said. She thought, briefly, of all the marriage offers she'd received — and the thousands Void claimed to have received. None of them had been interested in anything but the children she might bear. "He doesn't come from a royal family."

"I know," Alassa said. "Why do you think I like him?"

Emily stared down at the ground, one hand wiping away her tears. None of the princes had struck her as decent men; one had been a brain-damaged lunatic, one had been a lecherous swine, and the others had been somewhere in between. The thought of having to share the rest of her life with one of them was bad enough, let alone the thought of sharing a bed. And Alassa would have willingly accepted one of them, if it had seemed necessary.

But Jade? Jade was decent.

*And he is a good match for her,* she thought, bitterly. It still hurt. *They're both smart, they're both fond of physical exercise, and they're both...they're both determined. And who would try to pick a fight, in court, with a combat sorcerer?*

*And he doesn't share the problem of inbreeding...*

And yet, it still hurt.

"My father would have had me marry you, if you had been a boy," Alassa said. "He knows I need someone formidable as a husband. Jade...is formidable, without actually being a threat to me — or to my father."

Emily flushed. Zed had offered her, perhaps in jest, a potion that would change her gender, permanently. A joke...or a subtle revenge on King Randor?

"I don't know," she mumbled. "I just don't know."

"I need you to help me," Alassa said. "Please..."

"Then why didn't you tell me?" Emily asked. She felt betrayed and isolated and abandoned and alone, in the midst of a heaving castle she owned. "Why didn't you tell me any of this?"

"Emily..."

Emily rose, and stalked towards the door. "I need to think," she snarled, as the wards resisted her passage. She tore them down with swift, efficient spells. "Leave me alone!"

Alassa came up behind her and rested a hand on her shoulder. "Emily, I..."

"*Leave me alone,*" Emily snapped.

The last ward came down; she pulled free of Alassa, and stomped out the door. Outside, thankfully, the corridor was deserted, although she heard the band playing in the distance. She walked down the corridor, away from the sound, and up towards the library. Baron Holyoake had resisted anything that smacked of learning, but Emily had insisted on receiving a copy of everything printed in her lands. Her library already had thousands of volumes, ranging from makeshift novels to textbooks and research papers. And it was still expanding...

"But why not now?" A voice asked as she entered. "We're engaged!"

Emily looked up. Gaius stood in front of Melissa, who leaned against one of the bookcases. She looked angry, her arms crossed just under her breasts. Magic crackled between them. It was all that was keeping Gaius from pushing further into her personal space, Emily realized, as they both turned to look at her. Gaius met Emily's eyes for a split second, then he turned and walked past her, out the door.

"Emily," Melissa said. She sounded both defiant and depressed, an odd mixture. "Tell me something."

Emily glowered at her. She didn't *like* Melissa. How could she, when Melissa had decided she was to blame for Alassa becoming a much more capable magician? And whatever Alassa had done to start a fight with Melissa had happened long before Emily had arrived at Whitehall. But she couldn't help feeling sorry for her, too. Gaius had clearly been trying to push his luck.

"What?" She snarled. "What can I tell you?"

"You're the sole child of Void, a Lone Power," Melissa said. "Is it easier being such a child than the heir to a magical family? To have one person to please, instead of hundreds?"

"I don't know," Emily said. At another time, she would have offered to talk, but now...all she wanted to do was collapse. "Void has been a very eccentric presence in my life."

"But I bet he's proud of you," Melissa said. "The Matriarch finds fault with everything I do, no matter how well I do. I could come back home with full marks, the praise of every teacher at Whitehall and an honor award...and I would still have her picking holes in my work."

She sighed, then walked past Emily and headed for the door. "You don't know how lucky you are," she said, bitterly. "To have a father who only shows himself from time to time. My father is dead..."

"I'm sorry," Emily said. "I..."

"My grandfather wouldn't object if the Matriarch ordered him to walk off a cliff... and he's meant to be the Patriarch," Melissa said. "And *she*...nothing ever pleases her."

She nodded once, and walked out the door. Emily stared after her, raised a ward to seal the library, and collapsed into one of the chairs. Alassa and Jade, Melissa and Gaius...her emotions were too mixed up for her to think clearly. Instead, she closed her eyes and tried to force herself to relax.

*It hurts*, she thought, again. It was a bitter thought. Logic told her she should be happy for her friends. There were no grounds for objection, save for the pain. *Why does it hurt?*

But her thoughts provided no answer.

# Chapter Twenty-One

SHE LOST TRACK OF HOW LONG SHE REMAINED SITTING IN THE LIBRARY, LOST IN THE TANGLE of her own thoughts. It seemed like hours, or perhaps only bare minutes, before she felt a familiar presence pushing against her ward. She wanted to channel the strength to keep Imaiqah out, but she couldn't muster the energy. Instead, she allowed the ward to open far enough to allow Imaiqah to enter the library, then closed it behind her.

"Emily," Imaiqah said. She walked over to where Emily sat, curled up in a chair, and sat down next to her. "How are you feeling?"

"Awful," Emily growled. "I...did you *know* about this?"

Imaiqah met her eyes. "That Alassa and Jade want to get married?" She asked. "Yes, I knew."

Emily wasn't surprised. Alassa and Imaiqah had become friends over the past two years...and, in some ways, they were closer than Emily was to either of them. They had more in common, including *Ken*...and besides, Emily had been at Mountaintop for part of Third Year. And besides, Imaiqah was far more perceptive when it came to emotions than Emily herself. She'd probably known that Alassa and Jade had feelings for one another before either of them had admitted it.

*And they shared a room*, she thought. *Did Imaiqah ever leave them alone together in the room?*

"They should have told me," she said, finally. "I could have handled it."

"Alassa was afraid to tell you," Imaiqah said, bluntly. "She...is not in a very comfortable position."

"I could have handled it," Emily repeated. But she thought she understood. Alassa might not have dared to get close enough to consider marriage — or a fling. There were definite advantages to the match, but also several weaknesses. King Randor might refuse to even consider the possibility. "Does her father know?"

"I'd be surprised if he didn't have someone here keeping an eye on them," Imaiqah said. "And he *has* been surprisingly indulgent with *both* of them."

Emily frowned. How many bad romantic movies were based around the bodyguard falling in love with the millionaire's daughter or the pop star with the awful singing voice? In hindsight...had King Randor known all along? He might just have given Jade the job so he could see what his daughter's prospective husband was made of.

She shrugged and looked at her friend. "Why does it hurt?"

Imaiqah looked back. "Do you want me to guess?"

"Yes," Emily said, flatly.

"I think part of you thought of Jade as *yours*," Imaiqah said. "He'd asked you to marry him, not the other way around. You thought of that as a commitment, even after he changed his mind and you *both* decided it would be better not to get married."

"But I didn't think of him as mine," Emily said. "I *knew* we weren't going to get married."

Imaiqah gave her a long considering look. "I'm not saying your feelings have to be logical, or smart," she said. "Men do the same with us, of course. If they think a girl is theirs, they will *keep* thinking a girl is theirs, even after they move on. I've had quite a few boyfriends who thought they had a claim on me, even after we broke up."

Emily flushed. "But...Jade's different."

Imaiqah laughed at her. "Everyone says that," she said. "Or something about how *she* is the only person who can make a good man out of him. Or about how everyone else doesn't know him the way she does. Or..."

She shook her head. "I think you have another problem," she added. "You have some...issues with abandonment, don't you?"

"No," Emily said.

Imaiqah ignored her. "You don't make friends easily. And you're hellishly loyal to the friends you *do* make. I think part of you thinks that Alassa and Jade will go off together and leave you alone, even though they're *both* your friends. And you reacted badly, even if you don't want to admit it, because you thought you were being abandoned."

She had a point, Emily admitted, privately. But...it still hurt.

"I don't think you can really say you have a claim on him," Imaiqah said. "Alassa was worried that you might feel you did, which is partly why she said nothing to you. But how do you feel?"

"Stupid," Emily said.

"That's a good answer," Imaiqah said. "Tell me. Do you want him?"

Emily shook her head, firmly. She couldn't envisage spending the rest of her life with Jade.

"Then what's the problem?" Imaiqah asked. "Apart, perhaps, from you feeling blindsided and stung because no one told you?"

"She said I was selfish," Emily muttered. "I..."

"Lots of people say things they don't mean," Imaiqah said. "Alassa is no different from anyone else, even though she's a princess. I won't say she isn't attracted to Jade, because she obviously is, but marrying him solves a great many other problems at the same time."

Emily nodded. Alassa was nineteen and, by the laws of Zangaria, had been of marriageable age ever since she'd started to have menstrual cycles. The longer she waited, the greater the chance King Randor would find someone for her to marry, someone who might not make a great husband. And time wasn't on her side. The low birthrate of anyone who shared the Royal Bloodline meant Alassa needed to start trying to produce a heir as soon as possible, preferably before the barons decided to try to cause trouble again. King Randor might delay proceedings until the end of Fourth Year, but she doubted he would delay them much longer.

"I've been stupid," Emily said.

"Far be it from me to disagree," Imaiqah said, dryly. "Consider yourself lucky. My mother would have been furious if I'd acted the way you did."

"Lady Barb will be, once she hears about it," Emily said. It struck her, suddenly, that there might already be rumors spreading through the castle. Both Gaius and Melissa had seen her here in the library, obviously upset. "I don't think I've treated her very well, either."

"No, you haven't," Imaiqah said. She stood and paced over to the bookshelves. "But then, Alassa didn't handle the matter very well. If she'd told you before the Faire started, you could have shouted at each other for a while, and then gone back to being friends. Or Jade...he could have told you, too."

Emily sighed. "Is it wrong of me to wish I felt nothing?"

"It depends," Imaiqah said. "Would you give up happiness as well as sadness, love as well as hate...?"

"You've made your point," Emily said, quickly. "But it isn't going to be easy to get used to it."

"I seem to recall *someone* demanding to know why I went out with so many boys," Imaiqah said, dryly. "Do you find that better or worse than Alassa courting Jade?"

Emily looked up. "Did *you* date Jade?"

"I try not to date boys who are more than a year or two older than me," Imaiqah said. "Jade is...what? Five years older?"

*That*, Emily knew, wouldn't be a problem. Alassa had been introduced to a handful of princes who were ten years older than her, while some of the others who'd sought her hand had been in their late fifties. Compared to them, Jade was remarkably close to her age. And he wouldn't be motivated by either a lust for power or a lust for her personally. A trained sorcerer could have his pick of young women looking to boost their bloodlines.

*And he likes her*, Emily thought. *That has to count for a lot, too.*

"I owe Alassa an apology," she said, as she stood. "Where is she now?"

Imaiqah didn't bother to pretend to be surprised by the question. "In her rooms," she said. "I don't think she's too happy, but at least she's not hexing everyone in sight."

Emily winced. Given what she'd said to Alassa, being hexed might be the least she deserved.

"Then we'll go see her," Emily said. "I need to talk to her."

"You could wait," Imaiqah said. "Talk to her tomorrow, when you've both had a chance to sleep on it."

Emily shook her head. "I just want to get it over with," she said. She hated the thought of fighting with her best friends. "Please."

"Then I suggest you clean your face, first," Imaiqah said. She produced a pocket mirror from her robe, and held it in front of Emily. "You look a mess."

Emily sighed. She'd never been vain — if she hadn't been cured of vanity years ago, living close to Alassa would have made sure of it — but Imaiqah was right. Her face was streaked with tears, while her hair had come loose and was hanging over her shoulders. And there were stains on her tunic.... Irritated, she wiped her face dry with a handkerchief, while Imaiqah helped clean up the dress. She might not look particularly regal, she decided, but at least she didn't look as though she'd been crying.

"Let's go," she said.

Outside, the music seemed to have grown louder. She glanced at her watch, realized to her dismay that the dance had at least another hour before it could be brought to a close, and followed Imaiqah through the stone corridors. Emily half-expected to see Jade, standing guard outside Alassa's door, but there was no sign of him. She couldn't help being relieved; right now, Jade was the last person she wanted to see. Imaiqah knocked on the door, then held it open.

"I'll see you both at breakfast tomorrow," she said, as she pushed Emily inside. "And try not to turn each other into small, hopping things."

Emily turned to glare at her, but Imaiqah closed the door in her face. Gritting her teeth, she turned and peered towards the bed. Alassa sat on the mattress, brushing her long golden hair with a gold-edged hairbrush, her blue eyes tired and wary. Emily felt a stab of guilt, followed by a bitter awareness that there was guilt enough for both of them. Neither of them had handled the situation very well.

She swallowed, unsure what to say.

"I'm sorry," she said, finally. "I shouldn't have snapped at you so badly."

"I shouldn't have snapped at you," Alassa replied. "I owe you so much."

Emily winced. Alassa had to have been having nightmares. If Emily had been feeling vindictive, she could have shattered the relationship, simply by bad-mouthing Jade to King Randor. The King would almost certainly have believed her and denied his daughter permission to wed. Or, perhaps, picked a husband himself and ordered Alassa to marry him before she returned to Whitehall.

She walked over to the bed and sat down next to Alassa, then wrapped her arm around her shoulders. "I'm sorry," she said, again. "I've been a right…"

"Pain in the posterior?" Alassa hazarded. "Or just someone who was caught by surprise?"

"I never realized," Emily said. "Even when you were dancing together, I just thought you were trying to avoid dancing with others."

"I wouldn't want to dance with others," Alassa said. "Jade's just the right height for some of the more…interesting dances."

Emily blushed. She'd learned the basic steps of formal dancing as part of her lessons in etiquette, but some of the more complex dances were as close as one could get to lovemaking in public without taking off one's clothes. Emily had never felt comfortable enough to try them, as they left her feeling too exposed.

"I hope you two will be very happy together," she said, finally. "But I wish you had told me ahead of time."

"We planned to tell you after the Faire," Alassa said. "But Jade thought you might have seen something earlier."

"I didn't," Emily said.

"I'm sorry," Alassa said. "I know you didn't need the stress."

"None of us do," Emily said. She looked around the room, wondering — once again — if being a baroness was worth it. "Have you told your father?"

"My father hasn't asked me any questions," Alassa said. "I find that worrisome."

Emily frowned. Alassa couldn't lie to her father, not directly, while lying indirectly was very difficult. A couple of questions from King Randor could lay the whole affair out in the open for all to see. And yet, Alassa *had* told her the King had interrogated her when she'd returned after First Year. For him *not* to question her now...Emily puzzled over it for a long moment, wondering just what it meant. Randor was far more perceptive than Emily, and might well have recognized that Alassa had deeper motives for putting Jade forward as Court Wizard.

*And if he didn't ask her,* she thought, *he gets to maintain plausible deniability.*

"I think he probably knows *something*," Alassa said. "But he will have to decide soon if he wishes to encourage it or not."

"I know," Emily agreed.

She sighed, inwardly. Alassa was caught between two worlds; the restricted life of a princess, even a Crown Princess, and the unrestricted life of a magician. Logically, she could protect herself against everything from sexually-transmitted diseases to an unwanted pregnancy, but King Randor and his court wouldn't see it that way. Alassa could not be allowed to publically disgrace herself. And it didn't matter, no matter how unfair it seemed, that royal princes had licence to fornicate as they saw fit.

*Hypocrites,* Emily thought.

But she saw the underlying logic. A bastard child with a whore could be acknowledged or denied at will, while a pregnant princess was much harder to hide. If Alassa became pregnant out of wedlock, she would either have to abort the pregnancy, which would make her a pariah if anyone found out, or give birth to a bastard. And *that* would be impossible to hide.

*And she would also have to cope with being pregnant,* Emily thought. *And help rule the country at the same time.*

She looked at Alassa, suddenly. "Have you slept with him?"

"I can't," Alassa said. "It isn't something I can do before we get married."

Emily nodded in understanding, although she could see advantages to getting pregnant before the wedding. If Alassa couldn't have children with Jade, and it was quite possible she simply couldn't have children at all, it would probably be better to find out before they were committed to one another. God alone knew how easy it would be for them to separate, given their position. Emily had a private feeling that quite a few of the aristocrats had been having problems with their wives. But then, all the *men* had to do was find a mistress and leave the legitimate wife at another estate.

"I'm very happy for you," she said, as she rose. "And I will speak to your father for you, when the time comes."

"I don't know which way my father will jump," Alassa admitted. "There are advantages to the match, but there are also disadvantages. The barons will mutter angrily because *they* didn't get to marry me."

"I won't," Emily said.

Alassa snorted. "You're a girl," she said. "You couldn't marry me...but if you had a son, you might be angry on his behalf."

Emily rolled her eyes. If she'd had a son, assuming she'd given birth as soon as it had been physically possible, he would be five years old by now. By the time he was old enough to wed, Alassa would be twenty-nine, perhaps older. The idea of convincing Alassa to wait ten years, losing the time she needed to give birth to as many children as possible, was absurd.

"On the other hand, the barons will all know that *none* of them got to marry me," Alassa added. "That will keep them from uniting against one of their number. And, as Jade isn't a foreigner prince, they can't claim we're threatening the independence of the kingdom. The only concerns they can raise is that Jade isn't an aristocrat, but as he's a combat sorcerer, that problem falls into nothingness."

She sighed. "But, on the other hand, marrying Jade would take me off the marriage market," she said, after a moment. "And several princes would feel slighted, feeling they'd been pushed aside in favor of a common-born sorcerer. They might cause trouble for father in the White Council."

Emily frowned. "And he would reject your choice on those grounds?"

"Father swore to put the kingdom first," Alassa reminded her. "If marrying his daughter to a common-born sorcerer threatens the kingdom, he won't do it."

"I see," Emily said. "Suddenly, I'm *very* glad I'm not a boy."

"Me too," Alassa said. She smiled, impishly. "You'd make a funny-looking boy."

Emily laughed, surprising herself. "I'm sorry for reacting so badly," she said. Somehow, talking to Alassa had made her feel better, even though she still felt guilty. "And I will do what I can to make up for it."

"Serve as a target for some new hexes I've learned?" Alassa asked. "I would be very appreciative."

"No, thank you," Emily said, quickly.

"I thought not," Alassa said, although it was clearly a friendly comment. "But I don't really blame you."

"I'll see you in the morning," Emily said. She looked down at the floor for a moment, then back at Alassa. "And...and I do wish you both the very best."

"I'll tell Jade you've forgiven us, then," Alassa said. "And Emily..."

Emily waited, lifting her eyebrows.

"I didn't mean to hurt you, either," Alassa said. "I'm sorry."

"It's all right," Emily said. The pain had faded to a dull ache, which she knew would go away in time. "See you in the morning."

She stepped out of Alassa's room and walked back to her own rooms. As soon as she was in the room, with the door closed, locked and warded, she lay down on the bed and stared at the ceiling. Her thoughts, no matter what she did, were still a mess. It had been far too long a day.

Dismissing the thought, she felt the battery in her pocket, closed her eyes, and went to sleep.

## Chapter Twenty-Two

"THERE'S A LETTER ON YOUR TABLE FOR YOU, YOUR LADYSHIP," JANICE SAID, AS EMILY stepped into the Great Hall. "I think one of the young men left it for you."

Emily frowned. The Great Hall was almost empty. Most of the guests were either sleeping in after a night of hard dancing, or had gone straight down to the Faire. Only Jade, Alassa, Imaiqah, and Frieda were seated at the High Table eating breakfast. Emily felt an odd pang as she met Jade's eyes, but told herself not to be stupid. There was nothing to be gained by shouting at him, too.

"Thank you," she said.

A simple cream envelope lay atop her empty plate, she noted after she sat down next to Alassa. She checked it automatically — some letters she'd received at Whitehall had nasty spells attached — and discovered a privacy spell, but nothing actually harmful. Slitting it open, she discovered a note from Steven, apologizing for being called away at short notice. It must have been very short notice, Emily thought sardonically, as she placed the letter in her pocket, but she didn't really mind. After last night, the last thing she wanted was a delicate conversation with Steven.

"Emily," Jade said. "I'm sorry. I..."

"Don't worry about it," Emily said. She didn't really want to talk to Jade, either. "I don't have any grounds to complain about you and...Alassa. I hope you will both be very happy together."

*And not forget me*, she thought, silently. Imaiqah had been right. No matter how she looked at it, a part of her felt abandoned. Alassa might not even return to Whitehall after Fourth Year, leaving her and Imaiqah behind. And who knew what would happen then?

"Thank you," Jade said.

He looked relieved, Emily noted; beside him, Alassa gave her a reassuring smile. In hindsight, it was clear just how close she and Jade had become. And yet, Emily wouldn't have to stop being friends with either of them, because of their relationship. She shook her head ruefully. Perhaps she should try and pay more attention to emotional undercurrents in future.

She sighed, knowing it wouldn't be easy, and ate her breakfast as quickly as she decently could. There was nothing on her schedule for the morning, so she intended to see if she could sit down with Caleb and rewrite the proposal until she knew it backwards. Imaiqah intended to go back to the Faire and assist her father, while Alassa and Jade planned to explore on their own. At first, Frieda looked down at the table, but rather than seeming excited after Imaiqah asked her if Frieda wanted to go down to the Faire too, looked doubtful. Indeed, she seemed oddly subdued.

"I'll take you there in the afternoon," Emily promised. She didn't know how long she'd have to spend with Caleb, but she had a feeling she would need a break afterwards. "Or we can go for a walk in the city."

"Everyone will know you there," Alassa reminded her. "Don't forget to use a glamor."

"I won't," Emily said, although she had her doubts. The paintings she'd seen of herself, scattered around the castle, were no more accurate than the paintings at Whitehall. They made her look like a brown-haired version of Alassa, complete with larger breasts and white dresses that called attention to her face. "You'd better do the same."

"She will," Jade agreed. "I don't want too many people to recognize her."

Emily smiled, then scribbled a note for Caleb, asking him to meet her in the work-room once he'd had breakfast. She passed it to a maid, who took it without hesitation, then smiled as she saw Markus entering the Great Hall. He looked tired, but there was a faint smile on his face that suggested he was pleased about something. Emily put it aside for later contemplation, bade her friends farewell and headed up to the workroom. Lady Barb was already there, sitting on a wooden stool and studying a set of notes.

"Emily," she said. She looked tired, yet slightly amused. "Are you all right?"

Emily frowned. Lady Barb knew...of *course* she knew. "Did everyone know but me?"

"Probably," Lady Barb said. She shrugged, expressively. "They *were* quite discreet, but you know how rapidly rumors can spread through Whitehall. I imagine most of the school knows by now."

"I didn't," Emily said, crossly. "And..." She swallowed. "I said horrible things to Alassa last night. Things I should never have said. If Imaiqah hadn't come to talk to me..."

"You might have lost your friend," Lady Barb finished.

"Yeah," Emily said.

"I don't blame you for being shocked," Lady Barb said, after a moment. "Or for los-ing your temper when you finally found out."

"It was worse than that," Emily said.

"I didn't hear," Lady Barb said. "There are advantages to the match, as you know. An infusion of fresh blood might be just what the Royal family needs."

She rose to her feet. "But I suggest you concentrate on something else, for the moment. Last night could have been disastrous in many different ways."

"The families could have gone to war," Emily said.

"Quite," Lady Barb agreed. She looked past Emily. "Good Morning, Caleb."

"I thank you," Caleb said, as Emily turned to face him. "I got your note."

"I'll leave the pair of you alone," Lady Barb said, as she walked past them. "If you need to talk, Emily, I will be down at the Faire."

"Thank you," Emily said. "I'll see you there later."

Caleb eyed her curiously as Lady Barb closed the door behind her. "What was *that* about?"

"I'll tell you later," Emily said. She didn't want to discuss Jade and Alassa with Caleb, or anyone else for that matter. "I was looking at the proposal notes..."

She walked over to the bookshelves and picked up the notes. "I was thinking we could draw out flow diagrams first," she said, as she put the papers on the table and motioned for him to sit down facing her. "It's quite similar to spell incants, but it would allow us to plot out the magic without those pesky start points and end points."

"Or accidentally triggering a spell," Caleb said, thoughtfully. He raised his eyebrows. "Flow diagrams?"

"Because the magic flows through the spell mosaic," Emily said. She tapped one of the sets of notes, feeling an odd burst of pleasure at how quickly he was catching on. "We build each component out of pieces of mosaic, then bigger sets to represent the entire spell, and finally start magic flowing through them as you planned. If we fiddle a little here, we might even be able to ensure the spell changes, depending on the feedback."

"It still leaves us with the main problem," Caleb said, after a moment. "Each piece of mosaic has to be charmed individually."

"Maybe," Emily said. She'd pulled one thing out of her memory from Aurelius's books. "But if you used subtle magic, you could produce a number of components at the same time, if you didn't mind waiting a few hours. You could even enhance the ambient magical field if you used a ritual..."

Caleb gave her a sharp look. "How do you know about rituals?"

Emily cursed, inwardly. Lady Barb was going to kill her.

"It's something I was encouraged to study by my father," she lied, finally. She didn't want to lie to Caleb, yet she saw no choice. Lady Barb might have taught her the basics, but Whitehall's students were rarely shown how to use rituals until they entered Fifth Year. "He thought there were ways to use rituals to power runes without burning them out."

"You *would* burn them out," Caleb said, although he still looked doubtful. How did *he* know about rituals? But then, his mother was an experienced sorcerer. "It just wouldn't last..."

"It would if you made them out of iron," Emily said. "Have a team of ordinary blacksmiths make them for you according to a plan you devise. You could hire quite a few in Dragon's Den for a handful of pieces of gold. Then just keep repairing or replacing them, as necessary. I think if you raise the level of magic in the compartment by a fraction, the results would definitely be better than you expect."

"Or it might explode in our faces, again," Caleb said. He tapped the diagram thoughtfully. "I never thought of combining the different sets of magic like this."

"I only saw it recently," Emily admitted. There was another possible use for the technique, she suspected, if it happened to be combined with a battery. But that would have to wait until she actually had a moment to sit down and work through it herself. "We might need to get special permission to use a ritual."

"It's brilliant," Caleb said. "They might not let us do it in Whitehall itself, of course, but they should definitely let us take it out of the school. There's quite a few outbuildings that could easily serve as a base."

Emily grinned. "I made a few additions to the proposal," she said. "But we'll have to redraft it for the Grandmaster."

"Give me a moment," Caleb said, as he scanned the sheet of paper. "You seem to have altered the variable search incants too."

"I was getting to those," Emily said. "If we poke and prod at it, the entire system might actually start learning from experience."

"You'd need one hell of a source of power," Caleb said. "I think it wouldn't be possible to use such a capable system without a nexus point. Even Whitehall has had problems with developing self-learning wards."

Emily nodded, slowly. The nexus provided a vast source of power — Mountaintop had never been able to match it, even with the sacrifice of thousands of students — but the wards weren't self-aware. There were so many layers of complexity written into the system that she had a private suspicion there were more cracks in the defenses than anyone cared to admit. Shadye might have been reduced to trickery to get through the wards, but Void had been able to walk in and out of the school as he pleased.

"We might be able to find a nexus point," she mused. There had to be some in the Blighted Lands, although it was possible the necromancers had destroyed them...if, of course, they could be destroyed. But then, Shadye had gone for Whitehall, not for one of his fellow necromancers. "Or perhaps find another source of power."

"There isn't one," Caleb said. "Even necromancy wouldn't be enough."

"Probably for the best," Emily said. Would her *battery* be enough, if she kept charging it? She briefly considered swearing him to secrecy, but dismissed the thought. As nice as Caleb was, she barely knew him. "But what we have—" she pointed to the first set of proposals "—would be more than enough, right?"

"Probably," Caleb said.

He pulled a notebook out of his pocket and started to write in crisp, even sentences. Emily absently admired his command of Old Script, wondering just when his military father had permitted him to learn to read and write. Even Imaiqah's father had hesitated over teaching his daughters the basics...and Alassa, who had never been pushed by her parents, had only ever mastered a few basic words. But then, English letters were so much simpler.

"I'll have to send this back to the school tonight, through the portals," Caleb said. "Once the Grandmaster approves it, we can start planning our working schedule."

"Fourth Year is going to be busy," Emily said. She would have Charms, Alchemy, Healing, Subtle Magic and several other courses to complete, as well as a new Martial Magic program. Aloha had said they were going to get a new tutor...absently, she wondered who it might be. Lady Barb would make a good, if unforgiving, teacher. And it would keep her close to Sergeant Miles. "I think we might have to wait until we know our classes before we start making specific plans."

"There's always at least one afternoon a week put aside for joint projects," Caleb assured her. "If we have to make some special arrangements, we will need to request them before we go back to Whitehall. I was told that if the arrangements weren't requested at least a week before school reopens, we wouldn't be getting them."

"Joy," Emily said. "A place to work outside the school, if necessary...what else?"

"Whatever else we can make a case for," Caleb said. He winked at her. "Do you think a solid gold bracelet would be useful for our project?"

Emily smiled, toying with the snake-bracelet on her wrist. "I don't think so," she said. "What happens if we can't justify our requests?"

"I imagine the Grandmaster will mark us down for it," Caleb said. He shrugged. "But half of the project is working out what we might need, explaining why we might need it...and then explaining afterwards why we *didn't* need it."

"Oh," Emily said. "And what if we need something we *didn't* anticipate beforehand?"

"We get marked down," Caleb said.

He smiled at her, and finished writing down his notes. "I'll try and rewrite the entire proposal this afternoon, then pass it to you before I take it to the portals," he said. "You'll need to read it carefully, then sign it. At that point—" he shrugged expressively "—the die is cast."

"Thank you," Emily said. She would have loved to help, or at least she felt as though she *should* have helped, but she knew his Old Script was far better than hers. "Will you have time to go to the Faire?"

"I may go tomorrow," Caleb said. "The Grandmaster won't get back to us for a few days, even if he starts work at once. He'll need to run it past my Advisor, then the supervisors, who will probably question everything with a gimlet eye."

He shrugged. "But I do want to go see the railway trains again," he admitted. "They run without magic!"

"They do," Emily said. She'd promised to explain them to him, when she had a moment — and she did, now. "Does that surprise you?"

"Oh, yes," Caleb said. "I wouldn't have believed it possible."

There was a tap on the door. Emily rose, and opened it. Lady Barb stood there.

"Emily," she said. There was a dark tone to her voice. "Caleb, can I borrow Emily for a moment?"

"Of course," Caleb said. "I have to go rewrite the proposal anyway."

He bowed to Emily, and walked out of the room.

"I do trust you're planning to read the entire proposal, once it's rewritten," Lady Barb said. "Your grade will depend on *his* work — and vice versa."

"I will," Emily said. She swallowed. "I accidentally told him I knew about rituals."

Lady Barb pursed her lips. "I'm surprised *he* knows about rituals," she said, after a moment. "I was unaware that Stronghold taught them to Second Year students."

"His mother might have told him, or he might just have read ahead," Emily said. "There are a handful of references to rituals in the books at Whitehall."

"But you wouldn't know what they were talking about without the prior knowledge," Lady Barb said, curtly. "You know, because I taught you, but how does *he* know?"

She shrugged. "That's a problem for another day," she said, "and we will *discuss* your...lack of discretion later. I will need someone to help clean the classroom every day next term, perhaps."

"I'm sorry," Emily said, quickly. "I covered for it. I blamed it on Void."

"Glad to hear it," Lady Barb said. "It's a good explanation, for now. But sorry isn't always enough."

She sat down, waving a hand at the other chair. Emily sat, relieved. She wasn't entirely sure if Lady Barb could sentence her to a term's worth of detentions while school was out, but there was no point in tempting fate. Besides, Lady Barb was right. She'd accidentally revealed something that could be used against her, at a later date. The Grandmaster would not be pleased, even if the cover story was firmly in place.

"I have received a message," Lady Barb said. She sounded thoroughly displeased, but the tone was not aimed at Emily. "There is a...problem I need to deal with, before it gets out of hand. I will be away for at least a week."

Emily stared at her. "You can't stay?"

"I believe that's what I said," Lady Barb reminded her, primly. "Master Grey has agreed, reluctantly, to continue to work with you as Head of Security. I would have preferred Jade for the role, but there's no way he can be put in command of his former master."

"And he needs to stay with Alassa," Emily said. "Is there no one else?"

"Under the circumstances, you're very lucky to get *anyone*," Lady Barb snapped. "These events are normally organized months in advance, with a small army of magicians arranged to help keep order."

She rose to her feet and began to pace. "I would prefer to stay here myself," she admitted, "but the request is actually quite important. It isn't something I can leave with anyone else, even if someone was available."

She stopped in front of Emily, staring down at her. "Time to stand up and do better," she said. "I can't hold your hand any longer."

"I know," Emily mumbled.

"Miles said he may be down in a couple of days, but no promises — and you're not to rely on him either," Lady Barb warned her. "I've done my best for you, at very short notice, but I can't stay here any longer."

She paused. "Keep charging your battery, and think of a way to use it if necessary," she added. "You may have a few other tricks up your sleeve, but be careful. There are too many witnesses here."

"I know," Emily repeated. She rose to her feet, unable to escape the sense that she had been abandoned again. "I didn't mean to put you to any trouble."

"I'll be using you as a live subject next term, if you're not careful," Lady Barb warned. "You do know there are limits to what can be learned if you work with a homunculus, don't you?"

Emily flushed, embarrassed. She had no idea how Lady Barb had convinced a handful of volunteers to strip down and allow a class of students to examine them, but she was damned if she wanted to do it herself. Third Year Healing had seen most of the idiots and wannabes removed from the class — Lady Barb was strict with everyone — yet it had still been an embarrassing day. And none of the students had actually *known* any of the volunteers.

"I'll do my best," she promised.

Lady Barb clapped her shoulder. "Sometimes, we learn by being dumped in hot water," she said.

"Yeah," Emily countered. Most of Whitehall's teaching methods were far superior to Earth's, but some of them left something to be desired. "And sometimes people are scalded to death."

# Chapter Twenty-Three

IT WAS NEARLY LUNCHTIME BY THE TIME EMILY FINISHED CHANNELING MAGIC INTO THE BAT-tery, although it took her some time to realize it. Somehow, the sensation of brushing against her own raw magic was relaxing, even if the effort of channeling and expending so much magic left her feeling utterly exhausted afterwards. As soon as the ring had cooled down, she placed it in her pocket, ate several ration bars in rapid succession, and after she felt like she had a bit of energy, then finally walked to Frieda's rooms.

"Jade told me he feels guilty," Frieda said, as soon as Emily stepped inside. "Guilty for what?"

Emily shook her head. "It doesn't matter," she said. She held out her hand. "Let's go down to the Faire."

The Faire looked busier than ever, she noted as they walked through the gates and into the mass of stalls. She'd half-expected to see that some of the stalls had closed, as they had to have sold most of their goods by now, but instead there seemed to be even more stalls open than before. They must have been bringing in new stock through the portals, she reasoned, as she perused one of the old book stalls. Sergeant Miles had made her study the logistic effects of portals on the Allied Lands and they tended to work a little like railroads on Earth, although they had their limitations. Nothing larger than a small cart could be moved through the gateway.

She found herself relaxing as they walked from stall to stall. Hundreds of young children ran around, playing elaborate games of tag while their parents chatted, browsed, and bought supplies to take home with them. It was interesting to see just how easy it was to separate out the different social castes, Emily noted, despite her only having spent three years in the Nameless World. The aristocracy wore fine silks, the magicians bright colors and the merchants plain, simple garments. But there were other differences, too. The aristocracy walked around with their heads held high, while the magicians kept their eyes fixed on the other magicians; the merchants seemed to adjust their attitude, depending on who they were speaking to.

*But that makes sense*, she thought. *A nobleman wouldn't buy from an uppity com-moner, no matter how much he wants the product.*

It bothered her to see such social divisions, even at the Faire. Who was actually winning when a cringing merchant talked a proud aristocrat into buying something for twice the going rate? The aristocrat, because the merchant bowed and scraped, or the merchant, because he walked away with the money? And yet...she couldn't help thinking the aristocrats deserved to lose their wealth. It was rare for them to bargain, even when they were poor. They felt they had to make a show of being rich and powerful.

*Which explains some of the problems facing Zangaria*, Emily thought. *The wealthy and powerful are often not as powerful as they seem.*

Frieda poked her. "What are you thinking about?"

"Money and power," Emily said. She noticed a magician bargaining with a merchantman and smiled. They were torn between ten silver coins and eleven. "And how some of the people who claim to have both have neither."

Frieda gave her an odd look. "What does that mean?"

Emily shrugged — it wasn't something she wanted to discuss at the moment — and led Frieda over to watch a performer. The young man — he couldn't have been any older than Frieda — tossed burning torches in the air, catching them one by one, without the aid of protective spells. The crowd cheered loudly as the performer caught the final torch, bowing to his audience. A little girl — his sister, Emily hoped — carried a hat from person to person; Emily dropped a bronze coin into the hat, and watched as the girl carried it back to the performer. He grinned at the small pile of coins, and performed a whole series of backflips, carrying two torches in his bare hands.

"I could learn to do that," Frieda said. "Couldn't I?"

"Get Sergeant Miles to teach you the Sword Dance, if you want to do something insanely dangerous," Emily said. The sergeant had taught Jade and several of the older boys, but he'd refused to teach Emily. Looking at how the boys had moved their swords, thrusting and parrying in a complex series of motions that could get someone stabbed if they messed up, it was hard to blame him. "One single mistake and you'd be dead."

Frieda frowned. "But I could be healed, couldn't I?"

"Healed from *death*?" Emily asked. "No magic can bring back the dead."

"Healed from having my arm cut off," Frieda said, throwing her a cross look.

"Maybe," Emily said. She had never been *that* good with a sword. "But is it worth the risk?"

They moved on to the next set of performers, a band who sang songs about great battles, heroic love affairs, and a ballad about a mundane man who killed an evil magician. Emily was mildly surprised they dared to sing the latter at the Faire, where most of the clientele were magicians, but she had to admit it was a catchy tune. Besides, as she listened to the words, it became apparent that the magician had been an idiot, someone stupid enough to take a pratfall again and again. She couldn't help wondering if the magicians enjoyed listening to a story about someone so stupid, he embarrassed everyone else.

"And then the dragon opened its mouth and blew fire towards me," a voice she vaguely recognized boomed. "I ducked under its jaw, and stabbed up with my sword."

Emily peered over at the next crowd and blinked in astonishment. Farmer Giles — *former* Farmer Giles — was standing there, wearing a mercenary suit of armor and telling an outrageously tall story about a battle with a dragon so large it had to have grown into intelligence. Emily shook her head in disbelief — she'd actually *met* a dragon, which was more than could be said for most magicians — and listened with growing amusement. Giles was a surprisingly good storyteller, even when he was describing how he tamed the dragon by pulling a thorn out of its scales. Emily knew that next to nothing could actually *harm* a dragon, save for magical weapons and other tricks...

"Alassa said you actually rode on a dragon," Frieda said. "Is that true?"

Emily nodded, smiling, as Giles brought his story to an end. The crowd cheered, tossing a handful of coins towards him. Giles scooped them up, loudly promising another story in an hour or two. He would definitely make a fine author, Emily decided, as long as one didn't happen to look too closely at his plots. She had no idea what would happen if a person pulled a thorn out of a dragon's scales, but she doubted it would lead to lifelong friendship. The dragons were simply far too long-lived to give much of a damn about humanity.

*And at least he found a way to support himself*, she thought, as she gave him a coin herself. His eyes went wide when he saw her, then he looked away. *He might make a career out of storytelling.*

"You should tell stories yourself," Frieda said, as they walked off towards the food stalls. The smell of cooked meat was growing overpowering. "You're good at telling stories."

"No, I'm not," Emily muttered.

She sighed, inwardly. Every story she'd told Frieda, to help the younger girl sleep, had been from Earth. There was no one in the Nameless World to enforce copyright — she could write out *The Lord of the Rings* if she wanted to, and sell copies — but it still felt wrong to steal. Besides, there was no particular reason why someone couldn't actually produce a whole series of magic rings, with one ring to bind them all. The story would only give unscrupulous magicians ideas, Emily was sure, and she knew from Lady Barb that they had too many ideas already. But she had never told Frieda the truth.

"You should," Frieda insisted.

"I have too much else to do," Emily said. Besides, even high fantasy like *The Lord of the Rings* would need to be revised to fit into the Nameless World. Putting semi-humans like hobbits as the heroes? It would not go down well. And then she would have to explain Gandalf and the other wizards as something other than angelic creatures of light. "But you can do it, if you like."

Frieda frowned. "Can I?"

"Of course," Emily said. She clapped the younger girl on the shoulder. "Don't let anyone else tell you what you can and cannot do."

"Unless they happen to be tutors?" Frieda asked. She gave Emily a sly smile. "Or older students?"

Emily was still chuckling as they bought pieces of pizza and settled down to eat. Perhaps Frieda *would* make a great storyteller...and, by the time the story was written, it would be very different from the original. Or perhaps she would find something else to do with her life. The Nameless World wasn't ready to support an author trying to earn a living wage through writing. But she could always write in the evening, after doing her job...

*Maybe she can write about the courtship of Jade and Alassa*, she thought. She'd read a few stories of past courtships, only to dismiss them as romantic nonsense. But there was probably a method in the madness. Romantic stories helped disguise the ugly truth, that all royal marriages were business arrangements first and everything else second. King Randor was fond of his wife, Emily knew, but he would still have married her even if he'd hated everything about her. His father wouldn't have let him welsh out of the contract.

Frieda looked up, sharply. "What the hell is that?"

Emily blinked, then listened. Someone was barking like a dog...no, *several* people. And others were shouting...

"Stay here," she ordered. Whatever had gone wrong, she had to deal with it. "I'll be back as soon as I can."

She tossed the remains of the pizza into the bin, rose to her feet and hastened towards the source of the sound, cursing her dress as she moved. It just wasn't designed to allow her to move quickly.

*Do you want a slit in it so you can actually run?* Her own thoughts mocked her. *And show your legs to the crowd?*

She almost ran into Master Grey as she turned the corner around one of the larger tents, and blinked in surprise. A handful of children, ranging from seven to fourteen, were running around on the ground, barking like dogs. It would have been funny, Emily was sure, if it wasn't for the panic in their eyes. And in the eyes of their parents, who were staring at their children in horror. She shivered, remembering the girl who'd served as a test subject for compulsion spells at Mountaintop, and looked up as she heard the sound of someone giggling. A young boy was perched on top of the tent, looking at the children and cackling madly. It took her a moment to place him as Maximus Ashfall, Markus's younger brother.

Master Grey glanced at Emily and made a show of stepping backwards, leaving the matter in her hands. Emily fought down the urge to glare at him, then returned her attention to Maximus. It didn't need Sherlock Holmes to deduce that he was behind the chaos, even if there hadn't been a number of parents looking at him, their faces torn between fear and rage. But he was eleven, wasn't he? He couldn't have magic of his own...

*Potion*, she thought, as she saw the bottle in his hand. *He must have tricked them into drinking something that made them act like dogs.*

Summoning her magic, she reached out for Maximus and *pulled*. The boy let out a yelp as he was torn from the tent and dropped to the muddy ground in front of Emily. He let go of the bottle of potion and turned to run. Master Grey stepped forward, arms crossed, and pinned Maximus in place with a glare. Emily couldn't help feeling a flicker of envy. If only she had the presence to match her reputation. It might save her a great many problems.

"It was only a joke," Maximus said. "I didn't mean for them to actually drink it..."

"I'm sure you didn't," Emily said, as the parents closed in. "What did you give them?"

"They didn't believe me when I told them I was a magician," Maximus said. "So I gave them Dogbreath Potion."

Emily shuddered inwardly. Professor Thande had taught them to brew Dogbreath Potion in First Year. It didn't actually turn someone's breath into foul-smelling gas, despite some ribald comments from her fellow students; it actually make them act like a dog, at least until the potion had worked its way out of their system. A powerful magician might be able to push the effects aside, given enough mental discipline, but someone without magic would find it very hard to resist the potion. She looked at the barking children and shuddered, again.

"It was funny," Maximus insisted. "And..."

Emily had to fight down the urge to throw a fireball right into his smirking face. She hated bullies; she'd *always* hated bullies. Maximus would come into his magic and go to Mountaintop, she was sure, where he would spend half of his time picking on the children from non-magical families...and then his Shadow, if someone didn't give in to the temptation to feed him something lethal before Third Year. It would be so easy to wipe the brat's smile off his face...

"I will take you back to your parents, who will deal with you," she said, instead. "And you will *not* return to the Faire."

Maximus opened his mouth, either to object or to pretend it had only been a joke, but Emily didn't give him the time to say anything. Instead, she cast a spell, turning him into a tiny statuette of himself. The parents looked torn between relief and fear as she picked up the statuette, tucked it into her pocket, and turned to the children. They were still gambolling around like dogs.

"Take them to the healer's tent," she ordered the parents, quietly. Professor Thande had *also* told them what to do if they drank something they shouldn't. "Tell the healers they will need a dose of purgative. If they try to charge you for it, have the bill sent to the castle and I'll forward it to the brat's parents."

"Thank you," a terrified-looking mother said. "I..."

She broke off as she saw through Emily's glamor. "Lady Emily!"

"See to your child," Emily ordered. She hadn't wanted to be recognized. "I'll deal with *him*."

She sighed, inwardly, as the parents dragged their children towards the tent. It would have been nothing more than a prank in Whitehall or Mountaintop, nothing more than a harmless jest. Emily had lost count of the number of times Melissa and her cronies had pranked her...and of the number of times she, Alassa, and Imaiqah had pranked them back. But for these children, even if they recovered without permanent harm, it would blight the rest of their lives. Everyone would remember them acting like dogs even when the potion wore off.

"Not the nicest of people," Master Grey observed. "But what can you expect from an Ashfall?"

Emily rounded on him. "You could have handled it."

"You were the superior here," Master Grey said, with a glint in his eye warning her not to presume on it under other circumstances. "It would have been insulting for me to take the lead."

He shrugged. "I dare say Master Ashfall will not be too concerned," he added. "It was only a prank."

"Played on someone incapable of defending themselves," Emily countered. "It could have been really dangerous."

"It will be worse now," Master Grey commented. "But really, what can you expect from an Ashfall?"

Emily scowled at him. "Are you allowed to show a link to your former family?"

"Sometimes," Master Grey said.

"Then tell me," Emily said, "what are the *other* stories about how the feud started?"

Master Grey gave her a long, considering look. "Some people are told that the Ashworths wished to keep the family following the old traditions, while the Ashfalls wanted to rewrite them to suit themselves. The family was split between two factions, both so large that neither could claim a consensual victory. Eventually, the Ashworths stayed where they were, while the Ashfalls stormed off to set up their own family. And the feud spread from there."

It sounded believable, Emily decided. And yet...was it really likely that the split had been even enough to allow half the family to leave the other half?

He snorted. "In the old days, there would have been no contact between the magical families and common mundanes," he added. "This would not have happened."

Emily rather doubted it. From what she'd read, both the mundane aristocracy and the magical families had once been tied together under the emperor. It had only been after the death of the last emperor and the fall of the Empire that the two had separated, which was probably why powerful magic had popped up in Alassa's bloodline. But then, she had never really been sure just how powerful King Randor was, or indeed if he was a magician at all.

"I'm sure it wouldn't," she said. "If you don't mind, I have to take the brat back to the castle and hand him over to his father. I'm sure he will deal with him."

Master Grey looked for a moment as though he were about to say something, but instead shrugged and walked off towards the bookstalls. Emily glowered after him, collected Frieda, and began the walk back to the castle, mentally planning out what she would say to Marcellus. Maybe the Ashworth Patriarch would see it as a joke too, but *Emily* didn't. One way or another, Maximus would not be allowed back to the Faire.

"He won't like you telling him this," Frieda warned, once Emily had told her what had happened. "Fathers always believe the best of their sons."

"I know," Emily said. In Markus's case, Marcellus might have been right. "But I saw what happened, and I have Master Grey as a witness. And I told them all that I would not tolerate anyone abusing my people."

Frieda gave her a strange look, but said nothing.

# Chapter Twenty-Four

"I WISH TO APOLOGIZE, ONCE AGAIN, FOR MY SON'S BEHAVIOR," MARCELLUS SAID, DURING the evening meal. "He has been soundly chastised."

"As in, he's been told very loudly that he's been very naughty and he's not to do it again," Fulvia put in. "There's nothing to be gained by allowing one's children to run free."

"Except free-thinking magicians," Marcellus countered, crossly. "But I suppose you wouldn't want people thinking for themselves."

Emily sighed as the two magicians sniped at one another. They weren't the only ones; rumors had spread rapidly, of course, and now the two families were bickering constantly, while the other guests were trying to stay out of the line of fire. Both Markus and Melissa seemed to have made themselves scarce, while Gaius looked cross, and his two cronies were glowering around the room, as if they were searching for someone to blame.

"I don't care about what you do elsewhere," she said, sharply. "But I do care about what you do here."

"My son has been taught a lesson," Marcellus assured her. "He will not be abusing your people again."

"Good," Emily said.

"My son would not have had to be told," Fulvia commented. "He *knows* not to pick on the small, weak, and helpless."

"Your son is old enough to have grandchildren," Marcellus snapped. "How does your granddaughter behave?"

Emily sighed and prayed, inwardly, that the meal would come to a quick end. Perhaps she could arrange for the next dinner to be held outside the castle, or perhaps come up with an emergency that required her urgent attention. Or...she cursed inwardly, already knowing what Lady Barb would say. She didn't dare risk giving offense by *not* hosting the dinner every night.

*After this, I am damned if I am hosting anything else,* she thought, crossly. *The next Faire can be held on the other side of the world.*

Dinner, thankfully, came to an end without bloodshed, although there were a number of moments when Emily feared all hell was about to break loose. She watched the servants prepare the dance floor, and headed up to the balcony to rest while the guests danced the night away. Jade and Alassa were dancing; it bothered her to watch them, even though she wasn't sure why. They looked happy together... no, more than *happy*; they looked *right* together. Part of her envied her friends that happiness.

"My lady?"

Emily turned to see one of the maids, a young girl she barely knew. Like so many of the others, she was a younger daughter and had gone into service, rather than trying to find a husband or a life of her own. Emily knew that most of her maids would leave in a few years, with enough money to be sure of finding either a husband or a place to set up their own business, but it still felt wrong, as if people had been dealt a poor hand simply by being born.

And it galled her she couldn't remember half of their names.

"Yes," she said. "What can I do for you?"

"There's something...*funny*...about the library," the maid said. "I'm meant to clean it...ah...I kept meaning to do it, but every time I went close to the library I forgot what I was doing and walked away. And it kept happening."

Emily frowned. It sounded like an aversion ward, one tuned to grant privacy without calling attention to itself. Anyone who walked too close would miss it, or remember something urgent they had to do elsewhere. A powerful magician might sense its presence, if he were looking for it, but others might just be repelled without ever realizing they'd been pushed away. Mountaintop had once been shrouded in such wards.

"I'll see to it," she said. It wasn't *her* work and her friends were down on the dance floor, enjoying themselves. One of her guests had to have raised the ward. "Leave the library until tomorrow, please. The books will keep."

The maid bobbed a curtsey and hurried off. Emily watched her go, then turned and hurried down to the library. She felt the ward pressing gently against her mind as soon as she reached the door, trying to nudge her away. It was a skilled piece of work, she had to admit; if Lady Barb hadn't made her work overtime to recognize the existence of such magics and counter them, she might have missed it entirely. She gritted her teeth — the maid would have wound up in hot water for not doing her job — and pushed against the ward. It didn't actually fit into *her* wards — that would have been a step too far — but it was close enough that most people capable of noticing the ward would have assumed that *Emily* had put it in place.

*But that would tell them I had something to hide*, Emily thought. She had no illusions about how many magicians had been sneaking around her castle. Most of her notes were heavily protected — and the battery was sealed in her pocket — but that wouldn't stop some of her guests from trying to snoop. *They would think the ward was hiding something of mine.*

She pushed right though the ward and opened the door, silently promising herself that whoever had created the ward was going to get a piece of her mind, then stopped dead. Markus was sitting on a chair; Melissa sat on his lap. And they were kissing...they jumped apart, Melissa hastily standing up, as they saw Emily. Emily braced herself as Melissa lifted her hand, ready to cast a spell, but she dropped it again. Behind her, Markus rose to his feet.

"Emily," he said, gravely.

Emily looked from one to the other and found herself fighting down a giggle. Melissa's lips were swollen...and, from her rumpled clothes, it was clear they'd been doing a bit more than *just* kissing. She remembered Imaiqah looking like that, after the party they'd held to celebrate the destruction of the Mimic...her friend had admitted, later, that she'd had more than just a kiss with a boy.

"This isn't what it looks like," Melissa said.

Emily lost control and started to giggle, inanely. Melissa looked torn between anger that she was being laughed at and relief, maybe because Emily hadn't screamed for her great-grandmother, or even her grandfather. Markus stepped up behind Melissa and rested an arm on her shoulder, protectively. He genuinely cared for her, Emily realized, even though they had only just met. But then, they did have a great deal in common.

"If it isn't what it looks like," Emily managed to say, finally, "what is it?"

Markus and Melissa exchanged glances, as if they were uncertain what to say. Emily found herself giggling again, even though she suspected that both families would be outraged if they found out. Markus and Melissa were the respective heirs of their families, the people who would eventually inherit control of their wealth and influence. To have them making out with *each other* would be horrifying. They could be homosexuals, without any inclination to produce children, and their families would be less outraged.

"We started talking," Markus said. He'd managed to gather himself while Emily giggled. "You know, just after *we* were talking. And then we kept talking. And then..."

"We started kissing," Melissa said. She rubbed her lips. "And everything went on from there."

Emily shook her head, slowly. "I assume your families don't know?"

"No," Markus said. He paused. "Are you going to tell them?"

Emily hesitated. She didn't *like* Melissa, but she liked Markus. Head Boy of Mountaintop or not, he had offered her good advice, even if she hadn't taken it. And besides, if she did tell, it would almost certainly lead to a fight between the two families in her castle. Hundreds of people would be caught in the middle, including herself, and be killed. Or suffer a fate worse than death.

"I won't, as long as you two are discreet," she said. Quickly, she erected another set of wards around the library. "Do you realize just how much trouble you could get into if you are caught?"

"I don't care," Markus said. "If they kick me out of the family...it would be worth it."

"The Matriarch has already ruined my life," Melissa said bitterly. Her hand was resting on Markus's arm. "Why should I care what she wants?"

Emily sighed, inwardly. She distrusted strong emotion, with reason. Were Markus and Melissa truly in love...or had mutual disgust with their relatives, and perhaps their prospective partners, driven them into a relationship? It was hard to blame Melissa for wanting to spite Fulvia, not after meeting Gaius, but Emily wasn't blind to the potential for disaster. What would happen if — when — the families found out?

"Because she could make your lives miserable," Emily said. "Or get a great many people killed."

She looked from one to the other, thinking hard. "What are you going to do when they do find out?"

"Tell them that we love each other," Markus said. "And dare them to kick us out."

He sighed. "I can make a living on my own, if necessary," he added. "Melissa can join me after she finishes her schooling."

*Is that genuine feeling*, Emily thought, *or romantic claptrap?*

"And we could unite the houses, once again," Melissa offered. "We're the heirs. A great many arrangements would have to be discarded if they kicked one of us out, let alone both of us. They might find it easier to accept that we were married and reunite the families."

Emily had her doubts. By now, whatever had caused the original split, there were far too many differences between the two families for them to reunite easily. It would be like expecting Britain and the United States to reunify in 1805, even with the threat of Napoleon breathing down their necks. Neither one would fit easily into the other's system.

*And plenty of people on both sides who would object to the reunification*, Emily thought, coldly. *What would happen to Fulvia and her counterparts if the two families become one?*

"It would end the feud," Markus said. "I was raised to hate the Ashworths, Emily. I was told that they..."

"Ate babies for breakfast," Emily said, sharply.

"And more, much more," Markus said. "Eating babies was about the least of it. But Melissa isn't a monster."

Emily eyed him for a long moment. "How long were you thinking of ways to end the feud?"

"Ever since my grandfather was killed," Markus said. "He was lured into a challenge he couldn't win by an Ashworth, who was killed in turn by one of my family. If the feud hadn't existed, he might still be alive today."

*And so you asked me about Melissa*, Emily thought, grimly. *And that raises the question of just how sincere your feelings are towards her. Do you want her for herself, or because marrying her would give you the clout to end the feud?*

She shivered. It wasn't a question she dared ask.

"I was told worse about the Ashfalls," Melissa said, quietly. "But Markus isn't a monster, either."

"His brother is a little brat," Emily said, tartly. "You'd better be damned careful he doesn't realize what you're doing."

"I heard," Markus said. "My father was less than pleased about him, if that's any consolation."

"Not much," Emily said. She needed time to think, to process everything. "Picking on people who are defenseless isn't something to be encouraged."

"My father corrected him," Markus said. "But we will be careful not to let him anywhere near us."

"I never had siblings," Emily said, "but Imaiqah says that she rarely had true privacy from her family."

"Imaiqah grew up in a very poor household with only a handful of rooms," Melissa said, sharply. "We both had plenty of room to hide from our siblings."

Markus sat on the sofa, pulling Melissa to sit next to him. "Emily...please, will you keep this to yourself?"

"I thought I said I wouldn't tell your families," Emily said, as she sat facing them. There was something about the way they leaned together that suggested their feelings were genuine, despite the potential disaster looming in the future. "But I want you to do something in exchange."

Melissa eyed her. "Emily, I know we haven't been friends, but..."

Emily held up a hand. Tempting as it was to extort a price from Melissa in exchange for her silence, she had something else in mind.

"You're both magicians," she said, "so you have the ability to...enjoy yourselves without lasting consequences. But...your families are not going to be amused when they find out, and they will, eventually. I want you to come up with a plan to handle it when they do."

She sucked in a breath. Magicians could enjoy themselves — it crossed her mind that she had no idea if Melissa had had any prior relationships at Whitehall — but she had a feeling that Markus and Melissa had crossed one of the few lines. Even if the relationship didn't last the summer, it would still return to haunt them if anyone found out. And *would* it last? They might discover, once the thrill of making out in secret faded, that they had little in common. Or they might be kicked out of their families and break up under the stress of living as independent magicians...

"And I don't think faking your own deaths would work," she added, remembering *Romeo and Juliet*. She'd always thought that Romeo and Juliet were idiots who'd allowed love to blind them to the significance of their actions. It hadn't been until she'd entered the Nameless World that she'd grasped some of the forces driving them. "There are spells to check if someone is actually dead, or faking it."

"We could just run away," Melissa suggested. "Leave a note behind and make our escape."

"And where," Emily asked, "would you go?"

She thought about it, briefly. Markus was a qualified magician, but all of his papers said he was Markus Ashfall. Finding work without them would be tricky, although there was so much demand for trained magicians that it was likely some people wouldn't look too closely if Markus offered to work for them. Zed had told her, after all, that a person who could brew *Manaskol* reliably could practically write their own ticket. But what if the two families colluded to deny them a place to live?

"I don't know," Melissa said. She looked down at the carpet, then up at Markus, her eyes shining. "But at least we would be together."

Emily was tempted, sorely tempted, to simply order them to leave the castle. They could walk down to the Faire the following morning, and vanish. A couple of steps through a portal could have them halfway around the world before anyone noticed they were gone...and yet, she didn't want to tell them to leave. If they actually *did* manage to reunite their families, one of the major problems keeping the Allied

Lands from working closely together would fade away. But was the game worth the risk?

She sighed. Poker had become a fad at Whitehall, but she'd never liked it. Students gambled, and found themselves running into debt. Thankfully, the tutors had imposed limits on just how *much* could be gambled, yet there were still problems. Aloha had told her, privately, that she wished she'd never devised the first set of accepted rules. And here, Melissa and Markus — and Emily — were playing poker for the highest possible set of stakes.

"I think you're being idiots," she said, finally. "You could push your families into actually fighting each other, right here and right now. And you could get a lot of people killed."

"But we love each other," Markus said.

Emily winced. Alassa and Jade loved each other...and *that* might end badly, too. And now there was Melissa and Markus.

"I wish you both the very best of luck," she said, shortly. "But I still think you're being idiots."

Melissa half-rose, then stopped and settled back down. "What would you do in our place?"

Emily hesitated. Perhaps, once upon a time, she would have liked the idea of a grand romance, but she had known it would never come. All the romantic stories she'd read had always glossed over the truth, that grand passion came at a price, that Mr. Right would change as time went by. She'd never been one to have strong emotions...

...And yet, she practically envied both couples.

"I don't know," she admitted. Alassa had pointed out, cold-bloodedly, that Jade posed no threat to either Emily or Alassa herself. But what if Alassa had fallen for one of the princes? Or maybe even one of the barons? She would have to choose between her love, with all the risk of political disaster, or choosing a husband for political reasons. "Be careful, please."

She looked up as the wards around the library tingled. "I think someone is trying to come inside, right now."

Melissa paled as she sensed the magic. "Gaius!"

Markus leapt to his feet. "Is there another way out of here?"

"Behind the bookcase," Emily said. She stood, tapping the bookcase in just the right place, opening a passageway she knew led to an empty room. "I suppose you want me to distract Gaius? If it *is* Gaius?"

"Yes, please," Melissa said, as she rose. She sounded nervous, despite her magic. But then, Gaius enjoyed the support of her great-grandmother. "And thank you."

Emily sighed, cursing herself under her breath as she closed the bookcase behind them. Just what had she managed to get herself into now?

*You could just abandon them*, her thoughts offered. And then she realized the implications of her knowledge. *But now that you know, they'll blame you for not telling them.*

# Chapter Twenty-Five

"OH," Gaius said, as he opened the door. "I thought you were Melissa."

"I don't look anything like her," Emily said, waspishly. She held up a book she'd picked from the shelves, randomly. "I came in here to read, not to be disturbed."

"*Legends of Honor*," Gaius said, reading the title. "I think most of those stories were made up."

"Most stories tend to be embellished along the way," Emily said. She sat down, placing the book on her lap. "Can I help you?"

Gaius sighed. "Can you help me find Melissa?"

"I still can't alter the wards to track individual people," Emily said, knowing she was prevaricating and not particularly caring. "The castle was never designed to have proper wards."

"*Fundamentals of Wardcraft* says you're wrong," Gaius said. "You would just need to place a couple of dozen anchorstones throughout the castle, then retune the wards to resonate through the stones."

"My financial balance says I can't afford it," Emily said. Anchorstones were expensive, at least the ones that supported permanent wards. "And besides, I don't know if I will be staying here."

"I see," Gaius said. "I apologize for disturbing you, Lady Emily."

He turned towards the door. "Wait," Emily said. "Can we talk?"

Gaius turned back to her. "What do we have to talk about?"

*Good question*, Emily thought. Gaius still had the strange vibe of being torn between declaring himself a master and admitting that he was a slave. It was odd... and, perhaps, she would have felt sorry for him if she hadn't known he'd tried to push himself on Melissa. But he might be able to answer a question for her.

"I wanted to hear your thoughts on the feud," she said. "Why do you think it started?"

Gaius sat down, facing her. "I was told that there were two twin brothers who were both in line to become Patriarch," he said. "One of them was a thoughtful, reflective type; the other a violent berserker. The berserker attempted to kill the other brother, one day, only to discover that the thoughtful brother was the stronger magician. And then he fled, taking some of his allies with him, to found House Ashfall."

Emily's eyes narrowed. "And is that true?"

"It is what I was told," Gaius said. "The Matriarch discourages questions about the past."

Somehow, Emily wasn't surprised. Fulvia was perhaps the only person still alive who actually knew the truth. The story might well be nothing more than propaganda, without any seed of truth at all; indeed, it made little sense. There was no such thing as magical twins, a berserker magician would probably be killed by his own magic...and besides, why would so many people *follow* a berserker? Gaius really ought to know those facts. He'd known about magic for longer than Emily had been alive.

"I see," she said. The whole story shouldn't hold up for a moment. "And what does she say when you ask?"

"People normally get cursed," Gaius said. "They learn to keep their mouths shut pretty quickly."

Emily frowned. "What's your relation to House Ashworth?"

Gaius looked oddly relieved at the question. "House Arlene has been closely allied with House Ashworth for decades," he said. "I spent many happy hours with the children of House Ashworth."

"That must have been fun," Emily said, doubtfully. "How did you get engaged to Melissa?"

"My father and the Matriarch made the contract," Gaius said. "It is my honor to wed the Ashworth Heir."

Emily met his eyes. "Why you?"

"I beg your pardon?"

"Why you?" Emily repeated. "Why did the Matriarch settle on you?"

"She thought I would be a good husband and father, I assume," Gaius said. "The Matriarch was very keen that we should start producing children at once. She assured me that Melissa would welcome my advances. But she seems to spend most of her time away from me."

Emily shivered. There was a plaintive note to his voice, mixed with a sense of entitlement that worried her. Gaius seemed to think that merely signing the contact made Melissa his, without regard for her feelings. The formal wedding was just a formality, as far as he was concerned; they were already linked together. But it was clear that Melissa was far from happy with the arrangement.

*Of course it's clear,* she reminded herself. *You caught her practically having sex with Markus!*

"Her grandfather tells me I should press my case," Gaius said. "But it only seems to make her more resistant."

"Her grandfather is a man," Emily snapped. "I don't think he understands women very well."

"Her grandfather had five children, three of them girls," Gaius countered.

"It isn't the same," Emily said. "Melissa is a living, breathing person. She cannot give her heart to you because of what is said in the contract."

"She should," Gaius said.

Emily glowered at him. "Did you try to court her?"

Gaius blinked. "That would have been presumptuous."

*Men,* Emily thought. Part of her wondered why she was bothering to try to explain. Gaius wouldn't understand a word she said. He'd been raised to consider children like himself commodities to be exchanged on the marriage market. He had no objection to being sold to House Ashworth and he had no idea why Melissa was objecting. But it was different for women.

"Melissa is a young woman, like me," Emily said. "Can I offer you some advice?"

Gaius nodded, curtly.

"The contract doesn't matter," Emily said. "What matters, right now, is how she feels about being told she has to marry you. She has lost control of one of the most vital aspects of her life. And you, rather than trying to prove yourself to be a good husband, have been pushing her away from you."

Gaius leaned forward. "I will be a good husband," he said. "I can give her children."

Emily sighed, inwardly. Did Gaius think his only role was to be a stud bull? But then, it was quite possible. Alassa might have to worry about her husband usurping her power, but Melissa wouldn't have such a problem. The magical families judged by strength of magic, not gender. Gaius would be expected to father children, but not to lead the House...

*Which might be what Fulvia wants*, Emily thought, in a moment of insight. Balbus was a non-entity when his mother was there, while his oldest son had died when Melissa was very young. Gaius might be able to claim the title of Patriarch, but he would never be able to wield power. *And if she picked Gaius specifically...*

She shuddered, suddenly, as everything fell into place. Melissa was young and strong, perhaps strong enough to challenge her great-grandmother. But until she was twenty-one, she was still considered immature by her community. Fulvia could marry her off to someone who would make her a mother, but not encourage her to seek power for herself. Or, if the death of Melissa's father hadn't been a stupid mistake, father a few children and then arrange an accident for Melissa. Gaius was nothing to House Ashworth without his wife.

*And what*, she asked herself, *do I do about that?*

If she was right, and it *felt* right, Fulvia would *never* consent to Melissa marrying Markus and having his children. Markus was the Ashfall Heir...but even if there had been no feud, he was still strong enough to protect his wife and support her if she wanted to challenge her great-grandmother. And he would have strong ties to a House that would seek revenge, if *both* of the youngsters turned up dead.

"Lady Emily?" Gaius asked. "Are you all right?"

Emily nodded, curtly, and looked at Gaius. Young enough to be biddable, old enough to dominate his wife, trained enough to respect Fulvia as his superior, conceited enough to believe that Melissa had been given to him...yes, he was the perfect husband for a girl the Matriarch wanted to keep under her thumb. And he would play his role to perfection, never wondering if he was a pawn in a deeper game.

*I'll have to talk to Melissa about this*, she thought. *And Alassa.*

"I would advise you to try to court her instead," she said. "Why not see what she likes and try to share her interests?"

Gaius stared at her in honest bemusement. "But why would I try to court her when we're already engaged?"

*Because she doesn't consider herself engaged to you, you ninny*, Emily thought.

"Courtship is for magicians who do not have families to arrange a match," Gaius continued. "I was always told my parents would decide on my bride."

"If that was true," Emily said, "I wouldn't have been sent letters asking me to consider marrying into one family or another."

"I'm sure my parents wouldn't have sent such a letter," Gaius said, doubtfully. "It would be a dreadfully ill-bred thing to do."

Emily shrugged. Void had never bothered to give her a list of who had sought her hand in marriage — and she'd ended up burning the letters she'd been sent personally, after writing a short reply stating that she was not currently interested in marriage. It had been flattering, but also creepy. People she barely knew — or didn't know at all — were interested in marrying her, merely because she was a strong magician. They only wanted her for her genes.

"Do you want to be happily married," Emily asked, "or do you want to be fighting with your wife every day?"

"I don't think happiness is the issue," Gaius confessed. "The issue is merely producing children."

"Which you will find difficult, if your wife can't stand the sight of you," Emily snapped.

Gaius scowled at her. "Lady Emily, I asked you for help, not for...not for unwanted advice that offends my sense of how best to proceed."

*Hodge had his own sense of how to proceed*, Emily thought. *And look what happened to him.*

She sighed. It was tempting to point out that Gaius's approach wasn't doing anything but driving Melissa away. But she had a feeling that he wouldn't have understood any good advice, even if she hadn't been uneasily aware that Melissa was effectively dating Markus, despite their families. Gaius would be mortally offended if he ever found out, feeling that he'd been made a fool, while Fulvia would go ballistic. And somehow, she doubted Markus's father would be very happy either.

"I think you should give her some space," she said, firmly. "And learn to relate to her as a person, rather than a...an object."

"Those two pieces of advice contradict one another," Gaius said. He rose, peering down at her. "I must act as I see fit."

Emily was tempted to suggest that he ask Fulvia for advice, but she knew it would be disastrous. One thing she *had* learned from the attempted coup in Zangaria was that women who climbed to positions of power rarely did it because they had sisterly feelings for other women. The Iron Duchess had been prepared to condemn Alassa to a fate worse than death, just to ensure she kept a firm grip on power. Fulvia, too, had no motherly feelings for her great-granddaughter. Instead, she wanted Melissa married off before she could challenge her.

*You could be wrong*, she thought, as Gaius walked out of the library. *And what would you do then?*

She shook her head, cursing — once again — the decision to hold the Faire in Cockatrice, then turned and walked out of the room herself, dismantling the ward on the way. Hopefully, Gaius would assume that *Emily* had erected the aversion ward, rather than anyone else. But the fact he'd been prepared to try to break it down was worrying. What would he have done, Emily asked herself, if he *had* found Melissa? What if he'd found her with *Markus*?

The thought made her shiver. *Hodge* had thought he had rights over every girl in the village...and every traveling girl without a powerful protector. The thought that someone might stop him had never entered his mind. And if Gaius, who was a capable magician if he had graduated from Mountaintop, thought *he* had rights over Melissa...it might well get ugly very quickly.

*Melissa is a fighter,* Emily thought. Certainly, Melissa had never been scared of *her,* even after Shadye had died. *But she isn't fighting Gaius. Why not?*

She walked back to the balcony and looked down at the dancers. Most of the guests had headed back to their rooms, leaving only a handful of dancers remaining on the floor. Somehow, Emily wasn't surprised to realize that Jade and Alassa were still dancing together, while Imaiqah had found a young man from the Faire. Emily leaned on the balcony and watched, feeling oddly wistful. It was something she would have liked to do, perhaps, with a young man of her own.

*I could find Caleb,* she thought, *and ask him to dance. Or someone else...*

The thought echoed tantalizingly in her mind for a long moment, then faded away.

*Or perhaps not,* she added, mentally. She'd been less unsure of herself around men after Hodge — or, rather, after she'd knocked him down and turned him into a pig. *As if I don't have enough distractions right now.*

She caught sight of Fulvia, sitting on a chair like a queen holding court, and shivered again, but looked away before the ancient women could catch Emily staring. Was Fulvia really so unconcerned about her great-granddaughter's happiness? Or was Emily completely wrong about her motivations? Maybe Fulvia thought Gaius was the ideal husband for Melissa, someone who could be retrained to follow her without question. Or...

The dance came to an end. Emily looked down for a long moment, and turned and headed back to her rooms. There wouldn't be another disaster tonight, she was sure, even though Markus and Melissa were still together. Or were they? They might have had one last kiss before they went to their separate rooms. She shrugged, dismissing the thought. There was no way to know.

She sighed, inwardly. Gaius had been right about the need for more anchorstones and, despite what she'd told him, she could probably afford them. But it would have made it harder for her to pretend ignorance of what was going on under her roof if she had better wards. Markus and Melissa could be tracked easily, even monitored. Whitehall's Warden existed, at least in part, because of the *dangers* of overusing such powerful wards. The inhuman Warden had no real interest in human affairs.

*And if you go into a magician's house,* she recalled Lady Barb saying, *you are bound by his rules.*

She unlocked the wards protecting her door and stepped inside, sealing the wards behind her. No one had tried to break in, as far as she could tell, although she knew she was far from a perfect wardcrafter. Someone like Void could have dismantled the wards, searched her rooms and then rebuilt them so perfectly she couldn't tell they'd been touched. Or someone more subtle might have tinkered with the access permissions. The more people she added, the easier it would be for someone else to add more.

Shaking her head, she undressed, washed quickly in the bathroom and pulled on a nightgown, before falling into bed. It had been far too long a day, but her thoughts were so tangled she had to force herself to clear her mind before she could relax. Markus and Melissa, Jade and Alassa...when would it ever end? Sleep fell over her...

...Only to be broken by a faint tapping at the door.

Emily stiffened, sat up in bed, and reached out towards the wards. Frieda stood outside, knocking on the door as if she couldn't decide if she wanted to be heard. Emily frowned, but opened the door. A faint glow from a light spell illuminated Frieda as she stepped into the room.

"I couldn't sleep," she confessed, as Emily used magic to close and relock the door. "My room is just too empty."

"I understand," Emily said. She'd had less time for Frieda since the holidays had begun, which wasn't entirely fair to the younger girl. They had planned to spend time together before she'd realized that the Faire would claim most of her attention. "But it is *your* room."

"I know," Frieda said. She gave Emily a pleading look, one that made her look younger than her seventeen years. "But could I sleep here tonight?"

Emily hesitated. She'd never really *liked* sharing a room with anyone, even though she had to admit she'd learned a great deal through rooming with Aloha and Imaiqah. But Frieda had grown up in a tiny house, then roomed in a dormitory at Mountaintop. Sharing a room came as naturally to her as breathing.

And she felt alone. Emily understood that more than she cared to admit.

"You can," she said, finally. It was her castle. And, as a magician, she could do whatever she liked in the privacy of her own home. "But don't tell anyone."

Frieda looked surprised, but hastily climbed into Emily's bed. Emily sighed inwardly, and rolled over to give the younger girl some room. Magicians weren't supposed to confess to any vulnerabilities, if they were so gauche as to actually have them. Frieda might have been bottling up her feelings ever since arriving at Cockatrice. If she'd been feeling lonely...

*Because vulnerabilities lead to weaknesses,* she thought, bitterly. There wasn't much she missed from Earth, but the suggestion that mental problems and depression could be handled was definitely one of them. *But coping with madness might make necromancy practical after all. And if a necromancer could remain sane...*

Pushing the thought aside, she closed her eyes and went to sleep.

# Chapter Twenty-Six

"I'M SORRY ABOUT LAST NIGHT," FRIEDA SAID. "I DIDN'T MEAN TO WAKE YOU."

"Think nothing of it," Emily said. Sometime during the night, Frieda had cuddled up to her, which would have embarrassed the young girl hugely if she'd known. Emily had managed to extract herself before Frieda had woken and panicked. "I know how you felt."

She stepped into the bathroom, washing and dressing rapidly. She'd have to alter the wards, she reminded herself, to make it easier for the maids to set out some of her new clothes. It was so much easier back at Whitehall, where they could put their used clothes outside their doors for the servants to pick up and clean, but here.... She shook her head, reluctantly. Perhaps she could simply ward her bedroom, leaving a room outside the wards for the maids to enter and leave at will...

*And perhaps have them clean the room, too,* she added, thoughtfully. She hadn't stayed in the room for very long, but dust had already started to settle on the bookshelves and tables. *But they won't want to do it.*

She walked back into the bedroom. Frieda was sitting up in bed, looking lost and lonely. It definitely hadn't been easy for her, Emily saw, to move to Cockatrice. Emily might have told her that it was Frieda's home, but Frieda wasn't used to living in a castle. She sighed inwardly. Next time, perhaps she would have more time to spend with the younger girl.

"I need to catch up with Alassa," she said, glancing at the clock. Alassa and Jade had always headed down to the Faire as soon as it opened, spending their days wandering from stall to stall before returning for dinner. "Will you be all right here?"

"I should come with you," Frieda said, scrambling out of bed. "Can you wait for me?"

"If you hurry," Emily said. Thankfully, Frieda wasn't any more inclined to waste time washing and dressing than Emily was. Mountaintop's Shadows weren't encouraged to develop a sense of vanity. "I don't want to have to chase them down at the Faire."

Frieda nodded, rushed into the bathroom, and started splashing water on her face.

Emily smiled. Thankfully, people would think nothing of it if they came to breakfast together, shared a room, or even a bed. It wasn't common for magicians to share beds, but it did happen. And poor families like Frieda's were often forced to huddle together, just to share body heat.

While she waited, she picked up a book and glanced at the title. It wasn't one she had chosen; Bryon had simply picked a couple of dozen titles from the library and transferred them to her bedroom before she returned to the castle. Like many others, it was a dull flat book, suggesting that the writer had a long way to go before he came close to Tolkien or Peter Hamilton. Absently, Emily wondered what would happen if she wrote books set on Earth, with cars in place of carts and airplanes buzzing through the sky. Would it be considered a form of fantasy?

"I'm ready," Frieda said. She'd exchanged her nightgown for a simple white dress that hung to her ankles. "Shall we go?"

Emily nodded, checked to make sure she was carrying the battery, opened the wards and stepped out of her room. Frieda followed, and watched as Emily closed the door and resealed the wards, before they started to walk down to the Great Hall. As always in the morning, it was nearly deserted; most of her guests had danced the night away, and were sleeping in. Emily thought, briefly, of Mistress Irene's reaction when one of her charges overslept, and smiled. There was no way *she* was going to start waking people up before they were ready.

Frieda caught her arm. "What's so funny?"

"At school, we would be in trouble for getting up so late," Emily said. It wasn't easy, either; the beds were spelled to push someone out of bed, if they were too late getting up. "Here...the longer the guests stay in bed, the better."

"Funny," Frieda said, thoughtfully. "But I would have thought they wouldn't want to miss the day."

Emily shrugged. Frieda had grown up on a small farm, where not a single hour of daytime could be wasted, then moved to a school that kept her busy every waking hour. But for older magicians, the chance to sleep in could be a pearl beyond price. She could be tempted herself, once the Faire was over, just to lie back and sleep for a week. She was the baroness, after all. If she wanted to sleep until noon, no one would say anything – at least, publicly.

*But it would be a waste of a day*, she thought, as she joined Alassa and Imaiqah at the table. *And I could do so much else here.*

"Master Grey insisted on taking Jade down to the city," Alassa said, before Emily could ask. "Said it would be good experience for later life."

Emily nodded. "Does he know about...?"

"Us?" Alassa asked. "I don't think so, but he is observant. He might have noticed something."

"Probably," Emily said. Yet again, her thoughts mocked her; in hindsight, it had been all too clear. "When's the announcement?"

"I have to convince my father first," Alassa said. She shook her head. "And that isn't going to be easy."

Emily frowned. "I thought you listed the advantages and disadvantages."

"I did," Alassa said. "But my father may have other ideas."

Frieda leaned forward. "Ideas about what?"

Alassa exchanged a glance with Emily, and sighed. "Jade and I are planning to get married," she said. "But my father may object."

"Oh," Frieda said.

"You're not the only ones," Emily said. She'd promised not to tell their parents, but she'd said nothing about her friends. "Guess who I found kissing in the library?"

"Marcellus and Fulvia," Imaiqah said. "The way they snipe at each other, I would have thought they were lovers, once upon a time."

Emily grimaced. Fulvia was ancient, while Marcellus was probably somewhere in his late fifties. The thought of them actually *kissing*...she shook her head, determinedly. Maybe older people could get married and do all the things that married couples did, but she didn't want to think about it. Besides, they hated each other. If they had been somewhere else, they might well have been hurling curses rather than verbal snipes.

"No," she said. "Markus and Melissa."

Alassa stared at her. "Damn," she said, finally.

*She picked that up from me*, Emily thought. She'd introduced so many ideas and concepts to the Allied Lands, but she hadn't intended to introduce swearwords too. Or at least ones that came from Earth.

"That's so romantic," Frieda said, her eyes going wide. "That's..."

"You're serious," Imaiqah said, cutting Frieda off. "Are they really going out?"

"They were kissing," Emily said, remembering Melissa's swollen lips. How many times did someone have to kiss to make their lips swell? She had no idea. "They think they're in love."

Alassa shook her head slowly. "And to think I thought that considering Jade as a consort was likely to worry my father."

She had a point. King Randor might object to Alassa marrying Jade...and, if he did, the whole idea would be buried. But it would be harder for Markus and Melissa to split up without heartache, now they'd moved to a physical relationship. How far had they gone together? Had they managed to find somewhere in the city they could make love without fear of detection? Or had they only just begun?

"It's *very* romantic," Imaiqah said. "But what concern is it of ours?"

"It's political, not romantic," Alassa snapped. Her face darkened. "Send them both home, Emily; you can come up with something that will serve as an excuse. You don't want this to explode in your face."

Imaiqah gave her a sharp look. "You're only saying that because you don't like Melissa."

Alassa sneered. "Do *you* like Melissa?"

"Not really," Imaiqah said. "But..."

"Have you forgotten," Alassa said, "who it was who rigged the chairs so we couldn't get up, making us late for class? Have you forgotten who managed to turn us into rats and hide us in a cage for an hour? Have you forgotten who *accidentally* stole our notes and..."

Imaiqah slapped the table. "Have *you* forgotten who it was who turned *them* into stones and left them hidden outside the school?"

Alassa frowned. "What's your point?"

"She's been pretty awful to us, but we've been pretty awful to her," Imaiqah said. "Does that justify telling her parents and *really* screwing up her life?"

"She turned you into a cow," Alassa snapped.

"I got better," Imaiqah said. "And so did you. Tell me: does everything she did justify telling her parents and *really* screwing up her life?"

"No," Emily said, before Imaiqah could repeat the question for the third time. "But there is a political implication, too."

She sighed, and outlined the problem as she saw it. If the affair remained a secret, well and good; if it came out into the open, the two families would likely go to war. Frieda stared at her openly as she spoke, her eyes wide; the others, more practiced in controlling their expressions, kept their faces blank.

"That's why I told you to send them away," Alassa said, once Emily had finished. "Get the problem out of your hair before it explodes."

"But they will want explanations," Imaiqah said, quietly. "What will you tell their families when you send them away?"

Emily looked down at the table. What *could* she tell their families?

"I don't know," she mumbled. Imaiqah was right. If she sent Markus and Melissa away without explanation, Fulvia and Marcellus would be displeased. But if she came up with an excuse, it would haunt their lives until the day they died. "There's nothing I *can* tell them."

"I think Lady Barb would say the same," Alassa said. "They shouldn't be allowed to risk the lives of everyone in the castle, Emily."

*And that is what they're doing*, Emily thought.

"If it was just Melissa, sending her home would be easy," she said. "But I don't hate Markus."

Alassa lifted an eyebrow. "A secret boyfriend?"

Emily felt her cheeks heat. "He was good to me, when he didn't have to be. I don't think he's a bad person."

"He was a decent Head Boy," Frieda agreed. "Many of us had a crush on him."

"He could be playing games with Melissa," Imaiqah said. "It doesn't really matter if she loses her maidenhead to him or not, but an affair here, right under Gaius's nose, will have repercussions for the rest of her life."

"You're meant to hate Romeo," Emily muttered.

Alassa gave her a sharp look. "Pardon?"

"It's from a play...a play where I come from," Emily said. Maybe she could write down a few Shakespeare plays, and try and get them performed. "Two feuding families, two star-crossed lovers...and a very stupid plan to escape their fate by faking their deaths."

"Oh," Frieda said. "What happens?"

"They both end up dead," Emily said.

But, when they'd been forced to study the play, one of her teachers on Earth had suggested that Romeo was meant to be the villain. He'd been a player, moving from Rosalind to Juliet, eventually deflowering Juliet to ensure she could never marry Paris. Some of the girls had objected, either because it wasn't romantic or because it made Juliet a simple victim, but Emily had found the argument surprisingly compelling. Romeo had been driven by hormones rather than common sense. God alone knew if Romeo and Juliet would have been able to forge a life together if they'd escaped their fate.

"I don't think either Markus or Melissa will be killing themselves," Imaiqah said. "But really...what else can you do, but watch and wait?"

"And hope it doesn't blow up in your face," Alassa said.

"Their families will notice," Frieda said, slowly. "*My* family always noticed when I was doing something wrong."

"She has a point," Alassa agreed. "Even in a castle, there are watching eyes."

Emily shivered. Alassa had never really known true privacy, even if she'd regarded the servants as less than human. And it had only grown worse as she'd grown older. Alassa's personal household, which was legally separate from King Randor's even though it was in the same palace, consisted of servants the king had chosen personally. Emily rather doubted they kept their mistress's secrets when their master ordered them to talk. If Alassa and Jade had kissed in the castle, word would have slipped back to the king.

She leaned forward. "How did you and Jade...do stuff without being noticed?"

Alassa colored as Imaiqah snickered. "We didn't actually *do* much stuff," she said. "I can't until the wedding."

*Double standards*, Emily thought.

"But I did manage to use some magic to give us some time together," Alassa added. "Subtle magic is quite useful for hiding things."

"I know," Emily said, grimly. She tapped the rune between her breasts meaningfully. "But only if the people have no protection."

Alassa cleared her throat. "If you're not willing to throw them both out of the castle," she said, "you should help them."

Imaiqah coughed. "*You* want to help *Melissa*?"

"It's the practical solution," Alassa said. "Look, they're close, right? They're already kissing, aren't they? So they're going to keep kissing and...going further until they either lose interest in one another, or get caught. And when they get caught, all hell is going to break loose."

She met Emily's eyes. "If you arrange for them to have a private room on the upper levels," she added, "they wouldn't be doing it in such risky places."

Emily shook her head slowly. "And you think that will help?"

"I think they will need to make some pretty hard choices soon enough," Alassa said, flatly. "Are they going to stay together? And if they do, what are they prepared to give up to do it?"

"You mean they'll be kicked out of their families," Imaiqah said.

"Precisely," Alassa agreed. She rested her elbows on the table. "You know Countess Morin?"

Emily shook her head.

"She's the youngest cousin of Baron Gold — the one who had his head lopped off," Alassa said. "Somehow, she managed to avoid being married off as soon as she became old enough to be entered on the marriage market. She reached twenty-one... and then married the young man of her choosing, without bothering to get anyone's permission to wed."

"How romantic," Imaiqah said.

"You keep saying that," Emily teased.

"She wasn't meant to do it," Alassa snapped, glowing at them both. "As a relative of the baron, he was meant to choose her partner and the king, my father, was meant to confirm his choice. Her marriage would always be a political issue, first and foremost. She could have been married off to someone who made her family stronger. Instead, she chose her own path."

Her face darkened. "The baron disowned her, of course," she continued. "The husband's family wasn't too pleased, either. She moved from riches to...poor cloths. They eventually moved to Beneficence and made a life of their own, well away from the aristocracy. And it could easily have been a great deal worse."

"But they were happy together," Imaiqah said.

"I don't know if they were or they weren't," Alassa said. "But at that level, marriage is never solely a union between a man and a woman. Two *families* are being united."

"If Markus and Melissa marry," Emily said, "will it stop their families from fighting?"

"It might," Alassa said. "Or they might both be kicked out — or murdered — and then the fighting would go on."

She shrugged. "Give them a room, let them get on with it...and hope it doesn't come to light before the end of the Faire."

Imaiqah swore. "Emily," she said, "when *are* Melissa and Gaius meant to get married?"

"I don't know," Emily said. "But the Ashworth Family *did* request the Great Hall for the last night of the Faire."

Alassa paled. "If that's when they are going to get married," she said, "Melissa will have to make a choice very quickly."

Emily wished, suddenly, that Lady Barb had stayed. She could have asked the older woman's advice. Instead, Master Grey was in charge of security...and he had ties to the Ashworth Family. If she talked to *him* about it, Fulvia would know by the end of the day, and then all hell would break loose.

*And was it a coincidence*, she asked herself, *that Lady Barb had to go?*

She tossed it around and around in her mind. Sergeant Miles had told her, more than once, that the more unlikely a coincidence, the less likely it *was* a coincidence. But she couldn't see how Lady Barb's departure tied in with Melissa and Markus's relationship. Unless Lady Barb had seen the problem looming and decided it would make a nice test for Emily...the older woman *did* have a "sink or swim" mentality.

But it seemed unlikely. Lady Barb might test Emily, she might push her mercilessly, but she wouldn't risk thousands of lives for a test.

"I'll find them a room," she decided. It would cut down the risk of the lovers being discovered before they'd made some decisions. "And don't mention this to anyone."

Alassa smirked. "As if I would," she said. "I do know how to be discreet."

"Just think of the favors she will owe you next year," Imaiqah said. "Or what Markus will be able to do for you."

"Or the trouble it will cause if all hell breaks loose," Emily said. She gave Frieda a sharp look. "You too, really. Keep it a secret."

"I will," Frieda promised.

After breakfast, Emily went to find Bryon. A room was assigned to Markus and Melissa on the upper levels, so it should be relatively safe, but she fiddled with the wards anyway, ensuring that it should be completely secure. She just hoped it was enough to allow them to decide their future before time ran out completely.

*If it isn't*, she thought, *I will need another option.*

# Chapter Twenty-Seven

THE NEXT FOUR DAYS PASSED RELATIVELY SMOOTHLY, MUCH TO EMILY'S SURPRISE. MASTER Grey kept her informed of a constant string of small incidents at the Faire, but reassured her that such incidents were common to all such gatherings. Magicians acting out old grudges, sorcerers carrying out industrial espionage, sellers trying to undercut their rivals...as long as it didn't lead to outright violence, it was reluctantly tolerated. Emily had her doubts, but kept them to herself.

Melissa also seemed to be keeping to herself, she noted. Emily had hoped to be able to have a discreet chat with her about Gaius and Markus, but Melissa was nowhere to be found. Emily couldn't help wondering if Melissa was avoiding her, or if she was just spending all her time with Markus, who was keeping himself out of sight. It would be an understandable thing to do.

She found herself dividing her time between Caleb in the mornings, and Frieda in the afternoons. Emily had never really had a chance to explore Cockatrice City, so she wrapped a glamor around herself and took Frieda down to see it. It was far smaller than any city on Earth, but it was blossoming rapidly. Hundreds of cheap houses and apartment blocks had been erected, while shanty towns were being taken down and rebuilt as people moved in from the countryside in hopes of finding employment. And there were opportunities everywhere. A peasant runaway from the next barony could train as a carpenter, a blacksmith, a printer, a steam engineer...

It made her think of what America might have been like in the days after independence from the British crown. There was fearsome injustice, but there was also a sense of hope, a sense that immigrants could work and become part of a new nation. Cockatrice was older, of course, but it had changed remarkably in two years. And much of it was due to the influence she'd had on the country.

"They seem to like putting up notices," Frieda said, indicating a large billboard someone had erected by the side of the pavement. "Why?"

"Because now half the population can read," Emily said. "It lets them spread the word quicker than hiring a herald."

She scanned the billboard, unable to conceal her amusement. It was littered in advertisements for everything from printing services to legal advice, as well as warnings from the Town Council. One note warned that anyone who threw slops into the streets would be forced to clean them with their bare hands. It wouldn't be pleasant, Emily knew, but it was necessary. Cockatrice, like most of the other cities on the Nameless World, had serious problems with sanitation. Diseases bred and spread where people didn't wash their hands, let alone bathe; people needed to boil water and clean up waste in the streets to avoid catching something nasty.

*Besides, there's a use for human waste in making gunpowder,* she thought. *The trick was finding a way for someone to profit in cleaning up the waste.*

Frieda didn't seem to like the city very much, Emily discovered, although she couldn't say she was surprised. Frieda had grown up in a tiny village before she'd moved to Mountaintop; a city with over a hundred thousand inhabitants was far too large for her. Eventually, they walked back to the castle, with Emily checking on Markus and Melissa before going to bed.

The following morning, she finally managed to chat with Caleb about steam engines.

"There are times when magic can be unreliable," she said, once they were sitting in her workroom with full mugs of Kava. "A magician who doesn't *want* to cast a spell may find himself incapable of casting it. Random factors and glitches can throw off any spell, if not handled properly. Technology, on the other hand, always produces the same results, time and time again."

"So does magic, if handled properly," Caleb objected.

"Not *all* magic," Emily said. "There are some spells that demand a virgin caster" — she'd never realized Caleb could blush so brightly — "and others that insist they can only be cast by male or female magicians. Technology does not make any such demands. As long as you get it right, it will work."

"Spells can be rewritten," Caleb said, stubbornly. "But would that make them the same spells?"

"Good question," Emily said. She took a sip of Kava, then picked up a sheet of paper and began to draw. Imaiqah had neatened up her original diagrams considerably, back when she'd just started; even now, no one would ever credit Emily as a draftswoman. "This is a pan of water, bubbling over a fire. Notice the steam coming up from the water."

"I see," Caleb said. "I thought it was a cow eating grass."

Emily blinked, but realized she was being teased. "As the water boils, it emits steam," she said. "In fact, the water is expanding to the point it becomes hot vapor. With me so far?"

Caleb nodded.

"So if you happen to seal the pan," she continued, drawing a lid over the pan, "what happens?"

"The water keeps becoming steam," Caleb said. He shook his head, doubtfully. "And then...?"

"The pan bursts," Emily said. "The water keeps expanding, pushing against the metal, until something finally breaks. It needs somewhere to go and, eventually, it makes a way out."

"I see," Caleb said. "You can't slow this from happening?"

"Not without magic," Emily said. She'd had to learn the hard way when she'd found herself having to cook her own meals on Earth. "Point is, the steam has to go somewhere."

She picked up a second piece of paper and drew out another pan, with a pipe leading up and out into the air. "You can steer the steam by providing a way for it to escape," she continued, as she added steam to the diagram. "The steam expands along the path of least resistance, but the pressure never reaches a point where the pan explodes because the steam is escaping."

Carefully, she drew out a wheel and placed it in front of him. "In this diagram, the steam pushes the wheel as it struggles to follow the path of least resistance. The wheel turns, which, through the *science* of clockwork, is linked to another set of wheels. Eventually, the steam can be used to move an entire train."

"It doesn't look as though it could produce enough power," Caleb said, doubtfully.

"You rode on the train," Emily said. "It didn't need magic to work."

"No, it didn't," Caleb said. "But I still have problems imagining it."

"The first models we produced were ramshackle things," Emily said. "They leaked steam, they only inched forward at the same pace as an elderly snail, but the designers eventually solved some of the problems and the trains moved faster. Now, they're planning designs that will actually be able to outrun a horse."

"That seems unlikely," Caleb said.

"Maybe not in the short term," Emily said. "But horses get tired. A steam train does not. Horses have limits to what they can carry; a steam train has limits, but they're much higher than any horse. Given time, there will be a network of rails running between cities, each one carrying goods and services from one place to another."

"Like the portals," Caleb said. He looked down at the sheet of paper. "Assuming your steam train could move at the speed of the average horse, it would take roughly nine hours to travel from here to Beneficence. However, I could step through a portal and arrive instantly."

"That would be true, in the short term," Emily said. "But portals require a great deal of magic to set up, while you can't move anything larger than a cart or a coach through them. A steam train would still have a very definite advantage."

She smiled. "There are other possibilities," she added. "The price of certain items tends to go up, the further the distance they have to travel. Steam trains will cut down that distance, allowing prices to fall."

"But they could still be brought through portals," Caleb protested.

Emily smiled. "In bulk?"

Sergeant Miles had discussed portals at some length, when he'd talked about logistics. It wasn't easy to set up a portal — two spells had to resonate together perfectly — and there were limits to how much could be stuffed through the spells. Something small and expensive, like Basilisk Blood, could be moved through the portals without incurring any economic penalty, but something that had to be moved in bulk was often easier to move by land or sea, rather than through the portals.

*And besides*, she thought, *the magicians who make the portals charge highly for their services.*

"I take your point," Caleb said. "But what about the long-term effects?"

"The world gets smaller," Emily said. "But maybe not as small as you would think."

Caleb looked at her. "I don't understand."

Emily sucked in her breath. She knew what had happened on Earth, but while the Nameless World was primitive in many ways, it had enjoyed the benefits of magic.

"The average person" — she gritted her teeth, remembering Hodge — "doesn't see much beyond his own horizons," she said. "A relatively tiny percentage of the entire population travels from place to place; only aristocrats, soldiers and magicians really see large parts of the world. The average peasant in the fields doesn't know anything about the world on the other side of the mountains, nor would he care if you tried to tell him about it."

"That's true," Caleb said. "My father always said that peasants were resistant when the time came for them to move."

"He would be asking them to give up their homes and farms," Emily pointed out. "And if they don't believe in the threat, why would they want to move?"

She shrugged, and went on. "If railways keep expanding, more and more people will be able to travel without leaving everything behind. It will become easier for people to go on holiday to somewhere else, perhaps somewhere hundreds of miles away, and return to their homes. So many people from so many different places, intermingling, will have all sorts of effects."

Caleb frowned. "I met people from all over the world at Stronghold, then Whitehall."

"They were a tiny percentage of the population," Emily said. "How many people from Cockatrice visit Alexis on a daily basis? I'd be surprised if *any* of them had visited the city more than once in their entire lives."

"I see, I think," Caleb said. "But news spreads faster, too."

"That's true," Emily said. "And peasants in nearby estates are seeing what I've done for my peasants, and are growing restless."

"You may have a problem with that, in the future," Caleb warned. "I don't think the other barons will thank you for stealing their peasants away."

"They won't," Emily agreed. "But I can't do anything to stop it — and they would be wise not to try."

Caleb looked down at her drawings. "All that from...*this*? It looks so simple!"

"Most technology is nothing more than new applications of old concepts," Emily said. "Waterwheels work on the same basic principle, using water rather than steam, and they've been around for generations. But it's not the only change, of course. Two years ago, it was a rare peasant who could sign his own name. Now, millions of people are learning to read and write using my letters and numbers."

She sighed. "The average peasant family would send a daughter to another family, perhaps in the next village, and never hear from her again," she added. It wasn't a pleasant thought, if only because she knew Frieda would probably have met that fate, if she hadn't had enough magic to win a place at Mountaintop. "Now, the daughter can write home to her parents, if she wishes. Ideas will spread far quicker than they can be stopped."

Caleb eyed her. "And that's a problem?"

"It could be," Emily said. "If the daughter was being mistreated, she could ask for help. Or if someone in the next village hears that a different baron is asking for less tax, or life in a city is so much better than being a farmer, word could spread rapidly. The effects will be unpredictable."

She looked directly at him. "And someone who sees my steam engine may have the insight to turn it into something even more workable."

"And you don't mind that," Caleb observed. "Why not?"

"Because...because I am not the only person who can have ideas," Emily said. There was the additional problem that *none* of her ideas were even remotely original, but she let that pass. "You might see the steam engine, then develop an improvement; I might see your improvement, and come up with an additional improvement of my own. The really smart engineers who have devised the latest steam engines wouldn't have done so without me..."

"They stand on your shoulders," Caleb said.

"*Yes*," Emily said. "And the people who come after them stand on *their* shoulders. And, because the laws of technology work for everyone, I couldn't stop them even if I tried."

"The same thing happens with magic," Caleb said. "You looked at the spell mosaics and came up with your own ideas."

"I wouldn't have if you hadn't showed them to me," Emily pointed out. "How many magicians willingly decline the protection of the Sorcerer's Rule?"

"Not many," Caleb said.

"Someone could try to duplicate your work," Emily continued. "But they would waste a great deal of time in merely reinventing your project. If you showed them what you had, they would advance faster..."

"Which might not be in my interests," Caleb said. "I wouldn't get the credit for their work."

"And at what point," Emily asked, "does it stop being *your* work?"

She sighed, inwardly. Could whoever had designed the first personal computer claim credit for himself or would he need to pass it back to Edison or Tesla or even Benjamin Franklin? Or, if someone ever cracked FTL, would he or she have to credit Albert Einstein with the invention? There might be hundreds of Great Men out there, ready to start turning out new inventions, but how could they proceed without basing themselves on the work of their predecessors?

*Lightning rods*, she thought, remembering Franklin. *I will have to introduce them, soon enough, and see what happens.*

"I see your point, I think," Caleb said. "But I don't think many magicians will agree."

Emily shrugged. "It may not matter," she said. Perhaps, one day, she would set up a research university, somewhere that combined magic and science. "Science marches on."

"So I see," Caleb said. "But people like my father won't be impressed."

"He should be," Emily said. "Think of the advantages of being able to move troops from one end of the country to the other in the space of a few short hours."

"I will mention it to him," Caleb said.

"Good," Emily said. She settled back in her chair, and smiled at him tiredly. "Do you have a moment to go over wards?"

"Of course," Caleb said. "I don't have much to do until the Grandmaster gets back to us."

"I'm sorry," Emily said.

"Don't be," Caleb said. "I get to explore the Faire, catch up on my reading, and stay away from my family."

Emily lifted her eyebrows. "You don't like them?"

"My brother has always been a prat," Caleb said. "The apple of father's eye. And my younger brother just completed his first year at Stronghold, to general applause. One of my sisters seems torn between becoming a combat sorceress in her own right or finding a suitable boy to marry, while the other moans and groans because her magic hasn't developed yet. I think they're better off without me."

"I know the feeling," Emily said. "What about your mother?"

"She keeps yelling at my sister, telling her to actually apply herself," Caleb said. "What's the use of having powerful magic if you're going to become a mere housewife?"

"Parents can be difficult at times," Emily said.

Caleb nodded. "What was it like growing up with Void?"

"He was always distant," Emily said. She felt an odd flicker of guilt at lying to him, something that puzzled her. Lying was never easy, but...why was it harder to lie to Caleb? "I didn't have much interaction with him until I turned sixteen and my magic flourished."

"My father tried, in his own way," Caleb said. "I know he meant well, but..."

Emily nodded. Fathers expected their sons to follow in their footsteps. She'd known fathers who thought their sons should do everything they'd done, from becoming doctors and dentists to chasing girls or remaining chaste until marriage. There might be magic in the Nameless World, and fewer opportunities, but human nature remained the same.

"He used to insist on leaving the books behind and going to kick a ball around the yard," Caleb added. "Casper was always great at football, too."

"I bet he was," Emily said.

"And he managed to become captain of the Regiment's football team, a year earlier than normal," Caleb added. "You know how he did it? I think father pulled strings on his behalf."

"Or he might just be good at it," Emily said. She loathed team sports, but Alassa and Imaiqah loved them. "Maybe he's an undiscovered talent."

"A discovered talent, perhaps," Caleb said. "Or a hidden talent at convincing people to support him, even though it isn't wise."

Emily smiled. "Did his team win the games?"

"I have no idea," Caleb said. He reached for a sheet of paper, but stopped. "Do *you* have any siblings?"

"Not that I know about," Emily said. It was possible she had a half-sibling or two, if her biological father had married again, but she had no idea if he was even still alive. "And I don't really want to know, either."

"Lucky you," Caleb said. "There are times when I wish I was an only child."

"And then your father would insist that you followed in his footsteps," Emily pointed out.

"Yeah," Caleb agreed. "There is that."

# Chapter Twenty-Eight

LEARNING FROM CALEB, EMILY DISCOVERED, WAS DIFFERENT FROM STUDYING WITH LADY Barb or one of the other teachers. Caleb seemed to veer between trying to help her work the subject out on her own or giving her the answers on a platter. Part of her didn't mind, but after three years of studying in magic schools she knew better than just to take the answers and write them down on her exam papers. She wouldn't be marked down for not showing her work, unlike increasingly annoying math exams back on Earth, but she would have problems moving ahead. Magic demanded a clear understanding of the basics at all times.

But it was a fascinating experience. Caleb understood wards far better than Emily and he was able to offer quite a few suggestions, although there were limits to what they could do in Cockatrice. The walls were solid stone, not bound together with *Manaskol* or anything else that could be used to anchor magic. She could channel magic through the stone, she was sure, but it wouldn't rest in place.

"Necromancers use stone knives," she muttered. "Perhaps it would work better if they used silver, or gold."

"They'd both explode in their hands," Caleb said. He didn't seem horrified at the mention of necromancy, even though it was a given he'd know the basic rite. "Which isn't such a bad idea, is it?"

Emily nodded. "We could use stone ourselves for the spell mosaics," she said. "Or perhaps..."

She broke off, considering the battery. If she rigged up a stone projector, she would be able to channel magic out of the battery and into a mass of spells. But if she did, she would drain the battery in one shot. The same rush of magic that tipped necromancers over the edge into madness would also render her battery useless. No, she told herself, what she needed was a *valve*, something that allowed her to control the flow of magic. But she wasn't sure what she could use to do that...

"What is that?" Caleb asked, as she sketched out the idea before she forgot it. "A mixture of wood and stone?"

"An idea," Emily said. She'd become better with her hands, over three years of Whitehall's ruthlessly practical education, but she knew she'd need help to build the valve. Yodel would be able to help her, if he didn't throw a fireball at her on sight. "Something I can't talk about yet."

Caleb looked hurt. Emily felt another pang of guilt, which she ruthlessly suppressed. She couldn't tell him about the battery, let alone the possible uses, without him swearing an oath to keep it to himself...and merely asking him to swear an oath could easily be taken as an insult. Lady Barb had offered her oath, without being asked, because she'd seen that Emily needed help, but Caleb? They were on an equal level...

"Not a piece of your technology, then," he said. "Something magic?"

"I'm afraid so," Emily said. She touched the battery in her pocket, surrounded by a haze of spells intended to both hide and protect it. "Very magical."

There was a knock at the door. Emily touched the wards with her mind and frowned, inwardly, as she sensed Markus and an unfamiliar magician. Caleb hastily gathered up their notes as Emily rose, then opened the door. Outside, Markus and Steven were waiting, patiently. Emily hadn't even known that Steven had returned to the castle.

"Lady Emily," Steven said. "I was wondering if we might have a brief word."

Emily hesitated, then nodded. "I'll meet you in the drawing room," she said, reluctantly. She turned back to Caleb. "Can I ask you to clear up here?"

"I suppose you could," Caleb said. He picked up the drawings of steam engines and peered down at them. "Can I keep these?"

"If you like," Emily said. "But there are diagrams and instructions for building your own on sale in any market place."

Caleb laughed. "I would rather get my information from the source," he said.

Emily blushed, then checked the wards, pocketed her own notes, and walked to the drawing room. It was one of the few rooms she'd managed to have redecorated; giant bookcases, most half-empty, had replaced the endless rows of slaughtered animals Baron Holyoake had hung on the walls. His table, a solid mass of wood, had been replaced by something smaller and lighter, while the hard-backed wooden chairs had been replaced with comfortable armchairs. She had no idea how anyone had been able to endure the previous layout, but perhaps no one had used it very often. Baron Holyoake had spent so much time hunting, either animals or maids, that Emily was privately surprised he'd been able to find any time to plot a coup.

*Maybe he was just good with time management,* she thought, a smile playing around her lips. *Or maybe he left management of his estates to his men.*

"Lady Emily," Steven said. He rose from his chair, then bowed to her. "I took the liberty of ordering Kava."

Emily sat in her chair and smoothed her dress down. "That's quite all right," she said, firmly. Privacy wards tingled into existence around the room as Markus cast them with practiced ease. "I could use a mug myself."

"It's been an interesting few days at the Faire," Steven said. "Quite apart from the guest list...well, it adds extra weight to what you told us before, in Mountaintop."

"I recall," Emily said. She'd told them that change was coming and that they needed to adapt, or be swept away when the changes built unstoppable momentum. "I'm glad you enjoyed your visit."

"I have learned much," Steven said. "And I have communicated all I have learned to the quarrel."

Markus cleared his throat. "Steven may no longer be the local head," he said. "But he is still very well connected."

Emily shot him a glance. Markus had to be in an awkward position. On one hand, his relationship with Melissa depended on Emily keeping her mouth shut, at the very least; on the other hand, damaging his relationship with Steven might have had unfortunate long-term consequences. Were they friends? She couldn't recall seeing them spending time together at Mountaintop. Or were they merely pushed together by events?

"You graduated last month, I assume," Emily said. "Did you do well?"

"High marks," Steven said. He smirked. "As if there was any doubt."

"I'm glad to hear it," Emily said. She looked up as Janice arrived, carrying a tray loaded with three mugs of steaming Kava. "How much of that was your own work?"

"All of it," Steven said, with pretended outrage. "Honestly, Lady Emily. Do you think I would have held the post I did if they thought I would abuse it?"

Emily shrugged. Markus had been Head Boy...but he was also the Ashfall Heir. Nanette had been Aurelius's personal project, a girl who had nowhere else to go. And Steven had been closely linked to Crystal Quarrel before being appointed its representative in the school. She rather doubted that academic credit alone had smoothed their paths to advancement.

But, at the same time, a magician who didn't know the source matter from cover to cover was likely to prove a poor magician in the future. Few quarrels would see any great advantage in giving their representatives marks they hadn't earned.

She picked up her mug and took a sip. "It isn't my concern," she said. "But I'm glad to see that you're doing well."

"Thank you," Steven said. "With your permission, therefore, I will skip any further pleasantries and get right down to business."

Emily had a nasty feeling she knew what was coming, but she merely nodded.

"You spent five months at Mountaintop, during which you attended a dozen meetings of Crystal Quarrel without actually swearing any of the formal oaths," Steven said, bluntly. "I do not believe you attended many other meetings...or am I mistaken?"

"I was not asked," Emily said, flatly.

The memory was thoroughly embarrassing. She'd found the whole arrangement somewhat amusing, although it was rather more than just another frat boy sorority house. Maybe the quarrels had more influence than she'd realized in the school, but it involved networking and making friends, two things she had never been very good at doing. And yet, in hindsight, it would have been easier to spy if she'd gained access to more quarrels.

"I imagine they thought we'd gotten to you first," Steven said. "We were not shy about our success."

"They weren't," Markus confirmed. "I think Steven did a little dance while crowing."

Emily smiled as Steven glowered at Markus before looking back at her.

"The point is this, Lady Emily," Steven said. "We do consider you one of us, but there are limits to what we can do with you unless you swear the oaths. There are many advantages to belonging to a quarrel."

Emily looked at Markus. "Do *you* belong to a quarrel?"

"The Ashfall Family *is* a quarrel in its own right," Markus said. "There's no room for joining a bunch of outsiders."

"You would also have the opportunity to work with other members in Whitehall," Steven added, gently. "The Grandmaster forbids recruiting until Fourth Year, but we do have representatives there."

Emily blinked in honest surprise. She hadn't known there were quarrels at Whitehall — apart from the one she'd formed herself — but it shouldn't really have been a surprise. If quarrels pervaded magical society to the degree Steven had claimed, they would definitely not have left Whitehall alone. Maybe Steven had moved so quickly to speak with her out of fear she'd go to another quarrel. After all, she *hadn't* sworn the oaths.

"You would probably rise to become the local head," Steven added. "You could recruit and train newcomers from the students, then pass the interesting ones on to us for further development. Your personal status would be enhanced beyond measure."

"I can't," Emily said, after a moment. "My father would not be amused."

"Your father is powerful enough to survive alone," Steven said. "Are you?"

Emily swallowed. "He is still my Guardian," she said. It was true enough, although Void had never actually interfered with her life. "I cannot defy his edicts without a very good cause."

Steven met her eyes. "The advantages of being part of a union of magicians?"

The hell of it, Emily knew, was that it was a very good deal. If she'd been what everyone thought she was, the bastard daughter of a Lone Power, the chance to ally herself with a quarrel would have seemed ideal. It would have given her friends, a family of sorts, and access to some of the highest places in society. But there would be a price. She would be expected to uphold the quarrel, forsaking all other concerns.

*And I already belong to a quarrel*, she thought. *The one my friends and I made.*

"My father would not be impressed," she said, firmly. "I'm sorry for putting you to so much trouble, Steven, but I cannot disobey his rules."

Steven's eyes glittered. "Do you think he'd punish you?"

Emily had no idea how Void would react, in real life, but it was as good an excuse as any.

"He is my Guardian until I turn twenty-one," she said. If Melissa could be pushed into a marriage because she was still too young, no one could dispute Void's far less significant edicts to his daughter. "I don't think he would be too pleased with me if I compromised myself."

"I'm sorry to hear that," Steven said, his eyes betraying a hint of anger, "but I do understand."

"That's why he got the job," Markus commented. "Someone else would be screaming curse words by now, demanding that you swear the oaths at once."

Emily sighed, inwardly. "I'm sorry, too." Once, the offer would have been very tempting, but like so much else at Mountaintop it had probably been a trap. "But you are welcome to stay for the rest of the Faire."

"I would be honored," Steven said. He took one last sip from his mug, then placed it on the table and rose to his feet. "I trust you will consider us, when you reach the age of maturity."

He bowed to Emily, nodded to Markus, and strode out the door.

"He wasn't too hopeful," Markus said, as soon as the door was closed. "Your father is not one to disobey."

"No," Emily agreed. "And what about yours?"

"The Old Man often lets me make my own mistakes," Markus said. "He was quite insistent that I proved myself in Fourth Year before he formally accepted me as his heir."

"Your brother is still young," Emily said.

"And still a brat," Markus agreed. "But my father believes that the strongest and most capable should take the lead at all times. If I had proved unsuitable, I suspect the Prime Heir would have become one of my cousins."

"I can't see Lady Fulvia doing that," Emily said. "She named Melissa as her Heir before she went to Whitehall, let alone passed Fourth Year."

"It might have been hard for Melissa to claim power," Markus said.

Emily shrugged. "I trust you are enjoying the room?"

"Yes, thank you," Markus said. "I wasn't expecting you to actually *help*."

"I didn't know *to* help," Emily said. She paused, then leaned forward. "What did Melissa tell you about me?"

"That you came out of nowhere and turned the school upside down," Markus said. "That you were both a good and bad influence on people, particularly Princess Alassa."

"I think that's true of most people," Emily mused. "Melissa has certainly been an influence on me."

Markus lifted an eyebrow, but said nothing. Emily had to smile to conceal her own amusement. Melissa's influence had largely been focused around encouraging Emily to learn counterspells and other tricks, including a large number of prank spells. There were times when it had almost been fun, pranking one another, but she'd never been quite able to rid herself of the horror she'd felt at some of the pranks. Turning someone into a frog and then dropping them into a lake was one thing, but actually risking their lives was quite another.

*Don't kick any animals at Whitehall*, she thought, remembering one of the rules. *You never know who it might be.*

"I'm glad to hear it," Markus said, finally.

Emily laughed, and met his eyes. "When is she supposed to get married?"

"The last night of the Faire," Markus said. "By then..."

"By then, you have to come to some decisions about what you want to do," Emily snapped, crossly. "Or do you intend to keep having an affair with her after she's married?"

"I thought you were on our side," Markus said.

"I am," Emily said. It was true enough. Neither Fulvia nor Gaius commanded her liking, let alone her loyalty. "But what are you going to do when you run out of time?"

She listed the options as she saw them. "Talk to both families and try to broker a peace? Run off together and find a place to live away from the maddening crowds?

Have one final kiss and then part, never to meet again?"

Markus glared at her. "Have you ever been in love?"

"No," Emily said, flatly. She loved her friends, and Lady Barb, but it wasn't roman-tic love in any sense of the word. They were her friends and the closest thing she had to a real mother. "I don't know what it's like to love someone, but...do you know you're in love?"

Markus's face darkened. For a moment, he looked so angry that she thought he was going to hit her.

"I could not live without her," he said.

"Then find a way to live *with* her," Emily suggested. Romeo had made similar dec-larations, had he not? And, in the end, he and Juliet had died together. But that wasn't romantic, not really. It was just stupid. "Talk to your families. Or run off together, leaving an insulting note behind. But either way, your time is running out."

She sighed, inwardly. Romeo and Juliet had been underage, by Earth's standards, although Shakespeare's audience wouldn't have seen anything odd in a thirteen-year-old girl getting married. But it underlined Shakespeare's original point: emotion, strong emotion, led to poor decisions. Both Romeo and Juliet had been thoroughly immature, and it showed.

*Not that one can't be both immature and over sixteen,* she thought. There were quite a few students at Whitehall, Melissa included, who Emily would have classed as immature. Hell, Imaiqah and the Gorgon were more mature by themselves than Emily and Alassa were put together. *And making Romeo and Juliet older in later pro-ductions might still make perfect sense.*

"I know," Markus said. "But I don't know what to do."

"Talk to her," Emily said. "Sit down one evening and have a long chat ..or would you like me to host you both for dinner? I could say it's a gathering for youngsters, and leave Master Grey in charge of the dance."

"Maybe for lunch," Markus said. "You couldn't just invite the pair of us, could you?"

Emily considered it, but shook her head. Imaiqah and Alassa already knew, but she would need to invite Jade and Caleb to keep her cover...and there were others in the castle of the same general age. The ones who weren't invited would think they'd been deliberately excluded...

"I'll invite you both for lunch, tomorrow or the day after," she said. She thought briefly about inviting Alassa, then dismissed it as a bad idea. Melissa would be hor-rified at the thought of *Alassa* offering her advice. "But I would really advise you to come to a decision soon, before you run out of time."

"I know," Markus said. "But it's so hard."

"You were Head Boy," Emily said. "Didn't you have to comfort anyone who'd been unlucky in love?"

"Yes," Markus said. He wrung his hands together as he spoke. "It was a lot easier when the problems belonged to someone else."

# Chapter Twenty-Nine

THE FAIRE SEEMED LOUDER THAN EVER AS EMILY AND FRIEDA WALKED THROUGH THE gates, even though many of the rarer books and potions had been purchased and a number of stalls had closed. Hundreds of magicians were in the crowd, a surprising number eying the railway train with the same mixture of fear and awe that Emily had felt when she'd seen magic for the first time. Beyond them, thousands of others were browsing through the stalls, or watching children nervously as they ran around, playing elaborate games that reminded Emily of Cowboys and Indians.

*They feel safe*, she thought. The Nameless World had its fair share of horrors, but parents didn't seem so inclined to try to wrap their children in cotton wool. *And they know the kids have to grow up sooner rather than later.*

"I need to talk to Yodel," she said to Frieda. The enchanter had set up a large stall, complete with two apprentices who were getting into the spirit of trying to sell everything from enchanted trunks to hands of glory. "Will you be all right out here?"

Frieda hesitated for a long moment, but eventually nodded. "I could always go look at the railway again. But you won't be long, will you?"

"I don't know," Emily admitted. It was quite possible that Yodel would be rather unhappy to see her again. "I'll be as quick as I can."

She watched Frieda run off towards the makeshift station, where Imaiqah and her father were showing off a larger steam engine designed to replace watermills, then turned and walked towards Yodel's stall. One of the apprentices eyed her with some interest — it was odd how it no longer sent tingles of fear down her spine — while the other, more politically aware, turned and rang a bell hanging from the side of a large tent. Emily couldn't help comparing it to a wigwam, but there was enough magic wrapped around it for her to suspect it was designed and built by Yodel personally. The flap opened, revealing the enchanter himself.

"Lady Emily," Yodel said. His voice was flat, completely expressionless. "What can I do for you?"

"I was hoping we could talk in private," Emily said. "I may have a commission for you."

Yodel studied her for a long moment before motioning for her to enter the wigwam. It looked barely large enough for one person from the outside, but Emily wasn't too surprised to discover it was much larger on the inside. A handful of tables were scattered around the interior, littered with tools, pieces of half-carved wood and dozens of different types of crystal. The walls were a strange, shifting grey; her eyes hurt when she looked at them for too long.

"You managed to expand the pocket dimension," she said. "I thought you couldn't live in one permanently."

"You can't," Yodel said. "But I can use it as a workshop."

He sat down on the floor and motioned for her to sit down facing him. Emily hesitated, then did as he directed, resting her hands in her lap. Yodel had every reason to be mad at her, she recalled, wondering if she'd made a mistake stepping into his place of power. It had been her fault that he'd had to leave Dragon's Den.

"I'm sorry I did not contact you earlier," she said, finally. "I should have written to you after...after they confiscated your book."

"I got it back," Yodel said. "The Grandmaster wasn't too happy, but he conceded I didn't know what you intended to do with it. I hope he striped you good and proper."

"Something like that," Emily said.

"But I was planning to leave anyway, as you know," Yodel added. He smiled, rather thinly. "Working here has been an eye-opener in more ways than one."

Emily smiled back, relieved. "Have you managed to drum up more business?"

"More than I can handle," Yodel said. "Your people seem to be richer than the rest of the country's population put together. I've had so many commissions that I've actually had to take four apprentices. Teaching them all together is pure hell."

*And to think Lady Barb had problems with me,* Emily thought. It was rare for a magician to take more than one apprentice at a time, let alone four. Teaching them all together would be immensely difficult, particularly as the more complex fields of magic required one-on-one teaching. *Is he taking on more than he can handle?*

"I didn't know you could take more than one," she said, out loud. "How are you coping with four?"

Yodel shrugged, expressively. "It's a slow process," he said. "We agreed that the apprenticeship period would be longer than normal, but that they would also be paid for their services instead of working in exchange for tuition. And they can leave, without fear or favor, if another enchanter should happen to need an apprentice."

"It seems they would have an advantage," Emily observed. "You would already have taught them the basics."

"Maybe," Yodel said. "Every enchanter has his own way of doing things. I could teach my apprentices something that would make another enchanter recoil in horror."

He shrugged, again. "But we're not here to talk about me, unless you've come to collect your taxes personally."

"No, sadly," Emily said. "But I do have a commission for you."

"I see," Yodel said, carefully. "And will this get me into trouble with anyone?"

"I don't think so," Emily said. She had no idea what, if anything, the Grandmaster or Master Tor had made public about the whole affair. "But I will be requiring an oath."

Yodel lifted one bushy eyebrow. "And if I asked for details *before* swearing the oath?"

"I would refuse to give them to you," Emily said, curtly.

"Then let me think," Yodel said. "I must say the Faire has been quite interesting, Lady Emily."

"Thank you," Emily said, refusing to be thrown by the abrupt change in subject. "Helping to organize the Faire is quite different from merely being a visitor."

"I can imagine," Yodel said. "They were talking about inviting me to be on the committee this year. I turned them down."

Emily frowned. "Why...?"

"Too much hard work to do already," Yodel said. He waved a hand at the overflowing tables. "I have a dozen trunks to finish and a number of other projects waiting in the wings."

"That's why you brought your workshop here," Emily said.

"Correct," Yodel said. "Let the apprentices handle the task of selling my wares, while I try to catch up with my work."

He cocked his head and smiled at her. "What sort of oath do you want?"

"An oath of secrecy," Emily said. "And an oath that you won't try to duplicate it for yourself."

"Interesting," Yodel said. "And how much would I be paid for this?"

"Five gold coins," Emily said.

"Ah, but I don't know what it is," Yodel said. "I reserve the right to haggle over the price after you finally tell me."

Emily gave him a long considering look. If Imaiqah had come with her, she could probably have haggled until Yodel agreed to do everything for a single gold coin. But Emily did have to admit that Yodel had a point. He had no idea what she was asking him to do.

"Very well," she said. "But you keep my secret even if we can't agree on a price."

"Very well," Yodel echoed. He held up his hand and swore the oath. "What do you want me to make for you?"

Emily reached into her pocket, feeling the reassuring weight of the battery pressing against her skin, and removed the diagram she'd drawn out earlier.

"I want something like this, something that will channel magic," she said. "It needs to be both strong and small."

Yodel took the diagram and studied it, thoughtfully. "This would make a very odd wand," he said. "If you intend to use a wand, you don't need to force your magic through stone."

"I know," Emily said.

"And I can't see this being any use to anyone, unless you plan to use a nexus point," Yodel added, slowly. "Or a ritual."

"Something along those lines," Emily said, evasively.

"You're going to be a Fourth Year," Yodel said. He gave her a probing look. "You do realize that asking for help from your fellow students, let alone an outsider, with regards to your project is grounds for being held back a year? Or being expelled, if they think your cheating was above the acceptable levels?"

"This isn't anything to do with my joint project," Emily said. "It's a personal project of mine."

"How curious," Yodel said. "What would you say, I wonder, if I told you the price wouldn't be money, but a full explanation of what you intend to achieve?"

"I would be forced to decline," Emily said, flatly. It would be nice to have a skilled enchanter working on the batteries, but she was all too aware that the more people who knew, the greater the chance of a leak. "This is too important to risk getting out before it's ready."

"I see," Yodel said. His dark eyes peered into hers for a long chilling moment. "In that case, the flat fee for producing this is twenty gold coins. You will also have to pay for the materials."

Emily blinked. The value of coins tended to be variable, something that caused no end of confusion, but twenty gold coins...she'd paid about the same amount for her first trunk, and a little more for the second. She could afford it, she knew, but it annoyed her to have to pay so much. She'd grown up counting every last coin before carefully buying the cheapest food, drink, and clothes she could.

"Five gold coins, plus the materials," Emily said. "How long will it take you to make it?"

"An hour or two," Yodel said. "Come back in three and it will be ready for you, barring disaster. But I can't do it for anything less than fifteen gold, plus the materials."

Emily sighed. "Ten gold, plus the materials," she said. "Or fifteen, counting the materials."

"Done," Yodel said, immediately.

"Oh," Emily said. She had the feeling she'd slipped up. "How much are the materials worth?"

Yodel glanced at the diagram. "Assuming everything works perfectly, one or two gold," he said. "But I don't mind the excess."

Emily sighed. "Very well done," she said. "If I return to pick it up in three hours, it will be ready?"

"Unless there is a complete disaster," Yodel said. "But I'm afraid I will have to ask for the gold in advance."

"I should pay you ten now and the remaining five when I come back," Emily said. "But I don't have time to worry about it."

She opened her pouch, counted out fifteen gold coins, and waited impatiently for Yodel to check each one individually. Not that she really blamed him for being careful. Fake coins were rare, she'd been told, but gold coins that had been diluted with some other metal were alarmingly common. The sooner someone set up a proper bank, and a proper mint, the better. But there were problems that would have to be solved before either could be made to work.

*Like how to keep noblemen from requesting loans they have no intention of repaying,* she thought, sourly. *Or all the other problems that the banking class caused the medieval world.*

The thought made her wince. Most of the early money-lenders had been Jews, which had been seen as a neat way to avoid the Church's prohibition on usury. Unsurprisingly, it hadn't made the Jews popular; smarter kings had used them as scapegoats, while stupider kings had been happy to allow pogroms from time to time. How much anti-Semitism had been born, she wondered, because working with money was the only avenue open to the Jews?

"Fifteen gold," Yodel announced, finally. "I'll write you a receipt."

He picked up a piece of paper and scrawled a note in Old Script, then passed it to her. Emily glanced at it, parsing out the words, and stuck it in her pouch. The charms would keep it from being stolen, she knew; Lady Barb had forced her to charm the pouch again and again until even she hadn't been able to take it without setting off alarms. She'd rigged similar protective spells around the battery itself.

"I would be curious to know what you intend to do with this...object," Yodel said, as Emily rose. "It seems to have no purpose, as far as I can tell."

"You'll be among the first to know," Emily assured him. She took a breath. "And I am sorry for any problems I may have caused you."

Yodel climbed to his feet, moving slowly and carefully. "I should not have given you that book," he said. "But what is done is done. Unless you can change the past...?"

"I don't believe it to be possible," Emily said. She'd checked the books at Whitehall, when she'd thought about some of the fantasy stories she'd read, but time travel didn't even seem a workable concept. Most people thought of a time machine as nothing more than a watch. "You can't undo the past."

"No," Yodel agreed. "All you can do is make the most of what happened to you."

Emily nodded as he opened the flap, allowing her to step back into the real world. The noise of the Faire crashed down on her — it had been quiet inside the wigwam — and she nearly stumbled. But she regained her composure and calmly walked out of the tent. Yodel's two apprentices — she wondered, absently, what had happened to the other two — both looked down at the ground. Clearly, the one who had recognized her had filled in the other while she'd been in the tent.

She caught up with Frieda at the railway, and they walked together to the zoo. The lion looked more aggressive than the first time she'd seen it, roaring and snarling at anyone who got too close, despite the protective spells. Beside it, in the next cage, a sleeping tiger-like creature snored loudly. Emily couldn't help wondering just what it actually was; if she'd seen it outside the cage, she might have mistaken it for a stuffed toy. But, judging by the teeth and claws, it might have been the last mistake she'd ever made.

"Eva was telling me that the old Baron used to kill these creatures," Frieda said. "They said he'd even killed a Mimic."

"I doubt it," Emily said. No one apart from a handful of people at Whitehall, including herself, knew the true nature of the Mimics. A man without both magic and understanding would be rapidly consumed, then replaced, if he tried to fight a Mimic. "Maybe he got replaced instead."

Frieda looked up at her. "Do you think that's possible?"

"I don't think so," Emily said. "He was hung, drawn, and quartered, then buried in several unmarked graves. I don't think a Mimic could have endured that without returning to its natural form."

"I hope you're right," Frieda said, suddenly serious. "Mimics have always scared me."

"They scare *everyone*," Emily said. She'd had nightmares about being replaced...and Imaiqah had confided in her that she'd had them, too. "But you don't have to worry about them."

Frieda gave her a worshipful look. "Because you'll protect me?"

*Because it's pointless*, Emily thought. *The Mimic would be indistinguishable from its target...and even it, when it was buried behind the duplicated personality, wouldn't know what it was. You could be a Mimic and never know it.*

"I'll do my best," she promised, instead. There was no point in giving Frieda nightmares too. "We did see one destroyed at Whitehall."

They moved on, past dozens of animals in cages. A handful of surprisingly mundane horses seemed to be very popular with the children, who were lining up to take short rides around the Faire. Emily puzzled over it for a long moment — she'd never been fond of horses, although Sergeant Miles and Alassa had taught her to ride — and then realized that the children would probably never have another chance to ride. Zangaria had strict rules covering horse ownership, banning anyone from owning a horse without good reason. Or the willingness to pay a fairly considerable bribe.

She rubbed the bracelet at her wrist as they stopped outside a glass case containing dozens of tiny snakes. None of them were Death Vipers, but she knew from Martial Magic that they were almost as dangerous. They could be eaten, Sergeant Miles had said, yet it was only as a last resort. Preparing them to be eaten was difficult and dangerous.

"If I were to look for a familiar," Frieda said, "could I start here?"

"Start at Whitehall," Emily said. She sometimes wondered what it said about her that she'd chosen a lethal snake as her familiar, but she really hadn't had a choice. "And perhaps with something less dangerous."

"I could choose a tiger," Frieda said, looking back towards the roaring lion. "Or a lion."

"You don't get to choose," Emily said. "You cast the spell and see if the creature responds to you. If it doesn't, you move on to the next one and try again."

Frieda frowned. "Didn't you try?"

"I did," Emily said. "But I found nothing willing to bond with me until I reached the Cairngorms."

She smiled, ruefully. Jade had told her that some boys refused to try to bond with creatures they considered unmanly, even if they'd been rejected by everything else. But then, what sort of combat sorcerer would want to walk around with a mouse or a hamster on their shoulders?

"You'll have your chance next year," she said. "And I'm sure you'll find something you like..."

She broke off as she sensed a surge of magic.

"What's that?" Frieda asked.

"Trouble," Emily said. There was another surge of magic, stronger than the first. "Come on!"

# Chapter Thirty

Even if she hadn't been able to sense the surges of magic, Emily discovered as she ran, it would have been easy to find the source of the trouble. Commoners were running in all directions, while magicians were hastily casting protective wards to protect their merchandise or allow them to watch the show in something resembling safety. Emily gritted her teeth as she ran past a pair of screaming teenagers, and came to a halt as she saw two groups of magicians facing each other.

For a moment, her heart almost stopped. Markus was standing at the head of one group, flanked by Steven and another boy she vaguely recognized from Mountaintop, facing Gaius and a small army of Ashworths. Had Gaius realized that Markus had been making love to Melissa? Or had something else happened? She glanced from side to side, seeing magic crackling over their palms, and realized that all hell was about to break loose.

"Get out of our way," Gaius bellowed. "We have the right to proceed!"

"We were here first," Markus shouted back. "The law is on our side!"

Emily gaped as Frieda ran up behind her. Had they just started to bicker like a gang of street thugs? Or was it nothing more than an excuse for a brawl? She could easily have believed both possibilities

"Go find Master Grey," she snapped, catching Frieda's arm. Where *was* he? If Emily could sense the magic, so could a fully-trained magician. "Hurry!"

"You murderous scum," a man shouted from the Ashworth side. Emily didn't know him, suggesting he was from a cadet branch. "You murdered my uncle!"

"You killed my brother," an Ashfall shouted back. "You killed him!"

Emily wanted to cover her ears as the two parties kept shouting, hurling out charges and counter-charges and accusations of acts she would have thought anatomically impossible. Both sides were buying time, the tactical side of her mind noted; they were both hastily preparing their spells for a fight, while summoning reinforcements. She looked around for Master Grey, or anyone else who might be able to help, but saw no one. Was he on the other side of the Faire? Or had he simply decided he couldn't get involved?

Markus raised his hand and shot a bolt of light towards one of the Ashworths. The target deflected it, with an effort, and threw back a fireball of his own. Steven caught it on his wards, absorbing the flames without noticeable effort. Other spells glimmered on the air, on the very verge of being cast.... Emily gritted her teeth, said a silent prayer and ran forward, placing herself between the two parties. Magic crackled around her, but faded as they realized they would catch her in their spells.

"The law is not on your side," she said, as loudly as she could without actually shouting. "And this isn't a place to fight!"

"Get out of the way," Gaius snapped. "We're going to teach those thugs a lesson."

"Not here you're not," Emily snapped back. "Fight them somewhere else, if you like, but not here. There are too many others who could get caught up in the fighting."

She tried to think of something she could do with the battery, if they started hurling spells at each other again, but everything she could think of required prior preparation. If Yodel had built her the valve...she shook her head, mentally, and concentrated on keeping the two sides from fighting. She didn't have the ability to separate them by force.

"They were blocking our way," Gaius insisted. "We have every right to remove them."

"We were here first," Markus snarled back. "You demanded we move!"

Emily wondered if she could knock their heads together. She hadn't liked Gaius from the moment she'd laid eyes on him, but she hadn't thought he was stupid enough to pick a fight in the middle of the Faire. Had someone goaded him into starting a pointless fight? Or was he merely trying to burnish his credentials before the wedding? Perhaps he thought that having experience of fighting the Ashfalls would be good for his future. Or perhaps he thought it would impress Melissa.

"Look around you," she said. "Do you really want to draw hundreds of others into your fight?"

Gaius hesitated, noticeably. "I..."

"He most certainly does not," a stern voice said. Fulvia was standing to the edge of the crowd, glaring at the Ashworths. Melissa was standing next to her, looking pale. "This is not a place to fight, Gaius."

"Nor should you let yourself be lured into a fight," Marcellus added. The Patriarch of House Ashfall looked tired. "Put down your spells and step back."

Markus hesitated. "But..."

"Do as he tells you," Emily said, meeting his eyes and trying to convey a message. *Do you think she would like it if you killed her kinsmen?* "You don't want to start a fight here."

"We offer our most sincere apologies for the disruption," Fulvia added, speaking to the entire crowd. "Ashworths, with me."

She turned and started to march back towards the castle. Gaius shot Emily a look that suggested murder, then strode after the Matriarch, followed by the other youngsters. Melissa remained behind, her eyes flickering nervously between Gaius and Markus, until Fulvia barked a command for her to come, too.

Emily felt a stab of sympathy for the girl. It couldn't have been easy to watch her secret lover prepare to fight her family. But why had it all blown up so quickly?

*Idiots*, she thought. *It would have been safer if they'd picked the fight in Whitehall.*

"I offer my apologies, too," Marcellus said. "Markus, you and I will discuss this matter once we are back in our rooms."

Markus colored. Emily felt a flicker of sympathy, knowing that Marcellus would not be kind or understanding. How could he be, when he didn't know that Gaius was more than just a potential Ashworth? Marcellus had no idea that his son was dating Melissa, or that Gaius was his rival. All he saw was a dispute between two hotheads that had nearly resulted in utter disaster.

*And worse, perhaps*, she thought, *if they had managed to kill me.*

"Markus," she said. "I would like to invite you to breakfast with me tomorrow morning."

Marcellus turned to face her. "My son will be busy," he said. "I will find him something unpleasant to do."

"Father," Markus said. Something unspoken seemed to pass between them. "I..."

"Very well," Marcellus said. "You may join Lady Emily for breakfast. But you will not be attending dinner tonight."

Emily blinked. He had changed his mind that quickly?

"Lady Emily, with your permission, I will keep everyone away from the dinner and dancing tonight," Marcellus added. "I do not feel it would be a good idea for my family to meet *them* when tempers are still running high."

"I understand," Emily said. If nothing else, an evening without dinner and dancing would be a relief. "I will cancel the dance altogether to let tempers cool."

She looked at Markus. "I will see you tomorrow."

Markus nodded. "Thank you," he said.

"You can discuss the nature of the favor you owe her," Marcellus added, as he turned away. "All hell could have broken loose today."

Emily nodded, once.

Markus bowed to her. "It will be my honor to perform one favor for you," he said. "And I thank you for saving us from our darker impulses."

He turned and followed his father before Emily could think of a response. Markus owed her more than one favor...and both of them had to sit uneasily on him. The magical community insisted that favors had to be repaid, one way or another, and few liked the thought of remaining in debt permanently. He would need to find a way to repay her, she suspected, before he took over as Patriarch. His family would not like him owing a favor to anyone.

She watched the rest of the crowd disperse slowly, muttering amongst themselves. The Ashworths and Ashfalls might be the largest parties here, but they weren't the only ones. A fight in the Faire would have drawn in other families, eventually ripping the magical society apart into open war. Could the Ashworths and Ashfalls, even combined, resist the remainder of the magical families? Or would the battle at Cockatrice merely be the start of a war with only one possible outcome?

*But the necromancers would have laughed*, she thought. *So many magicians killed in a pointless civil dispute.*

"Lady Emily," Master Grey said. He cast a privacy ward with effortless ease. "I was in the city."

Emily eyed him, suspiciously. "You were in the city?"

"One of the Ashfall bitches cast a particularly nasty spell on a young man," Master Grey said. He sounded annoyed at the question. "I had no choice but to go after him and provide assistance. It was not an easy task."

"I'm sure it wasn't," Emily said, tartly. "We nearly saw the start of a fight here."

"Putting Ashworths and Ashfalls together is like mixing Basilisk Blood with powdered Dragon Scales," Master Grey reminded her. "I *told* you that, didn't I?"

"Yes, you did," Emily said.

Master Grey met her eyes. "Then why did you invite them both?"

Emily gritted her teeth. "Because I didn't keep a close eye on the proceedings," she said, sharply. Had she even known? The first time she'd heard about the feud had been in Mountaintop, by which time the preparations for the Faire had been well advanced. "And because I didn't know what I was getting into."

"And *that* was incredibly careless," Master Grey said. "In future, I suggest you learn to look before you leap."

He was right, Emily knew. But it didn't make it any easier.

"You managed to get yourself entangled in a morass," Master Grey said. "The Ashworth Heir will be married in five days, at the end of the Faire. I have no doubt that the Ashfalls will do what they can to make it a night to remember — and curse. If you manage to get through that night without spellfire, it will be a miracle."

He pointed a long finger at her. Emily couldn't help noticing that it was covered in tiny scars.

"Your carelessness could have cost lives today," he added. "If you were *my* apprentice, or daughter, I would have dismissed you by now. Your carelessness is becoming legendary...and yet, you are at the heart of destiny itself. You cannot afford to be careless any longer, Lady Emily."

"I know," Emily said.

"Then go back to your father and tell him to give you some proper training," Master Grey snapped. "You need a crash course in everything from etiquette to how best to judge the political implications of your works. Or ask the Grandmaster to get you a *proper* tutor before you make a mistake that gets people killed. Your former Shadow, for example."

Emily glowered at him. "Where is she?"

"I sent her back to the castle," Master Grey said. "It was the safest place."

He dismissed the privacy ward and strode off. Emily watched him go, hastily casting a glamor to hide her feelings. His words had hurt her more than she cared to admit, because he was right. If she'd been paying attention, if she'd known what she was doing, she might have been able to prevent the Faire from becoming a looming disaster. But now she was committed to seeing it through to the bitter end.

She turned as she heard someone walking up behind her. "Emily," Jade said. "Are you all right?"

"I'm fine," Emily lied. "Where's Alassa?"

"Waiting in the food tent," Jade said. "I came as soon as I could."

His eyes narrowed. He could sense the glamor, even if he couldn't look past it.

"You're not all right, are you?"

Emily scowled, inwardly, as they started to walk towards the tent. Jade — and Travis and Cat — had seen her in Martial Magic. They *knew* her reputation was vastly overblown, even though she *had* killed two necromancers. Jade had come to care for her, in a way; Travis had just been a nasty bastard, while Cat had been hugely competitive. But the nastiest thing Travis had ever said to her had been after he'd been replaced by the Mimic.

And Jade could tell when she was upset.

*Lucky Alassa*, she thought. *He'll be there for her when she needs him.*

"Your former master just tore a strip off me," she said, bitterly. What was wrong with her, she asked herself, that she practically froze when someone was chewing her out? "And he was right."

"He yelled at me more times than I care to recall," Jade said. "There were times when I hated him. But he was always right."

He shrugged. "There's no room for weakness in a combat sorcerer. Or, really, in any kind of sorcerer."

"Lady Barb said the same," Emily said.

"She was right," Jade told her. "At the end of Fourth Year, you and Caleb will be expected to defend your project to a group of supervisors. They will tear you apart, examine every aspect of your project, force you to repeat yourself over and over again...you'll hate it. I did."

They stepped into the tent. It was larger on the inside than Emily had realized, although it didn't seem to be a pocket dimension. Alassa was sitting at a table, wearing a dark green dress that seemed to draw attention to her long golden hair. A faint glamor surrounded her, hiding her identity from anyone who didn't already know her; she looked up as Emily approached and smiled. Emily smiled back and sagged into a chair.

"I'll get the drinks," Jade said, firmly. "You sit down and relax."

"You're a lucky woman," Emily said, as Alassa reached out and took her hand. "Really, you are."

"Thank you," Alassa said. "How are you feeling?"

"Tired and weak," Emily said. "Yourself?"

"Trying to plan the wedding," Alassa said. "Would you be interested in being my Maid of Honor?"

Emily held up a hand. "Let me see what the job actually involves before I agree," she said, quickly. "I've managed to get into trouble that way already."

Alassa smirked. "You're learning."

She shrugged. "Basically, your job is to keep me from getting into trouble, organizing the bridesmaids and standing beside me when I give my vows," she added. "There isn't much else to do."

Emily smiled, tiredly. "Let's see," she said. "Turn you into something immobile, so you can't get into trouble; cast compulsion spells on the bridesmaids, so *they* can't get into trouble..."

"I have to ask every noble-born girl in the kingdom," Alassa said. "And casting compulsion spells on them would get you into trouble."

She paused. "Although you might want to consider it anyway. Half of them will be brats, and the other half stuck-up bitches."

"All of them?" Emily asked, choosing not to remind Alassa that *she'd* been a brat only three years ago. "How many is that?"

Alassa frowned. "Not all of them will be able to come," she said. "And I may have to prune their numbers if too many *do* come. But you'd have at least fifty to handle."

Emily blinked. "Fifty? Just fifty?"

"Bridesmaids have to be younger than the bride, by tradition," Alassa said. "And they can't be married themselves. They're also meant to be virgin, but no one asks for fear of the answer."

"I see," Emily said. "Let me think about it, *please.*"

Jade returned, carrying a tray of drinks. "Three chocolates," he said, as he sat down. "And some biscuits."

"Thank you," Alassa said. She took one of the mugs and took a sip. "No alcohol, I assume?"

"I checked all three," Jade said. "Drunkenness at the Faire would not be appreciated."

"No, it wouldn't," Emily said. She took a sip of her own drink and tasted warm melted chocolate mixed with milk. Somehow, it helped her to relax. "My family taught me the dangers of drunkenness."

"Prig," Alassa said, without heat. "There's some amusement to be had when a pair of barons try to drink each other under the table."

"The apprentices drank themselves senseless last year, after the Faire," Jade added, thoughtfully. "Master Grey was not amused."

"I bet he wasn't," Emily said. "What did he say?"

"He started out by calling me a stupid idiot, and it went downhill from there," Jade said. "I had the impression he didn't forbid me to go, purely so he could tell me off while I had a hangover."

"Maybe he just wanted you to make your own mistakes," Emily said. "Lady Barb said the same thing to me, once."

"You learn by doing," Jade said. "Or was it different for you?"

Emily shrugged. "I didn't have the chance to learn anything useful until I came here."

*Sure you did,* her own thoughts mocked. *History. Basic science. Everything else you've used to make money here.*

They drank the rest of their chocolate in companionable silence, then Jade rose. "I need to get Alassa back to the castle before nightfall," he said. "Emily?"

"Tell Bryon we're cancelling the formal dinner and dance," Emily said. "The guests can be served in the Great Hall, if they don't want to eat down here."

Alassa lifted her eyebrows. "And yourself?"

"I'll stay here for a bit," Emily said. "I need to think."

"A terrible habit," Jade said, dryly. He helped Alassa to her feet, and smiled at Emily. "Good luck."

Emily watched them go, feeling an odd twinge of envy. She didn't want Jade — that had been settled a long time ago — but she would have liked someone to be with her. And yet...who would put up with her?

She glanced up as someone loomed over her. "Lady Emily," he said. "Please, could I join you?"

# Chapter Thirty-One

EMILY STUDIED THE NEWCOMER FOR A LONG MOMENT, BEFORE NODDING AND MOTIONING TO the stool facing her. He was tall, but fat, easily the fattest man she'd ever seen. Indeed, he was so large that she couldn't help wondering if the stool could take his weight. His face was almost entirely hidden behind a bushy ginger moustache, which waggled invitingly as he sat down and smiled at her. She'd seen hundreds of strange outfits on magicians in the past, ranging from dark robes to chainmail bikinis, but she had to admit the newcomer wore the strangest outfit she could recall. He wore a golden hat, a pink shirt, orange trousers and strange, frilly shoes.

*Maybe he's color blind*, she thought, as the newcomer settled down. *Or maybe he's trying to make people underestimate him.*

"Lady Emily," the newcomer said. "I knew your father when we were young."

Emily had to smile. "What would you like to be called?"

"You may call me...oh, most people call me Fatty," the man said, without any trace of the horror someone from Earth would have felt at the word. "It's as good a name as any."

Emily frowned. "*Just* Fatty?"

"If you like," Fatty said. He slapped his chest, which wobbled like a plate of jelly. "Your father is a gaping emptiness, while I am pleasantly plump."

"My father never mentioned you to me," Emily said. "I don't know anything about his life before I was born."

"He never talks about his past," Fatty said. "But I didn't really come to talk about him, either."

Emily nodded, and reached out with her mind, trying to sense the magic surrounding Fatty. He was masking very well, she had to admit, but she could still sense the magic rolling and seething behind his wards. It reminded her of Void, or — perhaps — the Grandmaster. Fat as he was, Fatty was also very powerful.

*And there are few fat magicians*, Emily thought, puzzled. *Is he unable to burn fat while performing magic or...is he building up reserves for a battle?*

"You're a Lone Power," she said, out loud. "Aren't you?"

"Something of the sort," Fatty said. "I could never quite grasp the importance of being *alone*, you see, but yes, I am powerful enough to be counted as one."

He shrugged. "I enjoy magical society too much to exclude myself from it," he added. "But your father prefers his own company."

"I know," Emily said.

"But I came to talk to you," Fatty said. "I wanted to thank you."

Emily blinked. "Thank me? For what?"

"For keeping the Ashworths and Ashfalls busy," Fatty said. "It was a surprise to have them both attend the Faire, but you've kept them under firm control. I thank you."

He lifted his hat, revealing that he was going bald on top.

"You're welcome," Emily said, although she couldn't help being surprised. "Have you been making good use of the time?"

Fatty nodded. "The usual deal—making is going on in various tents," he said. "Of course" — he winked at her — "having to keep the problem children under control prevents you from attending the meetings. I don't blame you for wanting to skip them. Your father would not be pleased if you accidentally made the wrong deal."

*And if I had planned it that way*, Emily thought, *it might have been brilliant.*

"I thank you," she said, keeping her face straight. "Can I ask you a question?"

"You can ask any question you like, as long as it's a sensible question," Fatty said. "Or one that lets me show off how brilliant I am."

Emily sighed inwardly. "The feud," she said. If Fatty was as old as Void, he'd been around long enough to witness the separation between the two families. "How did it start?"

"A very good question," Fatty said. "But I could not give you a definite answer. Fulvia is, I think, the only survivor from those years. Far too many people on both sides have been killed before they could have children or even pick their own path in life. All I could tell you are rumors."

"Oh," Emily said. "Does *anyone* know?"

"Ask Fulvia," Fatty advised. "But you might want to do it from a safe distance. She might not be a Lone Power, but anyone who's lived so long as Matriarch will be hellishly powerful."

"Her family seems to be scared of her," Emily observed.

"She's had plenty of time to learn the tricks of the trade," Fatty pointed out. "I dare say she'll outlive them all."

He rose to his feet with ponderous grace. "I would like to advise you to attend a meeting tonight, but your father would be unhappy," he added. "Next time, perhaps, you will be able to attend with him. It would be nice to see him again."

"I'll pass on your words," Emily said. "And thank you."

"Thank *you*," Fatty said.

He lumbered off, steering his way through the tables with deceptive ease. Emily shook her head in droll amusement, wondering why he chose to remain so bulky, then rose and walked out of the tent. Outside, night was starting to fall over Cockatrice, but the Faire was still illuminated by glowing balls of light, casting an eerie radiance over the scene. Emily smiled as a gang of young children ran past, pausing as she heard the sound of someone singing in the distance. It was sweet enough to almost bring a tear to her eye, but there was no time to listen. She needed to find Yodel before he closed his stall for the night.

She had never been very sensitive to emotions, but even she could sense the tension in the air as she walked through the Faire. People exchanged glances with one another, while magicians were wrapping even more protective wards around their stalls, as if they feared another fight. They might have a point, Emily suspected; Gaius and Markus had both been reluctant to back down, even when their superiors had arrived. The next time, she might not be there to stop them before they started hurling curses at each other.

"Lady Emily," one of the apprentices called, as she approached. "You're just in time."

Emily nodded to him, pushed aside the flap, and stepped into the workroom. Yodel stood in front of a table, using a wand to fiddle with the interior of a trunk. Emily waited patiently for him to finish, her eyes sweeping the tables for objects of interest. But the only thing that caught her eye was a wooden frame, one that looked like it had been designed to hold a painting. A spell she didn't recognize glowed around it, working its way in and out of the wood.

"Someone wants to have an updating portrait," Yodel commented, as he looked up. "She wants everyone to know what she looks like at all times."

Emily frowned. "Does that include when she's in the bath?"

"It could," Yodel said. "She wants it fixed on her face, just in case."

"As long as she isn't pouring her darker feelings into the portrait," Emily said. How long had it been since she'd read *The Picture of Dorian Grey?* "Everyone can make a fool of themselves if they wish."

"You are too tolerant, Lady Emily," Yodel said. "People who make fools of themselves tend to lash out when they realize how stupid they've been."

He put the wand down and stepped away from the trunk. "This is your commission," he said, as he walked towards a table. "I actually designed two: the first one matches your request, while the second should be considerably more efficient. However, I do not advise you to use either of them as a wand. The magic would become dispersed before it entered the wood."

Emily picked up the first device and peered at it. It was smaller than she'd expected, little larger than a pencil, but tipped with enough wood to serve as a very basic wand. There was no way to guide the magic, save by pointing it at the target, yet she knew it shouldn't be a problem. If she was right.... She touched the wood, embedding a spell in the material, and smiled to herself as it took root and waited. Wandcraft was hardly her forte — she'd been taught never to use a wand unless it was absolutely necessary — but she knew enough to make it work.

*Nanette taught me more, by accident,* she thought, as she inspected the second valve. *And so did Shadye.*

"I trust they are suitable?" Yodel asked. "I was really quite intrigued by the task."

"They should be," Emily said.

"But I don't understand them," Yodel protested. "Even a Lone Power would have difficulty using them without wasting magic. Or do you plan to try to power them from a nexus point?"

"I'm not sure yet," Emily said.

"Please let me know when you work it out," Yodel said. "I would be curious to see just what you have in mind."

Emily nodded — it was clear he was *frantic* to know what she was doing, just from the way he kept looking at the valve — but kept her thoughts to herself. He was right, in a sense; no single magician could channel enough power to make the devices — she would have to come up with a proper name — workable. But combined with her batteries, it would give her the ability to cast a single spell with terrifying power. Unless it exploded in her pocket, of course...

*Or someone hexes you, and the battery comes apart,* she thought, grimly. *What would happen if so much raw magic poured into the world?*

"I thank you," she said. She placed both of the devices into her pocket, casting a handful of anti-theft spells over them. "I may ask you to make others, in the future."

"I always look forward to your commissions," Yodel said. "And I thank you for the challenge."

Emily nodded and stepped out of the wigwam. Night had fallen completely, leaving the city shrouded in darkness; even the castle, the heart of the barony, was only illuminated by a handful of distant lights. She couldn't help feeling a shiver as she looked at her castle, then back at the Faire around her. It was clear that they belonged in very different worlds.

She heard the singing again and turned to walk towards it. A young girl, around thirteen, stood in front of a caravan, singing sweetly to an assembled crowd. She was young, with pale skin and dark oval eyes, a strange mixture of white and oriental features.

*Jasmine,* Emily remembered. She'd met the girl last year, at the first Faire. *What's she doing here?*

She dismissed the question a moment later, silently cursing herself for forgetting Jasmine and her family. The girl had lost her parents at an early age and wound up living with her uncles and aunts. Emily had offered to pay her fees when — if — she wanted to go to Whitehall. But it had never crossed her mind that Jasmine would attend the next Faire.

*It should have,* she told herself.

"Lady Emily," a quiet voice said. "I was wondering if I could have a word."

Emily groaned inwardly — what now? — and turned to see the speaker. He was a tall, powerfully-built man, with long dark hair drawn back in a ponytail. His face seemed somehow ageless, yet lined enough to make it clear he was no longer young; his dark eyes seemed to glimmer as he peered at Emily. There was something about his stare that was more than a little unnerving.

"Yes, we can," she said, finally. The dark robes marked the newcomer as a sorcerer, but there was nothing to identify his speciality. "What would you like to be called?"

"I am Master Gordian," the newcomer said. He gave her a tight bow, as if he wasn't quite sure just how much respect she was due. "And I merely wished to see if you lived up to your legend."

"Very few people do," Emily said, as she curtseyed in return. She tried and failed to keep the tiredness out of her voice. "What can I do for you?"

"Nothing, at the moment," Master Gordian said. "I thank you for consenting to speak with me."

He bowed, deeper this time, and strode off. Emily stared after him, wondering just what he'd been playing at. Hastily, she checked her pockets and discovered that the battery, the devices and her money pouch were all still in place. She opened her mouth to shout after him, but thought better of it. Instead, she turned and started the long walk back up to the castle, using the night-vision spell to find her way in the dark. By the time she reached the gates, guarded by a pair of her men, she felt so tired that all she wanted to do was climb into bed and sleep.

"My lady," one of them said. "I welcome you to your home."

"Thank you," Emily said, absently. She turned and looked back at the Faire, wrapped in a blaze of light, then back at the guards. Their armor was now marked with runes to protect them from subtle magic. "I..."

She shook her head. She didn't belong here, playing lady of the castle. She didn't have the training, let alone the attitude, to govern hundreds of thousands of people. And yet, King Randor had tricked her, giving her the title and the lands without ever telling her what was involved. She should leave, she knew, and yet she was reluctant to give it up. She'd made so many changes she couldn't leave, without risking everything falling apart.

*Or so you keep telling yourself,* she thought, as she walked through the inner doors and into the castle proper. *Are you just trying to convince yourself that you want to stay, even though you don't want to stay? Or are you being greedy?*

She cursed herself under her breath. In Zangaria, land meant power...and Randor had given her enough land to make her very powerful indeed. He'd given her the resources to be a serious threat to him, if she'd wanted to make herself a threat. No one, absolutely no one, would turn down the offer of lands and a title. No wonder Alicia had been so desperate to have her title confirmed before the king married her off or organized her barony to suit himself. But Emily...Emily didn't *want* the barony.

*Then give it up,* her own thoughts mocked her. *Or are you just going to procrastinate until the shit hits the fan?*

"My lady," Bryon said, stepping out of a side room. "I have organized a simple dinner, without the formalities, for the guests."

"Very good," Emily said. She had a feeling that most of the guests would demand room service, or go down to the Faire to eat, but some would definitely want to be fed in the Great Hall. "Have there been any problems up here?"

"A few dirty looks from one family to the other, but no real problems," Bryon said. "I heard there was nearly a fight down in the Faire."

"There was," Emily confirmed. She had to fight down the impulse to start shaking, now that it was all over. She'd plunged right into the middle of the two groups... her wards were as strong as she could make them, but if she'd been attacked by both sides they wouldn't have lasted long enough for her to escape. She could have died there and then. "But I think it's over, for the moment."

"That is good, my lady," Bryon said.

Emily rubbed her forehead. She felt hungry, but there was too much else that needed to be done.

"Please send a message to Melissa Ashworth," she said. "Inform her that I request the honor of her company for breakfast tomorrow, in the blue room, at nine bells."

"I will see to it at once," Bryon said.

"We will also be joined by Markus," Emily added, "so please give him the same message. *Don't* mention it to either of them."

Bryon frowned, but nodded.

"I will have the maids deliver breakfast for the three of you, once you are ready to eat," Bryon said. "Will you be wanting anything in particular?"

"We'll order food tomorrow," Emily said, after a moment. Melissa and Markus would both want to choose their own breakfasts, while Emily had no idea what *she* would want at the time. Maybe something less fatty than bacon, eggs, and fried potatoes. "Are there any other concerns right now?"

"Lady Frieda is waiting for you in her rooms," Bryon said. "I promised her I would inform you as soon as you arrived."

"I'll see to her myself," Emily said. God alone knew what Master Grey had said to her, before he'd sent her off to the castle. He'd probably frightened her to death. "Let me know if there are any other problems before I go to bed."

She sighed inwardly, and started along the corridor to the stairs. A handful of maids and servants passed her, but there was no sign of any of the guests. Emily could pretend, just for a moment, that the Faire was already over. But the illusion shattered as soon as she passed a set of guest rooms and sensed the wards the occupants had erected to protect themselves. It was clear they didn't trust Emily's promise of safety.

*But who could blame them?* She asked herself. *They all know that their rivals won't hesitate to sneak in and out of their rooms if they have a chance.*

She walked up the stairs and tapped on Frieda's door. The door swung open, and Frieda practically threw herself into Emily's arms. Emily hugged her tightly, half-carried her into the room, and closed the door behind her.

"I was so worried," Frieda said. "You could have been killed!"

"I know," Emily said. "What did he tell you?"

"That you were going to do something stupid, as always," Frieda said, frowning. "I'm starting to think he doesn't like you."

Emily laughed, despite herself. "I'm starting to feel that way, too."

# Chapter Thirty-Two

"THE BLUE ROOM," MELISSA SAID. "RATHER AN...IMAGINATIVE NAME, ISN'T IT?"
Emily shrugged as she rose and walked around the breakfast table. The Blue Room was blue, all blue. Even the cups and saucers were blue. And if she'd stayed with her normal color of dress, Emily knew, *she* would be blue too.

"I think the baron's wife must have designed the room," Emily said, finally. Personally, she found it rather creepy. "Or maybe someone who thought that a unified color scheme was the way to go."

"Not a magician, then," Melissa said.

"Probably not," Emily agreed. She tried to imagine what it must have been like to be the baron's wife, then gave up in disgust. "But please take a seat. Markus should be along in a few minutes."

Melissa gave her a sharp look, then relaxed and sat down. "Why are you doing this?"

Emily shrugged. "Doing what?"

"Helping us," Melissa said. "It isn't like we're *friends*."

"Because...because it feels like the right thing to do," Emily said, after a moment. She walked back around the table and sat down facing Melissa. "And because I can't think of any other solution."

Melissa looked at her for a long moment. "And you're not planning an elaborate revenge?"

"No," Emily said. "I think you have enough problems without me making things worse, don't you?"

"Yes," Melissa said, slowly. "If you hadn't been there yesterday..."

"There would have been a fight," Emily said. She wondered, suddenly, just how much she was missing by being forced to keep an eye on the problem children. Fatty had practically thanked her for keeping the two families under control. "What happened?"

"I wish I knew," Melissa said. "The Matriarch was having me fitted for the wedding dress when we sensed the surges of magic. And then she yanked me out of the tent and ran towards the scene."

"You're meant to marry in four days," Emily said, incredulously. "And you're only having the dress made now?"

"There wasn't time for a proper fitting while I was at Whitehall," Melissa said, shrugging. "Besides, the Matriarch thought it would be better to purchase a dress here."

She looked down at the table. "I think she wanted to make sure I got the right dress, from the right person, at the right time," she added. "Someone probably owed her a favor and she meant to call it in. Or something."

Emily frowned, unsure if she actually *believed* Melissa. Alassa hadn't had much trouble having her dresses fitted, even at Whitehall, and there was no reason Melissa couldn't do the same. Could no one at Ashworth House make or fit a dress? Or was there a political reason to have the dress made at the Faire? The Matriarch might see it as patronizing someone whose career she wished to assist.

And how long did it actually take to make a wedding dress, anyway?

"Tell me something," Emily said. "What does your mother have to say about all this?"

Melissa glanced up. "My mother? My mother is powerless and has been so for years, ever since my father died. She's only an Ashworth by marriage."

Emily's eyes narrowed. "She can't refuse to marry you to Gaius?"

"It's the Matriarch who has the right to choose," Melissa said, bitterly. "My mother left *her* family after she married my father. If the Matriarch wanted to throw her out of the family, there isn't anyone who could stop her."

"I see," Emily said. "Even you?"

Melissa shook her head.

Emily considered it. She could see how Melissa's mother might be considered surplus to requirements, now her husband was dead, but it didn't seem wise for Fulvia to mistreat her so openly. *Melissa* could not fail to take note of how her mother was treated...and *she* was the Heir to the Matriarch. How long would it be, Emily wondered absently, before Melissa saw fit to rebel?

But then, she already had. Fulvia would *not* be pleased when she found out about Markus.

*And how much of your attraction to Markus*, Emily wondered, *stems from rebelling against your family?*

She rose as Markus entered the room. He looked tired, as if he hadn't slept all night, but his eyes were bright. Emily had a private suspicion that his father had probably told him off quite sharply, once they returned to the castle, before ordering him to stay in his rooms until the following morning. Given the tension in the air, it had definitely been a wise move.

"Markus," she said. "Please, take a seat."

"Thank you," Markus said. He sat next to Melissa, and smiled as Emily walked back to her chair. "And thank you for yesterday, too."

"I meant to ask," Emily said. "What happened?"

"Gaius and his mob of friends walked right into us," Markus said. "It was quite deliberate."

Emily met his eyes. "But why?"

"I don't know," Markus said. "He thinks he will be the next Patriarch. Maybe he feels he needs to prove himself."

"He's just an idiot," Melissa said, tartly. "If he caused a major clash with outsiders, the family would disown him rather than let him drag everyone into the war."

Emily eyed her, sharply. "Did you encourage him to cause trouble?"

"*No*," Melissa snapped. "Don't you think I have enough trouble of my own?"

"Yes," Emily said. "I apologize."

Janice appeared, carrying a menu and a small notebook. Emily had to smile at the concept of having menus inside her own home, but ordered scrambled eggs for herself. Markus and Melissa took it in stride, although *they* probably felt as though they were in a hotel. They both ordered large breakfasts, as if they expected to need the energy. Emily couldn't help thinking they might be right.

"I meant to ask," she said. "Why Gaius?"

Melissa blinked. "Why Gaius?"

"He's been chosen to be your husband," Emily said. "Why did the Matriarch choose him?"

"Because she hates me," Melissa said. "She has always hated me."

Markus scowled. "I think Gaius is biddable," he said, slowly. "Maybe not for Melissa, but the Matriarch would find him a useful tool. He wasn't raised to be an Ashworth, so he probably wouldn't try to turn his position into something with real power. Merely being an Ashworth would be enough for him."

"Then he can marry someone from one of the cadet branches," Melissa hissed. There was nothing but raw hatred in her voice. "I will not be marrying him."

"Then," Emily asked, "what are you going to do?"

Melissa exchanged a long glance with her lover. "I don't know," she said. "What *can* I do?"

"Tell your family that you're not going to marry him," Emily said, ticking points off her fingers as she spoke. "Cut your ties to the family altogether if they persist. Run off together and live somewhere you won't be recognized. Or..."

"I could challenge Gaius to a duel," Markus interrupted. "If I kill him, it would be perfectly legal."

Emily had to admit it was a tempting prospect. But there was one hitch. "And what if you lose?"

"That isn't likely to happen," Markus scoffed. "I was dueling champion for three years running. I don't think Gaius ever did more than put up a reluctant fight."

"I'm not so sure," Emily said. "He might have learned more after leaving Mountaintop."

Markus snorted. "Why would he?"

"To keep his real capabilities a secret," Emily said. God knew she'd hidden enough of her own skills, even if most of them couldn't be used as anything other than a last resort. "He could have had private training after leaving Mountaintop, or merely thrown every duel he fought in over the last few years."

"That would be stupid," Markus said. "Everyone knows that dueling champions are popular..."

*With the girls*, Emily finished. She wasn't sure if that was true of Whitehall, but she did know that the boys in Martial Magic or on the *Ken* teams did tend to get more attention from the girls than the boys who weren't. *But if someone was more interested in hiding their skills than picking up girls, why would they bother to try to win?*

"Not everyone is interested in being popular," she said, instead. "And wouldn't he be required to protect Melissa as part of the wedding contract?"

"He would hire a champion," Melissa said, disdainfully. "If, of course, he had the nerve to do even that."

Emily shrugged. Lady Barb had taught her, several times, that there were advantages and disadvantages to having a reputation as a skilled fighter. On one hand, people were reluctant to cross you; on the other hand, people tended to view you as a threat. Not that it would matter to her, she reflected. She already had a terrifying reputation, one that was so exaggerated she didn't recognize herself. It wasn't as if she actually *could* walk on water or make necromancers shiver at her tread.

*But you could walk on water with magic*, she thought. *You would just have to freeze it first — or adjust the surface tension.*

"If you did challenge him," she said. "How could you do it in a way that would make him accept?"

Markus gave her a puzzled look. "What do you mean?"

"You're talking about challenging him," Emily said, "but he has the right to decline."

"That's simple enough," Markus said. "You just issue a challenge he *cannot* decline. Or make him challenge you."

Emily sighed, inwardly. "And don't you think everyone will know it?"

"I beg your pardon?"

"You could call him a...a rapist if you liked," she said. "And he would have to accept, because otherwise people would wonder if the charge was actually true. But everyone watching would also think you insulted him in the hopes of having him issue a challenge."

"Or he might just run," Melissa said, vindictively. "That would be the best possible outcome."

Emily sighed, again. She didn't understand the dueling system at all. It seemed clear enough that the challenged could decline a challenge, but *failing* to accept a certain challenge could be just as bad as accepting it. The system was tailor-made for abuse, even with the quarrels and magical families keeping the balance and eliminating rogue duelers. Trial by combat had always been a stupid idea, if only because the guilty party could win and then silence his enemies.

"Or his quarrel might think you stepped over the line," Emily said. "Or the Matriarch might see it as an outright attack on House Ashworth and retaliate in kind."

Markus snorted. "So what do we do?"

"I think you need to make up your minds," Emily said. "I..."

She broke off as the food arrived and they tucked in. Explaining the concept of scrambled eggs hadn't been that hard, but sliced bread had been unknown in Zangaria before she'd introduced it. Making proper toast, as she saw it, was actually tricky, although the cooks enjoyed a level of skill and precision Professor Thande would have envied. But the results had definitely been worthwhile.

"You're running out of time," she said. "Are you going to talk to your families, run off together...or what?"

"*You* could talk to our families," Melissa said. "I'm sure they would listen to you."

Emily rather doubted it. Fulvia didn't seem the type to be impressed by her reputation, while Marcellus would suspect she had deeper motives. And besides, Fulvia had too much tied into marrying Melissa to Gaius to surrender easily, even if Emily truly lived up to her fearsome reputation. She couldn't hope to keep Melissa from having to face her great-grandmother, at least one final time.

"I don't think so," she said. "I think you have to make up your own minds — and fast."

Markus swallowed. "My father would not be pleased," he said, "but I think he would let me have my head."

"I hope so," Emily agreed. "But your brother is too young to take up the reins, if something happens to your father."

"There are others," Markus said. "I don't think my father would hesitate to name someone from one of the cadet branches to take over, if I happened to go."

Emily looked him in the eye. "Are you *willing* to go?"

"Yes," Markus said, simply.

"It's easier to consider running than facing my family," Melissa admitted.

"You may not have a choice," Emily said. "Your family — both families — could make your lives very difficult, if they chose."

"I know," Markus said. "But there are limits."

Emily shrugged. Markus could find employment anywhere, given both his qualifications and his obvious skills. There was a shortage of trained combat sorcerers, according to Sergeant Miles; Master Grey or one of the others might be quite willing to take him on as an apprentice, even if he was in bad odor. But it wouldn't be easy. People who would happily have loaned him money, knowing he was part of the Ashfall Family, would be reluctant to extend the cash if he was alone.

*And Melissa might have to leave Whitehall before completing Fourth Year,* Emily thought, morbidly. Part of her wouldn't be sorry to see the girl go; part of her knew that Melissa would find it even harder to live without her family. *She wouldn't have any real qualifications to her name.*

"You should be careful," Emily said.

"And what," Melissa demanded, "is the alternative? Giving up—" she waved a hand at Markus "—and marrying Gaius?"

"Put that way," Emily said, "you may have a point. I..."

She paused as Janice stepped back into the room, carrying a folded piece of paper. Emily took the paper and scanned it, scribbled a response on the bottom, and passed it back to Janice. It would have been good news, under other circumstances; Imaiqah's father was finally ready to show off some of his top secret work in a location several miles from Cockatrice. But now...she wasn't sure if she dared leave the castle and go anywhere, other than the Faire. Who knew what sort of disaster would strike the moment she turned her back?

*But I have to go,* she thought. *They can't keep the engineers here indefinitely.*

"Please ask the coachman to prepare my carriage," she said. "And ask Frieda to join me in one hour."

"Yes, my lady," Janice said.

Emily waited until she was gone, then looked back at Melissa. "You do have a point," she admitted. "But you also have to be prepared to take the consequences."

"I will," Melissa said.

Emily met her eyes. "You may be kicked out of your family," she said, flatly. "If so, will you be able to stay at Whitehall for Fourth Year?"

"I don't know," Melissa admitted. "My fees are paid until Sixth Year — my father organized them when it became clear I would develop strong magic — but that isn't *my* money."

Emily sighed. In some ways, *she* was richer than Alassa, even though Alassa was heir to the throne. Alassa's wealth was tied up in Zangaria; she couldn't use it as ready money, even if it produced money over the long term. Melissa...how much money did she have in her own name, and how much did she have tied to her role as the Ashworth Heir?

"The Matriarch might claw it back," Emily said. It wasn't hard to imagine the Matriarch being so vindictive. She vividly recalled her stepfather carefully counting his change and demanding to know where a handful of missing cents had gone, then questioning each and every item on the bill. "Or something else might happen."

"The Grandmaster might not resist," Melissa said. There was a hint of sullen bitterness in her voice. "He doesn't favor everyone like he does you."

"He doesn't favor me," Emily said.

"He does," Melissa said. "Anyone else would have been kicked out of the school after some of the stuff you've done."

Emily considered it. She knew Master Tor had demanded her expulsion, but the Grandmaster had overridden him. Anyone else...it was hard to see why she might have been favored, apart from being allowed to enter Martial Magic without any prior preparation. But she hadn't asked for it. She'd always assumed that Void had insisted on it, pointing out that Emily would need to learn to defend herself as quickly as possible.

"If that's true," Emily said, "I'm sorry. But I didn't ask for any of it."

"That doesn't make it any easier," Melissa said.

Markus touched her hand. "We will decide how to proceed," he said, formally. "And we would like to know we can count on your support."

"I don't know what else I can give you," Emily said. "This isn't Whitehall. There's no way to squash a fight before it can turn lethal..."

But that wasn't entirely true, was it? There *was* a way to do it.

*I'd need to embed the spell first*, she thought. Battling Nanette had been difficult enough; she'd need something much bigger if there were more people involved. *And then I will need to test the spell...*

"Just don't make matters worse," Markus said. He met her eyes for a long moment. "My father would be reluctant to start a fight here."

"I will do my best," Emily promised. She finished her breakfast, and stood up. "You can stay here for as long as you like, if you wish. Just...be careful."

Melissa smiled. "In this room, or in the castle?"

Emily shrugged. She might have mellowed a little towards Melissa, but she didn't like the other girl enough to want to keep her around indefinitely. On the other hand, she could think of at least two jobs she could hire Markus to do if he wound up looking for employment. A skilled magician would be very helpful.

"We will see," she promised.

# Chapter Thirty-Three

"SO...WHERE ARE WE GOING?"

"Somewhere," Emily said, as she played with Yodel's device. They sat together in the carriage, driving out towards an isolated farm on the edge of the Craggy Mountains. "It's a place we selected for some important research and development."

Frieda looked puzzled. "What *sort* of research and development?"

"Technology," Emily said. "The type of technology that shouldn't be developed anywhere near towns or cities."

Frieda snorted. "Be cryptic, why don't you?"

"I'd like to see what you make of it," Emily said. Being in the countryside seemed to relax Frieda, a little. "I need your first impressions."

She smiled as the carriage came to a halt and the coachman opened the door so they could climb out of the vehicle. The Craggy Mountains rose in front of them, peaks hidden behind dark clouds that threatened rain in the very near future. Emily took a long look, remembering the coal and iron seams running through the mountains, and turned towards the cluster of buildings at the base of the mountains. There had been few people living nearby until after Baron Holyoake had been executed, she recalled. Now, thousands of would-be miners flooded the area.

*But we haven't come here to see the mines,* she thought, as she led the way towards the central building. *We've come to see something much more interesting.*

A cold wind blew down from the mountains as they approached the building. Emily couldn't help shivering, despite the warm fleece she'd thrown over her dress. She shivered again a moment later, touching an aversion ward that would keep away almost anyone without business at the site. She took Frieda's hand and led her through the ward, right up to the door. It opened moments later, allowing them to walk straight into the building. Inside, it was mercifully warm.

"Lady Emily," a familiar voice said. "Welcome to Powder Mill."

Emily smiled at the speaker. Paren, Viscount Steam, was a short brown-haired man with a shrewd face and generous smile. It was clear where Imaiqah got her looks from, Emily recalled thinking the first time she'd met her friend's father, although it was clear that Imaiqah had picked up something from her mother too. Behind him, Imaiqah stood, holding a tray of warm drinks in her hand. She seemed relieved to see Emily.

"Take one of these before we go out in the cold again," she said, holding out the tray. "I think you'll need them."

"You will," Paren confirmed. "Have you been looking forward to this trip?"

"A bit, yes," Emily said. She took a mug and passed it to Frieda, then took another one for herself. "How have you been coping with the project?"

"Growing better as we learn more and about the...*scientific method*," Paren said, pronouncing the words as if they were a foreign concept. "There are some very skilled artificers involved in this work, Lady Emily. I have a feeling it won't be long before we see rival installations dotted around the world."

*Probably*, Emily thought. Whoever gained a copy of her notes, the notes Nanette had stolen, would have a leg up on their competition. Paren might be in the lead, at the moment, but that wouldn't last. The scientific method worked for everyone, not just magicians or trained engineers. Given time, everything born in Zangaria would spread around the Nameless World.

"We've been producing several barrels of gunpowder per day," Paren said, as they walked into a small lounge. Behind them, Frieda chatted quietly with Imaiqah. "Some of it was used to make the fireworks you saw at the Faire, some was used to help blast through the rock for the miners...and some was used for the *other* project. So far, there hasn't been *that* much interest from the king, but that will probably change."

"Undoubtedly," Emily said. She sat down on one of the chairs and motioned for Frieda to sit next to her. "Once he understands the potential, *everything* will change."

Paren nodded. "There were a great many accidents, Lady Emily," he said, "but we finally worked out a suitable design for *guns* and *cannons*. They are crude, I think, and there is a great deal of space for improvement..."

"You have no idea," Emily said. She didn't expect anything better than blunder-busses and cannons, but she knew there were many improvements to come. "Give them time."

"Of course, Lady Emily," Paren said.

He took a sip of his drink before he continued. "I have prepared a demonstration, as you asked," he added. "We can watch them fired after we've finished our drinks."

Emily nodded, and changed the subject. "How is your family coping with the move out here, Viscount?"

Paren sighed. "I'm not doing too badly," he said, "but the kids are having problems. They don't fit in with the grandees and they don't fit in with the merchants. Where are they supposed to go?"

"I wish I knew," Emily said.

She cursed the feudal system under her breath. Merchants regarded noblemen and aristocrats as enemies, while aristocrats looked down on anyone who hadn't been born and raised among the nobility. It wouldn't be easy for Paren and his family to fit in, even though Imaiqah was Alassa's close personal friend. They would be caught between two very different worlds, fitting into neither. Perhaps Imaiqah's children would have it easier, Emily thought. She was a magician as well as the princess's friend.

"And Lindsey doesn't fit in very well, either," Paren added. "But she does love living in a larger home."

"That's something, I suppose," Emily said. Imaiqah's mother had been a merchant's daughter, she recalled absently. She would be used to living with other merchants, not the nobility. "But it does help your family."

"Yes," Paren said. "However, I don't get to sit on the City Council any longer either."

He finished his drink and rose. "Let me show you what we've done," he said. "I think you'll be impressed."

Emily nodded him to lead them out the back door and into a large, open field. A cannon was placed just outside, its barrel pointing towards a set of targets at the far end of the field. Two young men, both apprentices, were sitting on top of the weapon; they jumped to attention as soon as they saw Paren, and hastily bowed to Emily. Emily nodded back, and watched as one of the apprentices produced a case and opened it, displaying a large musket.

"This is the Mark-VII," Paren said. He'd taken her handful of half-remembered notes and given them to his engineers, who'd turned them into a set of solid concepts. "It does have a tendency to jam if not cleaned regularly, but it does work. The accuracy, however, leaves something to be desired."

"Volume of fire might be more useful than accuracy," Emily said, recalling the early gunpowder wars on Earth. "You could break a charge of mounted horsemen with enough firepower."

"The grandees will *love* that," Imaiqah muttered.

Emily nodded. The aristocracy had had a fit when stirrups had been introduced, if only because they made it much easier for *anyone* to learn to ride a horse. What would they say, she wondered, when they realized that horsemen would become outdated soon enough, once there were enough cannons and guns to go around? They'd probably press for a ban on gunpowder weapons, only to discover that *anyone* could produce gunpowder or reason out the principles behind the weapons.

"Yes," she said. The Charge of the Light Brigade might have been magnificent, she quoted mentally, but it hadn't been war. "They will utterly *adore* the new weapons."

Paren raised his voice. "Prepare to fire the cannon," he ordered. "Lock and load!"

Emily smiled as the apprentices opened the breech at the rear of the cannon, then loaded in the cannonball and a large bag of gunpowder before closing the breech with a surprising gentleness. It puzzled her until she realized that a single spark would set off the cannon and cause an explosion that might maim or kill the gunmen.

Paren caught her eye and motioned for her to move back, along with Imaiqah and Frieda, as the apprentices aimed the cannon and lit the fuse. Emily covered her ears...

There was a deafening explosion as the cannonball was hurled towards its target.

"My ears are ringing!" Frieda shouted. "That was *loud*."

Emily nodded. The sound had been far louder than she'd expected, even though she should have known better. She knew more about gunpowder warfare than anyone else on the Nameless World, although she expected that to change in short order. The apprentices ran forward and opened the gun, hastily clearing out the residue despite the smoke, and prepared to fire a second cannonball. Minutes later, there was another explosion; this time, the cannonball struck its target.

"Impressive," Emily said. "But what are you going to do about the smoke?"

"We're still searching for the correct formula for smokeless powder," Paren said. "Do you know how to proceed?"

Emily shook her head. It had been sheer luck she'd remembered, with the aid of a few memory charms, enough to start them on the path towards gunpowder. And even then, she was all too aware of just how many people had been injured, or killed, before they had worked out a stable formula. There was no way she could recall the precise details of smokeless powder. They would have to work it out for themselves.

"Magic will help protect us from the smoke," Imaiqah said. "But it isn't really enough."

"No," Emily agreed. The study of basic chemistry, as opposed to alchemy, was in its infancy, but she knew it would eventually solve the problem. "We will solve it one day."

She sighed, inwardly. If she'd known she would be spending the rest of her life on the Nameless World, she would have memorized as many textbooks as possible on everything from medicine to military technology and tactics. Even looking at a page for a moment would be enough to create an impression she could dig up with a memory charm and put to use. But all she had was her very limited knowledge. Given time, the problem *would* be solved, yet she had no idea how long it would take. Earth had taken centuries to move from basic cannons to machine guns and nuclear bombs.

*But I built a small tactical nuke*, she thought. *Someone else could do the same.*

"Take aim," Paren ordered, as the apprentice lifted the musket and pointed it towards the target. "Fire!"

The apprentice fired.

Emily watched as he hastily reloaded his weapon — it wasn't remotely automatic, not yet — and fired again. She'd read that the Duke of Wellington divided his soldiers into two ranks, one firing while the other reloaded, but she hadn't understood why until now. For all of her talk about how the day of the horseman was over, a savage charge could break a line of infantrymen while they were busy reloading. And yet, if they fired enough bullets, it wouldn't matter if they needed to reload. The horsemen would be wiped off the field.

"No hits," Imaiqah said, quietly.

"It won't matter, if there's enough of them," Emily said. A memory surfaced in her thoughts, something to do with rifled barrels. She would need to meditate and see what came out if she concentrated on the thought. "But how strong will the impact be?"

The apprentice carefully cleaned his weapon, then turned to Paren. "My Lord," he said. "Will you have need of me later?"

"I do not believe so," Paren said. "Finish putting the cannon in the shed, then take the rest of the day off."

Frieda peered towards the targets at the end of the field. "Emily," she said slowly, "I could shield myself against...against one of those."

"Maybe," Emily said. "But you'd be expending magic trying to protect yourself."

"But..." Frieda shook her head. "I protect myself all the time."

"You protect yourself against hexes and jinxes," Emily said. She'd wondered that herself, back during First Year. "They're magic. Your protections are designed to break them up into unusable spellware. But a bullet would be a physical impact."

She scowled as another memory surfaced. Travis had knocked her down once, in a sparring match, and he'd done it despite all of her protections. It required more defenses to protect oneself from a physical blow, Sergeant Miles had said later, and it could drain one's magic quicker than anyone would prefer. Normally, a mundane posed no threat to a magician — there were no shortage of spells that would stop a non-magical person in their tracks — but now...how much magic would need to be expended to keep a magician safe from a swarm of bullets?

*And if someone can stop a pistol shot,* she thought, *could they stop a machine gun?*

"If that's true," Frieda said, "why don't more magicians use their fists?"

"Unmannerly," Imaiqah said, as they turned to go back inside. "What sort of magician would settle a fight by punching the other?"

Emily looked down at her hands, thoughtfully. On both Earth and the Nameless World, the strong tended to dominate, but the definition of strength was different. She thought of some of the bullies she had known on Earth and wondered, briefly, what they would do if she turned them into snails. The experience would shatter their minds. But, on the Nameless World, it was magic that defined strength. She could turn Frieda into a toad, if she wanted to expend the energy, but Jade? He would reflect the spell back at her, at the very least.

*Which is why we're not allowed to prank students younger than us,* Emily recalled. The Grandmaster had made it clear at the start of Second Year and the rule was enforced, vigorously. *No First or Second Year should be a match for a Third Year.*

"Because if you tried to beat up a stronger magician, you wouldn't last long enough to kill them," Emily said, slowly. "And if you faced a weaker magician, why use your fists?"

*To conserve your magic,* her thoughts answered her. *But what good is conserving your magic when you'll be having it drained to protect yourself?*

"We have around two thousand Mark-VII muskets right now," Paren said. "Training soldiers to use them has not been easy. Many of the hired swords I selected were reluctant to learn how to use the weapons. Even the ones that weren't reluctant were...unsure of themselves. It may take time for a full unit of soldiers to be deployed."

"The king will need to be kept informed," Emily said.

"He is," Paren confirmed. "But he's leaving it in our hands, for the moment."

Emily wondered, absently, just what King Randor was thinking. The temptation to just ban gunpowder and bury the new concepts had to be overwhelming. But he owed Emily — and Paren — and turning on his supporters was just *asking* for another coup. And besides, even without Nanette, the formula for gunpowder might already have escaped. It wouldn't be long before other kings started fielding their own gunpowder weapons.

*And the necromancers have their own armies,* she thought, remembering the horde of monsters Shadye had massed in front of Whitehall, then hurled into the school. *Muskets may tip the balance in our favor.*

"Keep me informed," she said, finally. "What about the cannons?"

"We have ten," Paren said. "But producing them should speed up, now we've worked out most of the kinks. The real problems lie in powder safety, so we've adopted the precaution of keeping the gunpowder isolated from everywhere else and putting the safety officer's apartment on top of the powder store."

Emily laughed. They'd done the same in Elizabethan England, if she recalled correctly. She didn't know if it had actually *worked*, but it would definitely tend to concentrate the man's mind on safety. On the other hand, if he happened to have a subordinate who hated him, he'd be in the perfect place for assassination.

"I'm surprised the king hasn't demanded more control," she said. The cannons weren't *that* powerful, but they could do a great deal of damage to a castle. "Does he know how fast you're advancing?"

"I think he has a great many other matters on his mind," Paren said. "Besides, we have yet to field a proper unit."

"Take volunteers from the cities," Emily advised. She knew next to nothing about military training, and most of what she *did* know was suspect, but she knew how hard it could be to unlearn something. "People who are willing to serve, yet don't have any prior experience."

Paren frowned. "Why?"

"Less to unlearn," Emily said. "They wouldn't have grown up thinking that swords and sorcery settle everything."

"There might be problems," Paren said. "The king would object to recruiting random commoners from the cities."

Emily sighed, inwardly. The base of the Royal Army — and the private armies the barons had enjoyed, before the coup — had been composed of former peasants, with a hard core of professional fighters. It made a certain kind of sense; the peasants might be ignorant, but they were used to following orders without question, as well as being immensely tough. But people from the cities tended to be more inclined to question orders.

"Then see what you can do without it," she said.

There was another concern, she suspected. The peasantry wouldn't question...and they wouldn't seek to duplicate the weapons for themselves. But city-folk, *they* might question — they might work out how to make gunpowder themselves, and then start designing their own weapons. And who knew where that would lead?

"I will try," Paren said. "For better or worse, I will try."

"Good," Emily said. "This will change the world."

She looked down at the floor, and smiled tiredly to herself. The gods might have made men, she misquoted, but perhaps she had taken the first steps towards making them equal after all.

*Not quite the same,* she reminded herself. *What sort of gun can turn someone into a frog?*

*But it might not matter,* her own thoughts answered her. *People always have different levels of skill.*

# Chapter Thirty-Four

THE DRIVE BACK TO THE CASTLE WAS SPENT IN PENSIVE SILENCE. FRIEDA SEEMED LOST IN HER
thoughts, while Emily thought hard about what she'd seen. Gunpowder had been
hard enough to reinvent, but guns? Matters were moving ahead faster than she'd
dared believe possible. Who knew *what* would happen when guns spread to the rest
of the Nameless World?

She was still mulling it over when the coach entered the courtyard and came to a
halt. As soon as the door opened, she jumped down to the cobbled tiles and looked
around, half-expecting to see some traces of disaster. But there was nothing, apart
from a pair of horses that eyed her with dark unpleasant eyes. Emily sighed — she
had never liked horses — and turned to follow Frieda back into the castle.

Inside, Bryon was waiting for her. "My lady, you have petitioners who wish to
speak with you," he said. "They have brought lawyers."

Emily blinked. She had never had much respect for lawyers, but she had to admit
she hadn't had much contact with them either. The Lawyer's Guild of Zangaria was
notorious for living down to the stereotype, yet it had managed to survive when the
Accountants had faded away and the Scribes had been forced to reinvent their business model. Emily would have been impressed if she hadn't known that King Randor
insisted that all major deals had to have a lawyer involved, even merely to draft the
contract. It ensured there was always work for the lawyers.

"I will be in the Great Hall in ten minutes," she said. She would have preferred
longer to freshen up, but if someone had been waiting for her it would be rude to
*keep* them waiting, even if they *had* brought lawyers. "Please have them brought to
me after I arrive."

Bryon bowed. "Of course, my lady," he said. "I will see to them at once."

Emily sighed, bid goodbye to Frieda, and walked back to her room, splashed water
on her face, and changed into a new dress. The weight of the battery in her pocket
mocked her, reminding her that she could be performing more experiments with
the devices Yodel had made, but she pushed temptation aside and strode back to the
Great Hall. Someone had been busy, she noted; the tables and chairs had been thrust
to one side, allowing the petitioners to stand in front of her seat. She sat down and
pasted a controlled expression on her face as Bryon entered the room. Whatever it
was, she would deal with it...somehow.

"My lady," Bryon said. "May I present to you Freeholder Jack, Freeholder Muick
and Misters Clermont and Darnel, of the Guild of Lawyers."

Emily sighed inwardly. Freeholders were a rank above independent farmers,
although they were liable to pay more taxes. It didn't exactly make them gentry,
Emily thought, but they enjoyed considerable status in their communities. They
also enjoyed exemptions from some of the other duties barons could assign to their
thralls, including military service. It was not a rank anyone would care to abandon, if
they had a choice. Both Jack and Muick looked prosperous; Jack was clearly several

years older than Muick, with hair going white at the roots. Behind them, the law-yers looked surprisingly like monks, complete with brown robes and tonsures. She couldn't help being reminded of Master Grey.

"Your Ladyship," Jack said. "We thank you for seeing us at such short notice."

"You are welcome," Emily lied. "Time is not on my side at the moment, so could you please move straight to the point?"

Jack and Muick exchanged glances. "Your ladyship, you became the baroness two years ago, after the late unlamented baron met his timely end at the hands of the king's executioner," he said. "You have made many changes to the law, for which we are grateful."

Emily sighed inwardly. *This* was getting to the point?

"However, your changes raise the issue of how contracts, signed and sealed in good faith, should be applied," Jack continued. "Some of those contracts are now due."

"I see," Emily said. She had a terrible feeling she knew where this was going. "And what do those contracts involve?"

"Your ladyship, I have only a daughter," Muick said. "My daughter cannot inherit the farm, by ancient law. It was my intention, therefore, to wed her to Jack's son and allow them to combine our lands into one. She was to wed last year..."

"But she is now underage, by my laws," Emily finished. "And even trying to marry her to someone against her will would also be against my laws."

"Yes, your ladyship," Muick said.

Mister Darnel stepped forward. "I have consulted the record books dating from the establishment of Zangaria as an independent kingdom," he said. "There is no dis-puting your right to change the law as you see fit, your ladyship, as long as the king's laws are not bent or broken. This was established when King Alexis I severed our formal ties to the remainder of the Empire, then reconfirmed when King Alexis III regained control over his kingdom."

He took a breath. "However, it could be argued that your changes *have* infringed upon the king's laws," he continued. "In choosing to declare numberless contracts invalid because they break your laws, you may well be breaking the *king's* laws."

Emily had to admire his nerve. Baron Holyoake would have summarily thrown Mister Darnel into the dungeons for daring to challenge his authority. Emily was almost tempted to do the same. No matter what he thought he was doing, he was upholding two acts that Emily held to be criminal beyond all hope of redemption: marrying a girl off without her consent, while she was still underage.

"The king has declared that contracts are to remain untouched," Mister Darnel said. "But you have declared them invalid."

"Yes," Emily said, flatly. She took a moment to catch her temper. Changing them into toads — would anyone notice the difference? — would not help. "However, I believe the king has yet to rule on this specific case."

She gritted her teeth in frustration. King Randor's father, if she recalled correctly, had wanted to use contract law to keep the barons under control. It hadn't worked very well, as the coup proved, yet...she hadn't expected to put her foot so firmly on a landmine when she'd started to rewrite the laws. The king could support her, which would call contract law into question, or undermine her. If the latter...she would leave, and the other barons would be emboldened to plot again.

"That is true, your ladyship," Mister Darnel said. "But legally, your law and the king's law cannot conflict."

"Which would insist the contract be enforced," Emily growled.

"Yes, your ladyship," Mister Darnel said. "Any future contracts could not infringe your law — and no one would complain about that — but signed contracts cannot be put aside on a whim."

Emily forced herself, firmly, not to say the first thing that came to mind. No one had said *that* to Baron Holyoake — at least, they had never said it *twice* — and yet they were prepared to say it to *her*? But Baron Holyoake hadn't been interested in his subjects, save for what tax he could extort from them. If they'd wanted to kill themselves in the streets, or turn into bandits, he wouldn't have given a damn.

"And so we must appeal to you," Mister Darnel said. "The contracts must be upheld."

"Tell me," Emily said, looking at the two Freeholders. "Do your children actually *want* to get married?"

"They have always known they *would* get married," Jack said. "There was never any question of them liking anyone else."

Emily supposed that made sense. If they'd grown up together in a tiny village, there would have been fewer partners than if they had grown up in a city...and fewer chances to stray, too. And if they'd known they were going to get married, one day, they might not have been looking for anyone else. And yet...

"If the girl is thirteen, the marriage can wait three more years," Emily said. "If, of course, she actually wishes to marry your son."

"There is no one else for her," Muick said. "And I do not wish to lose the farm."

Emily's eyes narrowed. "Why would you lose the farm?"

"If I die, with my daughter unmarried," Muick explained, "the farm will pass to my uncle's descendants. My daughter will remain an old maid for the rest of her life, while he takes my farm and uses it as he sees fit. This contract is her only hope of retaining the farm."

*And are you saying that because you think it is her only hope,* Emily asked silently, *or because you think it will influence me?*

She took a moment to compose herself. "And why can't your daughter inherit the farm in her own right?"

"She is a *girl*," Muick said, as if that explained everything.

"So am I," Emily said, simply.

Muick paled, but stood his ground. "You have magic, my lady," he said. "My daughter has nothing but a farm she cannot run in her own name. Should she be married when I die, the farm will continue and be managed in her husband's name; should she be unmarried, the farm will go to my uncles or one of their descendants. They will find her an inconvenience."

*And kill her,* Emily thought, *if they can't beat her into submission.*

She took a long breath, trying to recall what she'd read about land rights. Property rights were different — a woman could own her own property — but land always had to stay in the male line. Indeed, Jack and Muick were bending the law by marrying their children; arguably, Jack's son wasn't part of the male line. But he would be a man, married to the former owner's daughter, and in possession. And possession was nine-tenths of the law.

*Not here,* she reminded herself. *The law is what the aristocracy says it is.*

"I do not approve, now or ever, of allowing children to be married off before they can consent to the match," she said. "Nor—" she held up a hand as they took a deep breath "—do I approve of people marrying before they reach a certain age. I could, however, offer a compromise. In the event of you dying before your daughter is married, the land would stay in her name."

Mister Darnel twitched uncomfortably. "My lady," he said. "If you changed the laws concerning land rights, even for one farm alone, there would be trouble."

He was right, Emily knew. The fabric of inheritance law, no matter how unfair or sexist she considered it to be, would start to unravel. There were certainties written into the old laws, certainties that she should not alter without a very good reason. But while she thought she had a good reason, she knew that others would not feel the same way.

She considered other options, rapidly. It would be easy enough to gift the daughter a small sum of money, enough to ensure she could support herself if her relatives kicked her off the farm. Or she could arrange for the daughter to be offered a job at the castle or in one of the growing industries. Or...for all she knew, the daughter would turn sixteen and marry Jack's son before anything happened to her father.

*But if her relatives want the farm,* she thought, *they could murder the father and claim it, legally.*

It would be simple enough to change the law, she was sure, so unborn generations of women would have the same land rights as men. But it wouldn't help the current generation...

"I can offer another suggestion," she said, after a moment. "If they are betrothed, the land can go to Jack's son, if you die before your daughter is old enough to wed. He will keep the land as long as he marries her within a year of her turning sixteen, then merge the two farms as you planned. If he chooses otherwise, or she decides not to marry him, the land will revert to her."

"As she will effectively be a divorcée," Mister Darnel said, slowly. "I do not know how that will hold up in a court of law."

"But it might," Emily said. "Particularly if you talked up the inheritance rights."

She smiled, although she knew it might not endure. On one hand, the daughter was a woman and therefore legally barred from holding land rights; on the other hand, she had the right to keep her dowry, which *included* the land rights. Anyone who wanted to take the lands, because she was a woman, would have to find a way to appease farmers who would be suspicious of setting a dangerous precedent. And their wives would be furious.

*And maybe they would force their husbands to defend her,* she thought. *And turn their world upside down.*

"I would like to stay with the original contract," Muick said, stubbornly. "It is the only way to protect my daughter."

Emily ignored him. "How many other contracts are there with similar provisions?"

"I know of thirty-seven," Mister Clermont said. "Some of them have been scrapped, as the parties involved took advantage of this opportunity to change their minds. Others are still in force, but the actual marriages are several years off."

*And how many,* Emily asked herself silently, *were enacted without anyone knowing about it?*

It was a chilling thought. On Earth, it had been easy to get news from right around the world; everything was instant, everything was immediate. But the Nameless World had fewer methods of instant communication — she thought briefly of the parchment in her pocket — and it could be months or years before news spread from village to village. It was easy to imagine all sorts of horrors, only a few miles from her castle, passing completely unnoticed by her.

"Then we will offer similar provisions for such marriages," Emily said. It was a compromise, and not one she was comfortable with, but she had a feeling that things couldn't be pushed much further. "It will cushion the effect of the laws."

"But still call the king's law into question," Mister Darnel said. "I would fancy the matter should be put before the king."

"You may do so, if you wish," Emily said. It would be a brave man who tried, even if Emily *hadn't* butchered countless people for daring to have ambitions of their own. King Randor could jump either way. "However, I have no intention of returning the law to its previous state."

"Your decision is understandable," Mister Clermont said.

Emily looked at Jack, then at Muick. "Is this acceptable to you?"

"It is," Jack said.

"If there are protections for my daughter, then it is acceptable to me," Muick said, after a moment. "That is all I ask."

"I will have new contracts drawn up, then infused with magic," Emily said. Buying *Manaskol* would be expensive, but it was well to have a supply of her own on hand. If nothing else, Mountaintop had taught her how to design her own magically-binding contracts that could be applied to anyone. "You will be bound to honor your word."

"That would be suitable, Your Ladyship," Muick said.

"Thank you," Emily said, dryly. "I will have the contracts drawn up, then you will be summoned to sign them."

She called for Bryon and had the four men shown out, then picked up a piece of paper and started to write out a basic contract. Zed had taught her that the more complex the contract, the more magic it took to enact the terms; she'd need to have

Bryon and Imaiqah look at it before she wrote it out again, using *Manaskol.* The fewer loopholes she left in, by accident, the better.

"You handled that well, my lady," Bryon said.

Emily looked up. Bryon had returned to the Great Hall.

"It wasn't perfect," she said. *Perfect* would have involved everyone agreeing that she was right, but nothing short of compulsion spells would achieve that. "There were just too many tangled issues."

"That is true, but you managed to satisfy them," Bryon said. "I do not think you could have handled it in any other way without betraying your principles."

"I've compromised," Emily said.

She shook her head. Compromise was one thing when it involved her, but quite another when it involved people she had never met. She would probably *never* meet any of the others involved in the whole affair, yet she'd meddled quite freely with their lives. And if she'd screwed up, she might have *ruined* their lives...

"I trust that preparations for dinner are well underway," she said, instead. "There will definitely be a dance tonight."

"The cooks are getting the meal ready now," Bryon assured her. "There's still three hours to go before dinnertime. Everything should be fine."

"Then I will go to my rooms until food is served," Emily said. She rose, feeling her back aching from sitting on the solid chair. "Call me if there's an emergency, but nothing else."

"Of course, Your Ladyship," Bryon said.

Emily nodded, and walked towards the stairs, thinking hard. It was impossible to tell if she had done the right thing. The contract — the original contract — had been grossly immoral by her standards, but she was uneasily aware that the locals thought nothing of it. And, if Muick had been telling the truth, the contract was the only protection his daughter had. Emily knew, all too well, just how easily family could turn on family, particularly if there was money involved.

*I suppose I will have to wait and see,* she thought, tiredly. There was just time for a nap, if she used a spell to ensure she woke for dinner, after she had channeled yet more power into the battery. *Tomorrow will come soon enough.*

# Chapter Thirty-Five

"MY GREAT-GRANDDAUGHTER IS LOOKING FORWARD TO HER WEDDING," FULVIA SAID, AS the servants cleared away the tables so the dancers could move onto the floor. "It was kind of you to allow us to use the Great Hall."

Emily sighed, inwardly. Two days had passed, two days during which the tension had kept rising, with the families sniping and snarling at each other. Two days when she had seriously considered ordering both families out of her castle, even though they would only take the dispute down to the Faire. Two days...

*And two days until the wedding,* she thought, sourly. *And if they don't come up with a plan before then...I don't know what I'll do.*

"I'm sure she is," Emily said, neutrally.

She cursed under her breath as the band started to play a lively jig. Lady Barb had sent a short note, warning that she wouldn't be back for at least another week, while Sergeant Miles had sent a note of his own, stating that he would be unavoidably delayed. Emily had hoped — prayed — that one of them would reach the castle before the wedding, if only so she could beg for advice before it all hit the fan. What did it matter if she spent every free moment of next year in detention when two feuding families could rip apart her castle and kill hundreds of people in the crossfire?

"But she has been quite definitely avoiding her family," Fulvia added, breaking into Emily's thoughts and fears. "Is that normal for a girl?"

"How did you feel," Emily asked, "when *you* were getting married?"

"Satisfied," Fulvia said. "I had finally found my niche in life."

Emily frowned, inwardly. On the face of it, the answer was outrageously sexist, as if a woman was fit to be nothing more than a wife and mother. And yet...no amount of browsing the records had turned up an answer to the question of Fulvia's origins. Had she actually been born an Ashworth? If she hadn't, she might have had *very* good reason to be satisfied when she'd married the former Patriarch. She would have moved from near-obscurity, like Gaius, to the very center of magical life.

"Melissa is young," she said, finally. "Give her some time to grow accustomed to the thought of marriage."

Fulvia's face darkened. "It is my observation that giving youngsters *time* tends to result in problems."

And the hell of it, Emily knew, was that Fulvia was right.

She couldn't help a flicker of irritation as the bandmaster started calling the next dance. Jade was already leading Alassa onto the dance floor, followed by Imaiqah and a male magician Emily didn't recognize. Even Frieda had found a partner, a young magician from one of the smaller families, and was starting to dance with him. But *Emily* couldn't find anyone, not if she wanted to keep her eye on events. Next time, she promised herself, she was *damned* if she was hosting anything, even a tiny party. Someone else could do the work and handle the nerves.

"Lady Emily," Marcellus said. "I thank you for a wonderful dinner."

"You're welcome," Emily said. She was sure he wanted something, but what? "My cooks will be pleased to hear that you liked it."

"It is our intention to withdraw tomorrow morning," Marcellus said, "if you will not take offense at our departure. We do not wish to be here when the wedding takes place."

"Your consideration does you credit," Fulvia said. Her voice was so dry Emily was sure there was a hidden meaning buried in her words. "You do not, of course, wish to witness a shift in the balance of power."

"I would sneer, had I no sense of dignity," Marcellus said. "I do not imagine that Gaius will shift the balance of power in any direction. Marrying him to Melissa is a waste of her potential."

Fulvia shrugged. "Keep thinking that, if you like."

Emily cleared her throat. "You will all be leaving?"

"We will decamp to the Faire tomorrow," Marcellus said. "Tempers are already running high and the wedding, no matter how...*unimportant*, will only make them worse."

"I see," Emily said. If she hadn't known about Markus and Melissa, she would have been relieved. Having the two families so close was hair-raising. But as she did know about them...what would they do, if they knew their time was about to run out? Run away? Confront their parents? Or split up? "I thank you."

Marcellus gave her a wintry smile that said, very clearly, she owed him one.

"I thank you," Fulvia echoed. "No doubt you will make us pay for the favor in due course."

"No doubt," Marcellus agreed. He bowed to Emily and smiled. "Do you happen to know where my eldest son is?"

Emily looked around the hall. There were countless Ashfalls in the room, including several cadet families with tangled links to the main branch, but there was no sign of Markus. She cursed under her breath as she realized there was no sign of Melissa either, only Gaius, who was wandering around looking lost and out of place. Emily would have felt sorry for him if she hadn't known he'd passively accepted the marriage contract against the will of the bride.

"I imagine he's wandered off somewhere," she said, feeling the comforting weight of the battery in her pocket. "He may be exploring the battlements, or leaning on the balconies..."

Marcellus made a show of looking up. "I see no one on the balcony," he said. "Do you not have a way of tracking people in your castle?"

"No," Emily said. She was getting tired of answering that question. "I have no idea where he is, not right now."

"Well, I dare say I will see him when I see him," Marcellus said. He bowed again, and turned to leave. "And I thank you for your efforts, Lady Emily. It is nice to snipe without fear of death."

Emily watched him go, feeling more than a little bemused. Marcellus seemed less inclined to do anything about the feud, apart from sniping at Fulvia. But some of the stories she'd heard, of bloody massacres and stealthy assassinations, suggested otherwise. Maybe he'd just thought he had to be on his best behavior at the castle, she told herself, finally. Or maybe he'd just enjoyed the chance to bicker more than yet another battle.

"He is right, of course," Fulvia observed. "It *is* nice to snipe."

"But someone might say the wrong thing," Emily said. "And then you start a real fight."

"A magician without the self-control to remain *in* control is a poor magician," Fulvia said, primly. "And words cannot cause any true harm."

Emily shook her head, mentally. Words could always cause harm, even if they didn't inflict physical damage. She'd spent far too long listening to her stepfather telling her she was useless that part of her had believed it, despite all she'd managed to accomplish at Whitehall and Mountaintop. Beatings would have been kinder.

*If nothing else*, she thought sourly, *I could have shown the bruises to the police.*

She pushed the thought aside with an effort. Her stepfather was a dimension away, no longer a problem. She was free of him, free to build her own destiny as she saw fit.

"Lady Emily?" Fulvia said. "You've gone quite pale."

"Just an old memory," Emily said. She wasn't going to confide in this woman, whatever happened. Fulvia saw people as pieces on a Kingmaker board, not living beings with their own thoughts and feelings. God alone knew what she'd do if she knew the truth. "And, if you will excuse me, I have duties to attend to."

"The work of a host is never done," Fulvia said. "Just make sure you find some time to chat with people, Lady Emily. You could make some new contacts here."

And that, Emily knew, was good advice. But she'd never had the knack for small talk, let alone forming superficial friendships with people. All of her friends had met her by accident, even Imaiqah and Aloha. If she'd been assigned to a different room when she'd arrived at Whitehall, she might never have seen the relationship between Alassa and Imaiqah for what it truly was.

*And you wouldn't have made it better, either,* she thought, as she walked around the edge of the hall. *It would just have stayed poisonous...*

"Lady Emily," Gaius said. "I have been unable to find Melissa."

Emily scowled for a moment before pasting a concerned look on her face. "I'm sure she's fine," she said, tartly. "You'll see her at the wedding."

"By tradition, we are supposed to lead the bridal dance," Gaius said. "I need her here."

*Idiot*, Emily thought, although she wasn't sure if she meant Gaius or Melissa. The bridal dance was always held two days before the wedding, for reasons she suspected had something to do with fertility, and the prospective bride and groom were indeed meant to lead it. *Where the hell is she?*

"I'm sure she will be here when the dance starts," Emily said. She rather doubted Fulvia would take it lightly if Melissa failed to show, embarrassing her right in front of the Ashfalls — and the rest of her own family, for that matter. "You'll see her then."

She glanced around the room, looking for Markus, but saw nothing. Was he with Melissa?

"It is really quite annoying when one's bride refuses to talk to one," Gaius continued. "How am I meant to get to know her?"

Emily fought down the urge to put her head in her hands. They were idiots. They were *all* idiots. Markus and Melissa, for developing a relationship; Fulvia and Marcellus, for continuing a pointless feud; Gaius, for assuming that Melissa would happily abandon her life to follow orders and marry him. How could anyone just assume that their sons and daughters would be happy to keep feuding unto the end of time?

"I think you should wait," Emily said, crossly. She fought down the urge to just abandon the matter, to let the affair explode in their faces. "I'm sure she will be here for the dance."

She turned and stalked towards the stairs, walking up to the balcony. Down below, she saw as she turned to look, Jade and Alassa were following a complicated set of dance movements, while Imaiqah and her partner were literally dancing on air. Several of the other magicians were doing the same, although Emily couldn't help noticing they were only the ones who wore trousers. Everyone wearing a dress was remaining firmly on the floor. She smiled — she would never have the nerve to levitate herself in public, no matter what she was wearing — and then looked for Fulvia and Marcellus. The two family heads were standing at opposite ends of the hall, talking with their friends and allies. Emily couldn't help noticing that Fulvia seemed to be issuing orders, while Marcellus was actually chatting in a friendly manner.

*That seems to be their style*, she thought, mordantly.

She looked for Gaius and saw him, talking to one of the maids. Her eyes narrowed — no more incidents had been reported, but wiping memories was easy if one knew the spell — then she relaxed as it seemed to be a friendly conversation. She shook her head tiredly, wondering just what Gaius would have to say to a maid, and turned and walked towards the library, where it had all begun. If Markus and Melissa were together, they wouldn't have dared go too far from the dance.

*Unless they wanted to embarrass their families*, she thought. *Would Gaius refuse to marry Melissa if she showed him up in public?*

She gritted her teeth at the thought. Gaius *might* be humiliated enough to refuse to go through with the wedding, but he had plenty to gain and little to lose by marrying Melissa. It was unlikely *his* family would let him refuse, even if he wanted to walk away. And besides, Fulvia would be *furious*. Melissa could look forward to nothing, but painful or humiliating punishment for embarrassing the Matriarch in public.

*Silly girl*, she thought, as she reached the library door. Another aversion ward had been worked into the castle's wards, neater than the last one. If Emily hadn't known it wasn't hers, she suspected she would have been fooled; anyone else would have thought it was her work and thought no more about it. But it was a major security problem, she knew; someone nesting their own wards within hers was a potential disaster in the making.

She shook her head, dismantled the ward with practiced skill and stepped into the library. Melissa and Markus were standing beside the bookshelves, kissing. Emily felt her cheeks flush as they jumped apart, fighting down the urge to look away. They weren't naked, or even half-dressed, but she still felt embarrassed for intruding on a private moment.

"Emily," Markus said. She couldn't help noticing that he'd moved to cover Melissa, protectively. "What can we do for you?"

"You have a bridal dance," Emily said, looking directly at Melissa. "What are you going to do about it?"

"I don't want to go," Melissa said. She reached out and took Markus's hand. "I'm not going through the holy steps with...with *him*."

Emily fought down the urge to bang her head against the nearest wall. "Your family is expecting you to dance," she said. "You may not be required for any of the other dances, but you are required for *this*. What are you going to do about it?"

"She doesn't have to go," Markus said.

"And are you two willing to reveal your relationship now?" Emily demanded. Really, this was too much. "Are you going to run and hide? Or are you going to dance a farce of a dance?"

Melissa stared at her. "You don't understand!"

"I understand that you're running out of time," Emily said. Why couldn't they just have fled yesterday? They could have stepped through the portals or simply teleported to a private destination, and no one would have been able to find them. "Either go tell them the truth, or dance, or run, or..."

She broke off. Melissa was staring past her.

Emily turned slowly, already knowing what she would see. Gaius was standing in the doorway, staring at Markus and Melissa in absolute horror. Beside him, a maid stared at Emily, clearly aware she'd made a mistake. Emily cursed herself under her breath for missing the signs. Gaius hadn't been trying to flirt with the maid, he'd been asking her where Melissa was hiding. And the maid, quite innocently, had led him to the library.

"You..." Gaius started. "You..."

"I don't want to marry you," Melissa snapped. "I am *not* going to marry you."

"You filthy whore!" Gaius shouted. "You..."

"That will do," Markus snapped. He raised one hand, ready to cast a spell. "She isn't yours, and..."

Gaius launched a fireball right into his wards. There was a flash of light, and Markus was hurled back into the bookcases. Books fell from the shelves as he hit the ground, then threw back a spell of his own. Gaius dodged it, magic sparkling around his fingertips.

"Enough," Emily said. "You can't fight here!"

"You *knew*," Gaius snapped. "All that time! You knew!"

Emily had no time to react before he threw two spells at her. One froze her in place, while the other picked her up and threw her right across the room. The first spell cushioned the impact — there was no pain, even when she slammed into the wall — but she was briefly stunned. She heard Melissa scream in rage, then saw, as she fell, Markus blow Gaius right out of the room.

And then she hit the ground, unable to move. *Fuck*, she thought.

It took two tries to summon the mental discipline to break the spell. She'd underestimated Gaius, she realized sourly. Fulvia might have picked him for more than just an inability to question her, or family ties she could use to further her own plans. He hadn't tossed two separate spells at her, he'd actually *combined* them into a single spell. She would have been impressed if he hadn't used it to keep her from intervening.

The spell snapped and she sagged, for a long moment, before pulling herself to her feet. Melissa stared at her, her face despairing, wringing her hands as if she didn't know what to do, while Emily heard the sound of people shouting in the distance. Behind Melissa, the maid was frozen in place, caught in one of the spells hurled by the combatants. The wards were sounding a whole series of alarm bells in Emily's head, warning her that the guests were readying spells and protections as quickly as possible. They were on the verge of tearing her castle apart.

"Emily," Melissa pleaded. "What do we do?"

"You can help me fix this problem," Emily snarled. She reached into her pocket and touched the battery, then pressed her fingertips against the valve and embedded a spell into the wood, ready to be triggered. "Come on."

She swore as they reached the balcony. The families were separating rapidly as Gaius hurled accusations at Markus, accusing him of everything from rape to deliberately seducing Melissa. Steven stood next to Markus, holding a long staff in one hand, while two boys Emily vaguely recalled from the near-clash at the Faire flanked Gaius. Fulvia's face was dark with fury; on the other side of the room, Marcellus looked shocked. He hadn't known his son was courting Fulvia's great-granddaughter.

*But you already knew that*, Emily said, as dozens of magicians readied fireballs. *You knew he didn't know.*

"You bitch," Gaius shouted, as he saw Melissa behind Emily. "How could you?"

Markus snarled and threw a spell. As if that had been a signal, every magician opened fire or ducked for cover. Emily caught sight of Jade covering Alassa with his body — there was no sign of Imaiqah — and then reached into her pocket, placing the valve into the battery.

"Emily," Melissa said. A fireball struck the balcony near them, blowing chunks of debris into the air. Melissa hastily erected a ward to cover them both, redirecting the pieces of debris down to the floor. "What are we going to do?"

"This," Emily said.

Bracing herself, she triggered the battery.

# Chapter Thirty-Six

IT WAS IRONIC, PART OF EMILY'S MIND NOTED, THAT SHE'D MASTERED THE BASIC ANTI-MAGIC ward at Mountaintop, where most of the magicians in the Great Hall below had studied. It was simple enough — all it really did was break up spellwork, without any discrimination between different types of spellwork — but the ward demanded so much power that creating a blanket ward was impossible, at least without a nexus point. And they could be overcome, if someone had enough skill to adapt their spells to work within the ward's zone of influence...

She watched, grimly, as the ward's zone expanded outwards with terrifying speed. Fireballs winked out of existence, protective wards fractured and shattered; magicians hastily preparing spells to defend themselves or attack their foes watched in horror as their spellwork came apart, fading into nothingness. Emily wondered, vaguely, if there was a way to absorb the rogue magic into the ward, making it stronger, but pushed it aside as all eyes turned to her.

"If you want to fight like common mundanes," she said, knowing the insult would grab their attention, "you *can* fight like common mundanes!"

They stared at her in stunned silence. They'd had plenty of time, she knew, to work out just what sort of wards she used to protect the castle. They *knew* she'd never prepared the wards that would allow her to disrupt everyone else's magic, if she'd been able to anchor them in the stone walls — and that had been impossible. No magician should be able to channel so much magic, not even a Lone Power. And yet, they couldn't deny the evidence of their senses. She was holding the ward firmly in place.

*For a few minutes*, she thought. She honestly had no idea what would happen when the magic ran out. Or if they started trying to overcome the ward. She didn't have the connections to it that would allow her to counter their work. She'd hoped to test the battery first, before using it to save lives.

But time had run out.

"Look at you," she said. She pushed as much contempt into her voice as she could. "You're preparing to fight each other, ready to kill hundreds of people, over a stupid feud. How did it actually start? Do any of you even *know*?"

Several people looked at Fulvia, who said nothing.

"This is my castle," Emily said. "These are my people. And I will not let you harm them!"

"You allowed *him* to touch her," Gaius snapped. He waved a hand at Markus. "You let it happen! He seduced her, and you let it happen!"

Markus opened his mouth, either to retort or issue a challenge to a duel, but Melissa spoke first.

"I don't want to marry you," she said. "I *never* wanted to marry you!"

Gaius blinked in genuine surprise. Emily frowned, inwardly; had he believed

Melissa would want to marry him, or had Fulvia told him that Melissa wanted to marry him? She knew which way she would bet.

"The wedding is not going to take place," Melissa added. "I love Markus!"

"You are under the influence," Gaius said, desperately. "He made you drink a love potion, and..."

"As if we didn't have protections against such games," Melissa snapped. She sneered at him. "He couldn't have fed me anything without my consent!"

"And he defiled you," Gaius added, ignoring her. "This is a slap in the face..."

He pointed a finger at Marcellus. "He sent his son to seduce Melissa!"

"I most certainly did not," Marcellus said. He sounded torn between amusement and horror; his son, his favored son, had almost sparked off a fight that would cripple both families. "It never crossed my mind that the Ashfall Heir could act in so unthinking a manner."

"I love her, father," Markus said, simply.

His father scowled. "And are you ready to take the consequences of that love?"

"I am."

Fulvia's lips thinned. "Melissa is not free to give her love to anyone," she said. "What does love matter? Marriage is for the benefit of the families..."

"Then let them marry and reunite your families," Emily said. "End this stupid feud!"

"You are young and were raised in isolation," Fulvia said. "You could not understand just how much we have done to one another, in the name of the feud."

"And would you prefer to keep the feud going?" Emily asked. She felt the battery quiver in her pocket and swore, inwardly. There was no way to know how long it would last. "Each successive generation killing its counterparts, never even knowing *why* it was killing its counterparts, until one side manages to wipe out the other? Or the necromancers kill you all?"

Fulvia eyed her darkly. "I would not expect you to understand."

"You were there when the feud started," Markus said, suddenly. "I think you're the *only* person on either side who knows why the feud started. Why?"

Fulvia ignored him. "It seems we are to be embarrassed and humiliated," she said, curtly. "But at least the Ashfalls have been humiliated, too. We will leave."

She looked up at Melissa. "Melissa. Come."

Melissa stepped forward until she was standing next to Emily. "You killed my father!"

For the first time, Fulvia looked uncertain. "Don't speak of things you don't understand, girl," she snapped. "Your father died in an accident!"

"I can't prick my fingers in Ashworth House," Melissa snapped. "The wards are so complex that accidental harm is rare, almost impossible. How could someone drink enough of a disgusting potion to kill himself by *accident*?"

She glared down at her great-grandmother. "Why did my father die?

"I can guess. He was the direct-line heir, while *you* married into the family. Grandpa should hold real power, not you, but Grandpa always defers to you. My father must have wanted to claim power for himself, and so you killed him!"

"Do you really believe," Fulvia said, "that I would kill my grandson?"

"You were prepared to marry me off to...to that milksop," Melissa snapped. "Why *wouldn't* you kill your own grandson? And how long until I have an accident of my own?"

"Our marriage is for the best," Gaius said. "The families will grow stronger..."

"No, they won't," Markus said. "You don't have the strength of character to do anything but what you're told by superior authority. The Matriarch could keep you in line for the rest of your life."

"And what happens to the family," Melissa asked, "after you die?"

"The family will survive," Fulvia said.

"It won't survive if you keep killing or breaking everyone with the strength of character to lead the family," Melissa hissed. "Your son does what you tell him. I'd bet he doesn't have an original bone in his body. Your grandson is dead. I am to be married to a milksop weakling, while Iulius...Iulius is a brat. You've even been encouraging his bratty tendencies to make it harder for him to win friends!"

*You can talk*, Emily thought, silently.

"The family is doomed," Melissa said. "And I am damned if I will marry that man!" She jabbed a finger at Gaius. "I don't want to marry you, and if you were half the man you claim to be, you would respect that!"

"The family comes first," Fulvia said.

"What sort of family do we have," Melissa screamed, "if we bring our children up in loveless marriages?"

There was a long, agonizing pause.

"You overstep yourself," Fulvia said, finally. She made an odd gesture with her hand, but nothing happened. "You..."

"You can't use magic," Melissa crowed. "And what are you without magic? You can't punish me now!"

Emily winced, inwardly. How long would the ward actually last? She wasn't sure she dared test the battery, even though it was *her* magic inside the ring. Touching so much magic could drive her mad.

*And if Fulvia used magic to discipline the children*, she thought, *it might explain a great deal about Melissa.*

It crossed her mind, suddenly, that Fulvia could be in very real danger. She had to have used rejuvenation spells to keep herself alive for so long, if she wasn't stealing life energy from her family...had *that* been what had happened to her grandson? As soon as he'd sired a couple of potential heirs, his grandmother had turned him into a walking transplant? Or had it really been an accident? Accidents did happen, Emily had learned, and sometimes they looked more than a little suspicious.

*And if Fulvia can't use magic*, Emily thought, *what will it do to the spells keeping her alive?*

"We will not stay here," Fulvia said, instead. "Melissa. Come."

"No," Melissa said.

"Your marriage was agreed by the family council," Fulvia said. "You *have* to abide by it."

"Or leave the family," Melissa said. She reached for the icon on her dress and tore it free, then tossed it down to the floor. "I choose to leave."

"You're the Heir," an Ashworth Emily didn't know said. "You can't leave."

"Iulius can be the Heir," Melissa said. "Maybe he will live long enough to actually take on the role."

She eyed her great-grandmother, sharply. "Or maybe you will just seek to dominate him like you dominate your son," she added. "I wish him luck."

Fulvia looked furious, her eyes flashing with fire. "If you leave now, you will be cut off completely from the family," she snapped. "You will have no schooling, no contacts, no nothing...you will be alone."

"She won't be alone," Markus said. "I will be with her."

"No, you won't," Gaius said. He bunched his fists. "You sullied my bride!"

Markus dropped into a fighting crouch. Emily stared from one to the other, unsure of what to do. The ward wouldn't let her cast spells of her own, if only because there had been no time to tune it before she'd triggered the spell. And she couldn't stand between them again, not when Gaius hated her as much as he hated Markus. He was stronger than she'd realized, stronger and better trained...

*A woman is always at a disadvantage against a stronger man,* Sergeant Harkin had said, years ago. *And training can only go so far.*

Melissa ran forward and stood next to Markus. "Are you so desperate to have me that you are prepared to fight for me?"

Gaius stared at her, then at Emily. "I didn't know..."

"No, you didn't," Melissa said. "And maybe I should have talked to you earlier, but you never listened. You were so impressed with the idea of becoming Patriarch that you didn't even think to question what I wanted. What could I say that would dim the shining light in your eyes?"

"You are no longer part of the family," Fulvia said. Her voice was very cold. "Your destiny is your own. You'll excuse me, I trust, if I don't wish you luck."

"But..."

Fulvia ignored Gaius's protests. "But there is another issue here," she added. Her gaze sought out Marcellus. "Did you know your son was courting my great-granddaughter?"

"I did not," Marcellus said. He took a step forward, and held up one hand. "I swear this on my life and my magic."

"Then I must demand recompense, in line with the ancient traditions," Fulvia said. "The balance must be maintained."

Emily frowned. What was the ancient woman doing?

"I must decline," Marcellus said. "This was not deliberate harm."

"But you cannot deny it nearly proved disastrous," Fulvia said. "Indeed, were it not for Lady Emily, most of us would have died."

Marcellus's face tightened. "Markus," he said, never taking his eyes off Fulvia, "I cannot condone your actions. You knew she was the Ashworth Heir when you courted her."

"I understand, father," Markus said.

"And are you willing," his father said, still keeping his eyes on Fulvia, "to face the consequences?"

"I am," Markus said.

Emily looked at him. He seemed...nervous, but ready to do what his father commanded.

"I cast you out of the family," Marcellus said. It was a formal recitation. "You have no name, no kin, nothing but yourself. I will no longer speak with you, I will no longer hear you, I will no longer speak *for* you."

Markus sighed, but remained still as his father advanced on him. Emily watched, knowing she could do nothing to interfere, as Marcellus ripped his son's icon off his chest and dropped it on the floor, then ground it under his feet. Markus remained impassive, but Melissa stepped up to him and took his hand.

*They'll make it*, Emily thought, suddenly. *They do love each other.*

"The balance is maintained," Marcellus said. He looked at Fulvia. "Satisfied?"

"We are," Fulvia said. "And so we will take our leave."

She looked at Emily, sharply. "Thank you for your hospitality," she said. "Perhaps one day we shall repay you in kind."

And if that wasn't a threat, Emily thought, she had no idea *what* it was.

"We will not attend the remainder of the Faire," Fulvia continued. "Nor will we return to Cockatrice."

"I understand," Emily said. She wanted to demand to know, one final time, why the feud had even started. What did Fulvia know that she wasn't telling? But she knew she would get no answer. "I thank you for attending the Faire."

"Child of Destiny, they call you," Fulvia said. For a moment, she actually sounded her age. "I hope they will not say that this—" she waved a hand to indicate the wary families "—was destiny, too."

She bowed, turned away, and walked out. Emily watched the rest of the family follow her, some more hesitant than others. She couldn't help noticing the thoughtful look on the Patriarch's face, as if he was finally looking at his mother in a darker light. God alone knew what *that* would do, in the future. Would he start questioning Fulvia...or would he demand his power by right?

"We, too, shall take our leave," Marcellus said. "You could not be too displeased, Lady Emily, with the outcome."

Emily sighed, inwardly. Fulvia had been humiliated in front of her entire family — and her traditional enemies. She would not be allowed to forget it, not if there was anyone else with a spine within House Ashworth. It was quite possible that one of the others, perhaps her son, would mount a challenge to her power. Marcellus, for the price of disowning his eldest son, had the pleasure of watching Fulvia's humiliation. And, perhaps, the beginning of the end for his rivals.

"Do you know," she asked finally, "just what caused the feud?"

Marcellus shrugged. "My father told me that Lady Fulvia insisted her husband force certain members of the family to accept her as Matriarch," he said. "They were made to swear an oath to regard her as having been born an Ashworth. The younger brother, utterly outraged, left...and took half the family with him. Or so I was told."

"No one will ever know," Markus predicted.

His father ignored him. "I thank you for your hospitality, Lady Emily. And I shall hope to see you again, sometime."

He bowed, and left the room. Emily watched him go, then felt the ward collapse into nothingness. It had held out just long enough...

*Good thing they didn't challenge it*, she thought. *It would have broken the ward sooner rather than later.*

No one seemed to have much stomach left for dancing, she noted, as the room emptied rapidly. Most of the guests were probably going to spread the word to the rest of the world, starting with Fulvia's humiliation and ending with even more tall stories about Emily's power. But this time...at least it wasn't the nuke-spell.

"Thank you," Markus said. "But we, too, must leave."

"You can stay here for the rest of the summer, if you like," Emily said. "I dare say I will have the space to accommodate you."

"Thank you," Melissa said.

Emily watched them go before she sat down and watched the last guests leave the room. Jade and Alassa had vanished long ago; Alassa would be fuming at having missed the confrontation, but it was definitely for the best. She couldn't see Frieda or Imaiqah, so she hoped they'd had the sense to leave, too. It could have ended very badly.

"Lady Emily," Master Grey said. He strode over to her, his eyes fixed on her face. "I did not know you could cast such a ward."

"It took practice," Emily said, shortly. She felt too tired and drained to engage in a battle of wits. "What can I do for you?"

"Tell me something," Master Grey said. "Did you *know* they'd become lovers?"

"Yes," Emily said.

"Then you should have sent them home," Master Grey said. "Instead, you...just waited for disaster. Or did you plan to show off your power at the Faire?"

Emily shook her head.

"You could have started a fight that would have wiped out far too many magicians," Master Grey said. The cool contempt in his voice stung more than Emily cared to admit. "You're a child of chaos, not of destiny."

"Sometimes," Emily said. In hindsight, maybe she should have denied everything. "I thought it could be used to end the feud."

Master Grey snorted. "I've been training apprentices for years, Lady Emily, and I have *never* had one of them do something so stupid," he said. "*None* of them would have risked the lives of hundreds of people in hopes of ending a feud that has taken on a life of its own. You're a danger to everyone around you."

Emily gritted her teeth, but said nothing.

"And I also want you to know," Master Grey added, "that what you did was the most thoughtlessly arrogant piece of madness I have seen in my entire life. Your father would be proud."

He turned and walked away, not looking back.

Emily stared after him, feeling her heart pounding. She would have liked to deny it, but she knew he was right.

But what else could she have done?

# Chapter Thirty-Seven

THE CASTLE FELT EMPTY THE FOLLOWING MORNING WHEN EMILY ROSE FROM HER BED. IT took her a moment to remember that both the Ashworths and Ashfalls had left, along with half of the other guests. She sighed, rubbing her eyes, and turned her attention to the remains of the battery, which she'd dumped on a table before going to sleep. The ring was charred and broken, while the valve had shattered. It was clear that channeling so much power while trying to regulate the flow of magic had proven to be too much.

*But at least it proves the concept*, she thought, as she used a spell to reduce the remaining components to dust. *I can produce more, if necessary.*

She stepped into the bathroom, washed herself hastily, and pulled on yet another blue dress, before looking at herself in the mirror. Her eyes looked haunted, but she didn't look *too* tired. She briefly wished she knew more about makeup — if she went down to breakfast looking fresh and well, it would terrify magicians who knew how much power it should take to produce a ward — before dismissing the thought. Makeup was rarely worn in the country, outside whores and actresses. Who knew what people would have thought if they'd seen her painting her face?

*Whore*, she thought, remembering Gaius screaming at Melissa. *Or worse.*

There was a knock at the door. Emily concentrated, checking the wards she'd hastily rebuilt to protect her room, and opened the door with a flicker of magic. Outside, Janice stood next to a far younger maid, who quailed when she saw Emily. She'd been the one who, in all innocence, had pointed Gaius to the library. Emily gave her a questioning look before she glanced at Janice.

"Joan has something to say to you, my lady," Janice said, sternly.

Emily looked at Joan, who lowered her eyes. "It was my fault, my lady," she said. "I didn't realize they were in there together."

"Don't worry about it," Emily said. *She* hadn't thought to tell the servants not to say a word either, although she should have done. Joan hadn't known that Markus and Melissa had been making out in the library. "Really."

Joan stared at her. "But I..."

"It wasn't your fault," Emily said, tiredly. If there was anyone to blame, it was Fulvia, Gaius, Markus and Melissa, not a random maid. "Please go tell Markus and Melissa that I would like to see them in the Blue Room when they're up and dressed."

Joan bobbed a curtsey, and hurried off.

"She's new," Janice said. "She didn't know there might be a problem."

"It worked out in the end," Emily said. She'd be having nightmares, she suspected, about what would have happened if it *hadn't* worked out. "Tell her not to worry about it."

"She was so fearful of being sacked," Janice said. "Or worse, perhaps."

Emily shrugged. It was unlikely she could do anything worse than Baron Holyoake.

"Make sure she doesn't worry about it," she said, finally. "I'll be down in the Blue Room in thirty minutes."

It was nearly an hour before Markus and Melissa were shown into the room. Emily smiled at them both, indicating the chairs facing her with a wave of her hand. They'd clearly been enjoying themselves, now they could share a room openly; their faces were beaming with contentment and they were standing too close together, as if they couldn't keep their hands off one another. She just hoped it would last, when the strain of being cut off from their families finally started to bite. But, perhaps, she thought she had a solution to their problems.

"I received a formal note this morning, confirming that I've been disowned," Markus said. "My brother will be the Heir."

"My sympathies to your family," Emily said, dryly. She recalled Markus's brother far too well. "And to you, too."

"Don't be sorry for me," Markus said. "It feels oddly liberating, actually."

Emily smiled. "And you?"

Melissa looked back at her, half-defiant, half-afraid. "I didn't know you could channel so much power," she said. "Even a Lone Power would have had problems."

"She's the *daughter* of a Lone Power," Markus said. "Are you surprised?"

"She wanted me to make friends with you," Melissa said. "I never understood why until now."

Emily blinked. "You were trying to make *friends*?"

Melissa had the grace to blush. "You made Alassa into a competent magician," she said, softly. "I never thought of you as anything other than a rival."

"I know," Emily said. "What happened between you and her?"

"She's royalty, I'm family," Melissa said. "Or I was...anyway, we just got off on the wrong foot, and it went downhill from there."

"I can believe that," Emily said. She'd started off on the wrong foot with Alassa, too. "Still, I hope we can get on better in the future."

"If we see each other again," Melissa said. "The...Fulvia will probably try to reclaim my tuition fees from Whitehall."

"I thought she couldn't," Emily said.

"If anyone can, she can," Melissa said.

"And I need to find a job," Markus said.

"I know," Emily said. "I have an offer for you."

Markus gave her a sharp look. "A job offer?"

"Of sorts," Emily said. "You being...disconnected...from your family can only help, I think."

"I see," Markus said. He exchanged a look with Melissa, and leaned forward. "What do you want me to do?"

"Run a bank," Emily said.

"A bank?" Markus repeated.

Emily nodded, and plunged on. "There aren't actually that many banks in the world," she told him. "Most people, rich or poor, choose to keep their wealth in their own homes, if only to keep it where they can see it. The handful of banks that do exist are really nothing more than glorified storage sites, with the added disadvantage that the king's taxmen can see what you actually have."

"Or take it," Markus said.

"Precisely," Emily said. "The average peasant would not put his money in the bank, even if he had money, for fear of what would happen to it. This may let them keep their money secure, but it doesn't give it time to grow."

Melissa's eyes narrowed. "How does it grow?"

"If one hundred people have a single gold coin apiece," Emily said, "collectively they have a hundred gold coins. If that money happened to be gathered in one place, they would be able to use the money to buy what they wanted."

"But they would then have to share whatever they'd bought," Melissa said.

"I think I understand," Markus said, slowly. "They put the money in the bank, then the bank loans the money out at a low rate of interest, *then* they use the interest to repay the original lenders."

"Among other things," Emily said. "We would also be minting our own coins with a fixed value, perhaps even paper money. It would boost the economy considerably."

"By lending people money," Melissa said. "How?"

"You need to spend money in order to make money," Emily said. "If someone wants to open their own...oh, their own pub, they need to buy everything from the building itself to the tables, chairs, and barrels of beer. So the bank loans them the money, which is then repaid with interest once the business is a success."

"Assuming it is a success," Markus said. "But you could loan out the money to a hundred different people and still come out ahead, if half of the businesses succeeded."

"Precisely," Emily said. "At the moment, the only real source of wealth is land. If you happen to need a loan and you don't have land, you practically have to pledge yourself to the loan sharks. A proper bank would make it easier for people to take out loans without selling themselves or their children into slavery."

"And what," Melissa asked, "is to keep King Randor from simply taking the money?"

"The bank will be established in the free city of Beneficence, out of the king's reach," Emily said. "We will use charmed parchments to ensure that monies can only be drawn by established customers. Given time, we can probably offer special rates to the king, in exchange for him recognizing the independence of the bank. "Or come up with something else, if necessary."

She sighed. "I can show you my notes, if you like," she added. "I won't deny there are problems to be solved. There will definitely be issues with counterfeit coins and other pieces of unpleasantness, but I believe we can overcome them."

"And doing it in Beneficence will make it harder for anyone to interfere," Markus said. "My family may not take it any further, but Lady Fulvia was humiliated..."

"Yes, she was," Emily said. She could easily see Fulvia doing whatever she could to spite Melissa. "The city is neutral."

"Which is why the guilds rake in a hefty amount of cash," Markus said, dryly. "I could see them liking the idea of a bank, too."

He frowned. "We'd have to practically layer the whole building in wards, then devise binding oaths and contracts," he mused aloud. "Someone would be bound to try to steal something from the vaults, once we got them established. There are entire clubs of people who try to break wards purely for the hell of it."

"It will be a steep learning curve," Emily agreed, dryly. She leaned forward. "I can offer you a considerable wage, including enough for Melissa to complete her remaining three years of schooling, and a large lump sum to serve as the first deposit. You will also have a handful of shares in the bank, which you may buy and sell as you see fit."

Melissa frowned. "What's a share?"

"A share in the bank," Emily said. "Basically, ownership rights. A couple of people who happen to hold fifty percent, plus one, of the shares in any business can run it to suit themselves, but profits are paid out in line with the shares."

"So if I held ten percent of the shares, I would get ten percent of the profits," Melissa said.

"Basically," Emily agreed. It was a little more complex than that, but there would be time to discuss the difference between gross and net profits later. "I'd hold a number of shares, as would you. Later, we would sell them on, allowing other investors to join us."

"It sounds great," Markus said. "What's the catch?"

"I will be requiring an oath," Emily said, flatly. "This isn't something I can allow to get screwed up."

Markus eyed her for a long moment. "Very well," he said, finally. "Once you have an oath worked out, and we have agreed on the wording, I will swear."

Emily nodded. She would have to speak to Lady Barb, when she finally returned, and come up with an oath Markus could swear without compromising himself. Markus wasn't likely to swear eternal loyalty to her, or anyone. And besides, it would be insulting to ask him to do anything of the sort.

"You are welcome to stay for the rest of the summer," she said, again. "And I would be interested in talking about other ideas, too."

"I thank you," Markus said. "You're a very strange person, Lady Emily."

Emily couldn't deny it. To them, she had to look like a strange mixture of woman-child, genius inventor and eccentric romantic. She was nineteen, more or less, and she still thought of herself as a girl, where most children of the Nameless World would think of themselves as adults. But then, even Alassa was growing up as she started to accept the responsibilities that came with her birth. Emily could do no less.

"But a decent one, I hope," she said.

"Yes," Melissa said. "It must have been very tempting to betray us."

"It could have been," Emily said. "But I am not cruel."

Melissa nodded, slowly. "I'm sorry," she said.

"Me too," Emily agreed.

What would her life have been like, she wondered again, if she'd met Melissa first? Would Melissa have dragged her out of her shell and forced her to socialize, or would she have been allowed to study in peace, while Melissa and her friends continued their private war with Alassa and her cronies? But Melissa would have inevitably gained the advantage, as long as Alassa remained dependent on a wand. It would have only had one possible outcome.

"You never answered my question," Markus said. "What *should* I tell the MageMaster?"

Emily laughed. In all the excitement, she had quite forgotten Zed's proposal.

"Tell him that he can keep the books at Mountaintop for the moment, as long as he grants me freedom of the school," she said. There were books in the collection she wouldn't have cared to store elsewhere, even in Whitehall. "I will probably consult them, one of these days."

She looked up as the maid finally appeared, carrying three menus. "My usual, please," Emily said. "And you two?"

Markus placed his order before looking directly at Emily. "I think he will be satisfied," he said. "But he will probably want to give you something to allow you access into the school."

"He can send it to me here or Whitehall," Emily said. "And I hope he has forgiven me for everything."

"You made him MageMaster," Markus said. "I dare say he will forgive you, eventually."

Emily shrugged. Zed had been happiest as a researcher, probing the unexplored mysteries of alchemy; he probably didn't enjoy running the school. But, on the other hand, he hadn't had any long-term ambitions of his own. He might not have wanted the job, but he was the person Mountaintop needed.

"We will see," she said, as the food arrived. "But I'll try and stay out of his way for a while."

"You should watch your back," Melissa said. "Fulvia will not leave this insult unsettled."

"It might be hard for her to drum up support," Markus pointed out. "The only other person I've seen who made such a show of power was the old MageMaster, back in Third Year. There was an...an incident and he was not pleased."

Emily sighed. She'd shocked them all — and she had a feeling that most of the crowd had been glad of the excuse to avoid a fight — but anyone who thought about it might have been able to work magic *through* her wards. Or simply keep hammering on them until they broke.

Melissa smiled at him. "What happened?"

"A Fifth Year thought it would be a good idea to cast a curse on one of his classmates," Markus said. "The MageMaster went through the roof. Practically broke the idiot's spine as he dragged him out the door. I've never seen anyone expelled so fast."

*Expelled*, Emily thought, *or drained of power?*

She shrugged. There was no way to know.

"I'll watch my back," she said, finally. "But there's only so much I can do."

"Hire a bodyguard," Melissa suggested. Her voice became teasing. "I'm sure Jade would be a good match for you."

Emily snorted. "Don't even go there."

"It's a good thought," Markus said. "I could recommend a few combat sorcerers who might like the challenge."

"No, thank you," Emily said. Jade was spoken for...and besides, it would have felt weird to pay him for anything. And then there was Lady Barb or Sergeant Miles...the thought of hiring either of them was awkward, to say the least. She'd disliked Travis even before he'd been eaten by a Mimic, while Cat would still be in training. "I don't want anyone following me around."

"Apart from Frieda," Melissa said. "Does she still follow you everywhere?"

Emily sighed. "Sometimes," she said. "But she needs friends of her own."

"She has them," Melissa said. "And yet she really looks up to you."

"I know," Emily said. She shook her head. Who in their right mind would look up to her, when she had a remarkable talent for screwing up her life? And that of other people? Master Grey might have been right, after all, when he'd called her a child of chaos. "But what do I do about it?"

"Let her grow out of it," Markus said. "My brother and sister used to follow me everywhere, even when I threatened them. It was maddening."

"She is of the age when she needs someone to look up to," Melissa agreed. "And there are worse people for her to admire."

Emily blushed and changed the subject, hastily. "Like I said, you are welcome to stay here for the rest of the summer," she said. "But you might want to stay away from the Faire."

"It will be over soon," Markus agreed. "And then...we can start to work on the bank."

Emily rose. "Thank you," she said. "And...and I hope it works out for you."

"Thank *you*," Markus said.

"Tell me something," Emily said. She allowed her voice to darken. "Last night...did you *mean* to be discovered?"

Melissa and Markus exchanged glances. "Let's just say we knew it was possible," Melissa said, finally. "And we wanted it to be over."

Emily sighed. "I know how you feel," she said. "Even if I have never been in love."

She looked at the two of them, sitting so close, and felt another stab of envy. It would be nice to have someone so close to her...nice, but also dangerous. The whole affair could have gone so many different ways, all of which could have led to disaster. Romance...could be dangerous. It had blighted her mother's life beyond repair. She knew she shouldn't be considering dating anyone...

...And yet she had to admit it was tempting.

Turning, she walked through the door, warding it behind her to grant them both a little privacy. They deserved it, after everything they'd gone through.

*Good thing they didn't kill each other after all*, she thought. *The feud would just have continued with a new rallying cry. And that would have been the greatest tragedy of all.*

# Chapter Thirty-Eight

"THEY'VE APPROVED OUR PROJECT," CALEB SAID, AS SHE STEPPED INTO THE WORKROOM. "We're good to go."

Emily let out a sigh of relief. They'd worked too hard on it for her to entertain any other possibility, even though she knew nothing had been guaranteed. By now, rumors of the standoff between the Ashfalls and the Ashworths at Cockatrice had probably reached Whitehall, puzzling and alarming the Grandmaster. She was surprised that Lady Barb hadn't been ordered back to the Faire at once.

But, in the end, everything had worked out fine. To her relief, the Faire had reached its conclusion without any further incidents, either because of rumors of her power or simply because the two noble families had left immediately after disowning their former heirs. Emily had attended the final ceremony, then left the committee to organize the next Faire without her involvement. She was damned if she was wasting any more of her summer.

"That's good," she said. A week after the Faire had concluded, it was almost as if it had never been there in the first place. The only remaining traces were the iron rails, which had been left there to mark the spot. "Can we complete it in nine months?"

"I think so," Caleb said. He gave her a shy smile. "We could make a start on it now, if you want."

Emily hesitated — she liked spending time with Caleb — but shook her head. "I have too much else to do right now," she said. Now the Faire was over, she could actually spend more time with Frieda before she had to go back to Whitehall. "We can start once we're back at school."

Caleb nodded, slowly. "As you wish," he said. "It should be a workable project, even if it takes longer than we thought to work the kinks out."

"I certainly hope so," Emily agreed.

"My family wants me home for a few days prior to returning to school," Caleb added. "I don't suppose you have some reason to keep me here?"

Emily smiled. "I could chain you up in the dungeons, if you like."

"Don't tempt me," Caleb muttered. "It sounds heavenly right now."

"You don't want to go home?" Emily asked.

"My father will go on and on about my brother's achievements, my brother will go on and on about *his* achievements...I'll be bored stiff within the day," Caleb predicted mournfully. "Mother will ask why I haven't signed up for Martial Magic; my sisters will demand my return to Stronghold, so they have someone to help them when they go there."

"You don't fit in," Emily said.

"Not for a very long time," Caleb agreed. He sighed, then looked down at the papers. "I'll send most of my notes to Whitehall before I go, if you don't mind. We may as well ensure they remain safe."

"Of course," Emily said. She watched as Caleb packed up his papers, noting the smooth precision of his movements. He would be a natural in Alchemy class. But then, he had to concentrate to keep his hands from shaking. "I've enjoyed working with you."

Caleb smiled. "I've enjoyed working with you too," he said. "But I meant to ask: how *did* you produce such a powerful working, all on your own?"

"Magic," Emily said, deadpan. "Magic, and desperation. I couldn't allow them to rip the castle apart."

"They would have done it too," Caleb said. "That feud is legendary."

Emily eyed him for a moment. "Do you think I did the right thing?"

"I can hardly complain about two people wanting to leave their families," Caleb pointed out, after a moment's thought. "Maybe you could have handled it better, but I don't know how."

"Thank you," Emily said. It was odd, but part of her valued his approval. She still had no idea what Lady Barb would have to say about it. "I hope they will be happy, wherever they end up."

"Me too," Caleb said. He smiled, tightly. "It brings hope to the rest of us."

He rose, and bowed to her. "I'll have these sent off with a courier tonight, then leave the castle tomorrow. And then...I guess I'll see you in Whitehall."

Emily frowned. Part of her wanted to urge him to hurry up and go, part of her wanted him to stay with her, even though she needed to spend time elsewhere. She closed her eyes, trying to sort out her own feelings, but nothing made sense. Was this what Alassa had felt, when she'd first started to talk to Jade, or was it something completely different? She honestly didn't know.

"I guess," she said. She wanted to ask him to stay, but she felt too nervous to make the move. "And I look forward to turning the world upside down."

"Again," Caleb said.

He bowed to her a second time, turned, and walked out the door, carrying his notes under one arm. Emily looked down at the empty table, fighting down the urge to call him back. It wasn't like her to be so...*demanding* of another's company, she was sure, and yet...the impulse was almost overpoweringly strong. Maybe Imaiqah had been right, after all, and she was attracted to Caleb. He wasn't classically handsome, not like Jade, but that only helped. Or maybe she was just imagining things.

She sighed and reached out with her mind to touch the castle wards. It had taken days to repair them, even though she'd been able to ask for help from her friends. The ward she'd created had torn holes in the castle's protections, causing a series of failures that had eventually brought the entire network down. Jade had commented that he'd never heard of anything like it, while Markus had talked about the Fall of Mountaintop. Emily had a feeling that the problems had only just begun. The castle was definitely not designed to handle elaborate wards.

*Then I need a new castle*, she thought. It was annoying, but it had to be considered. Part of her still wanted to give up the barony, to walk away from Zangaria; part of her knew she could do a great deal more good with land and property under her direct control. *And I will have to talk the king into letting me build one.*

It wouldn't be easy. A castle was a symbol of strength — and dominance. If she held the castles in her land, she would dominate the land, perhaps even hold it against the king. There would be no shortage of reasons for Randor to refuse to allow her to build a new one, including fears of inciting the other barons to demand new castles of their own. But she needed somewhere she could ward properly, if she wanted to live there permanently. It was a minor miracle nothing of great importance had been stolen.

She looked up as someone knocked on the door. "Come in!"

The door opened to reveal Alassa, wearing a long white dress and a golden necklace that sparked with protections of one kind or another. Jade must have made it, Emily guessed, feeling a tinge of envy. It must be nice to have *someone* looking out for you, someone who cared for you as more than just a friend. Would he have been so considerate to her, she wondered, or would their relationship have been different? But there was no point in worrying about it now.

"I just received a note from my father," Alassa said. "He wants to see us all back at Alexis."

She swallowed, nervously. "This could be it, Emily."

"The moment you tell your father you want to marry a common-born sorcerer," Emily said, with some amusement. "Are you going to show more nerve than Melissa?"

Alassa shot her a sharp look. "I hope it won't come to screamed accusations and banishment," she said. "I missed the last part of the show. Jade dragged me out."

"Good for him," Emily said. She dreaded to think what would have happened if Alassa had been caught in the crossfire and killed. Zangaria had no other heir, no one else who could take the throne without starting a civil war. "What would have happened to Zangaria if you'd died?"

"It would have been bad," Alassa said. She sat down, primly. "My father should want me to get married as soon as possible. Jade...is the best candidate we have."

"He might not even let you return for Fourth Year," Emily said. She recalled Lady Barb saying that Alassa might be expelled, just to avoid having to put her exam results on the record. "And make you start churning out children immediately."

Alassa scowled. "I hope we *can* have children. But I can always find someone to adopt if worst comes to worst."

Emily winced. "I'm sure you will be fine," she lied. The Royal Bloodline was immensely complex and the Alchemists who'd designed it hadn't really known what they were doing. It was quite possible that King Randor's near-barrenness had been passed down to his daughter, eventually guaranteeing the extinction of his line. "I don't think there's anything wrong with Jade."

"I saw his records," Alassa said. "He's a healthy young man, only a few years older than me."

"And he can presumably sire children," Emily said. "You should be fine."

Alassa nodded. "Emily, there was an additional note for you," she added, as she held out a scrap of parchment. "Lady Barb is waiting in Alexis."

Emily's eyes narrowed. Lady Barb could teleport. There was nothing stopping her from jumping all the way to Cockatrice, rather than heading to Alexis and meeting Emily there, once Emily had traveled back to the city. It was odd, to say the least. What had Lady Barb been doing that had called her away from Cockatrice? And why had it also caught up Sergeant Miles?

Or was it a trick of some kind? An attempt to lure her out of the castle?

She took the note and checked it. Lady Barb had taught her how to sign her name — and, more importantly, how to read other signatures. Lady Barb had written the note, Emily confirmed rapidly, and she had done so of her own free will. It was no trick.

"I'll see her there," she said, although she was unable to escape the feeling that her life was about to change, once again. "Do you know if I will be coming back here?"

Alassa shrugged.

"I was under the impression you were going to go back to school early," she said. "But isn't this a little *too* early?"

"I don't know," Emily said. She sighed, inwardly. Deliberately or otherwise, King Randor had caused her a whole series of new problems. "The Grandmaster is the one calling the shots."

She rolled her eyes — she liked the Grandmaster — and then called for Bryon. When he arrived, she gave orders to have her coach prepared for immediate departure and then, on the assumption she would not be returning immediately, resume his duties as her steward. It wouldn't be hard, now the Faire was over; Bryon could handle all the minor problems, then forward the harder problems to her. She knew she would have to keep a closer eye on what was happening, in future, but she had no idea when she would find the time. Perhaps she should join Alassa and leave school after the Fourth Year.

*Don't be stupid*, she told herself, sharply. *Cockatrice will still be here when you graduate from Whitehall.*

They found Frieda in her rooms, reading an elaborate story written by a man who claimed to have sailed around the entire world. Emily had glanced at it, back when it had first been printed, but she'd had some problems believing some of the tales. Encounters with sea monsters were one thing — she knew there were all sorts of strange creatures in the world — but the writer had spent most of the book bragging about his experiences with women of all shapes, sizes, and colors. She was surprised he had managed to find any time for exploration.

"Hey," Frieda said, sitting up. One of the maids had been busy; instead of her twin ponytails, her hair had been reshaped into an elaborate arrangement that perched neatly on the top of her head. "Where are you going?"

Emily felt a sudden bitter stab of guilt. She'd promised to spend time with Frieda and now she was being called away, again. And she didn't even know if they were going to return to Cockatrice or not. Frieda could spend the rest of her life in the castle, if she liked, but it wouldn't be the same. She certainly wouldn't have anyone to explore the surrounding lands with, let alone study magic.

"Alexis," she said, shortly. "Would you like to come?"

Alassa poked her arm, gently. "Come with us," she said. "I can take you hunting, if you like."

She winked at Frieda. "Emily *hates* hunting."

Emily shivered. She disliked horses, she disliked riding through the forest...and she really disliked hunting wild boars that weren't actually wild boars. The tradition of turning criminals into animals and then letting them loose in the royal hunting grounds appalled her, even though Alassa and Imaiqah seemed to take it in stride. She hadn't realized until much later just how unnatural the boars had been, at the time...

*At least Jade didn't slaughter them with abandon*, she thought. The princes *had* slaughtered the boars, then gone on to hunt deer for the king's table. *There is that to be said for him, at least.*

"I don't know where I will be going afterwards," Emily said. "You could stay here, if you like, or you could go with Alassa."

"Stay with me," Alassa said, immediately. "I'll probably need someone to calm me down after mother starts twittering on about wedding dresses."

"Your mother treats me as a doll," Frieda protested. "Last time, she was trying to make me wear a glorified nightgown."

Alassa laughed. "She did that to me, too," she said. "And to just about every other young woman who entered the palace. I think Emily was the only one to make her escape."

Emily snorted. The queen's enthusiasm for dresses was terrifyingly strong. Emily wouldn't have minded so much if the queen hadn't wanted her to undress, practically in public, and don the latest in a set of private creations. There weren't many people who could say their dresses were made by a queen, but it was an honor she would have gratefully foregone.

"I always said you look like a doll," she said, mischievously. Alassa did sometimes look like a porcelain doll, although she wasn't quite as unreal as Barbie. "Dressing you up comes naturally."

Alassa made a rude gesture, then grinned at Frieda. "Come with us," she said. "You won't regret it."

"Very well," Frieda said. She clambered off the bed and glanced at herself in the mirror. "Eva will hate me for taking this down."

"Don't worry about it," Emily advised. She'd always disliked it when someone else tried to help her get dressed or do up her hair. "Just make sure you wrap up warm for the trip."

"And pack a bag of essentials," Alassa added. "My mother sometimes forgets the basics."

Emily snorted — there was a whole castle of maids, who would happily find anything Frieda needed — but kept the thought to herself. Instead, she left them to sort out Frieda's bag and walked back to the room Markus and Melissa were sharing. It was heavily warded, unsurprisingly, with a couple of wards that she wasn't sure how to remove. Markus had admitted, after he'd been disowned, that there were people in his family — both families — who might do whatever it took to kill them both. He'd wrapped so many protections around them both that nothing short of a whole team of assassins could get to them.

She tapped the ward lightly, and waited. It was nearly five minutes before Markus, wearing nothing more than a towel, opened the door and peered out, suspiciously. Emily blushed and looked away, embarrassed. Casual nudity didn't sit well with her at all.

"I have to leave the castle," she said, shortly. "I may not be back before school resumes, but you can remain here until you go to Beneficence. I'll write to you from Alexis to let you know what's happening."

Markus sighed. "Why have you been called away?"

"The king wants to see me," Emily said. Imaiqah and her family were already in Alexis. It was quite possible that Randor had already interrogated Imaiqah. "And then I may have to go straight to Whitehall."

"The Grandmaster's heard about what we did," Melissa said, walking up behind Markus and clutching his arm. Emily glanced at her and flushed. Melissa was wearing a towel too, which left very little to the imagination. "And he's mad at us."

"I don't know," Emily admitted. "But I just wanted to say goodbye before I left."

"Be careful," Markus advised. "And thank you, once again."

Emily nodded. Markus had sworn the oath, once they'd worked out a suitable wording. He would found the bank for her, then start issuing small loans. And then... she hoped and prayed that nothing went badly wrong. There were so many ways magic could be used to damage the bank's reputation.

*But we have the charmed parchments*, she thought, recalling how Aloha had agreed to let them borrow the concept in exchange for a handful of shares. *And we have other tricks, too.*

"I'll see you at Whitehall," she said, addressing Melissa. "And I wish you both every happiness."

Turning, she walked down to the courtyard. Bryon was waiting for her, along with a number of maids, servants and cooks. They all bowed in unison when they saw Emily, making her cheeks heat once again. She couldn't allow herself to get used to everyone bowing and scraping, she told herself firmly, or she might wind up yet another aristocratic brat. Who knew what that did to a child, growing up with everyone bowing to him?

*You don't need to guess*, she told herself, as she motioned for Bryon to rise. Thankfully, there had been no time to organize a proper ceremony. *Alassa was more than enough of a warning, when you first met.*

"I'll be back," she promised, as she scrambled into the coach. Frieda, Jade and Alassa were already there, Jade and Alassa holding hands. "For now, goodbye."

# Chapter Thirty-Nine

"BARONESS EMILY," KING RANDOR SAID, AS EMILY STEPPED INTO HIS PRIVATE STUDY. "Welcome back."

Emily nodded, and went down on one knee. "Your majesty," she murmured. "I thank you."

It was odd, but she'd never realized just how submissive kneeling could be, at least until she'd had to do it herself. Prostrating oneself was definitely submissive, but even kneeling carried a hundred unfortunate implications, each one darker than the last. By kneeling, she was admitting, at the very least, that the king was her superior...

"You may rise," King Randor said. "I understand that you wish to speak with me?"

"You summoned me," Emily said. She took the chair he indicated and sat, clasping her hands together to prevent them from shaking. "I assumed that you wished to speak with me."

Randor took his own chair, facing her. Even sitting, his presence seemed to dominate the room. It wasn't magic, as far as she could tell; it was the sheer force of his personality. And yet, there was something about it that offended her sensibilities. She respected Randor, even liked him to some extent...and yet she didn't think of him as her superior. How could she?

"But I was asked to summon you," the king said. "I assumed you wished to speak with *me*."

Emily felt her patience fray. "Alassa wished me to talk about a certain subject with you, yes," she said, wondering just what game the king was playing. "She must have told you I wanted to speak with you."

The king smiled. "She did."

Emily looked up at him and *knew*, beyond a shadow of a doubt, that *he* knew what Alassa had wanted her to say. But how much did he know? He'd carefully *not* asked Alassa any questions that might have brought her new relationship to life. And yet, if he'd been watching her and Jade, he might well have deduced the truth...she shook her head, feeling a headache starting to pound behind her temple. She was in no mood for games.

"She wishes to marry Jade," Emily said, bluntly. There was no point in spending the next half-hour dancing around the elephant in the room. "I think it would be a very good idea."

"An interesting statement," Randor observed. "Particularly as Jade's name was once romantically linked with yours."

Emily fought hard to keep her face under control, although she was sure that Randor could read *something* from her expression. The double standards had never seemed quite so hypocritical. Randor might have taken a hundred lovers, but he expected his wife to remain loyal and his daughter to remain chaste...and, too, his prospective son-in-law. Jade would hardly be the first person to have affairs before or after marriage and he would definitely not be the last.

"Jade and I were friends," she said, flatly. She might have liked the idea of a father figure — a genuine father figure — but Randor wasn't going to be it. "There was nothing between us, not really."

"Your father disapproved," Randor said. "Or did you?"

Emily hesitated, choosing her words carefully. "Jade is a good and decent person," she said, finally. "He's smart, a capable magician, and a trained combat sorcerer. But he is also not the type of person to meld well with me."

Randor smiled. "And you think he would meld well with my daughter?"

"There are many advantages to such a match," Emily said. "He would not involve Zangaria in foreign affairs, nor would he excite resentment among the barons, nor would he seek to take power for himself. And he would be capable of giving Alassa a level of protection, and care, that few others could match."

"But he is not a nobleman," Randor pointed out, smoothly.

"He is a sorcerer, which ranks him as equal to a nobleman," Emily countered. She shook her head inwardly in amusement. "And if he were to marry Alassa, the barons would not feel slighted because one of their number had been promoted, nor insulted because an inferior nobleman had been promoted above their heads."

"You haven't answered my real question," Randor said. "Do you think he would meld well with my daughter?"

Emily smiled, suddenly. Randor cared about Alassa! It had sometimes been hard to tell, but she saw it now. He might have had to use his daughter as a piece on the kingmaker board, he might have done his best to have a male heir...and yet, he cared about his daughter. She wasn't sure what to make of it, but it was there.

"Alassa is a very active person," Emily said. "She isn't stupid, far from it, but she prefers to be active rather than study. She loves to hunt, she loves to play games, she even set up her own team just so she could play *Ken*. She's immensely competitive and focused on getting what she wants..."

She hesitated, then went on. "Jade is much the same," she added. "He loves to hunt, to walk through the countryside, to climb mountains, even to play games. I remember him playing Scrum and carrying on, even with a broken nose. He and Alassa are well-matched. And he's loyal, protective, and caring."

Randor studied her for a long moment. "And you believe he will care for her?"

"Yes," Emily said. Jade had comforted her, shortly after she'd almost killed Alassa. And then, he'd tried to help her out of her shell. And he'd been one of the few who hadn't looked doubtfully at her after she'd killed Shadye. "Jade will be loyal and caring to whoever he marries."

"I'm glad you think so," Randor said. "But there are political considerations involved."

Emily took a breath. "There are more than just *political* considerations involved," she said, after a moment. "Your majesty, Alassa has *chosen* him. She is to succeed you as ruler of this country. What will happen if she takes the throne without a person she chose at her side?"

"I didn't choose my wife," Randor said, flatly.

"It's different for girls," Emily said. Actually, she had no idea how boys felt about arranged marriages, but they were granted far wider latitude than girls. "More to the point, how could she find a better match? How could she find someone who will complement her, rather than try to overshadow her?"

"An interesting point," Randor observed. "But should she be allowed the freedom to choose?"

Emily placed firm controls on her temper. Snapping at the king wouldn't help.

"Alassa is nineteen, pressing twenty," she said, "and a capable magician to boot. She is old enough to make her own choice, your majesty, and old enough to bear a permanent grudge if you choose badly. Jade offers her everything she wants and needs from a marriage."

"But he lacks the social polish of a born aristocrat," Randor said. "What happens when he has bastards?"

"Everyone has bastards," Emily snapped. God knew everyone thought Void, a sorcerer who could presumably use contraceptive spells, had at least one bastard. "I think Jade is much less likely to leave litters everywhere than some of your barons."

Randor smirked, unpleasantly. "Point," he said. "They do tend to cause problems when they grow old enough to know what they're missing."

Emily barely resisted the temptation to point out that Randor had presumably tried desperately to have a son, even a bastard son, of his own. The laws concerning illegitimate children were vague, deliberately so, but as long as the father acknowledged them they could be considered legitimate. And yet, the laws would complicate matters if Alassa had had an illegitimate child. Would the child still be part of the royal family if the father was definitely *not* a member?

"He saved her life at least twice, while she was at the Faire," Emily added. "I think you would not be able to find a better man to marry her. And she *wants* him."

"And tell me," Randor said. "How do you feel about it?"

Emily shrugged. She was damned if she was going to expose her feelings to Randor.

"I think they will make a wonderful couple," she said. "And I am very happy for them. I will be happy to support them, if necessary."

Randor peered at her for a long moment. "And you have no feelings for him at all?"

Emily blinked. "We are friends," she said, tartly. "And that is all we ever were."

It struck her, suddenly, that Alassa had to have been panicking ever since she'd fallen for Jade. A word from Emily to her father could ruin everything. Emily was a baroness, after all, and the person who had saved Randor's throne. No wonder she'd been so reluctant to talk about it. *She* might have known, or believed, that Emily wasn't interested in Jade, but her father couldn't have taken that for granted.

*Not when so much is at stake*, she thought. *The barons could unify round me to resist the match.*

"She loves him," she said, simply. "And he loves her. And they are good together, for all the reasons I bet she outlined."

Randor smiled. "And the dangers of insulting the nobility?"

"They can't *all* marry her," Emily said, remembering just how many suitors had clustered around Queen Elizabeth. She'd played them all masterfully but, in the end, she'd failed in her duty to provide England with an heir. It had been sheer luck that James I had been waiting in the wings. "If she marries Baron Silver, your majesty, Baron Bronze and the others will be insulted. Let her marry a complete outsider and spite them all equally."

"The only baron who would not think of marrying her would be you," Randor observed.

Emily wanted to roll her eyes. There wasn't a baron — apart from Emily herself — who *wasn't* married, with children. As far as she knew, the oldest Baron was easily old enough to be Alassa's father. But they would happily put their wives and children aside, just for the pleasure of being king. They'd have done it even if Alassa had been so ugly she looked like a toad someone had tried to transfigure into a human. The prestige of being king would be more than enough reward.

"I don't think I can marry her," Emily said, dryly. There were no actual laws against homosexual marriage in Zangaria, probably because no one had ever felt the need to write them. But open homosexuality wasn't highly regarded by anyone. "We certainly couldn't produce children."

"A terrible weakness," Randor agreed. "I will grant my consent to the match."

Emily blinked. That easily?

*He knew,* she thought. In hindsight, it was clear. *He knew, and approved all along.*

"I think they will be very happy together," she said. "And he would make a good consort."

"I should hope so," Randor said, tartly. He leaned back in his chair and stroked his beard thoughtfully. "I understand you have been asked to be Maid of Honor?"

"I would like to know more about the post before I agree," Emily said. "Last time I agreed to something before learning what it actually involved, I nearly got a great many people killed."

"Yes, you did," Randor agreed.

He studied her for a long moment before he went on. "Alassa tells me that you've been having doubts about being a baroness."

"Yes," Emily said. She knew she shouldn't turn down his gift, even in private, but she wasn't sure she wanted to keep it. "I do not think I am suited for the post."

"I could tell you stories about some of the other barons that would haunt you at night," Randor said. "You have caused problems, yes, but so have the other barons."

"I wasn't trained for the post," Emily said. "I..."

"*They* were," Randor countered. "And many of the ones who inherited from their fathers caused far worse problems for their subjects than you."

He shrugged. "I knew you would have problems coming to grips with the task," he said, after a moment. "But you have a long life ahead of you. You have time to learn."

"But I do not want to spend my entire life there," Emily said. "There's an entire world to explore."

"And magic to be done, I imagine," Randor said. He gave her another smile. "That's what managers are for, Lady Emily. Hire more, give them a basic set of orders, and then leave them to handle the job."

*Or set up some form of democracy*, Emily thought. She had no idea how well democracy would work, when there was no underlying agreement that everyone was theoretically equal, but it might be better than everything else. *Something that lets people handle their own affairs.*

*Yeah, right*, her own thoughts answered her. *And what would democracy say the next time you have to tackle an unsavory contract?*

"I will see what I can find," she said, reluctantly. "But I won't have managers abusing the population."

"Then don't let them," Randor said.

He reached out and clapped her on the shoulder. "You have a long way to go," he said, "but I am sure Alassa will be with you."

Emily nodded, slowly.

"But tell me," Randor said. "What are these *guns?*"

"They're something new," Emily said. "They will change the world."

She outlined the basic concept, keeping some of her thoughts to herself. Guns wouldn't just make it harder for the barons to defend their castles; guns would make it easier for the commoners to rise up against the nobility. It took months to train a soldier, and years to train a combat sorcerer, but how long did it take to learn to use a gun? If King Randor saw all of the implications, he might want to shut down the whole program.

*But Nanette's notes are still out there*, she thought, grimly. *Who knows who else might be making guns and gunpowder now?*

Randor frowned. "And why should I tolerate such a big change?"

"Because you need it," Emily said. "What happens when the necromancers come over the mountains?"

"Zangaria doesn't border the Blighted Lands," Randor said.

"But that could change," Emily said. "They could punch through Whitehall or a dozen other spots and march north. And then all hell would break loose."

She wondered, suddenly, what would have happened to Shadye if he'd been lured onto a giant landmine. It would be simple enough to hide the gunpowder, and detonate it when the necromancer was standing on top of it. Would it kill him, make him lose control of the stolen magic, or would it just make him madder? There was no way to know.

"We will see," Randor said.

He rose, signaling that the interview was at an end. "Lady Barb has requested permission to take you back to Whitehall tonight, rather than wait for dinner," he said. "Do you wish to remain here to eat?"

Emily hesitated. It had been seven hours since they had left Cockatrice, but it felt longer, even though she'd managed to catch some sleep in the coach. Part of her wanted to stay long enough to chat with Alassa, congratulate her and Jade on their impending marriage, and then make arrangements for Frieda. The rest of her didn't want to stay any longer in Alexis than strictly necessary.

"I think I should go with her," Emily said. If nothing else, she had a lot to talk about with the older woman. "But will you take care of Frieda?"

"I will ensure she is looked after," Randor said, gravely. "You may go."

Emily rose, hastily curtseyed, and walked out of the room and up towards Alassa's chambers. Somehow, Emily wasn't surprised to see Lady Barb when she entered, chatting with Jade and Alassa while Frieda read a book, boredom clearly written on her face. Emily smiled at her, and grinned at Alassa.

"Your father has approved the match," she said. "Good luck."

She looked away as Jade and Alassa embraced. She was happy for them, really she was, but part of her felt nothing more than envy. It would be nice to have a caring partner. Lady Barb shot her a sharp glance and rose.

"I have some preparations to make," she said, "so we will leave in an hour. Be ready."

Emily nodded, and turned to her friends. "Make sure you don't have *too* big a wedding," she warned. "You'll be overwhelmed."

Alassa sighed. "I have to invite everyone," she reminded Emily. "Or someone will start feeling left out."

"We'll survive," Jade said.

Emily hoped he was right, both for the wedding and for the rest of their lives. She'd only ever known one couple intimately — her mother and her stepfather — and that had been an awful descent into shouting matches and drunken crying fits. Lady Barb wasn't married...none of the adults she knew, apart from King Randor, were married. She had no idea how Jade and Alassa would live together, but she hoped they would do better than her mother...

*Alassa wouldn't tolerate anyone treating her like that*, she reassured herself. *And Jade wouldn't treat her like that.*

She turned to look at Frieda. "Will you be all right here?"

"I think so," Frieda said. "But can't I come back to Whitehall with you?"

"I don't think so," Emily said. *She'd* been allowed to stay at Whitehall for a few extra days, but only because of special circumstances. Somehow, she doubted the teachers stayed in Whitehall outside term-time. "But I can ask."

"Don't," Alassa advised. "I can take Frieda around and show her everything. And try to get her ready to play *Ken.*"

Emily laughed. "Are you trying to teach her how to play?"

"Yes," Alassa said. She reached out and ruffled Frieda's hair. "She's going to be a right terror in the maze."

Emily smiled, then stood up. "I'll get my bags, then write a few notes. And then I suppose I will have to wait."

# Chapter Forty

"WE NEED TO TALK," LADY BARB SAID, AS THE TELEPORT SPELL LET GO OF THEM. "NOW."
Emily nodded, clutching the older woman's arm until the world had stopped spinning. Teleporting didn't cause her as many problems as stepping through a portal, but it wasn't *that* much easier. She closed her eyes for a long moment, gathering herself, and looked up at Whitehall. It shone against the dark mountains, barely visible in the darkening gloom. And beyond them, Emily knew, the Blighted Lands waited.

"Tell me something," Lady Barb hissed. Eerie light flickered around them as she cast a light globe, followed by a privacy ward. "What were you *thinking?*"

She spun Emily around so she was facing the older woman. "What were you thinking when you allowed Markus and Melissa to fall in love under your roof? What were you thinking when you let it happen?"

Emily stared at her, feeling betrayed. "I didn't let it happen," she mumbled. "It just...*did.*"

"You were immensely lucky that they didn't call your bluff," Lady Barb said. "You used up the entire battery powering that ward, didn't you? You couldn't have maintained it if they had started to fight back!"

"I know," Emily said. She couldn't help feeling betrayed. Why had Lady Barb left her to face the crisis all alone? "I didn't ask for any of this!"

"You agreed to host the Faire, without considering the consequences," Lady Barb spat out. "You then allow your steward to expand the Faire, including your *technology.* You completely fail to lay on security until the very last moment, which means that everything has to be improvised at short notice...and then you allow a love affair to develop under your roof!"

"I didn't know," Emily snapped. She felt tears prickling at the corner of her eyes and brushed them away, angrily. "I didn't realize the problem!"

Lady Barb shook her head angrily, long blonde hair flapping around her shoulders. "You could have *asked!*"

"You could have told me," Emily countered.

"You *should* have asked," Lady Barb said. She made a visible attempt to cool her temper. "I don't expect you to know everything, Emily, but I do expect you to think about something *before* you agree to it!"

"You could have warned me," Emily protested.

"You're not a child," Lady Barb reminded her. "I don't understand you, at times, even knowing your origins. It's like...it's like you're a child trapped in a woman's body."

She might have had a point, Emily knew. Adulthood in the Nameless World came earlier, at least for non-magicians, than it did on Earth. A child of twelve could be married off, a child of sixteen could inherit his father's lands and property, a person of thirty could be a grandparent...and it was rare, vanishingly rare, for anyone without magic to last longer than sixty years, at least in the fields. There was no real awareness that teenagers were teenagers, and why should there be? The teenagers had no time to become teenagers before they were expected to be adults.

But, at nineteen, someone might still not be considered a responsible adult on Earth.

"I didn't think," she said. "I..."

"No, you didn't," Lady Barb said. She placed her hands on her hips, leaning forward intimidating. "And, because of you, two entire houses have been humiliated. You could have managed to get hundreds of people killed."

"You were there when I was asked to host the Faire," Emily muttered. "You could have warned me."

"I'm not your mother," Lady Barb said. "And if I was..."

Emily felt stricken. "I think of you as a mother," she interrupted. She had never been able to put it into words; no, she'd never really dared admit it. To have said it out loud might have ruined it. But it had to be said now. "I...I liked being with you."

"I'm not your mother," Lady Barb repeated.

"But you act like it," Emily said. She swallowed, then pressed on. "You helped me when I needed it, you advised me when I needed it, you...you even disciplined me when you felt I needed it. I thought you cared."

Lady Barb reached out and took her by the shoulders, gently. "Emily, there is a difference between caring and doing everything for you," she said. "A magician needs to learn to stand on her own, not...not depend on others. Even if I was your mother, you would be too old to have your mistakes corrected before you get your fingers burnt."

"I know," Emily said. "But it was nice to feel that I had someone who cared."

"I *do* care," Lady Barb said. "But I cannot do everything for you."

She squeezed Emily's shoulder, but went on. "You took me for granted, I think, and now I see why," she added. "I hadn't realized how you were feeling, and I am sorry for it."

"Me too," Emily said. "Should we have talked about it in the Cairngorms?"

Lady Barb gave her a sardonic look. "I assure you," she said, "that if *my* daughter had risked her life by taking a dangerous menace as a pet, said daughter would regret it for the rest of her days."

"At least you would have cared," Emily said. She remembered, bitterly, being seven years old and trying to cook. God alone knew how she'd avoided scalding herself, let alone accidentally eating something poisonous. "My mother didn't give a damn about me."

"And what about following me into the lair of a potential necromancer?" Lady Barb asked. "You could have died."

"I would have died trying to save you," Emily said. She gritted her teeth and went on before the older woman could interrupt. "And it would have been worth any amount of punishment just to see you alive again."

"You might regret saying that," Lady Barb said, darkly. "If I didn't happen to know you need every last moment of the coming term, Emily, you would be in detention so often that you wouldn't see the sun rise or set."

Emily swallowed. "I'm sorry," she said. "I thought I was doing the best I could."

"You should probably have done a little more research before agreeing to host the Faire," Lady Barb said. "Or simply asked my advice. I would have told you to hire someone like Master Grey to handle the security arrangements, then leave it in his capable hands. Or did you assume the committee would see to it?"

"They thought I would," Emily muttered. "And I thought they would."

Lady Barb poked her arm, hard enough to make her yelp. "But you were wrong," she said, flatly. "Next time, do a great deal of research before you agree to anything."

"I will," Emily promised. She took a breath. "What...what about...?"

"I would make a poor mother," Lady Barb said, tartly. "And even if you thought otherwise, I could not adopt you. It would raise too many eyebrows, given who everyone *believes* to be your father."

"I had a worse mother," Emily said. She'd known it wasn't really a possibility, but part of her had liked the idea of being adopted. "You care, at least..."

"Sometimes you scare me," Lady Barb said. "Your ignorance is staggering, all the more so as you are ignorant about things that we consider to be so obvious they are simply not worth mentioning. And then you blunder into worse trouble trying to fix your earlier mistakes."

She sighed. "There isn't a single person on the continent who would have invited both the Ashworths and Ashfalls to anything," she added. Her voice rose sharply. "Except for you. And then you manage to humiliate both parties..."

Emily wilted under her gaze. "I..."

"And if the grown-ups hadn't been looking for a reason to disengage," Lady Barb thundered, "you might have seen your ward torn apart, yourself the first victim of their spells. You were lucky."

She smiled, sardonically. "But at least it burnished your reputation," she said. "Both as a Child of Destiny *and* as the Necromancer's Bane."

"I don't care about that," Emily said. "I care about you."

"I cannot be your mother," Lady Barb said. "You saw Fulvia...and how the rest of her family reacted to her. Do you want to be Melissa, struggling against invisible ties? Or her brother, alternately praised and kicked? I cannot steer your life for you, Emily, and if I did there would be no guarantee you would like the results."

"I know," Emily said.

"But I can try and be there for you," Lady Barb added. "And *that* is something I can promise."

Emily nodded, one hand playing with the snake bracelet. Part of her wished that she could convince Lady Barb to marry Sergeant Miles, then they could both adopt her, but she knew it would never happen. Even if they did marry, even if Void raised no objections, Lady Barb was right. It would raise far too many eyebrows. And besides, Emily was nineteen. Even as a magician, she would be considered close enough to adulthood not to need adopted parents.

But it would have been nice to have parents, true parents.

"Thank you," she said, finally.

"The Grandmaster wishes to depart in two days," Lady Barb said. "That should give us long enough to talk about what you did with the battery, then find a way to improve it. There are all sorts of potentials in the battery."

Emily shrugged. She didn't really want to talk about it right now — or anything else, for that matter. It was nearly night — her mind, still operating on Zangaria time — insisted it had to be past midnight — and she wanted her bed.

"And you should start charging a new one," Lady Barb added. "It might come in handy."

"It will," Emily agreed. She swallowed. "It's been one hell of a summer."

"Better than last year," Lady Barb pointed out, dryly.

Emily nodded, and looked at the mountains. Shadye's lands lay on the far side, utterly untouched since his death. Aurelius had suggested that *Emily* was the rightful owner of those lands. But she knew, from experience, that mere ownership didn't always confer more than the title. Were the necromancers scared of her? Or were they merely biding their time?

*Or something so mad as to be utterly unpredictable,* she thought. *Shadye was completely insane by the time he died, and Mother Holly wasn't much better.*

She looked back at Lady Barb. "Where were you?"

"There was an *incident* with a newborn magician," Lady Barb said. "Someone had to tend to it."

Emily saw her pinched face and knew she wouldn't be told anything else, not now.

Lady Barb took her arm and started to lead her towards the school. "You will spend tomorrow cramming," she said, firmly. "Everything you can read about the Blighted Lands, you will read. And there will be a test. If you fail, you will not like the consequences."

Emily glanced at her. "Detentions?"

"Death," Lady Barb said. She nodded towards the mountains. "Who knows what's waiting for you on the other side?"

She paused. "And one other thing."

Emily looked at her, expectantly.

"You made several new enemies over the last month," Lady Barb said. "Marcellus is unlikely to be too disappointed by the outcome — he's young enough to have more sons, if necessary — but Fulvia is going to hate you. Balbus won't be much better, because you made him look like his mother's puppet. And Gaius will hate you worst of all."

"He was a better magician than I thought," Emily confessed.

"Never get on the bad side of a small man," Lady Barb said. "He will do whatever it takes to humiliate you, as you humiliated him. You destroyed his hopes of marrying into the Ashworths, but also made him a laughing stock — well, Melissa helped, I suppose. All the stories I heard agree that he was utterly humiliated. I expect you will be seeing him again in the future."

"I hope not," Emily said.

"You'll be lucky if you don't," Lady Barb said. "And one other thing?"

Emily blinked. *"Another* thing?"

"If you were my child, I don't think you would make the same mistakes," Lady Barb said. "I would have taught you from birth. But I am proud of you, despite everything. Your mistakes were bad ones, but you recovered. Few others would have done so well."

And that, Emily told herself as they stepped into the school, was enough.

# Epilogue

S HE HAD BEEN HUMILIATED.

Fulvia sat in her private room, protected by layer upon layer of custom-designed wards, and brooded. She had been humiliated. Worse, her mastery of the family had been called into question. All the little secrets, all the uncomfortable truths, were being dragged into the open and examined by the members of her family. Once, she had ruled without question; now, even her eldest *son* was considering how best to remove her from power.

*Child of Destiny*, she spat, mentally. *Child of Destiny, Child of a Lone Power...and the Necromancer's Bane.*

Fulvia hadn't been impressed when she'd first met Emily. The girl was young, only nineteen, and acted younger. Fulvia would have made something of Emily, she was sure, if she'd married into the Ashworth Family, but her father had resisted any and all blandishments designed to lure his daughter into Fulvia's clutches. There had been no trace of great power behind her smile, behind her clear nervousness at having to sit between Fulvia and Marcellus. Fulvia had come to the conclusion that the girl had been vastly overrated...

And then she'd cast a powerful ward and held it in place long enough to force everyone to calm down. A ward so powerful that even a Lone Power would have had problems holding it in place for more than a few minutes.

Clearly, everything had been an act.

The girl hadn't been nervous at all; she'd been amused, laughing at them. And no wonder! She'd been able to shut them down with a single ward.

It was galling, but the Ashworths were grateful. A fight in such close quarters, no matter the cause, could only end in mutual slaughter. Fulvia had never lost her hatred of Felix and his descendants, and she would happily have cheered if they had all died, but the prospect of losing her entire family staggered even her. Who would have *thought* that Melissa, obedient little Melissa, would have dared to fall in love with an Ashfall? And who would have thought she would have resisted her entire family for love?

Cold hatred prickled along Fulvia's spine. Melissa was not important. If she managed to retain control of the family, her son could always marry again and churn out a few more children, if Iulius was unsuitable. And if she didn't, the future of the family hardly mattered, not to her. Melissa had been right, even though she hadn't known it at the time. Fulvia had not been born into the family.

But all that mattered, right now, was revenge.

A figure stepped into the light, entering from a passage so old that only Fulvia and her closest allies knew of its existence. She looked up, then nodded slowly as the figure bowed to her, then sat down without being asked. He treasured his independence, or at least the appearance of independence, but he would do as he was told.

Fulvia had seen to that, over the years. A favor had to be repaid...

"There is nothing to discuss," she said, simply. "I have given you the opportunity. Lady Emily must die."

The figure eyed her for a long moment, then rose, bowed, and slowly retreated from the chamber.

Behind him, Fulvia smiled coldly. She had been ruined, perhaps, but she would have her revenge. Lady Emily would die...

...And then, once again, power would be hers.

End of Book VI

Emily will return in

*Trial By Fire*

# Afterword

When I was first forced to read through the script to *Romeo and Juliet* at school – I was the Friar – it annoyed the hell out of me. Romeo and Juliet were such *idiots*! They meet each other, fall in love and get married within the space of a very short period of time (depending on the producer.) And they don't tell their families, with the net result that Juliet is nearly married to someone else, Romeo loses his best friend and then kills one of his new kinsmen...and the young lovers (assisted by the Friar) stage an elaborate plot to fake their deaths, which turns tragic when they actually die. The only good thing about the whole affair is that it finally brings the feuding families to their senses.

I thought they were being stupid, as I said, for several reasons. First, they only just met; they certainly didn't have time to *know* if they had anything more than lust. Romeo seems to have a habit of lusting after girls, as demonstrated by his moaning over Rosaline (which stops abruptly once he sets eyes on Juliet), while Juliet is evidently a sheltered and virginal daughter. Second, they don't bother to tell their parents they'd married, which leads to disaster – Juliet's parents tried to push her into marrying Paris, unaware she was already married. And third, they killed themselves.

The problem with interpreting Romeo and Juliet is that we look at the play through the lens of our society. We see Romeo and Juliet as adults, free to make their own decisions and able to decide to marry without parental permission. Nor do we see them having problems telling the truth to their parents. Maybe their families are upset at their marriage, we think, but does it really matter to their children? Romeo and Juliet had every right to arrange their own marriage, sleep with each other and build a life together. Or not. Whatever happened would be their choice.

But *Romeo and Juliet* is a product of its time and place.

Romeo and Juliet were *young*. In Elizabethan England, girls could get married as young as twelve. Romeo was almost certainly underage too, by our standards; I rather doubt he was any older than fourteen. The whole play centers around the decisions made by two very young teenagers, below what we consider to be the Age of Consent, allowing their hormones to lead them into a deadly trap. To us, this is thoroughly unpleasant at best and so modern-day producers tend to imply that Romeo and Juliet are definitely over eighteen. But how can one reasonably expect thirteen/ fourteen year olds to think logically?

There were other problems. It was expected that Elizabethan parents would organize the weddings of their children, choosing husbands who would benefit the family as a whole (as Juliet's father chose Paris). Boys got some latitude; girls were expected to remain virginal right up until the wedding night. By marrying without her father's consent, Juliet effectively disgraced herself (as well as rendering herself unmarriageable) and sleeping with Romeo afterwards only made matters worse. Juliet could not go to her parents and tell them that she was already married without ensuring her eviction from the family. And, to some extent, Romeo would have the same problem.

Their marriage could easily have made the feud a great deal worse. What if Juliet's father assumed that Romeo had deliberately set out to make his daughter unmarriageable? Or what if Paris had demanded satisfaction? He'd been promised a bride – and one would not be forthcoming. The two lovers might have been exiled or murdered (Juliet's mother plotted to kill Romeo after he fled the city) and then the fighting might resume, with the eventual destruction of both families. The Prince had threatened to execute both of the family heads, after all, right in the first act.

The Friar is, in many ways, the villain of the piece. His decision to marry Romeo and Juliet (I have no idea if this was actually legal, but the young couple clearly believed it was) was a bad mistake, setting off the chain of events that eventually led to disaster. There were, I think other options than faking Juliet's death. He may well have believed that their marriage would end the feud – either that, or he was an evil old bastard – but I honestly don't see how he could have reasoned that to be true. It was far more likely, as I note above, that all hell would break loose. I do not consider him a holy man.

Most productions, I think, miss this point. To us, *Romeo and Juliet* is a story about a love affair and focuses on the romance. But the play is, in many ways, a warning about the *dangers* of unfettered feelings.

Your mileage may vary, of course.

## *About the author*

Christopher G. Nuttall is thirty-two years old and has been reading science fiction since he was five when someone introduced him to children's SF. Born in Scotland, Chris attended schools in Edinburgh, Fife and University in Manchester before moving to Malaysia to live with his wife Aisha.

Chris has been involved in the online Alternate History community since 1998; in particular, he was the original founder of Changing The Times, an online alternate history website that brought in submissions from all over the community. Later, Chris took up writing and eventually became a full-time writer.

Current and forthcoming titles published by Twilight Times Books:

**Schooled in Magic YA fantasy series**
*Schooled in Magic*—book 1
*Lessons in Etiquette* —book 2
*A Study in Slaughter* —book 3
*Work Experience* —book 4
*The School of Hard Knocks* —book 5
*Love's Labor's Won*—book 6
*Trial by Fire*—book 7

**The Decline and Fall of the Galactic Empire military SF series**

*Barbarians at the Gates*—book 1
*The Shadow of Cincinnatus* —book 2
*The Barbarian Bride*—book 3

Chris has also produced *The Empire's Corps* series, the **Outside Context Problem** series and many others. He is also responsible for two fan-made Posleen novels, both set in John Ringo's famous Posleen universe. They can both be downloaded from his site.

Website: http://www.chrishanger.net
Blog: http://chrishanger.wordpress.com
Facebook: https://www.facebook.com/ChristopherG.Nuttall

CPSIA information can be obtained
at www.ICGtesting.com
Printed in the USA
FFOW04n0221051016
28190FF